Hugh

with love from

Lucy

November 1999

365 SAINTS

365

SAINTS

YOUR DAILY GUIDE
TO THE WISDOM AND WONDER
OF THEIR LIVES

WOODEENE KOENIG-BRICKER

HarperOne
An Imprint of HarperCollins*Publishers*

HarperOne

HarperCollins books may be purchased for educational, business,
or sales promotional use. For information, please e-mail the
Special Markets Department at SPsales@harpercollins.com.

HarperCollins Web site: http://www.harpercollins.com
HarperCollins®, 🏠®, and HarperOne™ are trademarks of
HarperCollins Publishers.

Library of Congress Cataloging-in-Publication Data

ISBN 978–0–06–247349–3

16 17 18 19 20 RRD 10 9 8 7 6 5 4 3 2 1

TO JSB AND MSB

ACKNOWLEDGMENTS

To all those whose love, encouragement, and support made it possible for me to write this book, more thanks than I can ever express.

To John, who did everything so I could spend all my time in the company of the saints. I couldn't have done it without you.

To Matt, who always said, "You can do it, Mom!" I wouldn't have tried to do it without you.

To Bobbi, Debbie, and Kris, who had more confidence in me than I had in myself.

To the sons of St. Dominic, whose love and prayers constantly sustain me.

And finally, a special thanks to my mother, who always believed I'd write a book one day. One day finally came.

The Time Before You Die

LUCY BECKETT

The Time Before You Die

A Novel of the Reformation

IGNATIUS PRESS   SAN FRANCISCO

View of Fountains Abbey, Yorkshire, lithograph
Victoria and Albert Museum, London
Victoria and Albert Museum / Art Resource, N.Y.

Sodoma, *Story of Saint Benedict*
Detail of the monk dining in the refectory
Abbey, Monte Oliveto, Maggiore, Italy
Scala / Art Resource, N.Y.

Cover design by Riz Boncan Marsella

In memoriam

Alban Rimmer, O.S.B.

1911–1984

Contents

PART ONE

1518–1554

I

June 1518

Fray Bernardino de Mesa, of the Order of Preachers, ambassador to the court of King Henry VIII, in England, to Charles, King of Castile and Aragon and Count of Burgundy, in Spain; June 1518.

". . . Despite the rumours of plague, Cardinal Wolsey stops in London and has received many several times the ambassadors of the king of France. He has sent to me to return to London, whither I shortly go, hopeful as I now am of his true and earnest endeavours towards the universal peace of Christendom. The Princess Mary, your cousin, who is now two years old, continues in good health, thanks be to God; I am very sorry to hear talk of her betrothal to the dauphin of France. God grant it will be no more than rumour. The Lady Margaret Pole, the countess of Salisbury, is appointed the princess's governess; and a more devout and godly lady and a more loyal friend to the queen your aunt I know there is not in all England. The queen your aunt, who is again with child (God grant she bear at last a healthy son), has journeyed with her court to Oxford, to the shrine of Saint Frideswide, and afterwards to the town, where, at a goodly and sober dinner in Merton Hall, I saw her converse cheerfully with many doctors and scholars, among them Master Reginald Pole, who is son to the said countess of Salisbury and who, I am told, is excellently learned in Latin and Greek and conspicuous still more for his virtue than for his learning. He was as a boy put to school at the king's charge with the monks of the Charterhouse at Sheen, a house long in the royal favour. They say his mother would have him a churchman, and, indeed, such a young man, come to riper years, will surely be deserving of high place. The king is at Abingdon and hunts every day."

2

September 1520

"Robert, I shall not see you again in this life. There is something I would have you know before you go from here for ever."

Master Husthwaite stood at his parlour window, looking out at the autumn evening. Mist lay over the river. The sun had set and the moor at the head of the dale was turning from purple to black. The lay brother who had come from the Charterhouse with the letter sat eating at the table.

Robert Fletcher had looked forward to this letter, without impatience, for months. Now he was in a fever of haste, as if the prior of the Mountgrace might change his mind about the empty cell if he did not appear by nightfall. He sat down again unwillingly. He had wanted to leave at once, as soon as the man came to the priest's house, where he had happened to be, copying a book, because the harvest was finished. But there were twelve miles of sheep-path between Hawnby and the Charterhouse, and it would be dark in an hour. He must wait until the morning.

The priest went on without turning round, peering into the dusk.

"The better world we hoped for when I was young, the world in which ancient learning would so marry with Christian virtue as to bring forth civil peace and private holiness where there were ignorance and enmity before: Is that world even now coming into being? When the cardinal founds a college at Oxford and Greek is taught in the university, when the king and the queen show favour to scholars and England holds the peace of Christendom firm—is this the dawn we once thought to see?

And where am I in this new world? Hidden away altogether from them all, a priest for a handful of poor people in a northern dale, with my books and my long-sought peace, and nothing, after today, nothing. Getting through slow days towards death with my books, as your father does with his drinking.

"But you, Robert, being young, and setting forth tomorrow on a strait path to God that will give you nevertheless a freedom you will come to understand, you are a part of this new world. For it must keep secret within it, as the Carthusians are secret in their cloister, the best of the old. So that you are what I have done, Robert, all I have done, for the new world."

The lay brother at the table pushed away his dish. Then he got up, bowed to Master Husthwaite's back, and left the room. They heard him climb the stairs.

The priest crossed the room and embraced Robert Fletcher, holding him close for a long time. At last he took him by the shoulders and held him at arm's length.

"Farewell, Robert, my son. Forgive me my grief at seeing you go, and . . ." He made the sign of the cross on his forehead with his thumb. "One day, if you find you need to, forgive me for having burdened you with too great a hope." He turned back to the window. "Now go, boy. Go."

In the morning he could not find Will.

He had slept badly, his schoolmaster's high words echoing in his head like accusations. He meant to leave with the first light.

He woke his father, who smelled of ale and smoke as he always did, from sitting half the night over the fire, and whose shirt was sticky with dirt. He said:

"I am going, father, to the Mountgrace. I am going today. I shall not see you again."

Old Tom Fletcher sat up in his bed. Very slowly, his eyes dull, he took it in. He shook his head slowly, angrily, like a bull.

"You do that, lad. You get away from here. You should never have been born, that you should not. I sent you away, didn't I? Why did you ever come back?"

His eyes filled with tears as he went on. Robert gritted his teeth.

"But you did come back, and you've worked your share since you were a little lad, and no thanks from your brother or me, I daresay."

"Never mind that now."

"Get along with you, lad, with your priest's manners and your learning. Forget this place. Damned house. Only fit for dying in. Faded away, she did, my lass. Not a word she said. No house for the living. Tom'll bury me, have no fear, and glad to do it. Say a prayer for your mother now and then so she rest easy. Don't trouble yourself about me. I'll bide in this world as long as I may, to keep Tom out." He laughed with malice. "Only to keep Tom out."

The old man looked at him sharply, returning to the present.

"Where is it you're going then? Oh, aye, to the monks, the fat monks. Like carp, they are, fat carp in a pond, bloated on the rents of such as me."

"I'm going to the Charterhouse, father, not to the abbey."

"What's the difference? They're all monks, aren't they? Fine white bread and folded hands and never the sweat on their backs. Get away to your monks, damn you! Leave me in peace. I never wanted you here with her eyes and her soft ways. Get away and good riddance!"

He slapped the air in front of his face as if hitting at a fly, and Robert left him.

He went out of the house to look for Will. The sun had risen. The new day glistened with a dew not far from a frost. He walked over the sheep-cropped grass, his footprints dark behind him, and forgot them both, his father and the priest. It was his own day, the first day. His life in the Charterhouse was an empty page on which all the writing would be fair and even, a silver field he would cross in a straight line to the top where the moor began and the wind always blew, the spirit of God.

Will was nowhere.

He wanted to see him before he left, to look at him carefully once more so as to remember him, for all that Will would not return his glance.

He went back to the house and looked again in the loft, where Will would sit for hours, rolling the stored apples. He looked in all the buildings round the yard. He went down even to the river, although for years Will had not gone that far. When the sun was already high he met his half-brother Tom.

"Where is Will?"

"Are you here yet? You reckoned last night to be gone for a monk long by now."

"Where is Will?"

"I've more to do than know where Will might be. What does it matter to you where he is? He'll be back for his dinner right enough."

At dinner-time, Will had not come back.

Robert was afraid for Will, afraid that he had hidden, run away, got into danger somewhere, because somehow he had understood that he himself was going. Will, his other half-brother, was mute and called an idiot, although Robert knew that he was neither deaf nor witless. He had often watched him search the sky for curlews crying somewhere out of sight. He had taught him to blow on a blade of grass between his thumbs and make it squawk, and Will had even laughed. He had never got him to utter a word. Now and then rage would seize Will, shake him like a gale, and he would smash something, anything. The trough in the yard he had broken with a pick so that the water streamed down into the mud. A winter's heap of firewood he had pulled about him, flinging huge logs over his shoulder as if they were twigs. When a sheepdog took his tame duck in its mouth and left it on the ground with a broken leg, he beat the duck to a mess of bloody feathers with a spade and afterwards set fire to the barn so that all that year's hay was destroyed. But almost always he was quiet, frightened, and slow, never wandering far, afraid both of the empty moor above the farm and of the river winding under trees on the floor of the dale.

Until late in the afternoon Robert looked for Will, with fear hardening in his stomach. He did not find him. At last he left his father's farm, weeping. His feet when he left had become like stones, holding him back as in a dream.

He walked over the moors to the Charterhouse in silence, the lay brother walking beside him. As he walked he remembered the one other such journey he had made.

He had been seven years old, and Tom, already grown, already hating him, had fetched him away from Arden mill, the nuns' mill up the dale. Two days before, Robin the miller had died, carried in from the hayfield with a pitchfork stuck deep into his guts. The five nuns had sobbed. Then remembered him.

"What'll we do with the lad?"

"He'll have to go back to his father's house, poor bairn."

"Old Tom Fletcher's not fit to care for man nor beast, and no woman in the place."

"How can we keep him here with Robin dead?"

He had walked down the lane from Arden between banks of cow-parsley, following Tom, who stopped once and said:

"At Easterside you'll do as I tell you and never heed father. Do you hear? Once a bastard, always a bastard. And your mother no more than a servant girl, remember that, a little whore that came to scour pots after mother died."

For fifteen years he had worked at Easterside for Tom, at first minding geese and feeding hens, later ploughing, sowing, reaping with the men, tending sheep, out on the moor alone

looking for ewes buried in snow while his father sat sullen by
the fire and Will was only kicked and cursed. On idle evenings,
when Tom let him go, Master Husthwaite had taught him to
read and write, had taught him Latin in his warm parlour, read
with him the psalter and the Gospels and Virgil, Saint Bernard
and Cicero and Saint Aelred of Rievaulx, to whose great de-
cayed abbey down the dale his father sometimes went to wrangle
with the bailiff. So he had learned to live also in the country of
language, the country of those things which cannot be known
without the words that reveal them. The silence of the
Charterhouse to which he walked was to be filled with the
words of that country, the words and the silence of the Kingdom of God.

As he walked, he more than once looked behind him. The
hills changed their places and after a short time hid the dale.

Night had fallen when they reached the monastery of the
Mountgrace. The heavy gate was opened softly and shut behind
him without a sound. As he came through into the outer court,
he saw no lights from the cells ranged round the cloister. Then
he remembered, from his single visit two years before, that the
monks' windows looked out only to their own gardens. The lay
brother gave him bread and cabbage broth alone in the guesthouse, showed him a bed in a long room with other, empty
beds, and left him without a light, saying that he would be back
in the morning to take him to the prior.

He did not sleep at once. He lay in the dark, cold under a
thin, clean blanket, and thought of Will, who often slept beside
him on the straw of the fold-yard, in the steamy warmth of
cattle and dogs. He was afraid for Will, afraid all at once for
himself. He tried to pray. O Lord God. For God he had left
Easterside. The words of his prayer came back to him dry,
without meaning. He shivered in the alien bed. The faces of the
priest, his father, Will, even Tom, passed one after the other
before his eyes. It was as he had last seen them, these faces, that

he would now always know them. They would age and alter out of his sight.

But he slept, after all, a sound, dreamless sleep.

3

August 1522

Pietro Bembo, scholar, in Padua, to his friend Gasparo Contarini, ambassador of the Republic of Venice at the court of Emperor Charles V, King of Castile and Aragon, Count of Burgundy, hereditary lord of the Netherlands, Austria, etc., etc., in Spain; August 1522.

". . . Meanwhile the dog-days pass pleasantly enough here in the country. My little boat rocks at anchor on the tree-shaded stream that flows past my house, and not far away, on the margin of my fields, the graceful Brenta follows its course towards the lagoon. A friend has discovered for me a portrait said to be of Laura herself, to hang beside my Petrarch on the east wall of my library; whether or not the lady be indeed Laura, it is a fine thing and fills to better advantage the space from which poor Boccaccio has had to be banished to the ill-lit south wall. I wish you were here with us, my dear Contarini, to admire the Attic vase and the bronze figure of Hermes, un-damaged in all parts, which I have acquired from my watchful friend in Naples, well rewarded for his vigilance, since you left us to pursue the more virtuous but no doubt less agreeable paths of public duty.

"A most remarkable young man, who arrived in Padua earlier this year to advance his studies under the guidance of our good old Leonicus, has joined our circle and visits my house fre-quently, spending many hours in the examination of my collec-tion of antiquities and manuscripts. Reginald Pole by name, he is a near cousin to the king of England; the English ambassador,

Signor Pace, tells me that he has even been spoken of in his own country as a likely husband for the king's only daughter, who, in the absence of a live male heir, must one day to the great anxiety of all inherit her father's realm and power. This young Pole is already adept in the discipline of Ciceronian eloquence and, although by nature reticent to the point of taciturnity, acquits himself in companionable discourse with intelligence and grace. I flatter myself that his increasingly elegant use of the Italian tongue owes not a little to my own tutelage. But the polish which the best of trainings has applied to noble birth and a gentle disposition is only the most apparent of his many merits. Indeed, I would go so far as to say that he is possibly the most virtuous, learned, and grave young man in the whole of Italy today, and I should be most gratified if you were to form an acquaintance with him on your return, not far distant it is to be hoped, to Venice. The years will, I have no doubt, prove him to be a man worthy of the affection of the most refined spirits . . ."

4

October 1522

The day before Robert Fletcher was to be professed as a monk, the prior came to his cell, slowly, walking with a stick, to hear his confession. In his own oratory he knelt in front of the old man and told him of his impatience, his restlessness, his grief at finding himself, after two years, no closer to the peace he had entered the Charterhouse to find.

He said: "The day Master Husthwaite brought me to see you, that first day, I stood in your window looking out over the cloister. I saw the cells of all the monks, the closed doors. I listened to Master Husthwaite describing me to you, telling you that I was patient, faithful, obedient. It was not true, none of it was true. But I promised myself before God as I stood in your window that if only I should be allowed to come here I would make it true. I thought that alone in my cell I should have the time, all the time for God. And now, it is less true than ever it was. It is not that I . . . that I . . . Sometimes I wish that I had committed some great sin for which I could be sorry all my days."

With tears in his eyes, he stared down at the knots in the planks that made the swept floor on which he knelt.

"Indeed I am ashamed. And yet I know not . . ."

He could not find the words. The words he had carefully prepared in the days before he did not utter, because they seemed to him now an account of someone else's soul. He had a sense of strength, of power within himself that thus far in his life every day had no more than scattered and wasted; he yearned to gather it together, the whole of himself, his whole soul and body, and lay it before God.

"I have done nothing. Neither good nor evil. And now I shall not . . ."

It was not what he meant to say. Then he saw what he meant.

"I am afraid that what I wish for is to die."

After a long silence the prior said, very softly, very slowly: "Mean by sin a lump. You yourself, body and soul, indivisible, are that lump. And I myself also, and every man. We can do no more than know ourselves as we are, and offer ourselves to God who has already accepted us, already forgiven us. Who takes away the sin of the world."

The words floated towards Robert Fletcher like leaves on the surface of a stream.

"My child, believe, believe what we have so many ways been told. His mercy is on them that fear him. His mercy is. It is not for you to deserve, only to trust, only to accept what is there, for you, for us all, for you only. Every hair on your head has been counted."

Like leaves on the surface of a stream he heard the words, like leaves, two or three among countless leaves, as if it did not matter which the old man chose to speak. He knelt, bowed to the ground, as the leaves floated by.

Quietly the prior went on. "Our names are written upon water, and all that we do and say, but the water is God's time. In him there is no movement from the past into the future. The flow of the water is our impression, the mark we make and its unmaking; in him is no unmaking, only the creation of the always new which afterwards he will not let die. To him we are bound; our end is in him, and therefore is no end. What you have done, what you will do, signifies nothing, nothing, except inasmuch as it takes you further from him or closer to him. The rest is in the eyes of the world, and what are the eyes of the world? Dead men's eyes. To live well is never to despair of him, never, for he did not, he does not, he will not despair of you.

"We are fallen men and having lost God's glory we live in the world and stray, terrified, on dark paths towards our certain deaths. But if we had not been wretched, there had been no need for Christ to come. And unless we know our wretchedness, unless we weep for it, he does not come. There is a veil upon our hearts. But if we turn always to him, the veil will thin and fade. The veil will be taken away. With an open face one day you will see the glory of the Lord.

"You will live, child of this house of God, you will live. Whether for an hour or for fifty years, you will live always on the edge, between his time and ours, and I pray that one day you will cross that edge for ever without fear."

The prior stopped speaking. After some minutes, in a firmer voice, he pronounced the words of absolution over him and blessed him. Robert Fletcher stood up. He put out his hand to help the old man from the chair in which he sat. When the prior was upright, he did not at once let go of Robert's hand but stooped and kissed it.

"Thank you", the prior said. "Come with me. It is time for Vespers."

They went out into the cloister. The bell began to toll, and other monks appeared at their doors. The prior took him out across the wide grass towards the church. They stopped in the middle of the cloister garth, where the nut-trees were beginning to lose their leaves, and the prior said: "One thing I would have you remember. It is easy to mistake love for faith. You can love what you know but in what you do not yet know you must have faith. Faith is for the night, for the cold weather. If a monk does not recognise the difference between love and faith he will lose heart when the days shorten, as they will."

He leaned on his stick and waved his other hand at the yellow woods above them.

"If a wind gets up tonight, there'll be scarcely a leaf left by morning. Our life here also has its seasons."

"Here?"

The bell ceased. Smoke curled out of a bonfire in the orchard and thinned slowly, scenting the air. Light from the west, which had already left the cloister, gilded the trunks of the oaks on the hillside like paint.

"Here in this Charterhouse. Here on this earth." The prior smiled at him. "When I am dead," he said, "I commend you to the care of Thomas Leighton, who has been a monk of this house almost as long as I have."

The old man suddenly raised his head and pointed at the sky.

"Look there! Imagine how small we must appear to him, a little patch of stone and grass, a few monks running about, not to be told one from another, like rabbits in a paddock."

High up, in the last sunshine, a hawk hung, scanning the earth for his prey.

The prior smiled and nodded as they walked on towards the church. Robert Fletcher shivered.

On a December morning in the same year, laid on a cross of ashes and surrounded by his monks, the prior died. He was buried next day in a nameless grave according to Carthusian custom. Afterwards they elected a new prior, Master John Wilson, an honest man, sober and just in all his dealings. Thomas Leighton, an old monk of fierce aspect to whom Robert Fletcher had never had cause to speak, cast his vote for Master Wilson with the rest.

5

August 1527

Don Iñigo de Mendoza, ambassador to the court of King Henry VIII in London, to Emperor Charles V, King of Castile and Aragon, Count of Burgundy, hereditary lord of the Netherlands, Austria, etc., etc., in Spain; August 1527.

". . . While Cardinal Wolsey remains in France, I am able from time to time to speak alone with Queen Catherine your aunt, from the which privy speech the said cardinal, when in England, did all things in his power, both mannerly and unmannerly, to hinder me. The said cardinal believed himself despatched not only to sign those treaties with the king of France against your Imperial Majesty of which you are aware, but also to arrange an infamous match between King Henry and the Princess Renée of France, against such time as King Henry will have contrived to procure from Rome the declaration of his marriage to the queen's grace as sinful and void. At this present, however, the queen informs me that the cardinal is forbidden to treat of any such French marriage, not, alas, because the king has altered his mind concerning his union with the queen's grace, but because he is resolved to marry with a certain lady of the English court, one Mistress Anne Boleyn. It pains me grievously to send this news to your Imperial Majesty. I am requested by the queen, however, to inform you that she has no mind to yield to the king's request that she meekly retire herself into a nunnery. She is, on the contrary, entirely and wholly confident of the lawfulness, innocence, and virtue of her marriage with the king, and of her right and duty to remain at his side as his true wife, for her own sake and for that of the Princess Mary her daughter. She rests with full hope upon the expectation of your Imperial Majesty's help and succour in her affairs (trusting in particular that the presence of your armies in Rome cannot but assist her cause). Meanwhile she bears herself with the dignity and courage natural to so great a lady, appearing at court with the magnificence to which she has long been accustomed, as for example upon the occasion, several days past, of the return to court of Master Reginald Pole, who is cousin to the king and a young man, as I am told, of much promise in affairs of state. He has been abroad these seven years, studying with the most famous masters in Italy (whence he has returned on account of the late disorders in Rome), and the king and queen together greeted him, with every appearance of warmth and kindness, which, in these uncertain times, it greatly gladdened my heart to see. It is my own opinion that if the queen holds firm and treads a watchful path, the king may yet desist from these his most wicked intentions. Long may the cardinal be detained in France, for I doubt not that he, to keep his high place in the king's favour, must do his utmost to further the king's design."

6

1528

In the Charterhouse of the Mountgrace time passed with an order, measured by the tolling bell, that gave to many years the semblance of one. The seasons followed each upon the last, bare wood, green shoot, bloom, and mealy fall, with the often repeated singleness of Christmas, Passiontide, Easter, and Pentecost, each signifying all those that had been and were to be.

Robert Fletcher became, very slowly, a Carthusian monk. Vespers and the night offices the monks sang together in the church; on Sundays the prior, or another of the priests in the monastery, celebrated the conventual Mass for all the monks, the lay brothers, and any guests there might be; on Sundays also the monks ate together in the refectory; once a week the prior summoned all the monks to the chapter-house. Otherwise Robert Fletcher was alone in his cell, his cottage of two rooms and a loft, his garden with walls too high for him to see over.

He learned to live within himself. At the same time he discovered that he had always to push outwards, towards God, for his manifold anxiety that he would fail God had narrowed to a simple terror that God might fail him. Used as he became to the nearness of God, God the hearer of his every silent word, God the witness of his every unobserved action, he more and more feared those hours when it seemed to him that God, constantly so close in his solitude, had crossed the boundary of his soul and become after all no more than himself, and so had ceased to be.

During these hours he lay on his bed, staring at the dead figure hanging on the cross, and saw only death. He would live shut up in his cell from the world for no cause, for nothing, only to die at the end after empty years muffled from the necessities of other men, privileged for no reason not even to labour for his bread.

Once this death lasted for five days. He turned the proper pages of his psalter and his breviary, and did not read the words. He walked through the cloister to the church at the proper hours and watched the other monks perform the liturgy, bow to a stone, supplicate nobody, kneel before a flat cake and a silver cup of wine. On the fifth day he asked the prior if he might seek counsel of Master Leighton in his cell.

Master Leighton listened as he told him of the light gone out, the ashes in the hearth, Jesus no more than a good man dead.

When he had finished he looked across the cell.

The old monk sat upright at his table, his eyes closed. When he opened his eyes they were keen, a little mocking, not unkind.

"The fool said in his heart, there is no God", Master Leighton said, and laughed. He leaned forward and clasped his hands on the table.

"You'll do, Robert Fletcher, you'll do very well, my lad. We'll make a monk of you yet. Not everyone who goes under the name of monk is a monk, let me tell you, any more than everyone who calls himself a Christian is a Christian. But never forget this: no one but God knows which is which. No one. Now: Do you understand that? No one but God knows which monk is truly a monk or which Christian is truly a Christian."

"Aye, Master Leighton."

"If you understand that, you are already there, though you may not understand why. For in that 'knows' and in that 'truly', God is. Is he not, Master Fletcher?"

Robert was bewildered. He shook his head. The old monk laughed again.

29

"Let us travel by a gentler path. 'The fool said in his heart there is no God.' Can you repeat the words that come after? No? *Dominus de caelo prospexit super filios hominum, ut videat si est intelligens, aut requirens Deus.* The Lord looked down from heaven upon the children of men to see if there were any of them understanding, or seeking God. Now you, according to all you have said today, do not lack understanding. You understand two things many do not. One is the blindness of faith. We see but through a cloudy glass. If I tell you that Britain is an island, you believe me, not because either you or I have walked about its coasts and seen for ourselves that it is nowhere joined to France, but because we know that other men have made such a proof of its nature and we might do the same. But if I tell you that God in Christ's Resurrection has saved you from death, there is no such proof to be had. There are words only, nothing but words in a book, however often repeated and however venerable the book. You believe me because you choose to, blindly, in faith. You believe me, if you do, because your belief changes everything for you, death into life. Or, rather, it changes nothing but your understanding, the meaning, for you, of life and death, and that is everything. This, the greatness of the change, is the second thing you understand.

"No doubt you did not know it at the time, no doubt both you and your good schoolmaster would have been scandalised to hear it said, but you became a monk in order to discover whether God is or is not. A monk, after all, is a man; but he is a man who finds himself at the extreme point of what it is to be human. Every man needs God, to rescue him from the meaninglessness of his mortality. '*Requirens*', seeking, aye; also, needing. A monk has shed all that other men may hide behind. Houses, land, possessions; coupling, wife, children; the liberty to wander through the world, always to try something new, even the liberty to dream that he might try something new; even his own will: he has shed them so that he may have no covert into

30

which he may creep. If God is not, what has the monk to keep him from the cold? And the Carthusian, a hermit bounded even from his fellows by silence and the walls of his cell, has least of all.

"So that the darkness you have seen these past five days is a true darkness, the darkness of a man's life without God. But take courage. It is the light that shows you how dark the darkness is. In this world we shall not know God as we know that Britain is an island. We may only lack him, need him, seek him, understanding that, if he is not, we have no souls and are but flesh and will. We are here to listen to his words, which have all been spoken in the language of men except that once, that single day, when Jesus was raised from the dead and God justified his word to us for ever. If Christ be not raised, your faith is vain."

Master Leighton stood up and spread out his hands.

"You will forget what I have said. My words are nothing. They are gone already. Dust. Air. Go back to your cell and believe. Read the Acts of the Apostles and ask yourself why those men, no wiser or braver than you are, who had every one of them fled in despair from the cross, afterwards worked in this fallen world miracles of faith of which we have not yet seen the end.

"You are a monk, Master Fletcher. You are close against the truth. But I am promising you no easy passage. Many times you will have to fight, though you are out of the world, battles as hard as any that are fought in it. Some of them you will lose. But you are close against the truth, a weaned child against the cheek of God."

The old man stopped speaking. His head dropped as if he had fallen asleep as he sat at the table. He said in a weary voice:

"Go back to your cell. Pray also for me."

He went, light-hearted, cured, for the time being.

Soon he indeed forgot much of what Master Leighton had said to him. Sometimes the hours of drought came back. When they did, he filed into church or chapter-house with the other monks and fixed his eyes on Master Leighton's face until he recovered the force of his words that day, though not the words themselves. Once at Vespers Master Leighton met his glance across the light of a single candle and smiled. Robert Fletcher bent his head, in token of thanks.

7

March 1529

Robert Fletcher stepped back from the rosebush to see the
shape his knife had made. He had been kneeling on the damp
earth, too close to see the whole bush, peering at each shoot to
choose the bud he would favour, the bud above which he would
make his neat cut. He felt the blade of the knife with his thumb.
He picked up the whetstone from the path and sharpened the
blade until it was so keen that it rustled as he drew his thumb
across it. He stood, stone in one hand, knife in the other, and
looked at the bush. It was lop-sided. He had cut into the wood
more ruthlessly, with more decision, as he had gone on, so that
the side on which he had begun was taller and looser than the
side where he had stopped. He made a shape in the air with the
hand that held the knife, describing the perfect outline that he
meant to impose on the bush.

A chaffinch flew from the wood outside to the high coping
of the wall beyond the rose. He stooped slowly, keeping his eyes
on the bird, and put the whetstone back on the ground. He
straightened, as slowly, so as not to frighten the chaffinch, and as
he did so he forgot the intricate problem of the bush, the
pruning that he meant to make perfect. He breathed in deeply.
The air was mild with the first mildness of the year. His hands
were not cold, although he had been working outside for—he
glanced up at the sun—more than two hours. Birds were singing in the oak trees the other side of the wall, trees that he could
not see from where he stood. He sniffed. A raw, clean smell rose
from the earth, dark and soft at last after the winter, a smell as of
the very sap rising in the old trees and in the uncurling primrose

leaves close to the ground. The chaffinch flew away, out of the garden, back into the wood. He felt the spring stir in himself also, warming him through. It was the Wednesday of Holy Week, and he felt the lightness of the coming Easter as if he already breathed the air of that new world.

He saw some blades of grass that had sprung up through the earth near to the rosebush. He went over to them, put down the knife, and sank his fingers in the earth, which was still cold. He pulled gently, to snap nothing off, and out of the earth came eighteen inches of villainous white root, here and there along its length clusters of smaller roots clutching at the soil as he pulled, and young shoots that would become matted tufts of grass: creeping quitch grass: quick, Robin the miller at Arden had called it, quick because it would not die. The smallest piece of root left in the ground would send out a tangle of growth creeping into the roots of innocent plants, choking them of life. Seven years ago, when he first came, his garden had been overgrown and wild because the monk whose place he had taken had been infirm for years before his death. He had had to dig up all the plants, what was left of them, lavender and catmint, pinks, rosemary and rue, and sort out with his fingers the frail black roots from the fat white ones. He had pulled out yards of quitch, ground-elder and bindweed, too, and yellow nettle-roots that stung as much as the leaves, and burned them in grisly, spitting bonfires with the ivy he had torn from the wall. But he had never dared to dig up the old rose, and the quicks still lurked among its roots, waiting for every spring.

He stood in the March sunshine holding the length of root in both his hands. In the wood outside the garden quitch grass and nettles killed nothing. The forget-me-nots and the wild garlic, the bluebells and the willow-herb held on as strongly as they to their own patches of ground, and the branches of the oaks shaded them all with an equal shade. There all and none were weeds. He looked at the rose-prunings lying in a heap where he had thrown them and wished that he had not cut out so much. There were buds there that would have become leaves and flowers, that had the scent of summer already folded in them. Now they would only burn.

It was Martin who had told him to prune the bush, Martin the lay brother, who sometimes brought him plants, seedlings, cuttings, scraps divided from clumps of herbs. The plants had begun to appear not long after he had cleared his garden of the worst of the weeds. They had been left beside his dish in the hole in the cell wall where every day a lay brother left his food. The hole was right-angled so that the monk inside the cell could not catch even a glimpse of the man who brought his food. He would never have known who had left him the plants if Martin had not said one day as he dumped a load of firewood in the corner of his cell:

"How does the winter savory do for you then? You should put a bit to your dish of beans, my lad."

Much later, this last autumn, he had brought his firewood again, and this time he had said:

"Needs cutting back hard, does the old rose, hard as you like, every odd year or so. Do it nowt but good."

These were the two things Martin had said to him.

So he had cut back the rose.

He frowned as he stood with the quitch root in his hands. He loved his garden, his bushes reduced to orderly shapes, with the bare earth beneath them. Why did it trouble him that in the wood beyond the wall, which he could see from the window of his loft but had never walked in, not once, there was no bare earth, and in autumn the traveller's joy hung in grey swathes over the unpruned briars?

From across the cloister the bell began to ring. He tossed the root, with unnecessary force, over the wall into the wood and turned towards his cell. It was the hour for Sext. The office-book lay open at the right page on the reading-desk in his cell.

35

He went to the tap by the door, to rinse the earth from his hands. But the bell did not stop after six strokes. He paused to listen, water dripping from his hands and the scratches smarting that the rose-thorns had made. The strokes of the bell went on, twelve, thirteen, fourteen, more, and it seemed to him that it was being rung faster and louder than usual. It meant, in any case, that the office was to be said in church. He looked down at his habit, muddy from where he had knelt to prune the rose. He dried his hands and dabbed at the marks with the cloth, making them worse because they were still damp. The bell stopped. He threw down the cloth, picked up the heavy office-book as he went through his cell, and opened the door into the cloister.

He almost knocked over Master Leighton, coming slowly down the cloister with no book and his hands folded under his habit. The old man, lately much aged, gave him a sharp look as he passed, signifying disapproval both of his haste and of the mud on his habit. Robert stepped back, to give him a lead of a few paces, and looked out over the great cloister-garth.

There was the sheen of new growth on the grass. Finches flew about among the twigs of the apple trees and the hazels, the soft gold of the catkins hazy over a drift of yellow crocuses. He sighed. All this shining and breaking open of the spring, the breaking open of bud, seed, shell, sheath, winter sleep . . . He turned to follow Master Leighton to the church.

He saw the prior emerge from his cell on the far side of the cloister. He quickened his pace so as to reach the church before the prior, then slowed it in surprise. The prior had stayed at his door, holding it open behind him with a gesture of courtesy. A stranger came out, a layman dressed in black, a gentleman, and walked with the prior towards the church.

The monks sang the office in choir as if it were Sunday, with the sunlight falling in bars on the north wall. Today, a weekday, they should not have met in the church until Vespers. He sang with the rest, paying no heed to the words he sang. The stranger was out of sight, in the nave beyond the narrow door under the tower. He wondered as he sang who he was, this young man whom the prior had accompanied with a deference beyond his usual gravity, and why he had come.

At the end of the office the monks filed into the chapter-house, and the prior, with a raised hand, signed to them to stay there. They waited in their habitual silence. The prior went back into the church and returned a moment later with the stranger. Then the prior said:

"The midday office has been sung in choir so that you might know that Master Reginald Pole, cousin to the king's grace, is here as our guest for the days of Easter. Master Pole has been a scholar in the universities of Oxford and Padua and is much at the court. He comes to us, so far in the north, so far out of the world, from the very centre of the world. But he has lately been living among our brethren in the Charterhouse at Sheen, where he also was for some years as a boy, so that he is no stranger to our quiet days nor to the tenor of our lives in the cloister. We are glad, we are very glad, to see him here, and his coming does us great honour."

While the prior was speaking the young man's eyes travelled round the faces of the listening monks. There was in his glance a warmth, a gentleness, that touched Robert Fletcher as the spring weather had already done. When the large eyes met his own, he put up a hand to his cheek as if to hide behind it. Master Pole's black clothes and clear gaze made him suddenly aware of his tangled beard, his big scratched hands, his coarse bleached habit, which smelled of sweat and earth.

After the prior had finished, the young man bowed to the monks with a brief smile that seemed to lighten the quality of the silence from which they watched him and left the chapter-house. The monks went back to their cells.

Robert Fletcher crossed the grass of the cloister-garth instead of following the rest down the shadowed walk. He stopped among the crocuses and looked down at them as they bent, together, in the light wind. There were daisies in the grass too— many more daisies than crocuses—that had also opened in the morning's sunshine. He picked a daisy and, with some anguish, twisted the stalk in his fingers until the head broke off.

"Noble metal to our base", he muttered as he walked on, to his cell. At his door he paused with his hand on the latch and straightened his shoulders as if there were someone inside whom he needed new courage to face.

On Sundays the monks dined together in the refectory. That Sunday, because it was Easter day, there was wine to drink, watered according to Carthusian custom, and flowers in little jugs down the middle of the table. The reading was one of Saint Bernard's sermons, on the Resurrection of Christ. A novice read it, nervously and too fast, so that the mighty Latin rattled forward like a river shallow over pebbles. Robert Fletcher was not listening to the sense of the words. He ate the meal without pleasure, although there was white bread instead of black and cream cheese with the baked apples, and watched, from the far end of the table, Master Pole eating and listening in a remote stillness, stiller than that of any of the monks. He had the impression that their far-come guest had in spirit already left the monastery and was somewhere else, in the midst of trouble.

At the end of the meal the prior called Robert Fletcher over. "Master Pole has asked to see one of the gardens of the great cloister. Will you show him yours, since I know that it has been your particular care?"

He bowed and, without a word, led the young man in his black clothes out into the air and across the grass to his cell. He opened the door for him, and Master Pole passed through in silence, accustomed not to open doors for himself. But when they came out into the garden he smiled with pleasure and said:

"Ah—you have a good, big garden. And sunshine." He turned round where he stood, looking at the sky. "Both a south and a west wall. You should plant a peach on that wall, or at least a plum. I have seen them in Italy grown against a south wall, forced into the shape of a fan and cut back every year. They bear a heavy crop. You are fortunate to have these warm walls. Aye . . ."

He put the flat of his hand on the stone of the wall and looked Robert full in the face. His voice altered.

"You are very fortunate. I could wish that I had been allotted such a garden." He hesitated, dropping his glance, and said softly, "And indeed, such a life, far out of the world, as your prior said, under these hills. Nothing can touch you here, your books, your peaceful days." He looked up. "What manner of life did you quit, to enter the Charterhouse?"

"My father is a tenant of the abbot of Rievaulx, sir, holding a deal of land, sheep-grazing most of it, that my brother will hold after him. I laboured for them and learned Latin from the priest at Hawnby, twelve mile from here."

"Peaceful days also. You are a happy man."

Robert said nothing.

Master Pole smiled and turned to the rose. He bent down beside it, took hold of its gnarled main stem, and rocked it a little in the ground.

"A fine rose, and full of vigour still, though it must be thirty years old. About my age. And yours. Does it carry white flowers?"

"Aye, sir, it does, a pure, clear white."

The gentleman in his neat black clothes stood looking at the pruned branches to which a few withered leaves were still attached. The new year's shoots were about to break. Robert suddenly saw fear in his guest's face and took one step towards him. But Master Pole looked down at the earth for a moment and smiled, after all, once more, as he raised his eyes.

39

"Perhaps it is a good omen", he said. And, as he held out his hand, "God be with you, sir."

Then he went away quickly, opening the door for himself.

January 1532

Messire Eustace Chapuys, ambassador to the court of King Henry VIII in London, to Emperor Charles V, King of Castile and Aragon, Count of Burgundy, hereditary lord of the Netherlands, Austria, etc., etc., in Italy; January 1532.

". . . The king rode out early, from Hampton Court, for the chase, as he is used to do. The Princess Mary, now much disregarded on account of her mother's marriage being cast into question, watched him go, humbly kneeling as is her wont, from the platform above and greeted of none. Until the king, turning by chance in the saddle, of a sudden took off his cap and bowed to her, at which they all followed. I saw this with my own eyes and did rejoice at it; but she, I have heard, retired to weep in her chamber as she does continually.

"The son of the princess's governess, Reginald Pole, he that these two years past went into France to further the king's cause, though much unwillingly as I am told, could not until yesterday obtain licence to go again abroad for the pursuit of his studies. It is said that he refused the archbishopric of York after the death of the cardinal because he would not adopt the king's opinion concerning the divorce and that he greatly angered the king by the intemperate manner in which he then spoke, although they were alone. He has lived this past year in retirement at the Carthusian house at Sheen, in the very rooms occupied by the cardinal after his fall from power, and has long desired to return to Italy, where, Sir Thomas More the Lord Chancellor has informed me, he is esteemed for his learning and virtue more even than for his noble birth (for he is of the blood royal and in any realm but England would bear a prince's title). It is said that yesterday he told the king that if he remained in England he must attend the Convocation, he being dean of Exeter though yet a layman, and that if the divorce were there discussed he must speak according to his conscience. On this, the king immediately gave him leave to go and promised to continue his pension of four hundred ducats. They say that, to make up his quarrel with the king, he secretly wrote him a letter during this last summer that set forth with such goodly wit and eloquence his reasons against the divorce that the letter was instantly destroyed by Master Cranmer for fear of the hurt it might do the king's cause should it become known among the learned of the Kingdom.

"The queen your aunt has said to me that the king's seeking of a divorce is a judgement of God for that her former marriage with Prince Arthur was made in blood, meaning that of the earl of Warwick, the White Rose, who was executed thirty years since on the orders of her father-in-law King Henry VII to clear the succession of the House of Tudor but at the instance, she swears, of the ambassador of Spain. I begged her to believe all not yet lost and reminded her that the said earl of Warwick's sister, the Lady Margaret Pole, and her sons are now, so far from being her grace's enemies, among her most faithful friends. But she was not to be comforted."

1534–1535

During the autumn strangers arrived at the monastery more often than before, and Robert Fletcher watched a change come over the prior as marked as that of the leaves of the oak trees turning from green to purple and gold. Master Wilson had ruled for twelve years in peace a peaceful house. Now his shoulders, as he walked, were hunched under a weight of care. In chapter, while the ordinary business of the monastery was discussed, he sat in silence looking from face to face, as if he would have liked to ask for help but dared not. His monks, by long use accustomed to resigning decisions to their prior, lived through the days not knowing what news each letter from London brought or who had clattered out through the Charterhouse gate carrying his noise away into the world.

Robert Fletcher, meanwhile, was in love with a book. A bundle of books had lately reached the Mountgrace from the London Charterhouse in exchange for a bundle that he himself had packed up and sent away. Among those that had come was a small volume, old and badly transcribed so that many words were difficult to read, which seemed to him to have been written for him alone. It had made of every day a wonder and a joy too short for all that the wakeful silence between himself and God might hold. He went into chapter, into the cloister, into choir for the night offices, and found himself with surprise there among his fellow monks. He did what they did, said or sang the same words; but he was all the time busy with a new work, the work set him by the book. The book was in English. It was called *The Cloud of Unknowing*. No author's name appeared in its clumsily sewn pages.

"Look that nothing live in thy working mind", the book said, "but a naked intent stretching into God. Cease never in thine intent; but beat ever more on this cloud of unknowing that is betwixt thee and thy God with a sharp dart of longing love, and loathe for to think on aught under God, and go not thence for anything that befalleth. If thee list have this intent lapped and folden in one word, take thee but a little word of one syllable. Such a word is this word Love. Fasten this word to thine heart. With this word thou shalt beat on this cloud and this darkness above thee. With this word thou shalt sink down all manner of thought under the cloud of forgetting."

Love, he said to himself over and over, love, love, as he woke in the dark, happy, to the bell ringing over the cloister, and walked across the wet grass to the church.

During this time the warning the old prior had given him on the day before his profession never once came back to him. Love, he repeated. *Faith* was a word he no longer needed.

Then, one morning early in the winter, the king's commissioner came to the Mountgrace. He sat at a table in the chapter-house and, without glancing at the monks in their places, read quickly through the legal phrases of a document declaring, on oath, loyalty to the king's choice of an heir to the realm. Robert Fletcher, watching the prior's downcast eyes, scarcely listened. What was the king's heir to him, to any of them there? Had they not left the world to dwell in the desert?

The commissioner put the document down on the table in front of him, turning it round so that it faced the monks. He pushed the quill and the ink further forward. Then he read, loudly, from another paper, the prior's name.

In silence the prior rose, walked to the table, and signed his name. The quill scratched. When he laid down the pen someone coughed. The prior sat down. He looked at no one.

Other monks, Robert Fletcher among them, followed the prior in the order in which their names were read out.

"Master Thomas Leighton", the commissioner called.

There was no movement. Robert Fletcher looked up sharply. Master Leighton was sitting in his place, his piercing eyes fixed upon the commissioner.

"Thomas Leighton!" the commissioner repeated, louder, looking round at the cowled figures, not knowing to which of them the name belonged.

Master Leighton was not deaf. He stood up at last, looked round the chapter-house at each upturned face, and said:

"I'll not swear your oath."

The commissioner stared at him, laying down the paper in his hand. The prior stood up. Before he could speak Master Leighton went on:

"The pope has judged the king's marriage to Queen Catherine good. If the marriage was good, the king has not the right under God's law to cast the Princess Mary off and put a bastard in her place."

The commissioner cleared his throat and said with deliberation:

"It is not for monks to meddle in these matters, but freely to signify their obedience to the king's highness."

"If it is not for monks to meddle in these matters, why do you come here asking from us oaths we are forbidden to swear?"

The prior raised his hand. Master Leighton would not be stopped.

"I will tell you why. You come from London to our cloister and call us from our cells, not because you want an oath for the king, but because you want an oath against the pope, and I for one"—he glared round the chapter-house—"I for one will not swear it. You can go back to London without my oath, and much harm may the lack of it do you!"

He sat down. The commissioner looked at him coldly for a while longer but at last shook his head and read out the next name. As the rest were called, the prior looked across at each in turn, and the monks came forward one by one and signed. The last, a young man called Geoffrey Hodson, only lately professed, stood when his name was read, bowed to the prior and said:

"I stick with Master Leighton."

The commissioner shrugged his shoulders, gathered his papers together, and left the chapter-house, followed by the prior.

The monks looked from one to another. They looked at Master Leighton, who sat in his place staring straight ahead, his jaw firm. His defiance crackled in the air. As if to escape its dangerous presence, some of the others went out, too quickly, pushing through the door. Robert Fletcher leaned forward.

"Master Leighton . . ."

Slowly the old monk fixed his gaze on him.

"Well, Robert Fletcher", he said. "I thought better at least of you. What have you done? Aye, there we have it. You do not know. But I tell you that one day you will be compelled to know what you have done, to see it for what it is. All of you!" He shouted the last three words, and a monk leaving the chapter-house jumped in the doorway and turned back, his mouth gaping.

"Fools!" Master Leighton roared at them. They flinched where they stood. They had never heard a voice raised in anger in the chapter-house. "Following one the other like sheep through a gap in the wall, and for what cause? Like sheep you have no minds of your own and run where you are led." He stopped short, halted by the scandal of his own contempt for the prior's example. The young monk who had refused to sign his name raised a hand to his mouth in fright.

"Let that be", old Leighton muttered. But as Robert continued to lean towards him, amazed, seeking an explanation, he spoke again. No one moved.

"Nay, and I will not let it be. The king has sent to us and the likes of us, up and down the land, so that he may fetch back to London a great heap of our names, sworn to uphold him in his unlawful marriage, and then say to the world that the conscience of the realm has judged these things well done. For that is what we are, all of us and each one of us, the conscience of the realm, and our voice is not to be overlaid by respect for persons, be they even the person of the king himself."

"Master Leighton", Robert interrupted him. "We are monks. We have left the world, the kingdom of men. It is not our duty to think on these things. Our duty is rather to forget them, to leave them to others whose concern they rightly are. What is it to us if the king should choose to alter his inheritance?"

"We are here to cast off our sins, Master Fletcher, not to cast off our wits. Listen to me, all of you. We are monks, aye; we are churchmen therefore. We are Englishmen also and dwell under the king's law. But as churchmen we dwell under the pope's authority, which is God's authority upon earth. While the king's law is consonant with the pope's authority, well and good. If the king proposes a law flat against a judgement the pope has made, then it is for us to follow the pope's judgement and do nothing that might ease the king's path. We should refuse our oath of loyalty to this one law, not because we mean to do aught in disobedience to it, but because it is fashioned of the king's lawlessness. We owe this to the pope and the Church; we owe it to England too. A monk—do you recall, Master Fletcher?— may not conceal himself anywhere from God. No more than in all those hiding places that he has renounced may he seek refuge in mere obedience to the king. To seek refuge is to betray—"

The prior reappeared in the doorway of the chapter-house. Master Leighton fell silent and got to his feet. Robert Fletcher saw, with a pang that pierced his own anger, the old man's stiff and painful movements as he rose. All the monks who remained in the room also rose. The prior looked from face to face.

"I am to tell you", the prior said quietly, "that every monk in the eight other Charterhouses of the English province has given his oath of loyalty to the king's grace. Master Leighton, Geoffrey Hodson, do you persist in your refusal, or will you now sign your names?"

"I will not", Thomas Leighton said, looking still at Robert Fletcher.

Geoffrey Hodson looked from the prior to Leighton and back.

"I will sign", he said at last.

Leighton raised a hand in the young monk's direction and let it fall.

"Master Leighton, you are confined to your cell until such time as I send you word that you may come to choir and chapter."

The old man's head dropped forward in assent.

Robert Fletcher went back to his cell out of temper, though not with himself. A Carthusian monk belonged to no realm, no kingdom, no temporal state. He knew that this was so. It was his fresh, his shining knowledge. "Look that nothing live in thy working mind but a naked intent stretching into God." What had a king's marriage to do with that intent? Master Leighton was wrong. Robert Fletcher was glad that the boy, Hodson, had obeyed the prior. He wished only for familiar peace to settle again upon the monastery. He picked up his book and shook his head violently, to clear it of the resentment he felt at the disturbance Master Leighton had caused.

When the monks went to the church for Vespers the commissioner and his servants had left. Thomas Leighton's place in choir was empty.

In the months that followed, the visit of the commissioner was not spoken of. After six weeks Master Leighton was seen again in choir and chapter-house, his face stubborn, closed. He did not meet Robert Fletcher's glance.

But the monks were not left alone in their desert.

During the spring and summer more messengers came from London and York, more guests, unknown to the monks, whom the prior, sometimes in the middle of the night, was summoned to receive. As if from a remote height, Robert Fletcher watched anxiety increase in the house. The hours that were not filled with ordered prayer and the work of his garden he spent reading over and over again, until he knew them by heart, the words of his book. Or simply emptying his mind of all words whatsoever.

In the tattered pages he found the old prior's phrase. Mean by sin a lump. Many times he stared at the ill-written words, overcome by an understanding that he had been far from when he had heard them spoken. Led by the book to leave behind him, as he had once left behind Easterside and before that Arden, not only the walls of his cell, the oak-wood and the flowers in his garden, and the many words he was required to pray, but also his very self, his past, his future, the insistence of his body, in wordless silence, he knew that he reached more nearly to God than he had ever done. More and more often he withdrew to an empty place filled only with attention. There he was alone and not alone.

When he tried in confession to describe to the prior this nearness and farness, this blinded sight, the prior did not understand and took him to mean that he had seen visions. He saw nothing that was not there, but what he saw he saw from a great distance. He climbed a long way.

From the height he attained, he looked down and watched them in the cloister, the chapter-house, the church, becoming afraid. He knew, himself, that the intrusions of the world into the defenceless monastery, the king's demands as to laws and oaths, were part of the lump of sin that must be pushed down under the cloud of forgetting. He watched the monks move through the days at their measured pace, no less quietly than before. But it was as if he stood on the high moor in the last of the sunlight and watched them scurrying in the shadowed dale below. He saw clearly. What he saw troubled him scarcely at all. His soul was not there but somewhere else. He would obey the prior. Was it not in obedience that freedom was to be found, the freedom Master Husthwaite had spoken of long ago and which he now recognised as the freedom releasing his soul to beat upon the cloud of unknowing?

That spring, Thomas Leighton was dying. Very old, gaunt and wasted, he persisted in carrying out every obligation imposed on him by the habit of fifty years. Monks rising in the small hours at the bell for the night office would find him already almost at the church door, gasping for breath on his two sticks, as if he had not slept at all but lain awake counting the hours through until it was time to begin the slow walk from his cell. In chapter he lowered himself into his place, his knuckles white on the sticks, and sat, his eyes shut, motionless as a stone. Robert Fletcher, always aware of his presence and of his relation to himself, with mixed feelings watched him little by little fail.

Deep within him he kept the memory of his first encounter with Master Leighton. Then, the old man's strength had supplied his own weakness, implanting in him an understanding which had afterwards grown to occupy all the room there was in his soul. Now, that understanding had become his own, himself, and Master Leighton had been left behind, outside, like a dying oak beside a tree in its prime with the sap ringing to the tips of its branches. In the matter of the oath-taking Robert had seen how the old man was still caught in the concerns of the world, while he had grown free of them. When he saw Master Leighton hobble from church or chapter-house into the cloister, he would follow him, slowly so as not to overtake him, but with a proud spring to his step, conscious of the strength of his body, of a health, a contained and dedicated vigour, that he would retain for many years yet.

Robert Fletcher was thirty-seven years old that spring, tall and heavy, with a brown spade of a beard and broad, thick hands.

From time to time he remembered the visit of Master Pole to the Charterhouse. When he did, he no longer thought of him as noble metal but, with some scorn, as a fine, slight youth, pale in his black clothes, too soft for the monks' diet of beans and black bread. In his backwards glance, the high-born gentleman from the king's court grew younger and younger. The green boy he had been himself, bent over the Georgics at Master Husthwaite's parlour table, thin and strong and sunburned, he did not remember at all.

One day in May the prior read to his monks a letter that had come from the Charterhouse in London. It said that the London prior and two other Carthusian priors had been hanged, drawn, and quartered as traitors before a great crowd at Tyburn for refusing to acknowledge the king as head of the Church in England. It also said that the London monks had been threatened with the dissolution of their house if they continued to follow the example of their prior's refusal.

The sun streamed in through the windows of the chapterhouse. The only movement was the tremble of the letter shaking in the prior's hands.

Geoffrey Hodson suddenly rose to his feet and said with violence:

"It was a martyr's death, and if they come to take us we should not be afraid to go."

There was a murmur of assent. The prior bent his head, covering his eyes with his hand.

Robert Fletcher stood up in his place and said:

"We are here in this cloister to dwell with God on his holy mountain and to pray for the souls of the faithful dead and that the sins of the living may be forgiven. Our peace is not of this world, and we have no worldly power to defend it. Our everlasting trust is in God; our mortal trust must be in mortal power. If the pope's power does not protect our cloister from the king, we must look to the king. If the king's men take our priors and hang them, if the king's men dissolve our houses, our cells and our choirs will stand empty, there will be none out of the world to ask forgiveness for the sins of the world, the souls of the dead will go unprayed for, and on his mountain God will dwell alone. But if we yield to the king, in this matter of the pope as in the matter of the succession, then the king, as head of the Church, must surely in all justice and reason defend our house."

Thomas Leighton opened his eyes and said in a hoarse voice, without moving his head:

"*Nolite confidere in principibus.*"

"The pope also is a prince, Master Leighton."

The prior motioned him to sit down, and he obeyed.

"If the king's men come here again, Master Leighton," said the prior, "what would you have us do?"

Thomas Leighton, still seated in his place, bowed ceremoniously to the prior. Robert Fletcher winced at the irony of the bow. The prior's face, anxious and open, did not alter. After a pause Thomas Leighton spoke:

"The honour of this house was laid low when the oath to the succession was sworn. They will come again. God grant I shall be dead before they come. When they come, to seek your assent to the king's usurpation of rule over the Church, I beg you, Master Prior, to recall that the safety of this house and the lives of the monks in your care are not your first charge. This house is wood and stone; these monks are flesh and blood; mortal, both house and monks. Our souls are bound for heaven, I trust, however we meet death upon the way thither. But to choose good against evil, to sort the truth of God from the deceits of men and to cleave to the truth, there is our first charge. There is any man's."

They waited for him to say more, but he clenched his jaw and stared over their heads.

Robert Fletcher cleared his throat.

"Master Fletcher?" the prior said.

"Master Prior; brethren", he stood up, looking round at the bent heads of the monks in the sunshine. He loved them all. He thought of the butchery in London, the blood horribly spilled for a foolish, human cause. He knew that he was right.

"I say that these brave priors have died for affairs of state and that God's truth, which, indeed, Master Leighton, we must use all our strength to discern and to cleave to, is not, in the king's new law, anywhere in question. The king is no heretic; has he not fought in every way the evil teachings of Luther? Has he not had heretics burned and even himself written a book defending the holiness of the seven sacraments? Surely this matter of temporal power over the Church may safely be left to parliament and the king to settle. Monks of the Charterhouse are innocent of all power and removed from the world's changes to live with God in his eternity. For them to take upon themselves this disobedience to the king is to return into those very toils of time and chance which they have been called by God to leave behind for ever. I see no wickedness in civil obedience to the civil power. The king, in asking us to acknowledge him head of the Church in his own realm, is asking us to give up nothing that is ours to give.

"What do we have that is our own, that we must never give up however hard we are pressed? We have our rule, the order of our days, which encircles our peace, guards us from all worldly dangers and distraction, and frees us to approach God in the silence of our souls. Let us protect that peace, at any cost save that of God's truth, for our peace is a part of God's truth, our own peculiar part as hermits in the desert."

He sat down, his heart beating fast, pleased with what he had said.

Thomas Leighton looked straight at him, his old eyes icy, and said: "*Credo in unam, sanctam, catholicam et apostolicam Ecclesiam.* An article of faith, Master Fletcher."

Robert Fletcher jumped up again.

"But the king is a faithful son of the Church."

"Then why does he care so much for oaths to his new law that he will kill blameless men to get them?"

"For the peace of the Church! Have not all the bishops and abbots sworn the oath? Should we not copy them, greater and more learned men than we are, rather than our own brethren who had far better have held their peace, obeyed the king, and stayed in their cloisters where they could do only good?"

Master Leighton appeared to have abandoned the argument. He sat, his eyes again closed, without stirring, his hands grasping his sticks.

Robert Fletcher, triumphant, looked at the other monks once more, and last of all at the prior, and said, slowly and with final weight:

"Loathe for to think on aught under God, and go not thence for anything that befalleth."

He sat down quietly, thanking God for the words which had come to him, the right words.

In the silence that followed, the prior sat for a while with bowed head. At last he opened his mouth to speak. A low growl came from the corpse-like lips of Thomas Leighton.

"You spoke, Master Leighton?" the prior said.

"I said, 'I come not to bring peace, but a sword.'"

Thomas Leighton died in June, before they heard that three more monks had been slaughtered in London, and then Bishop

Fisher, and then Sir Thomas More, who had been Chancellor of England; before the hottest weeks of the summer, when strangers arrived every few days to question the prior and often the monks also; before two monks ran away and were caught on the road to Scotland and brought back with their hands tied like common thieves; before the prior went away to York to see the archbishop and came back with a book proving the pope's authority to be no greater than that of any other foreign bishop.

In August they learned that a monk of Jervaulx, not fifteen miles away, had been hanged in chains at York for upholding the supremacy of the pope on the word of Master Leighton of the Mountgrace, which he would not forsake. But when the monks of the Mountgrace were asked to swear the second oath, the oath of loyalty to the king as head of the Church in England, they swore it, all of them, with soldiers eating round the fire in the guesthouse, their weapons on the floor beside them.

Robert Fletcher knelt in his cell that day with *The Cloud of Unknowing* open in his hands and thanked God for the saving of his monastery from a needless end.

10

November 1535

Master Edmund Harvell, merchant, at Venice, to Master Thomas Cromwell, Secretary to King Henry VIII, in London; November 1535.

". . . I have myself delivered into the hand of the said Master Reginald Pole your letter requiring him to make answer at the king our sovereign's express commandment to those things which have been asked of him and signifying to him your desire that this same answer may be to the honour of God and the satisfaction of the king's grace. He read in my presence your letter and the letters of the king's chaplain bearing the same commandment of his grace and put them away privily, saying to me never a word. One in my pay, whom (after many several vain endeavours to overcome with gifts the silence of his servants) I have at length placed within his household here, informs me that he is now much occupied in the writing of a book, an answer, it may be understood, to the king our master's repeated requests for his opinion concerning the king's proceedings as to the divorce and the casting off of the bishop of Rome's yoke. He is said to be altogether turned away from his books of philosophy and to have told the young men about him that theological learning is alone truly deserving of their study. He makes much of certain grave and illustrious men, his elders by many years, Signor Gasparo Contarini and the Abbot Cortese and Bishop Carafa of Chieti among them, with whom he spends long hours at the abbey of San Giorgio, discussing, as my informant has it, reforms needful in the bishop of Rome's church. Which way, after all such studies and deliberations, he will tend in the matter of his answer to the king's grace, time will surely uncover, which I cannot. Care for the dignity and safety of his mother and brothers yet in England will surely weigh heavy against such pronouncements to the king's dissatisfaction as he, in his regard for the bishop of Rome, may falsely judge to be to the honour of God.

"A rumour I have thus far been powerless to verify holds that the said Master Pole has received from the emperor himself a letter encouraging him to hope for succour in an invasion of England that would have as its end the placing of the Princess Mary upon the throne with Master Pole as her husband. If this be indeed the case, Master Pole is already deep in such traitorous dealings with Messire Chapuys as those for which Bishop Fisher lately met his end. It is certain that Master Pole did take very ill the news of the bishop's death and that of Sir Thomas More, and that rasher voices in his household than his own compared their deaths to that of Thomas Becket in ancient time. The Signory of Venice, however, has been not greatly troubled by the English news, caring, as is its long-known custom, much for the consideration and protection of the wool trade and little for the bishop of Rome's honour and dignity. If the said bishop of Rome publish the bull against the king's highness that I am told has been prepared, upon my word as a merchant trading in the port of Venice, the Signory will put the profit of the republic before whatever duty it may owe to the said bishop."

11

1535–1538

After the summer of 1535 more than four years passed in which the monks of the Mountgrace were again left undisturbed in the peace of the cloister. Once, in October 1536, a servant to Sir Thomas Percy dismounted from his horse at the gate and demanded of the prior that he and two of his monks should ride forth with their best cross to join and succour the great pilgrimage then afoot against the king's plundering ministers. The prior called the man into the chapter-house and said before the assembled monks that it was not the business of monks of the Charterhouse to march with men under arms, whatever their cause. The messenger rode away alone. A month later they heard that the pilgrimage had been cruelly put down and that the pilgrims, called rebels by the king, had dispersed into the far corners of the north whence they had come. During the following spring and summer further letters from London and York brought news of the executions of all the leaders of the pilgrimage, though the king had pardoned them, including Sir Thomas Percy and the abbot of Jervaulx. The monks said prayers for the dead men's souls, thankful that their prior had kept them from danger within the walls of their cells.

Their peace was not as it had been: it was soured, curdled, with fear.

In the summer of 1537 they heard that ten monks of the London Charterhouse, who for two years had refused to swear allegiance to the king's supremacy over the Church, had been taken from their monastery and chained to posts in the dark in Newgate gaol, where one by one they died of hunger and disease.

The news that frightened them the most, because they understood it the least, came early in 1538. The Charterhouses of Coventry and Sheen, where no offence had been committed nor any disobedience shown, were surrendered to the king by their priors, and the monks dispatched into the world to find, each man for himself, where to lay his head.

The monks of the Mountgrace prayed for the safety of their house.

12

March 1538

Messire Eustace Chapuys, ambassador to the court of King Henry VIII in London, to Emperor Charles V, King of Castile and Aragon, Count of Burgundy, hereditary lord of the Netherlands, Austria, etc., etc., in Spain; March 1538.

". . . Much though it is to be wished that King Henry will indeed contract the Milanese marriage, with all the advantages to your imperial grace's interests in the Low Countries that we have before this time set forth, I fear that it would be over-sanguine to hope for his true firmness of purpose in this matter. The infant Prince Edward continues in good health and, having satisfied after so many years his great longing and desire for an heir male, the king at this present approaches the devising of a further union with a levity that is the despair of his councillors.

"I have discerned a most dire change in the dealings of Master Cromwell, the Lord Privy Seal, with the religion of this realm. Following the forfeitures of some few abbeys and priories in the north, as retribution for their complicity in the great rising, Master Cromwell has lately received the surrenders of many several more in all parts of the realm, innocent of any resistance to the king though these have been. Further, the monks of these last-surrendered abbeys and priories are no longer given leave to pursue their religion in another house but are cast upon the world with but a meagre pension to keep them from beggary. Despite letters despatched by the said Lord Privy Seal this very month to all the abbots and priors of

England signifying that the king intends no suppression of any house yet standing except they desire such suppression of themselves or else misuse themselves contrary to their allegiance, I reckon these fair words in truth no more than threats to them that they must keep such goods and rents secure and whole as they now possess, for the future enrichment of the king's store. For the word at court is all of a general dissolution, and those who would advance themselves by the purchase of abbey lands from the king are even now sharpening their pens.

"Cardinal Pole's vain endeavour to assist the rising in the north has earned his family much grief and danger in these last months, and I have heard that his mother, the Lady Margaret (who, your grace will recall, was so good and faithful a friend to the late Queen Catherine, your aunt), was constrained to write him letters condemning him as a traitor and avowing her earnest wish that he had never been born (though in her heart I do believe her most anxious for his safety from spies and assassins despatched by the said Lord Privy Seal), proud as she must in truth be to know a son of hers prince of the Church and ever close to the pope himself."

13

June 1538–May 1539

Robert Fletcher glanced every day at his precious book, which was never sent back to the London Charterhouse, but opened it no longer. It seemed now not to have been written for him but for someone else whom he had once known. He had come down into the shadows with the rest, and, like them, he waited, watching the prior, while all over England monks were taking their pensions and leaving their cloisters, putting off their habits and setting forth to scatter their bones across the land.

In June 1538 the Charterhouse of Axholme fell, whose prior had been one of those disembowelled in 1535. In November 1538 the last monks in the London Charterhouse, those who had yielded to the king, were turned out. Their cells were used to store the pavilions, banners, and gilded tents that decked the field for the king's jousts. In March 1539 Witham and Hinton, in Somerset, the oldest of the English Charterhouses, were surrendered without protest, though the prior of Hinton had written to the Mountgrace in February that he would never give up that which was not his to give but dedicated to Almighty God.

Robert Fletcher had once been sure of the course the prior should take. After the assault of all this news, his sureness had altogether failed. When yielding was to save the house, there had been a reason for yielding. When nothing could save the house, what reason was there for resisting? He saw none. He shared the fear of all the others.

They lived through the days as they always had, in their cells, in choir, on their knees. But they were moving in an emptiness. They had died to the world; they had been called to live only towards their own deaths, towards the thinning of the veil that separated them from God. Time for them had been folded up in God, folded up no less in death. They were monks. They were not going to die as monks. This they now knew. Therefore what was slowly lost its meaning for them because what was to come had already been taken from them.

As martyrs they could have died as monks. Little by little they understood that the occasion for such a death had slipped by without their grasping it. Robert Fletcher knew that by some of them he himself was held to blame for this.

One day in May 1539 he heard Geoffrey Hodson, crossing the cloister, tell another monk that Master Fletcher had seen a vision announcing that the Mountgrace was to be saved and that the prior had believed his story to the ruin of them all. It was loudly said, in order that he should hear. He walked back without pausing to his cell, climbed the ladder to his loft, and stood at the window, angry, looking over the wall into the wood. It was not true; but what profit could there now be in more words of his? The moment was past, the time when they might have chosen another way.

He ran a finger along the familiar lifting grain of the rough oak window frame. Perhaps what the young monk had said was after all not far from the truth. He thought of Master Leighton and of his own certainty that the old man had been wrong in the stand he had taken, lacking an understanding of the true end of Carthusian life. Now his own understanding, his own certainty, had dissolved with the dissolution of the naked intent stretching into God by which he had set so much store. God seemed infinitely far away and careless, after all, of the fate of his monks, who were to be loosed into the world in a terrifying freedom that had about it none of the warmth of obedience.

Was it that old Leighton had been right? And yet what purpose would their deaths have served?

He stood at the window for a long time. He opened the casement, and mild sweet air came into the musty loft. He looked out at the new green leaves of the trees, the stars of the garlic, the blue forget-me-nots, blooming beneath them, the slanting sunlight breaking through them, and knew that he was glad. Whether or not it was his own doing, however much or little he was to blame, he was glad, glad not to have died, not to have starved to death chained to a post in Newgate. And he knew in the same instant that it was not the pain and the filth and the dark that he was glad to have escaped but death itself, the leaving of the world, before, before—

He watched a bumblebee blunder from starry flower to flower of the wild garlic. Before what, he did not know. But he laughed to himself as he stood there, looking at the wood beyond the wall, the scrambling briars, the green sprawl of the traveller's joy, the spikes of the foxgloves, the tall nettles, taller every day, outside the garden where no one cut them down. What ruin, he asked himself as he breathed the soft air. What ruin?

He looked up the hillside under the oaks and saw a deer, a young stag, knee-deep in garlic and bluebells, regarding him with a clear gaze. He held his breath. But the stag bucked suddenly, plunged its antlered head forward, and bounded away up the hill, disappearing among the tree trunks.

Robert Fletcher bent and kissed the unplaned casement frame, which was warm in the sun.

14

October 1539

Master Edmund Harvell, merchant, at Venice, to the Lord Cromwell, Lord Privy Seal and Lord Great Chamberlain of England, at the court of King Henry VIII in London; October 1539.

" . . . I have lately travelled to Rome, at much charge to myself and pains upon the way thither, being not well pleased with the diligence of him whom I during the past year, at your lordship's behest, have retained to spy upon the traitor Pole and to discover his purposes against the king's majesty and realm.

"The said traitor Pole returned to Rome last month, his journey to the emperor in Spain and to France in search of aid and comfort in his seditious enterprises against the king's highness having been, most happily, not one whit more fruitful than that which he undertook two years since. He expended much time, and all to waste, in Toledo and afterwards with an Italian bishop close to Avignon; in like manner on the former occasion he was forced to lie for weeks idle in Liège, which is neither a French nor an imperial city, since neither the emperor nor the king of France cares to receive the sworn enemy of the king's highness, be he even the bishop of Rome's cardinal-legate with never so great a train. The said bishop of Rome may thunder as he will; his commission appointed to punish the king's grace for the destruction of the idolatrous shrine to the traitor Thomas Becket is already dissolved for lack of work to do, nor has his minion Pole the power to act in his master's evil designs without succour from the emperor or from France. The cardinal's traitorous purposes against his native land being thus now in check, he talks away the time, or so I learned in Rome, with other cardinals of like mind, among whom Cardinal Gasparo Contarini, of the noble family of Venice, is his nearest friend, in vain attempts to further the cause of a general council of the Church. It is my belief that such a council will never come to pass, for so deep in iniquity are sunk the most part of the bishops and cardinals that they will never countenance such light upon their dealings as a general council would shed abroad. If there be any council, it will rather be no more than that assembly of ambitious manciples, of men sworn to popish lusts and gains, that your lordship has written of before this time.

"While thus constrained in Rome the traitor Pole has few means by which he may harm the king's majesty; nevertheless by the same token he is in Rome protected from those captains as have been bruited in all Italy to serve his majesty in the matter of the said cardinal's apprehension. It is certain that he went in fear of his life upon his several travels of the last years, but by disguise and feigned roads and other such tricks he has up to this present devised to evade and escape all these his pursuers.

"When I left Rome he lay ill in his house there, though not, I fear, sick unto death. One of the lowest servants of his household, whom by lavish gifts I at length enjoined to speak, told me that he grieves much for the deaths of his brother and kinsmen and for the imprisonment of his mother, as well he may, knowing naught but his own foolish pride and black villainy to have brought all about. The having upon his soul the ruin of so great a family and the base ingrate malice with which he has used his natural prince and country were enough long since to have persuaded to a more conformable mind one less hardened in evil intent than he.

"I am now come again into Venice, where my own affairs have suffered not a little loss from these two months' absence in your lordship's business. If my pains and charges therein were to be speedily requited, the damage were soon set to rights. There is great scarcity of wheat in Venice, and it is my advice that licence granted by his majesty for the free exporting of wheat and other grain from England into Venice would earn the more gratitude of the Signory, which it is ever to the advantage of the realm to foster."

15

December 1539–April 1540

Thomas Leighton was the last monk who died in the priory of the Mountgrace.

In July 1539 Beauvale Charterhouse in Nottinghamshire was surrendered; in November, Hull. The Mountgrace was left, for six weeks, the only Charterhouse in England.

They came there, the king's men, in December, in the bitter cold. The sky had been overcast for days with the sickly heaviness which precedes snow. In the cells at midday it was too dark to read.

Four of them came, in the afternoon. Horses were stabled, fires lit in the guesthouse, meals prepared. Soon the tolling of the bell summoned the monks to the chapter-house. They listened as the document was read that surrendered the priory and all its possessions in the counties of York, Lincoln, Warwick, Nottingham, Leicester, and Norfolk, lands that had been given in the past by this man and that so that prayers might be said for their souls for ever. This time, again, all of them signed the paper. Later they sang Vespers in the church. The commissioners did not appear. The monks shivered in the choir, and a north wind howled in the hanging woods as they went back to their cells.

In his cell Robert Fletcher stood in front of the stack of logs that had been given him to fuel his fire for the whole winter. He gave the stack a furious kick, and several logs toppled to the ground. He remembered Will, in the yard at Easterside, tossing great lengths of tree trunk behind him so that no one could come near, and shrugged his shoulders. Then he piled on to the embers in the hearth more wood than he should burn in a week and sat up all night beside the blazing fire, never lying down to sleep. The hour for the night office came and went. No one rang the bell.

In the morning labourers arrived, the commissioners' hired men, blowing into their cupped hands in the cold, and began to strip the lead from the church and the wainscotting from the cells. The monks went again to the chapter-house and were given clothes and some money. In the church a man on a ladder was taking the panes out of a window. Books were stacked on the altar, and on a table chalices and patens were pushed together beside a pair of scales. Outside, a group of men and boys from the farms, and one or two old women, waited to be paid. In the cloister, on the grass, was a heap of bedding.

Robert Fletcher went back to his cell with his new clothes in his arms. He saw that the door of his cell was open. In almost twenty years he had never once come back to his cell and found the door open.

A man came out, edging through the doorway a big, splintered piece of panelling. A second man followed, carrying the stool from inside the cell, with a pile of bedding folded on it, and several books perched on the bedding. As the man leaned back against the door to hold it open, something slid from the top of the pile and dropped with a clatter to the stone floor. It was the crucifix that had hung on his wall. Robert Fletcher threw down the clothes and bent to pick it up. He held the wooden cross for a moment in his hands before he saw that the figure of Christ had come off the wood as the crucifix hit the ground. It lay on the flags, face down, sprawled like a man punched from behind in a brawl. He stood aghast, staring at the small silver Christ, stretched in the dust.

The first man propped the length of wainscotting against the wall and stooped, putting out his hand. Robert Fletcher snatched the figure up before the man touched it.

"We're to take all t' silver to be weighed together", the man said.

"Not this, you're not. Not this!" The words burst from him.

He pushed past the second man and went straight through his cell into the garden. He knelt on the path and dug a hole in the frozen earth with his bare hands. There were tears running down his cheeks. When the hole was long enough he buried the figure, right way up so that it looked up at him, its arms outstretched, as it had all that while looked down, and piled the earth in on top of it. The cloud of forgetting, he muttered to himself as he made the grave; the cloud of forgetting, as the magnitude of his loss poured over him.

Later the monks stood and watched while the bell was brought out of the church. Eight men lowered it to the grass, where it remained, on its side, fallen in a stillness that, after many thousand hours rung to summon them, seemed at last to dispatch the monks more finally than any order from London, so that some of them backed away from it in fear. Robert touched its rim. The metal was so cold that he took his hand quickly away as if he had been burned.

While the monks were preparing to leave, snow began to fall, white thick flakes hiding the sky and the hills, coming down with the early dusk over the emptying buildings.

An hour later Robert Fletcher walked alone out of the gate. The wind had dropped, and the snow covered the grass, the church, the cells, the forsaken bell, with quiet. When he had walked two or three hundred yards up the path through the wood, he looked down. He could not see even the outline of the great cloister, the outer court. He could see no light. He was alone under the trees in the falling snow as if the priory of the Mountgrace had never been. He thought of the bared stone walls of his cell, the books gone, the fire out. He thought of his garden, the plants cut down for winter, the ivy and the nettles beyond the wall in wait for the spring.

That night he walked only as far as the neighbouring village, knowing that ten miles of open moor lay between him and Easterside. He slept in a shepherd's cottage, thankful for a place by the fire with the dogs. The next morning, his new clothes still drying out as he walked, he set out over the snow-covered hills in glittering sunshine. The cold and the brightness made his eyes smart, and he trudged with his head down, angry at the stupidity of what he had seen the day before, at how little there was for anyone to gain from the destruction of the Charterhouse compared to the scale of what was lost, angry for the fear of the tenants and their families, who were used to fair treatment from the monastery, angry most of all for the frightened old men turned out of their home into the winter world.

But as he neared Easterside, at last saw it from the other side of the dale, small on the flank of the hill with a thin line of smoke rising, he forgot his anger and his pulse began to race. What would he find there? After nineteen years, what would he find?

A woman he did not know opened the door to him. From behind her a cowed girl of about ten peered at him, frightened.

"Is this Thomas Fletcher's house?"

"Aye."

"Is Thomas Fletcher here?"

"He's out wi' t' sheep and won't be back while dinner-time. What do you want wi' him?"

She looked at him more closely, with some suspicion.

"Who are you?"

"Is old Tom Fletcher dead?"

"He's dead these seven year and more, and good riddance to him."

He saw an idea occur to her. Her face hardened.

"Be you—Who be you?"

"I am his son, Robert Fletcher. I have been a monk at the Mountgrace since I was a lad. Yesterday they—"

She drew back a step and began to shut the door.

"Don't shut the door. I won't hurt you. I shall ask nothing of him, only to tell me—"

The girl retreated to the back of the room. With the door half shut the woman said:

"There's nowt here for you. He said you would be coming here one of these days. You're to go away and not come back, he says. He won't have you begging here."

"Where is Will?"

"There's no Will in this house and never has been", she said, and slammed the door shut. He heard her bolt it, at the top, at the bottom. He heard her shout at the child and the child begin to cry.

He turned and walked away down the hill, his footsteps creaking in the snow, to where the beck flowed black and swift under icicled branches. He stopped on the plank bridge and watched the water.

Where was Will? Dead? If not dead, where was he? Where could he have gone, who had to have his food set before him like a dog or a small child? And Master Husthwaite, who must have been as old as his father, perhaps older? Surely he must be dead?

He looked at the black water flowing and thought of the village on the slope of the further hill, the church among the trees by the river. Either the village held an old man whom he had known, by whose fire he had sat winter after winter all his youth, or it did not. If it did not, what reason was there for staying here? And if he went on, where was he to go?

He looked up from the water. His freedom oppressed him. The midwinter sun was already well down in the sky, but the length of the day weighed on him, an unfamiliar load. In the monastery he had lived light, from one ordered hour of prayer to the next, his silence full of words, a certain number of pages to be turned measuring each day as the liturgy's turning of sorrow and joy measured each year. Even his body seemed heavy, as if he had been swimming downstream for a long time and had at last begun to wade ashore, the weight of his limbs increasing with every step against the pull of the water.

When the sun had almost set behind Murton moor and he was very cold, he left the bridge and walked uphill again towards the village. He met no one. Smoke rose into the clear, icy air from the cottages in the village and from Master Husthwaite's house.

For a long time he stood in the road, motionless, afraid. Afraid of what? Perhaps only of another stranger opening the door.

When it was dark enough for the glow of the fire to be visible through the panes of the window, he went up to the door and knocked. No one came. He knocked again. He heard a voice inside the house say: "The door is open." The voice had altered, become higher and thinner, but he recognised it. He pushed open the door and went in.

He drew back at once. There was a smell of dirt and poverty in the house, and for a moment he almost turned and left. He must have been wrong about the voice.

"Who is there?"

He had not been wrong. He walked further into the room, facing the window, the last of the light, so that he could be seen. Master Husthwaite, gaunt and hunched, with a long tangled beard, sat in his chair by the glowing fire, staring straight ahead of him.

"Who is there?" the old man said again, not turning his head.

"It is I."

But he said once more: "Who is there?" and did not turn his head.

He was blind.

The shock made Robert Fletcher almost fall, and he put out a hand to the wall to steady himself. The wall was sticky with cobwebs and grease. After a while, taking the time to speak gently, so as not to shock in his turn the old man sitting there, he said: "It is Robert Fletcher, sir, come back from the Mountgrace, which was yesterday suppressed by the king."

Master Husthwaite did not move, nor did his still and hollow face change at all.

"Do I know you, Robert Fletcher?" he said at last.

"You knew me many years ago, when I was a boy. You knew me well. I was the lad from Easterside. You took me in. You taught me. I helped you in the church. We read books. I went for a monk, at the Charterhouse. But now—"

"My books are all sold", the old man broke in. "They were nothing to me at last, nothing, for all the care I had. Are we not taught to set no store by worldly things?"

He spoke in a slow, toneless voice.

"Books. So much dust."

In the firelight Robert Fletcher saw two tears trickle from the sightless eyes. He took a step forward. The rushes on the floor were matted together with dirt.

"Do you remember me, Master Husthwaite?"

The old man said: "Have you brought my supper?"

A little later a cottager's wife, a woman Robert Fletcher thought perhaps he remembered, came into the house carrying a bowl of soup with pieces of bread floating in it. She started, almost dropped the bowl, seeing him standing there. She did not recognise him.

"I am an old friend of Master Husthwaite", he said. "I knew him long ago."

He took the bowl from her and gave the old man his supper, feeding him spoonful by spoonful from the bowl, kneeling in front of him on the filthy rushes. The woman watched.

"Poor soul", she said, as if Master Husthwaite were also deaf. "Poor old man. He didn't know you, sir, I'll be bound."

Afterwards he helped her put him to bed, a narrow truckle-bed without sheets, which stood where once the table had been at which he had copied thousands of lines of verse.

He slept on the floor himself, in front of the hearth, wrapped in a blanket that the woman brought when she came back with more soup, for him.

"You must be half-starved, sir, travelling in this weather."

He stayed for three months.

He washed the old man every day. He kept the room clean. He bought better food, eggs, cheese, white bread. He bought shirts and firewood and another truckle for himself, since the house was quite empty. He spent nearly all the money that the commissioners had given him. He talked to the old man, read to him often from the English psalter, which was the only book left in the house, twice or three times recited to him such lines of Virgil as he could remember. Not once, never once, did he reach, behind the simple demands of the present, which were those of a dying animal, the man he had known. Where was he now, that man, with his long past, and the much longer past which had given him all his subtle sense of who he was? Where was he now? Already with God although his body still lived?

He learned that the blindness had come upon him suddenly, five years before, and that since then he had scarcely stirred from his chair. He was no longer able to walk and refused to feed himself. Another priest had had to be paid to do his work. He had sold everything, saying that his blindness was the judgement of God upon all that he had loved and that he was fit only for the grave.

Never in those three months, as the life left in his body slipped day by day away, did Master Husthwaite give any sign of knowing who Robert Fletcher was, nor did he once call him by his name.

One Sunday in March, when he knew the end to be not far off, Robert Fletcher went to hear Mass in the church by the river. He stood at the back, as he had as a boy, and listened to the long-familiar words which he had himself countless times repeated in the Charterhouse. Words. Was it not words that Master Husthwaite had shut from his life in his despair, and were not words everything, everything of God that man may know, the water of life? And the bread and wine on the altar? The word of God made flesh? God's word—or only more words?

After the Mass he went out into the chilly sunshine. The villagers were going home, walking away up the path between the graves. He turned from them and watched the brown river flowing as in the past. He noticed a dead tree in the field across the river. All its twigs, its slender branches and fine shoots, which should bud into leaf in the spring, from which it might yet grow, had gone, so that only the thick, bare boughs, black and stark, remained. The tree would fall in a gale one day, and the great boughs would be found to be light and rotten, good for nothing but burning.

The woman who had brought the soup on the first evening touched his sleeve.

"How does Master Husthwaite do?"

"Not well. These last few days he has sunk very low."

"And him such a holy man. I am very sorry, Master Fletcher, we are all sorry, to see him die so. More years than I can count he's been Hawnby priest. There's many in the dale will not remember the time before he came. Mind you, too fine for us he always was. A man like him, with all his books and that, and a gentleman, wanting for nothing, the Lord knows why he shut himself away at the back of beyond, wasting among poor folk what he might have made much of in the great world, even in London, I shouldn't wonder."

"He did not think it waste." He spoke quietly, and she did not listen.

"And to be so brought down—I always say a thaw is evil weather. When the days warm . . . But then, what does he have to stir himself for now?"

He did not answer, and they stood side by side in silence. He did not raise his eyes again to the tree but stared down at the rushing water.

"The river's well up", he said.

"There's been a deal of snow to come down off the moor. They say the bridge at Laskill's gone. Though the water's nowhere near as high as it was the day, it'll be six or seven years back, about this time, the middle of Lent it was, when old Tom Fletcher was drowned at Shaken bridge."

"Old Tom Fletcher?" He looked up sharply.

"Oh, Master Fletcher, I beg your pardon, sir. I had quite forgotten—you never did seem like one of them, somehow, and with you being away so long. Though you have a look of your father, now I come to think."

"I haven't spoken to my brother since I came back. He will not see me. Tell me what happened at Shaken bridge."

"You mean to say you never heard?"

He shook his head. Every night at the Mountgrace, every single night to the very end, he had prayed for his father, thinking of him crouched over the dying fire.

"'Well, sir, it was a Friday, about this time of year, as I say. He'd gone to market early in the morning. That was the one thing he never let young Tom do in his place, not ever in all those years. And he'd left for home long after dark, late even for him, as came out after."

It had been one of his tasks at Easterside to listen far into the night on Fridays for the sound of the wagon lumbering into the yard. He had had to take the horse from the shafts and unharness it after the slouching figure of his father, wrapped in an old blanket and too drunk to hold the reins, had slid to the ground and stumbled, cursing, off to the house. Sometimes he fell on all fours into the mud, and he had to drag him to his feet and push him through the door into the smoky kitchen.

"There'd been pouring rain all that day and all the night

before. And what with the snow melting too, the river came up and up all the time he was away. Rising as you watched, it was, even here in the village. And of course by the time he set out, not taking a lot of notice, as you might say, of the road, the bridge at Shaken was down, washed right away, and the water through the ford eight or ten foot deep in the middle. The horse, knowing the way home as he did, must have taken the wagon straight into the river at the ford and tried to swim, perhaps, shafts and all. But the force of the water had brought rocks down all over the ford bed, the wagon stuck fast in the boulders—and there they found them in the morning, drowned both, horse and master, your father fallen half out of the wagon into the water, being asleep I daresay, in the dark."

The day after Master Husthwaite was buried, he left the village.

He walked down the dale, his step firm on the road, and rejoiced in the strength of his limbs, in the openness of the unknown world before him. The day was full of weather, blue sky and clouds, sunlight and rapid shadow, a soft wind blowing little squalls of rain. In the old man's house he had almost come to share his blindness. Now he had come out of the dark, and seeing with his own eyes the showery day, the spring, filled him with delight. The dale widened under the sky; he saw calves in the fields, lambs playing, and the river broadening as it flowed between trees.

He had been released from bonds, and his garden at the Mountgrace that day seemed to him a narrow plot, walled in, neat and small, a constraining pattern foisted upon God's earth.

16

September 1542

Messer Marin Giustinian, ambassador of the Republic of Venice at the court of Pope Paul III in Rome, to the Signory of Venice; September 1542.

" . . . Letters will already have reached Venice bearing news of the sudden death on 24 August of our illustrious countryman and friend Cardinal Gasparo Contarini. The sad disappointment of all the hopes placed in him for some adjustment with the Protestants at Ratisbon surely lay heavy upon him during his last months, as did the neglect, so plain as almost to deserve the name of disgrace, into which his reputation here in Rome had lately fallen. It has been observed by many that since the failure at Ratisbon the pope has swung very far towards the other party (for you must understand that the cardinals who a few years ago laboured together for the reform of the Church are now sorely divided among themselves). Cardinal Carafa, who sees heresy lurking everywhere in the Church, has the pope's ear; it was he who secured from the pope in July the bull which opened the way for an Inquisition to be established here in Rome, and now I learn that, without waiting for the proper provision of money from the Curia, he has fitted up a house at his own expense, where he presides daily over sessions of the said Inquisition.

"His companions of old are not exempt from the suspicion in which Cardinal Carafa holds all but the fiercest of his own supporters. I have heard that even Monsignor Pole, who earlier this year travelled as cardinal-legate to Trent for the council that never assembled, so that he returned as empty-handed as Cardinal Contarini from Ratisbon, has had the orthodoxy of his opinions called into question. Whether or not there is any substance in this rumour I have yet to discover; however it is certain that in his administration of the papal patrimony at Viterbo (that retreat from his enemies in which the pope graciously installed him two years ago or more), Monsignor Pole has acted with conspicuous leniency towards such heretics as have been there unearthed, saying always that he holds, with Saint Bernard, that the faith is to be maintained by persuasion and not by force. It is also true that the latest and most serious scandal, the flight to the Lutherans, in the very week of Cardinal Contarini's death, of the vicar-general of the Capuchins and the celebrated Augustinian preacher Pietro Martire Vermigli touches Monsignor Pole very closely, as the said Vermigli was a devoted friend of many years and took with him out of Italy a learned Jew of Monsignor Pole's household whom Monsignor Pole himself had converted to the Christian faith. (It need hardly be said that the apostasy of the Capuchin and the said Vermigli has added further fuel to the fire that Cardinal Carafa has set burning here in Rome.) All these things notwithstanding, I cannot myself believe that Monsignor Pole, who leads in Viterbo a life of almost monkish austerity and retirement, will ever abandon the fold of the Church for whose sake he has lived in exile from his native land these ten years and for which almost his whole family, including at last his aged mother, barbarously beheaded by the English king, have most unjustly died. I hear, indeed, that he has said publicly that he will not answer the letter he has received from Vermigli, in which the Augustinian attempts to defend his apostasy, and that he stays quietly at home mourning the death of our beloved Contarini, grieving more for him, and the failure of his cause, even than for the slaying of his family.

"It is agreed by all to whom I have had occasion to speak in Rome that any hope of reconciliation with the Protestants is now further distant than ever, not least because of the deep disagreements between Catholic philosophers, and that neither the emperor nor the pope is likely to yield on those points which have hitherto prevented the successful calling of a general council of the Church. The emperor would wish any such council to attend to the reform of discipline in the Church (thus sorely vexing the most part of the cardinals), in order to go some way towards healing the breach with the Protestants, which is causing him ever greater anxiety and grief in Germany; while the pope must compel a council to occupy itself with matters of doctrine in order to make clear what is and what is not to be judged orthodoxy, thus driving the Protestants still further into their obduracy. In short, I see no end to these troubles."

17

April 1545

Robert Fletcher sat with his book in a window of Saint William's College, where he lived with the other chantry priests, his breakfast piece of bread, a single bite out of it, forgotten on the bench beside him. He was aware of the morning crowd of people passing in the street outside, hurrying in the sunshine, not looking up; also of the ringing of the Minster bells, the full peal jangling and crashing above him as if for a special feast, although, as he afterwards remembered, there was none that day. Most of all he was aware of the sun striking, across the low clutter of the city's rooftops, the great east window of the Minster, transforming its huge height and width of glass into a fiery pool flashing above the people in the crowded street. He knew that they were there, the people, the bells, the dazzling glare on the window, though he neither looked nor listened but with trembling fingers turned back the few pages he had read, to the beginning.

He had bought the book because of the face of Valentine Vries, tied to the back of a cart with ropes and dragged through the mud.

When he saw that face and followed with the rest out to the Knavesmire for the spectacle, he had been in York only a few months. He had found without difficulty a place among the chantry priests in the Minster; he was better learned than most of the expelled monks who came to the city looking for work, and he discovered that the Carthusians, although he never met another in York, retained a respect that the other orders had lost. So he had slipped easily into the easy passage of days and weeks, saying the required number of Masses in the dusty little chapel in the Minster that was his chantry and on Sundays and feast-days singing with the vicars-choral in the high choir while beyond the screen the people came and went and children cried. He was grateful for bed and board and for the ordered regulation of his days. He had long been accustomed to obedience: not to choose, but to perform at the proper time the duty to which he was bound, and so to obedience he returned as if to a sleep from which he had woken, after all, earlier than was necessary.

One day at dawn he had come to the window hearing shouts and trampling feet in the street.

"They're burning the heretics today. Vries and his wife, a Dutch cordwainer . . . They pull them through the city, poor devils, over the bridge and up through the Bar . . . You won't see much for the crowd there'll be."

He went out, nevertheless, and joined the press of jeering, shouting people who, unlike a truly festive crowd, fell silent when what they had come to see passed by, so that he could hear approaching the rattle of wheels on the cobbles, and the bumping of the man's head. He saw the woman first, kneeling on the cart, her head hidden in her hands, and then the man, his ankles tied to the cart, the back of his head scraping the stones and his arms outstretched as if he had already been crucified. But the man's face was entirely alive and entirely at peace, as if he were lying under a tree on a hot summer day and watching the leaves move gently between him and the sky.

He followed the cart with the crowd, out under the Bar and down through the mud to the Knavesmire. Although he soon fell back in the throng and lost sight of the man's face, he knew that the expression on it would not now change. When he saw the two heaps of faggots, piled high above the people, he quailed and almost vomited. He turned back towards the city, running, but did not reach it before he was overtaken by the smell of smoke and burning flesh. He could not look back. He heard the woman scream three times, three dreadful shrieks carrying over the plain in the sunshine, but there was not a murmur from the crowd that had gathered to watch, nor a sound from the man who also died.

"A martyr's death. A martyr's death", he said to himself as he walked back, driving the nails of one hand into the palm of the other so hard that the marks did not fade for several days. It was of himself that he was thinking and of the death they had avoided at the Mountgrace by putting their names to the king's papers in the quiet chapter-house.

Some hours later, when the smoke had stopped rising from the Knavesmire and the people had all gone home, the difference struck him. The London Carthusians died, as the monks at the Mountgrace might have died, for the long past, for a good in the certainty of which they were sustained by the certainty of the ages. Something new threatened that good—the taking by the king of a power that had never been his—and they died to defend their own, their ancient ground. What was more, he himself had recommended yielding to the king so as to keep safe that very ground, although in the end the yielding was to no avail. But the cordwainer had not died for the past. The cordwainer had died for something new, something he had seen that others had not seen, and that he saw still as they dragged him through the streets and the blood from the back of his head stained the cobbles. And his new thing was not the king's, not by any means the king's, since had not the king ordered his death also?

No more heretics were burned in York, although it was well known that the number of those who owned to Luther's opinion as to how their souls might be saved was slowly growing, and that among that number were one or two of the richest men in the city.

The day after the cordwainer's death, Robert Fletcher said his

Mass as usual in the cold chantry. He pushed Valentine Vries to the back of his mind, but he did not forget him. Several times here and there in the city he listened to arguments about the sacrifice of the Mass or the existence of purgatory or the merit to be gained from pilgrimages and relics. Voices were raised, fists banged on tavern tables; old men in corners crossed themselves and crept fearfully away. In those who spoke with bitterness and fury against the Church he never caught even a glimpse of whatever it was that the cordwainer had seen.

Five years passed before he made a choice of his own.

He heard that a rich clothier, once a Halifax man and known to have shared the Protestant beliefs of his weavers, had died and that the widow was selling books she was afraid to keep in her house. He went to the house and bought the smallest of the half-dozen books she took from a chest that she first unlocked.

"And you a priest, sir", she said. "For shame, to give room to such wickedness." She locked his money away in the chest as if it too were tainted with evil.

He walked home with his heart pounding, nursing the book inside his coat. It was called *On the Liberty of a Christian Man*, and he knew that Luther himself had written it. The copy he had bought was a Latin translation, hastily written in a small, cramped hand with many abbreviations. He slept with it hidden under his bed, saving the reading of it for the morning light.

Now, the next day, the morning light glittered on the window of the Minster above him as he laid the open book down on the bench. He looked over his shoulder into the room as if he had never seen it before. They had all gone out, leaving dirty jugs and dishes among the crumbs on the table. He saw that the top of the table was after all a fine piece of oak, a fine smooth piece of black oak, well planed and beeswaxed, and the jugs and dishes shone among the crumbs, round and clear-glazed.

It was true. It was all true. It changed everything, all that he had been and now was, all that he had lived in the Charterhouse in the assurance of his virtuous days.

The phrases turned in his head as he sat there.

He took up the book again.

A Christian man is the most entirely free lord of all, subject to none.

A Christian man is the most entirely dutiful servant of all, subject to everyone.

In what manner does a man become just, free, and truly Christian, that is, spiritual, new, and inner? It is clear that no external thing, by whatever name it may be called, can in any way conduce to Christian righteousness or liberty, any more than it can lead the way to unrighteousness or bondage. This can be shown by a simple argument. What can it profit the soul if the body is well, free, and active, if it eats, drinks, and does as it likes, since in these respects even the most impious slaves of vice may stand very well? On the other hand, what harm can the soul take from illness, imprisonment, hunger, thirst, or any external discomfort, since in these respects even the most godly men—free men in the purity of their conscience—may be afflicted? None of these things touches the liberty or servitude of the soul. Thus it will profit nothing if the body be adorned with holy garments in the manner of priests, or live in holy places, or occupy itself with holy offices, or pray, fast, abstain from certain foods, and do whatever labour can be done by the body and in the body. A far other thing is needed for the righteousness and liberty of the soul.

He closed his eyes and saw the pile of habits on the frozen grass at the Mountgrace, a group of men beside it, in new clothes, some of them weeping.

"To clear the ground completely: even contemplation, meditation, and everything the soul can do are of no avail."

He saw *The Cloud of Unknowing*, tied up with office-books and psalters, to be taken to London with the silver and the lead.

> One thing, and one thing only, is necessary for the Christian life, righteousness, and liberty. It is the most Holy Word of God, the gospel of Christ, as he says: "I am the resurrection and the life: he that believeth in me, though he were dead, yet shall he live." Therefore let us accept it as certain and firmly established that the soul may lack all things except the Word of God, without which, in turn, there is no help for it at all. Having the Word, it is rich, lacks nothing: for it is the word of life, truth, light, peace, righteousness, salvation, joy, liberty, wisdom, power, grace, glory, and every inestimable blessing.

He stopped reading for a moment, to let this richness peal and clash about him like the bells ringing above his head.

> You may ask, "What then is the Word of God, and how shall it be used, since there are so many words of God?" I answer: the apostle explains in Romans 1 that it is the gospel of God concerning His Son who was made flesh, suffered, rose again from the dead, and was glorified through the spirit that sanctifies. To have preached Christ is to have fed the soul, to have made it righteous and free, to have saved it—provided the soul believed in the preaching. For faith alone is the saving and efficacious use of the Word of God: "If thou shalt confess the Lord Jesus with thy mouth, and shalt believe in thine heart that God hath raised him from the dead, thou shalt be saved."
>
> Nor can the Word of God be received and cherished by any works whatsoever but only by faith alone. Therefore it is clear that as the soul needs only the Word to live and be just, so it will be justified by faith alone and not by any works. For if it could be justified by anything else, it would not need the Word, nor in consequence would need faith.

He closed the book and went out into the street with it still in his hand. He was dazed by what he had read. Also he knew, and the knowledge jarred like a false note sung, that he had been told these things before, long ago. He could not remember who it was that told him. He had not then understood, and he knew now only that if he had understood, much might have been different. He shook his head, as if to banish the echo of the false note.

He walked slowly, looking at the people as they went by, faces marked with care, bent old women, young men swaggering, or hurrying close to the wall, older men weighed down with poverty or equally weighed down with wealth. They must hear, they must know, they must all be set free. The book he had read over and over again in his cell, his holy place, was only for himself, or, at any time, for very few. But this, this was for them all; no matter how poor or how encumbered with the things of the world, no matter how alone or how surrounded with parents, wives, children, they might be. This was for them.

He went into the Minster through the south door. Passing by his chantry without a glance, he walked through the arch beside the screen and up beyond the choir, beyond the high altar, to the Lady Chapel under the east window. There was no one there. The bells were still ringing. The tall silence lay undisturbed under their din.

He stood with his back to the great stone spaces of the church, with his book, among tombs. The light he had seen from outside, from the other side, striking the window into a blazing surface, he saw now pouring through the glass, split by the intricate lead, coloured red, green, blue, gold, purple, colouring the white stone where it fell, and quiet, as if the brilliance on the outside had been as loud as the bells.

He knew that now he had seen what Valentine Vries had seen.

It was not that everything had changed. Was it not rather that only he had changed and that what he saw looked new to him because of how he saw it?

That was it. Nothing had changed, yet all was new, because of his new understanding, his new eyes; as the wild light outside, reflected, cast back by the surface of the glass, was here given passage, cooled and coloured as it streamed in to the stone.

He stayed at the foot of the wall, the still light high above him, for a long time. With deliberation, he put what was past behind him, all the dead, his father, Master Husthwaite, the destroyed Charterhouse. He would take hold of what was to come even if it were not more than a day, an hour. He would let nothing darken his newfound sight, and in the freedom he had discovered he would do what he could that other men should know.

When he walked away, down the long south aisle towards the far, pale figure of Christ crucified in the window at the very west end of the Minster, the bells had stopped ringing. He came out of the cathedral into even, midday sunshine.

He walked briskly round the outside of the cathedral to Saint William's College. As he opened the door, a man rose from the bench by the window where he himself always sat and approached him, hand outstretched.

"Master Fletcher."

"Aye."

"Do you not know me, sir? I am Geoffrey Hodson, of the Mountgrace."

For an instant he stood as still as a stone; then he made himself smile, move forward, shake hands.

"Master Hodson—forgive me. After so long a time—"

"Not yet five years, Master Fletcher."

"Is it I you have come for?"

Hodson looked at him with stern, youthful eyes. He waited with foreboding, as if Geoffrey Hodson had the power to pull him back into all that he had thought to lay at last to rest.

"I come from the prior", Hodson said. "He is living, alone, in the hermitage above the Charterhouse, the cottage with his chapel beside it that the commissioners allowed him. He has sent me to seek out the monks yet alive, to ask whether any would be willing to return to the Mountgrace. Not to the cloister, which is ruined and slighted and overgrown with weeds, but only to his cottage, to dwell with him there in something near the old way. There is room for two or three, and his pension would support so few in the necessities of a hermit's life. I shall go myself, but, till now, I have found none other able—"

"Master Hodson", he broke in. "I am a chantry priest here in the Minster. I have also other work to do, fresh work, preaching the word of God. I begin to understand that to withdraw from the world as we once did, to wear the habit, to fast and repeat the office, cannot in itself free the soul, and that it is not works but faith itself that must bring liberty to all men, if only they may hear and believe the truth."

He faltered. His words, too newly learned, seemed to him to be without substance, to skitter on the surface of something else, more secret, darker. He gripped Luther's book tightly in his hand.

Geoffrey Hodson studied his face.

"Master Fletcher," the young man said at last, his voice hard, "you were the one whose return the prior most eagerly looked for. Have you forgotten the day of the first oath, and the day we heard of the martyrdoms in London, all you said then? And are you now inclined towards heresy? Justification by faith alone and meanwhile do what you will? I shall tell the prior—what shall I tell the prior? That you now believe your years at the Mountgrace to have been no more than wasted time? I will tell the prior that."

Hodson looked at him with contempt and went to the open door. He turned and said:

"Farewell, Master Fletcher. You were always for the winning side, that I do recall. God grant our paths do not cross again."

He banged the heavy door shut behind him.

Robert Fletcher sat down heavily by the long table, now bare and swept of crumbs. He remembered Thomas Leighton, who had laughed at him and said, "We'll make a monk of you yet." Then he remembered that it was from Thomas Leighton that he had long ago heard Luther's truth.

From his very depths, he groaned aloud.

He saw Thomas Leighton's freshly dug grave and the cowled monks standing round it singing in grey summer rain.

Recordare Jesu pie
quod sum causa tuae viae
ne me perdas illa die.

He thought of the pale figure on the cross in the west aisle window. He looked out of the window at the people still passing in the same street, unaware of his gaze.

Good Jesus, give me simple faith and free me from my sin.

He opened the book and began to read it once more, slowly and carefully.

18

July 1546

Don Francisco de Toledo, ambassador at the General Council of the Church assembled at Trent, to Emperor Charles V, King of Aragon and Castile, etc., in Germany; July 1546.

" . . . And so, in despite of our most strenuous endeavours to delay the discussion of doctrine until after the enactment of at least some such reforming decrees as would give satisfaction to the Lutherans, the Council has been engaged, these ten days past, in the early preparation of a dogmatic decree concerning the question of man's justification. I greatly fear that if, as seems likely, anathemas against justification by faith alone are shortly to be pronounced, all hope that the deliberations of the Council might open the path towards the reconciliation of the Lutherans to the Church must now be abandoned. Before the legates of the pope set the conduct of the Council in this unfortunate course, there remained some possibility that your Imperial Majesty's war against the League might appear to the world chiefly as the necessary suppression of rebellious subjects; now, although I have used all possible means available to me to prevent such an outcome, the Council's actions needs must give this lawful suppression the evil fame of a war of religion.

"The most unwelcome news of all is that the cardinal of England, Monsignor Pole, who alone among the princes of the Church, as your Imperial Majesty is aware, is regarded in Germany as holding the cause of the reunion of the Church truly at heart, has left both the Council and the city. The reason I have been given for this unlooked-for departure of him who, of the three legates of the pope, has always listened most attentively to my representations, is a severe pain in his arm from which he has suffered acutely already more than a month. Indeed it is true that he has of late looked very pale and much aged (I believe he is not above forty-six years old although in appearance a good deal older), but I think it by no means impossible that his indisposition is caused more by his distress at the turn events have taken here than by a mere affliction of the body. Your Majesty will remember that it was he who, in the first session of the Council, addressed the fathers with an impassioned plea for their own acknowledgement of guilt, as neglectful pastors who had led their sheep astray, to which the whole Council, though since showing little willingness to act upon his words, listened in astonished silence. It cannot be doubted that behind that address lay his earnest hope of guiding the Council towards such confession of grave fault and abuse in the past that the Lutherans might after all be persuaded to send representatives here. Furthermore, I have been told by one who was present that a month ago, when the list of errors to be condemned was being drawn up, Monsignor Pole insisted upon undertaking to answer for the Lutherans lest it be said that they had been condemned without a hearing. And at last, on the twenty-first day of June, when the present debate began, he implored the whole Council, considering, as it now is, the question upon which our salvation wholly depends (these were his very words), not to shun the writings of the Lutherans as the advised deceits of enemies and in all parts necessarily false, but to read them with an unbiased mind.

"From all these evidences it is clear to me that, watching day by day the destruction of those high hopes with which he entered upon the work of the Council and by which he has for many years set such store, he has succumbed to grievous disappointment, and that it is this which has broken his health and caused him to leave Trent. For, useful to your Imperial Majesty as his support has long been, he is all in all devoted to things of the spirit and no man of policy. He knows not how to alter his sail to any change in the wind and so has altogether left these dangerous waters, to the sorry weakening of your Majesty's interests here. This very morning I learned that the other legates sent to Signor Priuli's villa, where Cardinal Pole is lodged, to ask the said cardinal's opinion concerning an article in the draft decree under discussion and that he has refused to reply, giving absence, insufficiency, and indisposition as his reasons. (I have heard it whispered that he has himself inclined to certain Lutheran doctrines; but his well-known loyalty to the Church, unshaken by much personal tribulation, leads me to regard such rumours as slanderous and to conclude, rather, as I have said, that it is his deep desire for that unity of the Church which he even now sees slipping beyond hope of recall that has brought him to his present sad condition.)

"Meanwhile the debates on justification proceed with much display of learning, more rancour, and even more slowness (happily, for your Imperial Majesty's purposes), so that I doubt whether the decree will reach its perfected form before September or October, by which time your Majesty's present campaign will have its own tale to tell.

"The difficulty of supplying this distant city of the mountains, which now contains such an unwonted number of strangers, not to mention the avarice of the local tradesmen, has led to great increase in the price of meat, bread, wine, and fodder. If your Majesty would give instruction for the immediate transfer of funds from Augsburg or Venice, I should not be obliged further to diminish the household which your Imperial dignity requires me to maintain."

19

June 1549

"And therefore, my dear friends, now that the word of God in the Bible is given to you in your own tongue that you have known since you were children in your mothers' arms, now that the holy Mass is said for you in your own tongue that is as natural to you as the air you breathe, I beseech you only to listen, only to hear what God speaks anew to every man that comes into the world. It is not in the oft-repeated mumbling of old prayers half understood that we shall know God. Such prayers are no more than charms told over while our minds stray among the things of earth; but prayer may be speech between ourselves and God. And the Latin that is gone for the good English that you now hear plainly had no magic power in it; it was no more than an old tongue long since fallen out of use among the people.

"And so I beg you to listen with all your might, to hear and take to heart, today and henceforth, the word of God that will be given you. For it is not in coming dutifully to church, not in fasting or almsgiving or going on pilgrimage, though all these things are good, and not in anything the priest may say or do on your behalf, that you will know God. No, it is in yourselves, in your minds and understanding, in your sorrow for your sins and your love for Christ who has redeemed you from them, in your faith in him and your trust in the word that he is, that you will know God."

As he stopped speaking, he glanced along the few rows of people in the little church, his people, those whom he so much longed to lead into the path he had found for himself in these last years. Some of them were looking at him, most not. Two or three had mistrust, almost fear, on their faces. How could he soothe that fear from their eyes? What better words could he find, for the next time? He was there only to try to open their hearts. He did not want them to believe what he said because it was he who said it. He wanted them to grasp the truth for themselves and recognise it as their own.

He turned to the altar and picked up the new book, the book of the common prayer, which was the present cause of their suspicion. It had arrived two weeks before, its pages fresh and stiff from the printer, a heavy volume for each church in the whole land. He had read through it with joy. Smaller copies some of the booksellers in the city already had to sell, to anyone who wanted to buy one and had a few pence to spare. He had been given the proper tool, the very tool he needed for what he had to do, and he was grateful to the boy king in London and his council for it, and for all that had been done since King Henry died to clear away the old, overgrown, tangled hedge, the thickets of tradition and superstition and fear, that had stood between the people and the truth.

He knew that not many in York agreed with him. He knew that there were those who called him heretic and that some who should have been in his church today had gone to Mass elsewhere or not at all because they believed that what he would say to them came from the devil. But the archbishop himself, who was of the new opinion, had found him the living when the chantries were dissolved, and now that he had the new prayerbook in his hands and the people, some, at least, of those who could read, had it in theirs, surely they would begin to understand. All would be well. Surely all, in time, would be well.

He began to read the preface for Pentecost, for it was Whitsunday.

"Through Jesus Christ our Lord, according to whose most

true promise, the Holy Ghost came down this day from heaven, with a sudden great sound, as it had been a mighty wind, in the likeness of fiery tongues, lighting upon the Apostles, to teach them, and to lead them to all truth . . ."

He knew that it would take time. But had not much already been done? He would not have believed that King Henry's death could have seemed to him, an obscure priest serving his chantry in a forgotten corner of an ancient, cluttered cathedral, so like the lifting of a weight from his back. It was right that the chantries had gone. Had he not felt for a long time only encumbered by the law, by the obligations laid on him in the crabbed wills of those long dead, as he said by himself those hundreds of Masses for names that meant nothing to him, his muttered words rising in the empty chapel like dust in sunlight? And it was right that the English prayerbook should have come. In the city people might be afraid of the changes. "Woe be to thee, O land, whose king is a child", they said. But they were afraid only because they were unused to the liberty of the truth. They were like prisoners who, for the weakness of their limbs, cannot walk for a time after their shackles have been struck off. Slowly they would learn to stand by themselves, to walk in the sunshine, in the clear light, free men.

He was full of hope, his own past quiet in the shadow at his back, the darkness he had left behind.

The next day there was a riot in the city.

He was pushed into the doorway of a tallow-chandler's shop as a mob of men and boys, running, shouting, scattering people to huddle frightened against the walls, came pouring into the narrowest part of Petergate, iron bars in their hands, billhooks, hammers, mattocks, anything that would break and smash. One of them ran with a velvet altar-cloth over his arm, not noticing that the end of it trailed wet and heavy in the mud. Something in their faces as they went by, close to him but not seeing him, or anything else but the destruction afoot, reminded him—reminded him . . . A zeal for destruction, a glassy look in the eyes, a frenzied strength in unaccustomed arms and shoulders: it was Will that he, seeing them run, remembered. Then he saw Will.

He saw Will, taller than most of them, older than nearly all of them, running among twenty or thirty others with a huge crowbar in both his hands, held high above his head. The look in the eyes of the rest had in Will's reached a pitch of pure annihilating force that made the other faces seem only weaker reflections of his.

He watched him run by, his own legs powerless to move, trembling as he supported himself against the tallow-chandler's greasy threshold. He could not have stopped him or any of them. The shock had winded him, taking all his strength from him. He saw their backs turn the corner round the church of Saint Michael-le-Belfry. He took some gasping breaths and started to run after them, calling Will's name again and again, until he could not hear his own voice in the deafening clamour about him. He turned the corner.

They were gathered in a dense, roaring mass, in front of the bolted door of the church. He could not see Will.

They started to batter down the door.

He stood and watched. An old woman was standing beside him. When a panel of the door gave, with a rending split, she laid a shaking, frail hand on his arm. She raised her face towards his and said in a voice high with rage: "The great men from London! They've emptied the abbeys and taken the saints out of the churches and broken the chantry altars to pieces. It's them that's shown the way to waste and spoil. If the rabble do likewise, the archbishop and them's only got themselves to blame. They tell us we haven't to pray for the dead no more, my daughter says. And who'll pray for them when they're dead and gone, I should like to know?"

He looked at her, her sharp features, her sure old eyes.

"The dead are with God and do not need our prayers."

She looked at him with scorn.

"Not if they haven't been with God in this life, they're not."

She waved an angry hand towards the mob at the church door.

"Look at that. You look at that and tell me if that's the will of God. There's poor men there will suffer for the sins of their betters. The times will never be righted now, and that's the truth."

They had broken inwards the middle of the door and were jostling to get through the jagged hole. Then they fell back as one man came out again, stepping over the splintered wood, carrying a heavy load. There was a fresh roar as they surged forward, and soon above the baying voices and the outstretched arms books were tossed up into the air, one after another, leaves coming out as they fell and floating lightly to the ground.

"There was a time they'd never have dared lay a finger on a book", the old woman said.

Other people crept into the street from behind him and picked the pages out of the gutter. The books were psalters, old Latin psalters marked for singing, the words written out in the patient scripts of long-dead hands.

Now there were new sounds, cracking timber and the shatter of smashed stone, from the darkness inside the church.

He stood for a few moments longer, undecided.

Then soldiers appeared in the street, which at once emptied, and clambered in their turn through the black hole in the door, pulling their pikes in after them.

He could not bear to stay to see Will dragged out from the church and beaten in the street. He turned and walked quickly away into the maze of alleys and yards that lay towards the market and his little church. The streets were quiet, the people indoors, afraid. He knelt down at last in his empty church, alone and comfortless.

Later the same day, when he heard that some of the mob had been imprisoned in the city gaol, he went to look for Will among them. He was not there, and, although in the next few weeks he searched the city for him, asking in every yard and lane if Will had ever been seen there, he could find no trace of him anywhere.

Some time afterwards, passing the tallow-chandler's shop, he saw that a leaf from a psalter had been torn and glued to patch a broken window-pane. Rain had streaked the ink, and the words could no longer be read. People hurried along the street, pushing past his back. He stood in front of the window for several minutes, looking at the torn page.

20

January 1550

Messer Matteo Dandolo, ambassador of the Republic of Venice at Rome, to the Signory of Venice; January 1550.

". . . Although it is more than two months since the death of the pope, and although the air inside the Conclave is now so foul that the first physician in Rome has threatened the cardinals with plague on account of the filth and the charcoal fires burning in their cells, there is still no firm expectation of a new pope. Indeed, in the bankers' shops here they no longer make wagers on particular cardinals but only lay odds that a pope will not be made in January, by the middle of February, by the end of February, and so on. I have heard that already during this election one single banker has taken upwards of fifteen thousand crowns in wagers.

"In the past five weeks, since the arrival of the French cardinals, the number of votes cast in each scrutiny for the cardinal of England has neither advanced nor declined, but remained constant at twenty-one or twenty-two, those for him swearing that they will die in his support and the French answering that they will die in the service of their king, which is to say in the resolution to keep out the cardinal of England, he being the emperor's chosen candidate and having the whole of the Farnese party with him. Our own Cardinal Cornaro tells me that he has felt himself compelled to make apology to the French for his support of Monsignor Pole, whom he chooses not in subservience to the emperor but in satisfaction of his conscience, Cardinal Pole being a man of excellent virtue and a faithful friend to the Republic. But it is now plain that even without the opposition of the French, the votes cast for Monsignor Pole will never again reach the number pledged for him at the start of the Conclave when he once (on the fifth day of December) failed to attain the necessary majority by only a single vote. The reasons for the certain disappointment of those, including ourselves and the emperor's party, who were formerly convinced that they would see the cardinal of England pope are in my estimation threefold, and strangely contradictory in nature.

"The first reason is the fear of those cardinals most accustomed to the old ways of the Roman court that, were Monsignor Pole to become pope, the whole of Rome would be constrained to lead a new life, bishops would be compelled to reside in their sees, and many of the reforms no more than whispered of at the Council would be put into immediate effect. This fear, which does the college of cardinals but little credit, was brought into the open only three days ago, when Cardinal Pacheco, a firm friend to the emperor, charged the Conclave with rejecting a proposed candidate (by whom he meant Monsignor Pole) solely because he was too good a man, whereupon a storm of abuse broke out, with, so I am told, the language of the markets tossed from one side of the chapel to the other.

"The second reason for the fatal gulf that has opened between the cardinal of England and the papacy is singularly at variance with the first. It is the suspicion as to the orthodoxy of his opinions concerning justification, raised in the first instance by Cardinal Carafa, who charged him at the very outset of the Conclave with holding to certain errors in religion and of harbouring a nest of heretics in his household at Viterbo, by which were intended Marcantonio Flaminio, the poet, now mortally sick here in Rome, and my own friend Alvise Priuli, in whose house Monsignor Pole stayed when he was obliged to leave Trent and from whom he has seldom been parted these twenty years. It was not difficult for Monsignor Pole to refute these charges at their first making, since so many of his fellow cardinals are well acquainted with all that he has suffered in defiance of heresy in his own country and for the good of the Church; but it has, most unhappily, been equally easy for his enemies in the Conclave, and in particular for the French, to keep a degree of suspicion alive as a means of lessening his support. I have even heard that the young Cardinal de Guise openly accused him of evasion at the Council, saying that he left Trent in order to escape the debate on justification, whereas all who were present inform me that he was at the time in great pain from an affliction of the arm and shoulder and scarcely able to stand.

"The third reason for the failure of the cardinal of England in the Conclave, despite all the efforts of Don Diego de Mendoza, the emperor's ambassador, who leaves no stone unturned in his cause, lies within himself. He will say or do nothing on his own behalf; he will neither seek votes nor resign them to another; when on the fourth day of December he could have accepted the papacy, which then might have been bestowed on him by acclamation, he would not, although he was most earnestly pressed to do so (the vestments were already laid out for him, and the cells had begun to be dismantled), but only said that if it were the will of God he would be duly elected; since then he has not lifted a finger to dispel the doubts cast upon his opinions and his friends; in sum, he seems entirely passive in the matter, as if in truth he cares neither to be pope nor to refuse to be pope. One cardinal, compelled by sickness to leave the Conclave, told me yesterday that a more unfit person to be pope could not be chosen than the cardinal of England since he is a mere log of wood, neither the prospect of success nor the artifices practised to supplant him having the least effect upon him.

"Cardinal Carafa, meanwhile, has almost as many votes cast for him at each scrutiny as Monsignor Pole has, but as everyone knows that he is a candidate proposed by the enemies of the emperor and by the French only in order to keep Monsignor Pole from his majority, no one has the least expectation of his becoming pope.

"It would be rashness approaching that of those who stake money with the bankers to predict any early conclusion to this Conclave, already so unusually protracted: as long as the French cardinals remain, Monsignor Pole will not be elected; as long as the emperor's cardinals remain, Cardinal Carafa will not be elected. Plainly a third choice, acceptable to all parties, must sooner or later be made, and all those who wish to see no cardinal carried lifeless through the wicket must surely hope that some such candidate may be found before many more weeks have passed. There is no doubt that, whether later or sooner, Cardinal Farnese and Cardinal de Guise will come to some accommodation between themselves."

21

June 1552

He waited as he always did for the Minster bell to strike the hour before he raised his hand to the knocker. As he listened for the footsteps of the servant who would open the door, he straightened his back with pleasure and filled his lungs with the fresh morning air of an early summer day. This keen expectation of delight he now felt every time he stood here, twice each week at the same time, and it was this moment as much as any that would follow that he looked forward to all the rest of the week.

At the beginning, six months ago, when at this hour it had been scarcely light, it was the house itself that had been balm to him, the big new merchant's house with the fire always blazing inside the carved chimneybreast, clean rushes on the floor, and the heavy oak coffers shining with wax. The boys he came to teach, Master Goldthorpe's two sons, had more of their mother's gentleness in them than of their father's bold ambition; nevertheless they worked diligently for him, and he had soon begun to take a pride in what he was able to add to the grammar-school Latin that had been flogged into them as children. But it was Alice, their elder sister, Alice, who had begged her father to be allowed to join her brothers' lessons because she had already taught herself out of their schoolbooks more Latin than they would ever know, it was Alice whom he came for now. He knew it as he stood there, in Fossgate, in the morning sun, Robert Fletcher, priest of Saint Denis in the city of York and tutor to the family of Master Richard Goldthorpe, alderman. He knew it, and pure joy seized him so that he almost laughed aloud.

The servant opened the door and looked at him as if he were surprised to see him there.

"What is it, man? Is it not Thursday?"

"Aye, sir, 'tis Thursday, but—well, you'd best come in, Master Fletcher."

He crossed the threshold, moving his neck a little against the stiff linen of the shirt he had bought the day before. Age, which had flecked with grey his brown hair and beard, had thinned them not at all, and as he splashed his face and body with cold water that morning, he had looked down with satisfaction at his flat belly and shaggy chest, no less taut and strong than twenty years before.

He walked in these days, for the first time in his life, with a cock-bird's arrogance and glanced without shame at girls in the street who had something about them of Alice.

Alice.

The door shut behind him. The house received him. He breathed its clean smell. The panelling of the hall that had been warm and dark in the winter was today dark and cool, a haven from the brightness outside. There was no fire now but roses in bowls on the oak chests and a sheaf of lavender hanging upside down in the chimney. He crossed the hall to the small parlour where they had their lessons at a table in the curve of the window. He opened the parlour door.

Alice was there, alone, sitting on the seat that ran round under the window. She did not rise as he came in. She did not look at him. He shut the door very softly behind him so that the latch fell with hardly a sound. He came no further into the room. He thought that she must be able to hear the beating of his heart. She sat so still that he noticed the alarmed squawk of a bird in the garden outside, frightened, probably by a cat, as it flew off.

"Where are the boys?" he said at last, knowing as he spoke that they were not coming for their lesson, that they were not in the house, that he did not care where they were.

"They have gone to the Mercers' Hall with my father, to hear the Guild Court. My mother asked me to send John to say that you were not to come today. I did not send him."

Her voice was so low that he only just heard what she said. Still she did not look at him.

"Alice."

Then she looked at him, and at once he looked away. He thought that if he stayed where he was he might fall to the ground.

He walked towards the table. He cleared his throat and said: "Have you prepared some verses for me?"

He stood before the table, tracing a crack in the grain of the wood with his finger. She was looking up at him, but he would not meet her eyes. After a while she said, in a clear, firm voice, "I have tried the next twenty lines of book six. I found them hard, hard to—"

She stopped. He helped her.

"Is the book here?"

She moved for the first time since he had come in, taking the book from her lap, where she had held it, her finger marking the page. She laid the open book on the table. He had to sit down beside her. He left a space between them as if her flesh might burn him. She seemed scarcely to be breathing, like a child in a deep sleep.

"Read the lines first."

She waited for a long time, looking at the page in front of her as if collecting her scattered understanding of the difficult words. She began to read:

> *Tum pater Anchises lacrimis ingressus obortis:*
> *O nate, ingentem luctum ne quaere tuorum—*

The poet mourned the death of a Roman boy who had been buried by the Tiber fifteen hundred years ago, with armfuls of lilies and useless purple flowers. She read the lines as if the cut-off life were something that had slipped between the two of them as they sat in the June sunshine.

When she had finished, he sat motionless. He stared down at the table as if the grain of the wood had a message in it that he must decipher. A bee flew past them, through the open window, and out again, its buzz vanishing into the humming air.

Words came to him, one sentence, then another, and a third. He considered speaking them and decided not to. There was time to decide. Instead he said: "What is there for me to teach you that you do not find out for yourself?"

She said at once: "Many things", and then, more quietly, "A great number of things."

She had come with her old nurse to his church to hear him preach. He had seen her sitting there, near the back, her head bent. She had never stayed to greet him afterwards, nor said, in front of her brothers, anything about having visited his church.

Now he said: "Why do you come sometimes to hear me preach?"

She looked up at him so quickly that he was surprised into meeting her glance.

"Because I believe what you say."

He closed his eyes. What she had said bent his back, burdened him. He felt as if a heavy weight had been thrust into his arms and he had been told to walk on as fast as before. And yet was not this what he had wanted, what he had wanted from them all, for three, four years? As he opened his eyes he shook his head.

"It is not what I say—not me—you should believe. I am no more than—"

But the look on her face stopped him. She was not listening to his words. Her eyes had trapped his at last and would not let them go. He looked at her in wonder. Her mouth trembled a little. He put his hand on the open book, as if it might blow away. He would have liked to pick her up, to carry her out of the room, out of the house, into the sunlight and the world and never to come back.

He looked down at the table and immediately felt tears rise to his throat.

"Alice, why have you done this? Deceived your mother—"

"You know very well."

He shook his head again, to shake out of his eyes what he had seen in hers.

"Alice, dear child—"

He must do what he could.

"I am old. I am poor. I have nothing but a little learning, a few books. Your father is a rich man. Your mother is of the Fairfaxes and kin to half the gentlefolk of Yorkshire. You are their only daughter. And more, and most of all, I am a priest; and although your father wished me to come to his house and to teach his children Latin, there is no doubt that he would not—that he would never—"

She put her hand on his, where it lay on the book. She said: "You are alive, and free, and so am I", and, so softly that it was almost as if she had not said it, "The archbishop himself has married."

He looked at her hand lying on his, and the sight of it moved him more than its light touch. He looked at it, bidding it farewell. Then he said: "I am going now, Alice, out of your father's house. I shall not come back. Your father will hear that I am sick. And indeed—perhaps I shall be sick. And you are not to come to my church any more because I could not bear to see you."

She cried out as if he had hit her and covered her face with both her hands.

As he left the room he heard only her tears.

He walked out of the house into the sun, along Fossgate and Pavement past the prosperous houses and the merchants' halls, down to the crowded lanes by the river, the wharves where half-naked men were unloading bales of cloth from flat-bottomed barges under furled sails, the bridge with its cluster of roofs and casements leaning over the water. He did not believe that he was going to lose her. He was alive. He was free. The sun was striking glitter off the river and the houses and the backs of the barge-men gleaming with sweat. He was not going to lose her. He wanted to stop the people he met, any of them, all of them, and tell them that he was fifty-four years old and that never till now had he understood anything, had he known this wild glee, this drunkenness. He smiled at them as they passed by, and one or two of them turned to stare at him.

There was a gap between the houses in the middle of the bridge. He turned aside to the edge of the bridge and stood above the water facing the south, watching the shining river flow out of the city towards the sun. He laid his hand on the stone coping and looked at it as if it were an unfamiliar thing, new and strange, something discovered that he had never seen before. He saw again her hand upon it, felt it, light, warm. He closed his eyes against the glare and bent his head. The unreasonable happiness flooding his chest would choke him, would make him cry aloud. He clenched his hand on the coping and was pleased that the stone scraped his knuckles, drew a few scratches of blood. He was awed by her courage. That she had given him already, her courage.

He straightened, watched for a moment longer the dazzle on the water, and walked back up the hill towards the Minster, now looking at the people he passed with astonishment as if only he, and none of them, were alive and full of health and strength.

There was a shadow somewhere, not that he might lose her, something else; but he could not remember what it was.

Three weeks later the fine weather had not broken. It was the kindest summer anyone living had seen: rain fell several times at night, swelling the crops, keeping the gardens green, and washing the streets; every morning came clear and blue as the one before.

He lived through those days as if about to wake from a dream in which he could nevertheless choose to dwell a little longer. He did with ease all that he had to do. He spoke the right words without searching for them. He ate and slept little and was neither hungry nor tired. When there was no work for him to do, he walked out of the city into the fields with his English Bible under his arm and sat under a tree reading the psalms slowly and half aloud, as if he had written them himself and were pleased with every word he had lit on. He had not lost her. He kept away from her father's house and never went into the part of the city where he might meet her.

One night he started suddenly from a deep sleep, anxious and afraid. Something was wrong, had knocked him from peace in a single instant. He sat up, his shirt sticking to his back. It was a hot, dry night, and there was someone in his room.

"Who is it? Who's there?" His whisper sounded to him very loud.

She moved across the bare floor into a patch of moonlight.

He lay back and shut his eyes.

"Alice. What have you done?"

"This morning my father told me that he has betrothed me to Master Constable, a gentleman from Beverley who has several times been to our house." She spoke without haste, solemnly, as if she were telling a child of the death of someone he loved. "My father said that Master Constable is a fine gentleman who has built a fine house and owns so many hundred head of sheep.

"So I have come to you. If I stay even one night with you, they will say that I have lost all, brought disgrace on all. They will cast me off for ever and never let me come to my father's house again. And so—" She stopped.

He threw back the sheet and stood up. He did not touch her.

He did not look at her. He went to the window and pressed his forehead against the casement-frame, his back turned to her. It was now that he had to decide. Now. Luther had said that priests should marry. The parliament in London had said that they might. Many had. And monks?

He saw again the heap of lead on the grass at the Mountgrace, the bell on its side, the chalices piled on the chapter-house table, the king's spoil. He was no longer a monk. He should send her back to her father. That would be the end of it. Nothing, any more. Long-familiar emptiness. Empty arms. He should send her, and she would go, without a sound, as she had come. He pressed his head further into the rough, warm wood and moaned. He had never known such fear. The necessity to decide was so powerful that for a moment he could not support it. He saw himself, with disbelief, as if from outside his body. He saw a man leaning against a casement, a man who would choose one course or the other, now, in this endless instant. Now.

He lifted his head slowly, feeling the pain from the mark the wood had made. He looked out at the idle moonlight glinting on the cobbles.

"Stay", he said.

He turned and caught her as she ran to him. She was shaking from head to foot as if she were freezing cold.

When at last he let her go, he saw over her shoulder a bundle and a basket dropped by the door.

"What have you brought?"

"Most of my clothes. A cheese. Some strawberries."

"I am not so poor that I cannot feed you", he said, and both of them laughed.

That night they lay quiet, she in his arms, he dazed among crowding dangers. Triumphant pride such as he had never felt, and gratitude for what she had done, cut him to the quick as he held her there.

In the morning, with the sun slanting across their bed, he took possession of her body as though it were the whole world he so much loved. She cried, and laughed, and afterwards she slept, her peaceful limbs tangled with his.

He would carry her always.

He lay, woken from his dream.

22

October 1553

Don Juan de Mendoza, councillor and special envoy, at the monastery of Dillingen on the Danube, to Emperor Charles V in Brussels; October 1553.

". . . I this night concluded my conversations with Cardinal Pole, papal legate dispatched from Rome to England and for the furtherance of peace between your Imperial Majesty and the king of France. After staying here for the space of two days, during which time I have been courteously entertained by the legate in the name of the bishop of Augsburg, to whom this house pertains, and have talked three several times alone with the said legate, I shall begin my journey towards Brussels tomorrow, avoiding the cities of the Rhine that are said to be plague-stricken still.

"I communicated to Cardinal Pole at some length the substance of your Imperial Majesty's commission, that in your Imperial Majesty's judgement the time is not yet ripe for either legation to be proceeded with, neither the regulation of religion in England, Queen Mary having but in July ascended the throne and many of her subjects being known to regard the restoration of papal authority in England with distrust and fear for their ill-gotten spoils, nor the intervention of the cardinal, as the representative of the pope, in the pursuit of peace between your Imperial Majesty and the king of France. To my considerable astonishment, knowing as I do the singular marks of love and favour which your Imperial Majesty has bestowed upon him these many years past, I found the cardinal most unwilling to accept your Imperial Majesty's considered opinion in these matters, and most of all in the question of his return to England. Indeed, so firmly did he take his stand on the pope's instructions to him to proceed without delay to England for the settlement of religion in that realm, arguing that he himself, as an Englishman, knew the custom of the realm and the character of his countrymen well enough to judge better than your Imperial Majesty the ripeness of the time, that I was obliged to dispute with him for more than an hour as to which course would indeed most become your Imperial Majesty's honour and the quiet of all Christendom. Finding him immoveable as to his bounden duty to continue his journey towards England, I was at last compelled to inform him (which I hoped most sincerely I would not be brought to) that if he persisted in making his way northwards from here, he would be constrained by express orders from your Imperial Majesty to stop at Liège, or in some other place near to your Imperial Majesty's court, until your Imperial Majesty should be at leisure to give him audience, and that I had no means of assuring him how soon that might be. Hearing this, he asked for some respite to consider all that I had said, because I had pressed him for an answer as to his intentions, and later informed me that he preferred to stop here in the abbey of Dillingen to await further instructions from the pope.

"Several times in the course of our conversations I mentioned the question of Queen Mary's marriage, saying that in your Imperial Majesty's judgement the settlement of this question ought to precede the regulation of religion, for the better ordering of the same, and once suggesting that were the queen to marry an Englishman, discontent among the nobility might thereby be considerably increased. But on this matter he would by no means be drawn, except only to say that his own opinion was that the regulation of religion should precede all else. So that I could not tell whether he himself entertains any hope of marrying the queen; nor did discreet conversation with some of his household produce any better results, the news that your Imperial Majesty intends and purposes that the queen may take the prince your son as her husband being received only without surprise.

"I trust that your Imperial Majesty's ambassador in England will before now have contrived that the queen herself should write to the cardinal showing him the necessity of some delay in his journey and moreover that its successful conclusion will rest in large part upon your Imperial Majesty's pleasure. For the unlooked-for resolution of his replies and the ardour of his whole bearing lead me to suppose that his long exile from his native land, together with his austerity of purpose in worldly affairs, will make him difficult if not impossible to turn aside from his chosen course once he has arrived in England. So that it would be well for your Imperial Majesty's design as to the queen's marriage to be perfectly accomplished before that day; for who can tell what forces Cardinal Pole might be capable of mustering on his behalf should he present himself as the queen's suitor (to which end he might readily be dispensed from his deacon's orders)? And even if his sole purpose be the restoration of the Roman obedience in England, I firmly believe that your Imperial Majesty's ends will be better served by the English people's first having accepted the marriage of the queen to the prince of Spain."

23

April 1554

It was as cold as January. People walked quickly through the streets, their faces muffled, turned away from the raw east wind. The great walls of the Minster loured over the city, a sullen grey under the grey sky.

He opened the door of the baker's shop. The familiar gale of warm, yeasty air blew up at him.

"Shut the door, Master Fletcher! The cold wants keeping out."

"All well?"

"Aye, never fear. She's a while to go yet, poor lass."

He went through the shop and up the stairs at the back to the little room over the yard. Alice was sitting under the window in the grey light. As he came in she dropped her sewing in her lap. He looked at her, at the bed, the table, the two stools, the old chest the baker had lent them, the almost finished cradle in the corner, as if he had been away a long time. She stared back at him, her mouth half open, eyes wide, fearful.

He closed the door behind him and leaned against it. He was very tired.

"It's finished. Done. They've taken the living from me."

She raised her hand to her mouth and bit it, but the tears came all the same.

"As we knew they would, Alice. As we knew, we understood. They were not harsh, not unjust. There was nothing else for them to do. It is the law of the land, now."

"I don't understand. I don't. That such a law can be altered.

That they can punish you for nothing you have done wrong. For what was right and lawful when you did it. What will become of us now? And all because . . . because I . . ."

He crossed the room to her and knelt beside her, taking her hands.

"Hush. Don't cry. We knew it would be so. I shall be a schoolmaster. At the archbishop's new school it is laid down that any may teach who has learning, clerk or not, married or not. We shall not starve."

"I don't care if we starve. I care that they should take everything from you that you—everything, and for me, when I . . . The archbishop is in prison. They will alter the government of his school."

"If they do, there will be all the more need for schoolmasters. There are not so many learned men in York that I shall not be able . . ."

She looked straight at him.

"How did the rest do?"

He looked at the work lying in her lap.

"They", he searched for words not to hurt her. "They chose the other path."

Then she really wept, burying her face in his shoulder.

"I knew it. I knew it. You were the only one. You should have sent me back to my father. They would have had to take me in."

He held her against him, gently because of the child, and looked past her head through the small panes of the window at the leaden sky. Did she mean now? Or then, at the beginning, almost two years ago now? It didn't matter. She meant it. She had often said it before.

He waited for the storm of tears to pass.

Five of them had been summoned that day to appear before the special court in the Minster chapter-house, five married priests. He was called last because he had been a monk, and his offence was therefore the more grave. The other four had all admitted their fault and undertaken to put away their wives. He supposed this meant returning them, disgraced for ever, to their families. They were told that after a public penance had been performed, in the Minster and in their own churches, they would be restored to the priesthood.

When his name was called, he stood up without fear. Old Doctor Rokeby, the canon lawyer acting as judge in the court, asked him several questions. One was: "And did the said Alice Goldthorpe, of this city, have knowledge, at the time of the so-called marriage, of your monk's vows?"

"No."

Doctor Rokeby had looked up from his papers for the first time and given him a keen glance.

She had not known when they married that he had been a monk of the Mountgrace, and she did not know now. She did not want to know. Whereas he listened greedily to everything she could tell him of her childhood, her mother, her books, her old nurse, her dreams and nightmares, she wanted his life to have begun on the day he walked into her father's house to teach her brothers Latin.

She was afraid of the river, in which an apprentice of her father's had drowned when he slipped between the wharf and a moored barge. But he had taken her there on summer evenings when the setting sun turned the green water to a golden flood, until she liked to go with him to the bridge and watch the moving water. Once when they were leaning over the wall side by side, he had begun to tell her how he used to sit by the river under Easterside when he was a boy and watch the water flowing, and how that water, joined by many other streams, came at last to the city and flowed beneath the bridge and out to the sea. She had turned away from the wall and said: "That was long ago. Before I was born." They walked back to their room above the baker's shop, talking of other things.

It was as if she were afraid of discovering a rival, a different love. Perhaps she was right to be afraid.

"And are you now willing to put away the said Alice Goldthorpe your pretended wife to whom you are unlawfully married, to separate yourself from her and live apart from her and never more to seek her company, so that you may return to your priestly life and duty?"

"No. I am not so willing."

His words seemed to fall like stones into a new depth of silence. He went on: "I had rather live still with my wife and be counted no longer a priest, if it may so stand with the law."

They had muttered together for a while, and at last Doctor Rokeby had risen and said in a loud voice:

"You are deprived of the cure of Saint Denis in this city. You are no longer a priest of this see, nor may you be of any other in this realm. You will appear again before this court at such time as you may be called."

And so it was done. What was done? He knelt with Alice in his arms as her crying became the small, last sobs of a tired child and wondered what it was that had taken place in those few words he had exchanged with Doctor Rokeby. Was it that a truth had been declared? Or had after all nothing happened? So that if he were to go down to the church and say the communion service, forbidden in churches since the autumn, or, now, again, the Latin Mass, which he had said for twenty years of his life, and consecrate the bread and the wine, he would be breaking the law, aye, but would anything else have changed since yesterday? "Do this in memory of me." He was a priest, commissioned by Christ himself. What did Doctor Rokeby or all the laws of England have to do with that? And if it were true that nothing, nothing of substance, had taken place between himself and Doctor Rokeby, was he not yet, even as much as he was a priest, also a monk? If Queen Mary could not unmake his priesthood, had King Henry and King Edward unmade his monkhood, cancelled with the ruin they had decreed the vows that had been made between himself and God?

Alice had lifted her head from his shoulder and was gazing at him, red-eyed. He had forgotten her. She kissed his forehead because it was her turn to comfort him, and so he smiled, to show her how brave they were.

"Forgive me", she said. She had returned to the hour in which they were. "It's the child—that makes me cry so, when I should not."

It was not true that it was the child. She had often wept before, despairing tears behind which he could not reach her, and he knew that it was because she thought their marriage guilty, doomed to some retribution that she could not foretell. "I am to blame", she would say, sobbing as he held her; "I am to blame, and I shall pay the price, for you, for this, for everything."

Now she said: "The child has kicked a great deal today." She put his hand on her belly, and he felt the baby move. She laughed and said: "I daresay he's impatient to be born." But she bit her lip.

"Don't be afraid, Alice. You are young and strong, and your mother bore three healthy children and lost none."

He had said it before, and she was not listening.

"You will not leave me, will you, not now?"

She never called him by his name.

"I will not leave you."

She shivered.

"You're cold." He stood up and looked for her velvet cloak. Her old nurse had brought it the first October with some other winter clothes. Not daring to come in, she had left them with the baker's wife. Alice wore the cloak often in the cold weather; it hurt him to see her wrapped in it, in the little room.

"No. But light the taper. It's so dark. And no flowers yet, anywhere, since the snowdrops died."

He lit the taper and put it at the window so that when it was really dark the light would be doubled. On his way back from the Minster he had seen an old woman selling bunches of primroses from a basket.

"It's Monday. I'll go down to the market for some eggs."

She picked up her sewing and smiled at him.

"Come back soon."

It was colder than ever outside in the streets, and the wind whipped cruelly round the corners of the houses. He walked fast, his head bent, his hands tucked inside his sleeves.

A priest and not a priest, a monk and not a monk: somewhere, in some crack of the years, or perhaps only that morning, before Doctor Rokeby, he had lost himself. He had Alice; that was an unalterable fact. But between him and Alice there was no private space in which he truly existed, for them both. He was always with her and always alone because she feared the knowledge of him that he longed to give her, pushed it away. This knowledge was knowledge of the past. The past was where he himself, whatever of himself remained, was to be sought and found, and she wished only for the safety of the present. Guilt had eaten up the clear courage she once had, and he had been unable to take her guilt from her. She, who had first come to him because of the burning truths he had seemed to utter, could not any more believe in them, could not believe in all that forgiveness, all that love. She was bound to feel to blame, for ever, for the loss of his church, his preaching, his people. And the Mass? "Do this"?

He could no longer tell the good from the bad in what he himself had done. And without that judgement, without, therefore, repentance, how could he be forgiven? He walked through the streets and alleys. They grew darker, colder, emptied of people, until the very roofs and leaning walls seemed to close in upon him, full of menace. He bought the eggs in the market where the last street-sellers were packing up their wares among the rubbish of the day, the cabbage leaves and fish-guts, the offal and chipped bone from the butchers' boards. He bought the flowers. He turned for home. Was he forgiven? O God, he said aloud, and the certain words that had changed everything, the words of faith in which he had put his faith, he could no longer fit together. They were shattered propositions of which he had lost the meaning. He could not remember what they had to do with him.

At the corner of the Shambles he passed a beggar lying in the gutter, a huge, heavy old man with his head propped against a broken step, an empty dish in his hand. He passed him without attention. There were many such in the city. He walked more quickly. Alice was waiting for him, and he wanted to see her pleasure at the primroses. He needed to see it, to see her, to strengthen his hold on all that was left, Alice, and the child soon to be born.

A few yards from the baker's house he stopped suddenly. The beggar at the corner of the Shambles was Will. At the same moment he decided that it was not possible, that he had imagined the likeness to Will; Will, whom he had seen five years before in the rioting mob and then never again, although the city was not so big that in that time, had Will been there, he would not somewhere have come upon him. It could not be Will. Perhaps it had not been Will on the day of the riot.

He took two steps forward and stopped again. Had there been something familiar in the heaviness of the propped head that lay twisted, almost as if the neck were broken? In a misery of doubt he recalled his brief impression. He must go back to see.

He stood in the street, holding the primroses and the eggs. Close to him, over the lighted shop, there was Alice, and their fragile peace, and the baby. If it should be Will, how could he bring him in, drag him up the narrow stairs, to her, sewing by the one light? Yet to leave him there, in rags, on a night as cold as the dead of winter? He shuddered, putting the image from him. It was not possible that it was Will, not after so long a time.

He walked on, into the baker's shop, up the stairs, home.

He gave Alice the flowers, and she was pleased. After she had found a jug to put them in and filled it with water, she searched his face.

"You met someone?"

"No. Aye. I thought I saw a man I once knew. But it was not he."

She touched the primroses again, happily. She was always afraid that he might meet her father in the street.

She went downstairs, carefully because of the child, to cook their eggs and fetch the bread that they would eat with them. He picked up the sewing she had left lying on the stool, squares of cotton she was piecing together to make a coverlet for the cradle, and looked at her neat stitches. Then he rubbed the window-pane above the taper. A few flakes of snow were flying past in the wind. He knew that the beggar was Will.

24

May 1554

Messer Marc' Antonio Damula, ambassador of the Republic of Venice at the court of Emperor Charles V in Brussels, to the Signory of Venice; May 1554.

". . . Cardinal Pole returned from France three weeks ago and on the twenty-first day of April had audience of the emperor, who spoke to him with much anger of the discussions that the cardinal has conducted with the French king for the further-ance of peace, so that both the cardinal himself and others who were present understood that there is here little of either hope or desire for the accomplishment of the said peace. And even less, as it appeared from the roughness of his words on that occasion, does the emperor intend to allow Monsignor Pole to proceed on his journey to England for the restoration of the Roman obedience in that country, for the emperor concluded the audience with the pronouncement that the car-dinal might better have remained in France than come back to the Empire, where there is naught to his purpose. Since this audience with the emperor, whose unwonted harshness sur-prised many, Cardinal Pole has returned to the house in which he has lived since his first arrival in Brussels in January. He is said to be very low in spirits, on account of the long delays which he has been compelled to suffer (the better part of a year having now passed since Queen Mary ascended the throne), and even, believing it to be himself rather than his cause that displeases the emperor, to have offered the resignation of his legatine commission to the pope, who will doubtless refuse it, there being none other at Rome to replace the cardinal in the affairs of England.

"It is likely, however, that after the solemnisation of the marriage between the queen and the prince of Spain, who is expected shortly to sail for England, the emperor will at last allow the cardinal to proceed, for it is the emperor's fear lest the cardinal's presence in England should endanger the people's acceptance of the marriage that has led him to detain the cardinal so long from his native land. This fear is in my opinion groundless; I have several times, since the certainty of the marriage became known, heard the cardinal give his approval to the same, saying how greatly the alliance with so powerful a Catholic prince may benefit the unity of the Church, although it is true that formerly for many months he maintained a stubborn silence on the matter and once, I am told, dared to say to the emperor that the queen's marriage to a foreigner would never be popular in England and that in his opinion the queen had far better remain unmarried. But those days are now past, and if the cardinal be not permitted to leave for England after the marriage has taken place, it will be rather hindrance from England than any obstruction of the emperor's that will be the cause. For the cardinal lately said to me that in the affairs of England he is as a man walking in a meadow of unmowed grass, who sees the surface waving by the motion of a snake underneath, though he cannot exactly distinguish the spot where he lurks, by which he meant that it is the high passion rife among the nobility there, whose only desire is to retain and keep hold of the abbey lands they had of King Henry, that is the true obstacle to his admittance as legate.

"If he is forced to remain much longer idle and, as it were, imprisoned at Brussels by the devices of others (for even the pope does not stand firm to the purpose for which he despatched his own legate), I fear greatly for his health, though at present he appears well enough."

25

May 1554

He stood in the spring evening, in the warm rain, at the foot of Alice's grave. They had buried her that morning, very early, like a suicide, without a priest because she had married a priest. Her mother had been there, not her father, and he himself had watched from a long way off and walked all day in the fields outside the walls of the city, not wanting to show his face again in the streets.

The flowers her mother had laid on the grave were frail and wet in the rain. If he picked them up, all the petals would drop. Now she was free, free of her guilt, free of him—for had they not become one to her, himself and her guilt? Free also of fear. It was her fear, much more than the pain and the fever, that he had hated to watch in the last days, because her fear he should have been able to take from her. He could not. He had tried, again and again, and she had only fled from him, further and further into her terror because he was the cause of it. Now she was free, changed into something else. *Remanet nitor unus in illa.* That was it. Only the brightness remained in her, and this too Apollo loved. He had pursued her, like Apollo Daphne, into her fear, and she had escaped him. She had changed into something else and left him standing alone on the bank of the river.

He moaned aloud as he thought of her face on the first morning, nine days ago, happy, young, full of relief. The birth had been an easy one, so the baker's wife had told him, and Alice had achieved it with a courage that astonished him, sitting up to sew, with quick fingers, between the pains, until the baker's wife had sent him out to get something to eat, telling him not to come back for an hour. When he returned the baby was there, lying wrapped in linen, filling a space that he did not know there had been in the little room. Alice only smiled at him and then slept till the morning, waking with delight that it was over and that the child was strong and healthy, suckling hungrily.

For three days she was happy, nursing the baby when he cried, pleased at his earnest frown when he sucked and at the peaceful sleep that followed. Her fear had gone. He had thought that now it might not ever return. On the fourth day, with the start of the fever, it had come back, fiercer than it had ever been, savage and fierce, so that soon he could not tell whether it was sickness or fear that was the faster destroying her.

"It could not be—I said to you, I knew, I always knew it could not be. I shall die. I am punished for my sin. I knew it would be so. I shall not see him grow."

He was old and full of words, and she turned her face away and would not listen to him.

"Alice, Alice, listen to me. You will not die. The fever will pass. Alice—"

But the black dog had got her, had terrified her into a frenzy from which she would not hear him call her name; she refused to hear.

The bleeding had gone on and on, and the pain, until she was too weak to sit up to suckle the child.

He knelt down in the wet grass and began to pick the petals off the flowers where they lay on the upturned earth.

On the last day, the day before yesterday, she had said nothing at all, nor cried, but lay quite still, her eyes open, her eyes moving, following something that he could not see. Several times the baker's wife came upstairs and put the baby to her breast as she lay, and there was milk for him because he fed and then slept as peacefully as ever. He thought that perhaps she was better, that the fever had passed, but when he said so to the

128

baker's wife, she only answered: "Poor soul. Poor soul", and he did not know whether she meant Alice or himself.

Long after dark, when he was almost asleep himself, sitting at her side, she had said, still without stirring: "Fetch a priest."

Now, kneeling in the rain and slowly pulling to bits those flowers of the so late spring, he thought that he had never heard three words more ruinous. Her trust in him had gone, her belief in the words he had given her which had once set her free before God in faith and the assurance of forgiveness. *Simul iustus, simul peccator.* She had once felt, with him, the deep contrary pull of that tremulous certainty, the despair and the hope, the knowing and the not knowing, the loss and the finding. She had. Or had she? Had it not rather been, all along, only the love between them that had drawn her into accepting what he had told her? Had she ever understood, for herself, in herself? Did not these three whispered words, asking for some-one else to come, a stranger who with a few magic phrases would take away her sin, show that she had not?

He had gone slowly down the stairs and out into the night streets, bowed under the weight he had undertaken to bear on that first night when she had come to him, bringing her clothes with her, knowing he would not send her back.

A few magic phrases. What more had he offered her himself for the safety of her soul? Different magic phrases?

He had gone to the far end of the city to find a priest he did not know. He had knocked loudly at a strange door for several minutes until an old man had come grumbling from his bed. More minutes passed while the old man found a light and dressed, complaining that there were clerks enough at the Minster with nothing to do but eat and sleep and him an old man and half a mile from Goodramgate at that.

As the priest locked the door with two heavy keys, clumsily, still muttering, his impatience changed suddenly to fear.

"Follow me. I must make haste."

He ran back through the darkness, his footsteps echoing from the walls of the houses less loud in his ears than his own panting breath. Once he tripped over something alive on the cobbles and half fell. As he scrambled to his feet, his hand felt the warm, hairy hide of a sleeping pig. He ran on, at last into the baker's shop and up the stairs, gasping for breath.

She was dead, the taper still burning at the window, her bare arm hanging down over the side of the bed, her eyes open, afraid. Beside her on the bed the baby lay asleep.

He closed her eyes. Then he stood for a short time and looked at them both in the flickering light, Alice and her baby, the one, he knew, as utterly gone from him as the other.

He picked up the child, who startled as he touched him but did not wake, and wrapped him from the cold. He had never held anything so light. He laid him in the cradle and put over him the pieced coverlet. He did not hate him for his mother's death as his own father had hated him, and never would he. He carried the cradle down the stairs and through the streets to her father's house because there was nothing else for him to do.

Again he had to hammer on the door. The baby, in the cradle on the step, still did not wake.

He put the cradle into the arms of the sleepy servant who opened the door.

"Tell the master and the mistress that their daughter is dead this night of childbed fever. Tell them now."

Since then a day and a night and a second day had passed. He had not yet grieved. He had pushed grief ahead of him like an unwelcome guest, knowing that sooner or later grief would turn to face him. He had come here, to her grave, in order to stop walking, in order to let grief turn and meet him, and now he was only alone. Nothing was before him. No tears came, no prayers. Nothing.

He looked with surprise at what he had done to the flowers.

They lay on the earth with their stalks twisted and bent, every petal and every leaf torn off, a handful of trash thrown down for birds to peck among.

She had sent him for a priest because to her he was no longer a priest. And if he were a priest neither to her nor to the queen's court in the Minster, what was he?

A little limping rhythm beat softly in his head and after a while fetched up the words that belonged to it.

> Who'll be the clerk?
> I, said the lark,
> If 'tis not in the dark,
> I'll be the clerk.

It did not matter what he was. The truth that he had known had lately been hidden from him, but it was there yet, in him and if in him then somewhere between him and God. It had freed him once from the past, and it must free him again. The charge he bore, Alice, her fear, her death without the magic phrases she had sent him to fetch, he could neither escape nor lay down. He would bear it always, because it was what she had now become for him, in him. But she, she herself, who had been changed into something else, was free. Her he resigned to God. The sin he would bear. *Simul iustus, simul peccator.* Believe, believe. Surely, even now, as he accepted it for ever, God forgave the sin.

And the words of absolution Alice had longed for as she was dying? The priest through whom God speaks forgiveness? The priest in whose hands the bread and wine become Christ?

> Who caught his blood?
> I, said the fish,
> With my little dish,
> I caught his blood.

He shook his head violently. One day these questions—one day, but not today. He was worn out with running, chasing through thickets a quarry he had lost.

He started to sweep together with his hands the remains of the spoiled flowers. The wet petals stuck to the earth, so he had to leave them where they had fallen.

He would go away from York. He had twice visited merchants who in the past had brought their families week after week to hear him preach in his church. He had offered to say the English service of Holy Communion for them in their houses. They had shaken their heads and asked him to go at once, afraid of the new laws. None of those he had cared for in his parish, not one, had sought him out after his disgrace in the Minster. At Archbishop Holgate's school they had not dared to hire him. But he had heard that in London there were many faithful to the prayerbook and the new ways, many who were keeping their preachers in hiding from the bishops and were glad to do it. They would have a use for him. He would make of the time he had left, at last, a simple good. He would take to the Protestants who were standing firm what he knew of the truth and leave the past where it lay.

He got slowly to his feet. He was stiff and old, and his clothes were damp on his back.

The next day he packed up in a blanket his three books, his spare shirt, his winter shoes, and a little square he cut from Alice's velvet cloak, and he set out for London.

26

October 1554

Messire Simon Renard, Lieutenant of Amont, ambassador of Emperor Charles V at the court of Queen Mary and King Philip of England, for the time in Brussels, to King Philip in London; October 1554.

". . . I have but this hour left the house of the cardinal-legate, to whom I communicated all that your Majesty empowered me to say to him and from whom I received, upon the whole, replies that should satisfy both your Majesty and the parliament of England when it shall meet. I allowed the said cardinal (as your Majesty instructed me) to suppose that it was the ardour of his last letter to your Majesty imploring permission to enter England that had brought me to Brussels; thus he began by setting forth yet again his reasons against the further delay of his arrival in England, but expressed himself happy to recognise your Majesty's wish that he should now be given leave to depart from here and to resume his journey as soon as may be possible. He consented to enter England as an Englishman by birth, and as the ambassador of a great prince (the pope), but without the emblems and ceremonies of a legate, should such an entry be deemed expedient, and he further agreed that he would not attempt to use in England his legatine powers without the will and consent of your Majesty and the queen. As to the third matter, the enlargement of his powers so that he might, without reference to Rome, be able to remit the obligation of those who have obtained lands of the Church to return the same, he appears to be willing to seek such enlargement from the pope, but still somewhat evaded the question, saying that he would by no means have it appear that obedience to the Church should be, as it were, purchased by the offer of the Church's property. So that I shall return to this matter tomorrow, in order to have made your Majesty's conditions for his coming into England entirely clear to him.

"In conclusion I must add that I found in Monsignor Pole, who received me with the utmost dignity and courtesy, none of that silent obstinacy of which the emperor your father and the bishop of Arras have of late had cause to complain, but rather a noble simplicity which in my opinion cannot fail to call forth admiration in his countrymen (from whom he has these twenty years and more been separated) and must work greatly to your Majesty's advantage when at last he comes to England, as your Majesty's friend and servant, which he now warmly professes himself to be."

27

30 November 1554

Outside the palace of Whitehall the crowd stood twenty deep. They had been waiting more than an hour; they stamped their feet and rubbed their hands to keep warm. Breath came from each mouth in little clouds, and a cold mist seeped through the streets from the river. A row of torches burned above the open gate, lighting the nearest faces with a red glow. The courtyard was packed with more waiting figures, servants, horses, soldiers, priests, who moved about, stamped, and blew against the lit windows of the great hall and the open door, where people peered over each other's shoulders, trying to see inside. Now and then a scrap of news passed quickly from the door through the courtyard and out into the crowd.

"The king and queen are seated."

"Lord Paget speaks."

"The bishop of Winchester speaks."

There was a long pause after this. What the bishop was saying was not thought worth reporting, and the crowd began to grow restless, so that when the next piece of news came: "One of the old lords has swooned for the heat", it was greeted with a mocking cheer and a few cries: "We could do with a turn at his fire!" "Let him try the commons' air!"

Robert Fletcher stood with the rest. He was very cold and once or twice had wished he had not come, but the crowd was now too thick for him to leave before the end. His new friends, the group of firm Protestants, poor men and women, whose single-minded certainty had banished the doubts and griefs of the last months, had been surprised at his coming down.

"If the bishop of Rome sends his minion to strengthen the queen and the Spaniards, what is it to us? Let them do what they will. Let them put us under the old yoke, let them bring back the heresy laws and hunt us through the town, we shall never yield to the bishop of Rome. We shall never give up the new ways; we shall never stray from the truth. They'll not frighten us with their purgatory and their pains, so many Masses said for so many souls' rest, and all to line their pockets and keep the bishop of Rome in gold and silver.

"What do you want to go down there for, Master Fletcher, to see the great lords grovel to the cardinal from Rome? Not that they haven't feathered their own nests right enough and won't part with a penny for all they swear to be faithful Catholics now, to keep their place with the queen."

He said: "I saw him once upon a time, many years gone by. He was no cardinal then but a young man, as I was, though a lord. I showed him a garden."

They did not ask how such a thing had come about.

"You mark my words, Master Fletcher, this is an evil day for England. Better for us all if Romans stayed in Rome—and better for England if Spaniards stayed in Spain. The queen should never have married a foreigner. Never. An English church for the English people, that's what King Henry gave us; and the good bishops who gave us our English prayerbook are now in prison for their trouble and not likely to come out."

They were right. He knew that they were right. In two months their plain courage had refreshed him almost to a health as sound as theirs. Also their need of him. Most of the Protestant ministers had already left for Germany, and people too poor ever to leave, labourers and their wives, apprentices, widows, needed their services said for them, in the back rooms of inns and in houses along the Thames from which lightless boats could vanish swiftly on the dark water. They had work for him to do, and they joined together without question to pay for his bed and board. For as long as he was able, he would do what he could for them.

He had left York, and Alice, and his son, whose name he did not know, in the unrecoverable past, as he had left the Charterhouse.

And yet he had come to see. See what? The absolution of the realm from schism. The restoration of the Roman obedience. The queen and the bishops would still rule the Church. What were these but words that could be used to sanction the oppression of simple people who had understood that their salvation lay between God and themselves alone, in Jesus Christ's death upon the Cross and their faith in him?

But as he stood in the crowd and waited, as cold as the rest in the night air, he thought of Thomas Leighton, gaunt and furious in the Charterhouse, ready to die for those words, and of the monks who had been killed for them, disembowelled at Tyburn, the London crowd, this crowd, silent at the sight of the bloody habits.

There was a stir in the courtyard of the palace, then in the crowd.

"The king and queen kneel."

"The lords kneel all."

Those in the doorway knelt, and a few in the courtyard, still holding the bridles of restless horses.

"The cardinal speaks."

The crowd fell suddenly silent, awed, as if, at the last moment, the face of this prince of the Church speaking a few yards from them, though they could neither see him nor hear his words, impressed them more than they had expected.

Somewhere behind him in the crowd a sour voice said: "It's old Wolsey's ghost come to his own again, that's what it is. This was his house once, though all's forgot now, the cardinal's house, it was, and state kept then as was never seen. And they promised us there would never be such as old Wolsey again, and now—"

137

But his voice was lost in a low roar like a storm-wind, which came from the palace and spread outwards into the crowd, bringing people to their knees in hundreds in the dark.

"Amen. Amen. Amen", and then at once a great cheer from the hall, the courtyard, the crowd, wild cheers from the crowd, hats thrown in the air, and the servants scrambling to their feet to keep hold of the heads of rearing horses.

He did not kneel but stood, dead at heart, while about him people laughed, cried, embraced each other, called out, "God save England! God save the Queen! God save the old ways!" and the cheering went on and on.

The men in the doorway of the palace stood aside and bowed as the cardinal appeared, the scarlet cardinal in the flare of the torches, holding his right hand high and with many signs of the cross blessing the people.

"Fetch a priest", Robert Fletcher suddenly muttered to himself, watching. "Fetch a priest." He could not see the cardinal's face under the wide brim of his hat, only his beard, his long beard, almost white.

The queen came out, on the arm of the Spanish king of England, but he saw no more than their black clothes and solemn pause on the threshold before the crowd pushed forward and hid them from him. He saw nothing else, for the waving, cheering backs in front of him, until the procession came out of the gates and forced the people back from the middle of the road. He watched it move away through the night towards the abbey of Westminster, the jingling throng of horses, soldiers, lights; among it somewhere the king, the queen, the cardinal; around it and behind it still the crowd, noisy, exulting, boys and women running ahead to get a better vantage.

In the abbey church a Te Deum was to be sung, a hymn of praise in the royal church for Rome's forgiveness of England.

He waited in the road outside the palace until all the lights and all the cheering, following crowd had disappeared into the darkness. He turned at last and began to walk heavily towards the north, towards the Saracen's Head at Islington, where even now other men were met together to pray, in the upper room, with doors locked, where plays were sometimes given.

Lighten our darkness, we beseech thee, O Lord, and by thy great mercy defend us from all perils and dangers of this night.

Once he looked back and saw over the gate of the palace the row of torches still flaming in the dark, warming no one.

PART TWO

1558–1559

I

May 1558

He found that he remembered now as he had never before remembered, perhaps because he had all the time there was in the day. Arden, for example, Arden most of all.

That space between steep fields below the moor had made for a peculiar extremeness, a clarity in the weather: the short brilliance of the winter sun before it went down behind the western moor, and the chill interval of grey daylight that elapsed before the sky was tinged with the colours of a sunset that he could not see; the collected warmth of summer evenings, the long grass of the pasture, and gnats hanging in clouds over the cattle, as the light retreated up the hills before the line of shadow.

Now he was old. Perhaps the clarity had been within himself. What he had left of it was only a memory, an old man's memory of a certain place, long ago, the way the hills lay and the light fell, picking out every straw in the thatch, every unevenness in the stone, so that each cast its own shadow.

What he remembered was what he had seen. But the boy who saw it, where was he? He did not remember him, that boy, as someone else at whom he could look back across those many years. His were still the eyes through which he saw the narrow dale, the stone walls, the birch trees, the beck. If what he had seen and his seeing it, his lucid vision, were not even yet after fifty years put out, it was because they were here, nowhere else but here, and now, so late, no other time but now.

So he thought, because he had the time to think.

He got up from his stool and limped towards the window. With the rest he had run away when they came at last to take them prisoner. He was too old to run far. He fell down some steps, twisting his ankle. Two young soldiers arrived, out of breath from the chase. They had to put down their weapons and help him to his feet. They were not rough with him and let him limp in front of them, slowly down the lane from Islington through the cheerful May Day crowds coming out of the city towards the fields. He had feared his arrest more than anything except the rack, more than the burning itself. There would be a man each side of him dragging him, holding on to his arms, and women would come and pull at his coat and jeer. He had seen it. He had seen an egg thrown at an old man with white hair. It had broken on his cheek, and the sticky mess trickled into his beard, mixed with tears.

So that when they let him walk down by himself, at his own pace, he was glad that the sun shone, and smiled at the people passing in holiday clothes. At Newgate the soldiers were told to take him to the Tower, and they walked on. His swollen ankle did not hurt him. He might have been going to supper with a friend.

At the Tower he tried to give the soldiers the few coins he had, but one of them said: "Keep that for the gaoler; money may make a hard bed softer, even here."

Since then, thirteen days had passed. He had not been sent for. No one had come to question him. He had feared most of all that they would ask him for names and rack him when he would not give them; and that then he would give them. But as the lengthening days went by and he saw no one but the gaoler and the gaoler's wife, the fear began to fade. Was it even possible that he had been forgotten?

He tried, and found it easier each day, not to consider what was to come, what he would say in answer to the charges they would read; not to think, either, of the last years and months, why he had stayed to repeat for simple men words that had become no more than battle-cries shouted to keep the courage up in a war whose purpose both sides had lost sight of. He was tired. There was nothing, any more, that he could do. He slept well. He was warm. He had enough to eat. Idle and light at heart, he passed the days in a recovery from fear that was like a recovery from sickness.

He had no books. At the beginning there had been only the stool, a rough-hewn joint-stool, and a heap of straw to sleep on. He had asked for pen and paper, and the gaoler had told him that heretics were forbidden to write. Nevertheless next day, in return for one of the coins, he had brought him pens, ink, paper, a board, and a pair of trestles.

He had written nothing.

In Newgate they were chained hand and foot to the walls, sitting all day and all night in their own filth. He had peeled the shirts off their backs to wash them. Pieces of dirty linen he had not dared to lift stuck to open sores. Whom should he write to with words of fervour and strength when his letter alone might be enough to send a man there?

Outside, the summer had begun. The altered sounds and smells of the first hot day reached him faintly through the bars of his unglazed window. For being high up and not buried in the dark, in the dripping earth, he was most grateful of all. From his straw bed, from his stool, walking about the room, he could see only the sky, the fine blue sky by day and at night the stars moving across the bars. But if he moved the stool under the window and climbed onto it, he could see out. He would stand there, looking, like a child watching the street from an upstairs room.

"Whatever are you doing, Master Fletcher?" the gaoler's wife had said, coming in with his food one day. "You'll do yourself a mischief, clambering up there at your age."

"They're going to burn me", he said, but she was straightening the trestles of his table and did not hear.

From the stool he could see down into a yard. It was cobbled, but in the middle were two old apple trees growing in patches of earth. From the top of the taller one, some feet below his window, a thrush sang early in the morning and in the evening. The trees had been skilfully pruned, and against the sunny wall on his left a strange kind of plum had been trained in the shape of a fan. Once, somewhere, someone had told him of trees grown so.

Opposite to him was the next tower in the fortress wall, at its base a small door into the yard, lavender, a sprawling rosemary bush. On his right, beyond the battlements, was the river. He could not see it. But it was for the river that he climbed on the stool. The wide space above the water, full of the cries of gulls and the shouts of boatmen, he could see and hear, and at twilight lines of ducks flew westwards up the river, high over the water.

He was content to watch. Had he not lived in a cell before? A garden, and a fortress wall, and beyond the wall free air. The pigeons flying silently up through the oak trees, in and out of sunlight and shadow, over the nettles and the unpruned briars. In that cell he had reckoned to die, laid on a cross of ashes. From this cell they would take him out and tie him to a post over the stacked faggots. A few minutes of cruel pain: Was not that all that had changed?

He looked out of the window at the wall and beyond it at the bright air over the river where the gulls sailed. Perhaps he had been forgotten and would die here, after all, in his cell.

He would be glad for a day such as this to be his last day. He had not once been down on his knees. He had not prayed a single prayer. He had no Testament, no psalter. The words of all the prayers he had ever said, old and new, English and Latin, had left his mind as empty as if they had never been, as empty as the dazzling cloudless sky. The Mountgrace, the Mountgrace, he said to himself, as if they had taken him back there, for his death.

He was getting tired standing on the stool, a foolish old man gazing at nothing out of a high window. He would not get down until she brought him his meal. Cabbage soup, black bread, and water; he was hungry. As he realised that he was hungry, he laughed a little, at himself.

The day before there had been a mug of ale.

"A woman came with the ale and a clean shirt for you. She never gave her name."

She might have been one of a dozen women who came to the Saracen's Head under the pretence of hearing the play. Each time they brought food and clothes for imprisoned heretics they risked their lives.

"She said to see you had them, and she hopes you do well."

"If she comes again, tell her I do very well."

"Thank you, sir", said the gaoler's wife, as if she kept an inn.

The gaoler had told him that they had burned no one out of Newgate for several weeks past. Those who had been taken with him were still alive. If the hot weather lasted, there would be fewer in Newgate. They had chosen the fire. Were they to be cheated of their brave deaths, the awe-struck crowd, the cross of twigs tied together and held up for them, the murmur of pity and anger as they passed? Had the bishops after three years of burnings at last learned the lesson of those who, years ago, had left monks to rot to death in Newgate because the butchery of six of them had only persuaded the people of their goodness? If they had, it was too late. The fires, the smell of charred flesh, the howls of those who, in the rain, took an hour to die, had been an argument stronger than any book that those who ordered such deaths could not have the right of it. To a man who saw his neighbour burned on the pope's authority for worshipping God in words laid down by parliament a short time ago, the case was plain enough. The bishops were turncoats and murderers. Those among them who were men of honour had been burned themselves or had gone abroad to wait until the queen should die and the Spaniards be sent home.

He could have gone to join them. Twice since the burnings started he had been offered a place in a boat to Germany. "Take a younger man", he had said. Was he choosing the fire? Perhaps. Now he wished only that the long, light days of his imprisonment would not cease until he died.

But a year ago? Two years ago when they burned Cranmer? Had he not been certain then that he possessed the truth, that they could take away everything from him but his freedom to die for the truth? He had been brave then.

He had also been afraid, to travel to a strange country, to be trapped in silence. Once in York he had watched a Fleming in a tavern. The man's eyes shifted from face to face as he strained to pick out a word he knew. Some apprentices round a table laughed over a game. The stranger smiled. No one noticed. When he spoke, it was with the single words of a two-year-old child, but he was a man of fifty with a grizzled beard, dressed in the clothes of a merchant.

But it was neither courage nor fear that had made him stay. It was the charge he had to bear. Men who could not write their names, ignorant boys and women, were going faithfully to their deaths on account of words bandied about by the learned. Learned men had drawn the battle-lines. Learned men had chosen a few phrases from here and there, descriptions of mysteries too deep and close for any mind to comprehend, and had imposed them on the ignorant on pain of losing their immortal souls. "The truth is thus and thus", they said. "What that man tells you is idolatry." Or: "The truth is thus and thus. What that man tells you is heresy." Was it then for the learned to go away and leave the ignorant to fight alone? He had used such words himself. He had preached and taught. He had taken sides, certain that the side he had chosen was right and the other wrong. How could he have abandoned those who had followed others like him, and afterwards him, not because they understood but because they were led? Even after he no longer knew how much weight it was right for the great phrases to bear, he could not abandon those men and women. Them most of all.

He got down off the stool and carried it to the table, walking stiffly from standing for so long. For a while he sat motionless, a piece of paper in front of him. Then he took a pen and wrote:

"I, Robert Fletcher, being of sound mind and a prisoner of the bishop of London, do here set forth to my own satisfaction that:

"Item: The bishops who have, for the pope, condemned many to death by burning are turncoats, bloody butchers, and unpolitic.

"Item: Those condemned of the said bishops are innocent of sedition, faithful to the doctrine in which their betters have instructed them, constant, cheerful, and fearless in adversity.

"Item: It is not of necessity consequent upon the aforesaid articles that what the said bishops hold to be true is not the truth, or that what those condemned of the said bishops hold to be true is indeed the truth.

"Item: What is truth?"

He smiled as he wrote the last three words, smiled as he had when he noticed that he was hungry.

He added: "Written at the Charterhouse of the Tower of London the 14th day of May, 1558, and the fifth year of the Queen's Majesty's reign."

He crumpled the paper into a ball and put it in his sleeve. He rose, pushing back his stool with some force from the table, and limped about the room. It was for his own sake that he had not gone to Germany, not for the sake of those who were hunted through the back alleys of London and chained to slimy walls in Newgate. It was not because he was afraid to die in a foreign country, though he was. In the end it was least of all because he was sure even to the stake that he was right. He had stayed to wait. To wait for what? For his own certainty to dissolve, as it had dissolved again and again, all his life.

When he was seven years old a brother he did not know he had taken him from Arden, down the lane between the banks of cow-parsley. That had been the beginning. Since then he had built in every place, out of every place, a new certainty, deeper within himself, closer, perhaps, to God, and each one had gone down before the next. It was wholeness that he had waited for, and these had all been parts, only parts of the truth. If he had gone to Germany he would have chosen one part. The exiles in Frankfurt and Strasbourg wrote books reviling what he had loved for half his life and sent them back to England to uphold in poor devils with halters round their necks the belief that they were saints of God.

That was it. In riven England were the rifts of his own soul. A part, a side, a faction, one loyalty to be used against another; none of these could be the answer to the question he had just written down.

Now that he knew the question, would he be given the time to discover the answer? Pilate had asked the question and turned away. He would not. Now, he would not.

His idle peace had gone, and his lightness of heart. Though his ankle was hurting him, he walked back and forth, dragging his foot. He had lost the simple earth, the narrow dale before the beginning, and the garden of his cell at the Mountgrace, again. He was back in the unpruned wood among the nettles and the flying birds.

"God preserve me in this mortal life a little while", he said.

He was not going to burn, yet. He was not going to recant, for that would be to choose a different part, to join a different faction. But when they brought him to trial, he would hide between their questions, their phrases set to snare him, and they would have to send him back to prison, to his cell. He would wait a little longer in the world if he could. The whole was there, somewhere, yet to be found, and in it nothing should be lost, nothing that had once been known and loved betrayed.

He was no longer content to die.

At last he sat down again at his table and prayed to God for endurance and sharp wits. When the gaoler's wife came in with his soup he was asleep, his head on his folded arms.

2

June 1558

A month passed. No one came to take him before the bishop. Three times he was brought ale and clean linen, and once a dish of gooseberries, each time, the gaoler told him, by a different woman. He did not know who they were. He did not know who was left. They would never get to the end of them, not if the queen lived another ten, another twenty years.

There had been a week of grey, showery days. After that the weather had set fair. From his window he had watched the blue sky hardly change at all, hour after hour. The fruit on the fan-trained tree had begun to form after the blossom. One hot noon as he sat at his table he asked the gaoler about the tree.

"Lord Edward Courtenay planted it. Fifteen years he was here in the Tower, and only a lad of twelve when he came. The queen had him freed, being her cousin and a papist. I never knew how he fared after. A real gentleman, he was, but not in his right mind when he went from here, after all he'd seen. I did hear he died abroad somewhere. They beheaded his father. And his cousin, Lord Montague, that was, him that was brother to the cardinal. They killed near on the whole family on the cardinal's account, for his treason, they said, the cardinal that's now archbishop of Canterbury and the highest in the land. There's the wheel of fortune for you.

"Lord Montague's little lad, he was no more than four or five when they brought him here. I can see him now, playing out there in the yard. He sickened that bitter winter and died in less than a week. Must be twenty years ago and more. Then one summer, later, years later it was, they took the old lady out,

Lady Margaret, the cardinal's mother, a great lady in her day, she was, and she was beheaded, last of all. The block was up yonder, on the green. Her death was the end of Lord Edward. He was never right after that. Near seventy she was, and she died the bravest I've ever seen, and I've seen a few, I can tell you."

"And the tree?"

But he was thinking of the child, four years old, who had died of cold in the Tower, the same age as the son he had left in York, if he lived still.

"Oh, aye, the tree. It came with some books, from Italy, if I remember right. Done up in a sack, it was, with its roots in a crock of earth and moss and leaves packed round it. He would plant it, though I told him it would never thrive after coming so far. But it did, and there you are. It never fruited till after he'd gone. One of the guards looks after it now, and the apples. He thinks the world of a tree. He worked as a boy in the orchards at Evesham. They grew a lot of fruit, the monks did, down there."

The gaoler went away, and he sat on at the table, his head in his hands.

He saw old Martin the lay brother, dying, laid on the cross of ashes, the monks gathered about him, sunshine outside the open door. As he leaned down himself to give the ritual kiss of farewell, Martin whispered: "I have asked the prior to let you have my knife." A little pruning knife with a short, keen blade. Always afterwards he had used it for his apples, his roses, out there.

He shivered and wiped his forehead on his sleeve. This cell and that were not the same. Not.

It was the hottest day yet. The sky over London was no longer a clear blue but sultry with oppressive heat. Now and then thunder growled far away. The gaoler's wife had told him the day before that people were beginning to die of summer fever. He thought of the prisoners in Newgate and found that he could not remember the faces of men he had seen every day for months. They were part of a world he had lived in long ago, whereas in his cell in the Charterhouse, if he but opened his eyes, his crucifix, his books, would be there in their places, here—

His head was swimming, the air stifling. The water the gaoler had brought him to drink was warm and foul-tasting. His stomach turned, and he stood up, swallowing several times, a cold sweat on his face.

Perhaps in a few days he would be dead.

The thought gave him a pang, and he began to pace about restlessly, hot and shivering. He wanted to take his clothes off and plunge into icy water as he had often when he was a boy, in the river below Easterside. If he died, Easterside would die with him.

He thought of the last time he had seen Will and stopped in the middle of the floor, hitting his clenched fists together so violently that the pain made him wince. There were amends he could never make, not if he lived for a hundred years. Yet it had not been for his own sake that he had left him there, stretched out in the gutter in the cold. It had been for Alice's sake. Had it?

Had it not been to escape from his father, and Tom, and even poor Will, that he had gone to the Mountgrace? At Easterside there had been suffering, lovelessness, evil like a spreading infection, in him as well as in them, and he had run away from it. He had tried to leave it behind, and he never had. Thirty years later he had seen his brother in the gutter, an old beggar lying in filthy rags, and he had left him there because he was not brave enough to pick him up. That was the truth.

And Alice, who had died alone? And the child?

The gardener might weed and burn all day long, all summer long. The nettles were still there beyond the garden, and the brambles and the quitch grass, and at night they sent their yellow roots under the wall.

A phrase he had read somewhere came to him. We are all beggars, and that is the truth. The truth, the truth.

He groaned as he shivered again. His head ached and his throat was parched. A month ago he had set himself to find the truth. He touched the crumpled ball of paper in his sleeve. He had been going to use the empty days of his imprisonment, however many there might be, to discover the whole that he believed was somewhere, through the parts, the other side of them. Instead the fragments had become smaller and smaller. Only pieces remained, moments that came back to him so clearly that when they faded he looked round his cell, dazed, as if he had never seen it before. What they had died for, screaming at the stake, and what the others had killed them for, he could scarcely remember, and when he made the attempt only meaningless sentences formed in his mind.

Perhaps he was going mad. Perhaps they had shut him up alone to send him mad. But he was a monk of the Charterhouse. He had been alone for twenty years. He had always been alone. Had a month in the Tower, in the light, without the rack, without hunger, on the contrary, with straw to sleep on, a stool, a table, clean shirts, sent him mad?

He crossed the room, drank the rest of the warm water, and climbed on the stool after moving it to the window, to breathe in some fresh air. His legs were trembling, and he almost fell. The air outside was hotter and heavier than the air in the room. It had a sweet, dusty smell. A sparrow was hopping about in the grey earth under the plum tree, fluttering its wings and sending up little flurries of dust. Silence hung even over the river. Thunder rolled again in the south. He felt dizzy.

A sparrow in the dust. Two sparrows fighting in a dried-out rut, and him waiting, waiting, in the long grass for Robin the miller to die.

They had told him he was a child of God. Was that what they had told his son, in York? Or was he growing up as Master

Goldthorpe's son, his grandmother his mother, his grandfather his father, so that he himself might never have begotten him? He did not know. He would never know.

From somewhere close by, muffled by thick walls but not far away, came a scream, a man's scream, a long cry, Robin's death, after all, that he had waited for . . . He stared down at the apple tree, gripping the bars of the window with his hands. He would not go mad. The leaves hung limp in the heat. The scream came again, different, higher pitched and fainter. What was it? In God's name, what was it?

He remembered and gripped the bars tighter. The gaoler had said: "They brought a Frenchman off a Flanders ship last night. He's to be racked, very likely, for traitors' names. They say there are those going in and out of France who would like to see the Princess Elizabeth queen before Queen Mary dies a natural death."

He had never thought that he would hear the prisoner racked. Another scream. Why did the man not tell them, anything, lie to them, so that they would stop? He listened, sickened, sweating.

Nothing. Silence lay like a scarf over his ears, as it had all day. His hands let go their grip. Nausea filled his mouth with bile.

The door at the bottom of the next tower opened. He saw a child, a boy in a white shirt, come out and set up three skittles in a row on the cobbles. He stepped back two paces and knelt down on one knee. He had a wooden ball in his hand.

Robert Fletcher stumbled off the stool and vomited on the floor. He stood for a moment, shaking from head to foot. Then he fell onto his straw bed and wept.

Some time later the gaoler unlocked the door and said: "They've come to take you to the bishop. When you're ready, Master Fletcher, when you're ready."

Unsteadily, his limbs weak and trembling, he faltered his way down the stone stairs and out into the thunderstorm.

3

June 1558

He tried to stop his teeth chattering.

A clerk was also standing up, reading in a loud, level voice: "Robert Fletcher, sometime monk of the Charterhouse of Mountgrace in the county of York, sometime chantry priest of Saint Blaise in the cathedral church of Saint Peter in the city of York, sometime priest of the cure of Saint Denis in the said city, deprived for marriage in the year of our Lord 1554, twice afterwards in the same year contumacious, excommunicate in the same year, a preacher while unlicensed and excommunicate in the city and diocese of London, you will answer the articles that shall now be ministered to you."

He knew the voice was loud, and he could see the man standing there, not four yards away, reading from a paper. Yet the words seemed to float towards him from a great distance. He could see them coming past, pieces of ash. He watched them go by and tried to grasp them, but could not. They were light and black and entirely dead.

"First, that you, being within the city and diocese of London, have not, according to the common custom of the Catholic Church of this realm of England, come to your own parish church, nor yet to the cathedral church of this city and diocese of London, to hear devoutly and christianly Lauds, the Mass, Vespers, sung or said there in the Latin tongue after the common usage and manner of the Church of this realm."

The voice stopped. He knew that many faces were turned towards him, but he kept his gaze fixed on the clerk, for fear of falling. The clerk did not move his head but stood waiting, looking down at the paper. What was he waiting for? He became aware of a sound behind him, a crackling sound like the crackle of a fire beginning to catch. People were whispering behind him, quietly, only quietly, but the noise was so loud that he ducked his head and put his hands over his ears.

"Robert Fletcher, what have you to say to the article?"

The voice came from in front of him, above him. He took his hands from his head and looked up, almost losing his balance. There were four of them sitting there, behind a long table. On the table were papers, pens, ink, a big silver seal. They were dressed in black and white ecclesiastical robes and had black square caps on their heads. He could not tell which one had spoken. He looked from one face to the next. All four were staring at him, waiting. As he looked, the four black and white figures with their staring faces blurred in front of him and began to move, together, slowly from side to side.

"What have you to say?"

The same voice. Which face did it belong to? He tried to stop them moving, but could not. Another voice, from somewhere close beside him, said: "My lord, the prisoner can scarcely stand."

"Let him sit then. It's already late."

A chair was pushed forward. He flinched at the sudden scrape on the flags. He thought something was falling from a height, a burning rafter dislodging, crashing, bringing a shower of sparks down suddenly through silence.

He was helped into the chair. His clothes were soaked through, and the clammy shirt on his back made him shiver as he sat. The four figures at the table came to rest. The one on the right leaned forward and said, in a new voice, softer than the others: "We are waiting for your answer to the charge, Master Fletcher."

The crackling behind him had stopped. He turned towards the speaker and, after a moment, said:

"I am very sorry . . ."

He wanted to say that he had not heard the charge, or, rather, that he had heard the words but not understood them as they floated on the air.

"Is that all you have to say?"

The harsh voice again. The man who spoke he now saw more distinctly. He was the oldest of the four, though not as old as himself, and his chair had a higher back than the others, and carved, gilded arms.

"Very well. We shall proceed with the articles. You will address your answer to me."

This must be he. This man who sat with his hands eagerly clasped on the table and his head thrust forward, an expression of impatient attention on his face, must be Bishop Bonner himself, who had condemned so many to the stake and taunted them, he had been told, as they left the place where the sentence had been pronounced. This was that place.

The clerk began again: "Item: That you have not come to any of the said churches to pray, to go in procession, or to exercise yourself there in godly and laudable exercises."

Something in the bishop's face took him back. Back to Easterside and the fire Will started, the burning barn. Had he not seen, just now, the ash float upwards as the rain began? He was frightened when they told him to get the mare out of the stable, and she had reared and plunged at the flames and galloped away down the field, trailing the halter rope behind her.

"Have you any answer to make, Master Fletcher?" The gentle voice.

His eyes fixed on the bishop's face, he very slightly shook his head.

"Item: That you have not conformed yourself duly to all the laudable customs, rites, and ceremonies of any of the said churches."

"Item: That you have not been confessed of your sins at due times and places."

"Master Fletcher?"

The bishop banged the table with the flat of his hand. "Leave him in his accursed silence, Doctor Chedsey. We know him to be a persistent heretic, a liar, an oath-breaker. We need not press to speak a man whose word is only empty air, a blasphemer, a false prophet, a man vowed to most holy chastity who took a whore in pretended marriage and would not put her away when he was three times offered forgiveness by the always merciful Church. He will not recant. His silence condemns him more certainly than the vain words of the young men we had before us this day condemned them. Those young men, and many like them, have been fed lies by this old one. They have all been watched, and I tell you this, gentlemen: since last Christmas when John Rough was brought to justice, the heretics that meet in secret in this city and diocese of London have been nursed up and encouraged in their blasphemy and their disobedience by this same Fletcher that you see before you here. This Fletcher has made arrows of them to pierce the heart of the holy Catholic Church and the blessed Sacrament of the Altar too. If we burn the arrows, should we not with the more zeal burn the fletcher?"

The tinder flared again at his back, the joke repeated in whispers.

He said: "Did a sheepdog take your duck, my lord?"

At once he felt about him the fear of others. He was not afraid.

He saw the bishop's face harden with anger; he saw him choose to laugh. The court laughed also, following the bishop's lead, and he heard cowardice in the laugher, easy relief.

"You see how his sins have turned his wits? This is no simpleton, no fool like many we have had before us here, hinds let loose, men fancying themselves expositors of Scripture who can scarcely write their names. This is a learned man. We have it here . . ."

With feigned meticulousness, the bishop held up several papers, one after the other, and peered at each of them.

He heard them behind him, quiet, waiting to laugh again.

"Here. The surveyors of the chantries set it down. 'Robert Fletcher. Fifty years. Well learned.' There it is. Ten years ago he was well learned. He is brought before us as a heretic and a man of evil life, but we know he is well learned. For what, therefore, do we look? We minister to him articles touching on matters of faith and religion in which he is well learned, and we look to him for learned disputation, for the commentaries of a monk and the *quaestiones* of a scholar; we look to him at the very least for answers. And what do we find? A dotard who is shaking so with fear that he cannot stand. He sits and trembles, and we hear nothing from him, nothing, that is, except the chattering of his teeth, until at last he speaks and then . . ."

Obediently they laughed.

"Then he babbles like an infant in its mother's arms. We look for another Master Ridley, and he talks to us of dogs and ducks."

"My lord."

"One moment, Doctor Chedsey. I am in no doubt that his sins have sent him mad, but his madness shall not save him from his sins. Let the rest of the articles be read. If the prisoner does not answer, he is none the less guilty for his silence. Unless he chooses now to return from his wickedness and recant his vile heresies, he will burn for them whatever he may say or not say. Our blessed Lord has taught us that it is never too late to come home with the lost son, but I daresay it is too late for one who has lost his wits."

He said, very softly amid the noise of laughter and people leaving at the back of the court: "My lord, it is not I who have lost his wits, nor is it I who will burn."

For an instant Bonner stared. Then he shouted: "The articles! Read them!"

But the bishop's spite had woken Robert Fletcher as if from a dream.

"Item: That you have not received at your said curate's hands (as of the minister of Christ) absolution of your sins."

The fire was out. This time he understood the words. His whole body ached with fever. He longed to lie down. He longed for his pile of straw in the Tower, for silence. He bent his head.

"No. I have not", he said.

Had he not taught young men convinced by the evident truth of his words, and devoted women, that the contrite soul before God has no need of a priest's absolution, that the sinner's faith alone in the forgiveness and safety of God can loose him from his sins, that without this faith no prescribed words or deeds are of any avail, just as to it they can add nothing? Had he not himself sent out of the Minster scores of Easter penitents, their duty done, the sacrament received, their hearts still full of jealousy and greed that they had no light to see? With despair he had watched them go out into the streets, and with joy he had read later that no priest has power to remit sin.

He remembered all this without warmth, knowing that it had been so. He remembered also a November afternoon at the Mountgrace, the old prior, frail as the last oak leaves just cling-ing to the boughs, kissing his hand after hearing his clumsy confession, after absolving him.

The clerk read on.

"Item: You have not by your mouth, nor otherwise by your deed, expressed or declared in any wise that you without waver-ing or doubting do think and believe that the faith and religion now observed in the Church of this realm is a true faith and religion in all points."

Not without wavering or doubting. He smiled at the words.

Was any man certain of anything, after all the changes of religion in England, after all the ruin and waste, who did not hate more than he loved?

It was he who was old now, almost as old as the old prior, waiting for the winter gale. Would they send him back to the Tower? No. To Newgate, to the chains and the filth? He looked towards the man who had spoken gently. Doctor Chedsey's attention was elsewhere. He was writing. Several times he dipped his pen into the ink and wrote, with deliberation. He paused, fingering his beard.

He suddenly envied the old prior, with a deep envy that brought him almost to tears. That was how he himself should have died.

The clerk was still reading, but no one was listening now. Behind him they were waiting for the long tale of his offences to be done, for the bishop's sentence.

Doctor Chedsey continued to write.

The bishop was not looking at him but staring over his head. The fingers of his right hand silently drummed the table.

In a few moments the clerk would reach the end of the articles, Bonner would rise, speak, give him over to soldiers, who would hurry him away, roughly, by the arms. Tomorrow through the streets to Smithfield, the post above the faggots. Then it would be too late. He did not fear the flames. But he was saddened to the bottom of his heart that there would not be enough time. Somewhere almost within his reach was a whole, the whole that as a boy on his knees in the cell at the Mountgrace he had longed to lay before God. All that he had loved was part of it, the short grass in the summer and the sheep on Easterside, the woods above the Charterhouse, Robin at Arden carving a spoon out of a piece of cherrywood, the child in York who did not know his name. If he let them burn him now, the fragments would still be fragments. He would have lost his chance, his hope of understanding, his last hope of seeing as a single light the rays that had struck upon him again and again at different times, in different places.

His prayer flashed like a sword. Be merciful unto me, O God, for men would swallow me up.

"Item: That you have not faithfully and truly believed that in the said Sacrament of the Altar, there is really and truly the very body and blood of Christ."

"Oh, yes, my lord, I have."

He had stood up. His head was clear. His heart pounded. He was steady on his feet.

There was a gasp from many throats and then absolute silence. Doctor Chedsey stopped writing and looked up, his pen still in his hand.

"My lord, you have heard me charged with being a monk, long ago, and with being, after that, a chantry priest. So it was. The reason that I ceased to be a monk you know. The reason that I ceased to be a chantry priest you also know. You all know. In King Henry's reign parliament declared that there were to be no more monasteries. In King Edward's reign parliament declared that there were to be no more chantries. It is the duty of a subject to obey statute-law. Is it not, my lord? As a subject, I obeyed those laws. When I had ceased to be a monk, I read and came to believe that a man earns no merit by leaving the world and renouncing possessions, marriage, freedom; not because renunciation is evil in itself, but because we can earn nothing from God. Our salvation comes through faith in the merits of Christ freely bestowed. We have not deserved it, we do not, and we never can, deserve it. When I was still a chantry priest, I read and began to believe that the single sacrifice of Christ on the Cross was sufficient to redeem us all from sin and that nothing any other man may do can alter the judgement that will take place between each several soul and God, while every day I was offering Mass, alone, for the souls in purgatory. I did not want that power, my lord, and I became convinced that it was not a lawful power for man to take. So when parliament removed me from my chantry and took for the king the money I had been paid for Masses, I gladly laid down a task I no longer desired or understood.

"I had never preached before, but when I was fifty years old I became a preacher and went out to bring news of God to men and women who all their lives had received the sacraments of the Church but who had never heard in words they could understand of the darkness in their souls and the light that Christ brings. Saint Paul said that in the church he had rather speak five words with understanding, that by his voice he might teach others also, than ten thousand words in an unknown tongue. From the English Testament I read the Gospel to these men and women, and they heard for the first time the words that Jesus spoke to them. For you would not deny, my lord, that he did speak also to them? Yet you have burned them at the stake because they would not forsake the words they had received with understanding, for a tongue known only to the learned.

"These things I have done, and others too in accordance with the law as it then was, though not as it now is. But you know as well as I do, my lord, that no honest man could have obeyed the law in every point with the whole consent of his heart as it has changed and changed about these past twenty years. There have come to us all times in which we have had to see the law through the eyes of our consciences, and it is not the least honest of us who have from time to time chosen to disobey it.

"All this I grant; but a sacramentarian I have never been. I do believe that in the Sacrament of the Altar is really the very body and blood of Christ. This I have ever believed and ever shall, with the priest who taught me when I was a child, with the monks in whom I had my being half my life, with Archbishop Cranmer, with Luther, and with you, my lord. And transubstantiation is but a little word to call down a great mystery to the logic of the schools, and you do wrong to burn for it those to whom it is no more than syllables of a tongue they do not know."

The bishop rose, fury in his face.

"I thought as much! This Master Fletcher is mad. Nevertheless, like all his sect, he rails when he is stung. Indeed he is learned-mad and not too far out of his wits to pick and choose among his heresies like a lady over her silks.

"You will not save your skin, Master Fletcher, by bandying terms with me. Out of your own mouth you are condemned! You sever yourself from the Catholic and universal Church when you so much as speak of Luther, the arch-heretic, father under the devil of all the lies in Christendom. Salvation without works, away with purgatory, away with Latin, down with transubstantiation—all blasphemies, all lies, though you twist and turn between them like a running hare. Thomas Cranmer died a heretic and a traitor to the queen's majesty and you dare to say that he and I were one in the most holy Sacrament of the Altar!"

"So you were, my lord, so you were, at the beginning, at the middle, and at the end."

"He died a heretic and a traitor, and so shall you. So shall you, Master Fletcher, so shall you, but not until I have cooled your insolence."

Bonner stood up and shouted to the far back of his hall: "Take the prisoner, bind him hand and foot, and have him brought to Fulham. I shall see him there on Sunday, when he has passed a few days in the stocks."

Two men came and took him by the arms. They dragged him through the people, faster than he could walk, and as they went the crackling began again, very loud, as if they were at the heart of the fire.

4

June 1558

On the river his fever came back. At the wharf they tied his hands together, and his feet, very tight, with lengths of rope, They pulled him across the dirty cobbles and bundled him, almost threw him, into the bottom of the boat. He lay there, his back scraped, on a pile of chains, while above him the soldiers joked with the boatmen. They told stories, all three of them, and shouted with laughter. One of them had a flask, and several times they passed it round, each of them taking, he could hear, a long, greedy draught. He might have been an old sack at their feet.

After a while the heat—for the sun still burned through a heavy haze, and the storm had not cleared the air—the movement of the boat, and the throbbing pain in his head stunned him to near insensibility. He no longer heard the banter over his head and the slapping of the water on the sides of the boat as the oars rose and fell. His head was filled with the sound of his blood pulsing: when he moved a little to ease his aching limbs, the chains shifted and chinked under his ear.

He opened his eyes and saw against the purple sky a soldier with his head tipped right back and the flask to his lips. The pain in his head, his back, his wrists, his ankles, narrowed to a keen, desperate thirst. He raised his head and the chains bit into his shoulder.

"A drink", he said, twice before they heard.

"A drink? For you?" the soldier said. "Who do you think you are, you old heap of rags?" He poked him with his foot and laughed.

"Oh, give him a drink", said the boatman, leaning forward on his oars. "He's not long for this world by the look of him."

"It's finished." The soldier held the flask upside down and a few drops ran out.

"Give him some water, then."

"What for? He's wet already." A kick. "Aren't you? Soaking wet. Soaked to death."

But the other soldier grabbed the flask, filled it in the river, and bent down and held it to his mouth. He swallowed down a few gulps of water and immediately vomited. The second soldier poured the rest of the water over his face and over the chains he was lying on, to wash away the vomit. He looked up at him but could not speak, and shut his eyes again.

The first soldier said: "You don't want the fever, do you? Leave him alone. Can't you see he's got the fever? Dying like flies, they are, where he's come from. I'd rather go and fight their war in France than have this filthy job. Carrying lousy prisoners up and down the river and ending up dead ourselves very likely." He spat over the side of the boat. "Makes me sick."

"It's old men and children are getting the fever. We're young yet."

"Don't you count your chickens, my lad", said the boatman. "I've seen them all go down, young men and old men, boys and girls. You don't sleep safe in your bed till you're six feet under the ground."

"What about you then, greybeard?" said the first soldier. "Aren't you afraid the angels'll get you next?"

"I'll see you all out", said the boatman as he rowed. "Many's the dead man who's travelled in my boat. More than I could count."

The soldiers fell silent, except that after a few minutes he heard the voice of the first again.

"Toss you for Bess on Sunday after the bears."

But the other said: "You can have her", and then: "Is this the reach?"

But the boatman said: "You want a bit of patience. It's a long pull up against the tide."

The pain receded with the shore that they had left. From time to time he remembered that he was being taken up the Thames to Fulham, to the bishop's palace, but the fact meant less and less to him, until the names became like foreign phrases heard and not understood. He lay on the chains, drowsy, lulled by the water moving under his head and the lessening heat of the day. In his mind the words of the boatman came and went. Many's the dead man . . . Somewhere in the distance he saw on the bank of the river a thronging multitude. They stretched their hands out over the water towards the opposite shore, while behind them more came so that as he watched the crowd grew greater and spread further along the bank. And he was already in the boat they stretched their hands toward. The boat moved on, the oars rising and falling, and always as he looked back he saw the people flocking, smaller and smaller across the widening flood until he could no longer see them but only sense their longing for the shore.

Portitor ille Charon; his, quos vehit unda, sepulti.

Six feet under the ground. Many's the dead man travels in my boat.

He opened his eyes. The light was almost gone. Above him, against the livid sky, he saw the soldiers propped, as still as corpses, their halberds across their knees. Between them the boatman rowed on, tall and black.

Was it over, then, the fire? Had he passed through the end and forgotten it already? And all the people on the shore, were they the living? The dead?

O unjust God, to leave your children so.

As he watched the sky darken behind the boatman's head, there was a flash of lightning, and then another. A gust of wind came across the water, big drops of rain. The rain on his face, his side, his bound hands, recalled his pain. He tried to move away from it, but could not.

Both the soldiers sat up and pulled their cloaks over their heads. They looked like cowled monks, their heads hidden in their cloaks, bunched against the rain.

The boat went on, upstream, in the rain, until the night was dark.

"That's it", at last the boatman said. "Summer or no summer, there'll be a barrel and a fire lit, it's to be hoped."

He saw a row of half a dozen lights flickering in the darkness over the boatman's shoulder. They came closer and closer. The boat knocked against a wooden jetty, and the boatman threw a rope round a post and knotted it. Cursing, the soldiers dragged him up onto the wet planks.

"If you untie my feet, I can walk."

"Bound hand and foot, the bishop said."

"Where would I run to, here?"

"I'm not carrying him. Let him walk. If he can."

The rope had swollen in the rain, and it took the second soldier a minute or two to undo the knot. When at last he loosened it, the pain in his ankles became much sharper. He rolled over onto his elbows and knees. The soldier helped him to his feet, and he stood, swaying, as the blood left his head.

"Walk."

But he turned his head and looked back. He could see nothing but the utter darkness. Close to the jetty, the reflections of the lights wavered on the water, the rain pocking small circles in them as they moved. Out there somewhere they were still coming, flocking to the shore.

The soldiers took his arms, and he walked, through a hall where men sat, cheerful and noisy round a fire. Broken bread on a table, a ham, apples in a bowl. Two of the men looked up as they passed, laughed, and pointed. Glances from some of the others. One had a girl on his knee. They went down some steps into the dark. The first soldier swore and went back for a taper. A long passage. More steps. A door. They unlocked it, pushed him through it. It banged shut behind him. He stumbled and fell against a wall. For a moment while they turned the key and shot a bolt, the light from the taper showed under the door. Then, with their receding footsteps, it went away.

In the pitch dark he lay against the wall. He was very cold and shivered convulsively. He thought of the gaoler's wife, her care that he should not hurt himself falling off the stool, her hot soup, hot salty soup tasting of bacon and cabbages. If he had answered the bishop differently, no less truthfully but differently, they might have sent him back to the Tower. If he had said: "I faithfully and truly believe that in the Sacrament of the Altar there is present the very body and blood of Christ, and as to the rest I do not know. I once knew, I have known, but I know no longer", he might now be lying on his straw with the apple trees under his window.

Then he thought of the child in the white shirt and was glad they had not taken him back to the Tower.

Had there also been children on the bank, stretching out their hands over the water?

He was cold, and hungry because the fever had left him. He was not going to die tonight. He needed food. He crawled up two steps. His head met the door. He pulled himself up to his knees and struck the door with his bound fists. The hall was near enough for him to hear laughter, but his beating on the door sounded faint even to himself, flesh and bone weak on the heavy oak. He rested his head on his arms. The effort had warmed him a little.

He stank. The foul smell of his clothes, of his body, his painful crawling, brought back to him a picture from the far past. An old man, crawling... He lay in the dark, remembering.

171

He was fifteen or sixteen, walking with his father in the rain. Down the dale between steep banks where mist hung in the trees like wool, they walked to the abbey of Rievaulx, for his father to see the bailiff. His father left him at the forge, went away for many hours. An old man crawled into the yard on hands and knees, ragged, stinking, coughing. The old man sat against the dung-stained wall of the smithy and cursed the monks. Between every few words he coughed, spat lumps of bloody phlegm into the mud.

"All yon gold and silver, gold plate for my lord the abbot to eat off and a silver bit to his horse's bridle, and what do the poor get, while the fat monks go out hunting? A black crust and the bones from under the scullions' table. And the cold nights, starving cold it was, last night, in the stable with the rats running about, listening to them in there in the warm, laughing and drinking round their fire. Our holy mother the fat monks! Living off the fat of the land while the likes of us is left in the cold to die. I fought for the king, let me tell you, this last summer, for King Harry of England at Flodden Field, so that the fat monks should sleep safe in their soft beds, and what thanks do I get? We killed the king of Scots, do you hear, and half his knights. Too many to bury, they said, so we left them to rot, for the crows to pick at. They go for your eyes first, did you know that, boy? Don't run away! Don't leave me here to die!"

He was running, stumbling through the mud. The old man, on his knees, screamed after him: "Come back here! Come back! Don't leave me here to die! They peck your eyes out while your body's still warm!"

He ran as fast as he could from the yard, down a cart-track that led to the abbey stables. Round a corner against a wall he stopped to get his breath. He listened. He could hear nothing. After a while he peered out. The old man had not followed him. He could not see him anywhere. He waited some minutes longer. He walked on, towards the abbey.

The great buildings stood in a silence deeper than the silence of the rain. He walked in a leafless orchard, past a many-windowed hall. He walked through a garden, between rows of leeks and tattered cabbages, and up, under the east windows of the church, the glass in the lightless day as grey and blank as the stone. He followed the long north wall, passing many flat grave-stones. At the end of the church some steps led down towards the door. He stood out of the rain under the stone vaults of the porch and listened to the water running from the eaves. When he began to shiver, standing still, he gave the door a push. It opened without a sound, and he slipped inside, closing the door behind him.

The church was very cold, much colder than the rain. There were more tombs, sunk into the tiled floor. Huge pillars rose about him in the stillness, disappearing into the darkness of the roof. He walked down a side aisle past a series of dusty chapels. As he reached the vast shadowy space of the transept, he heard a small sound echo: pages being turned. He stopped, startled, and from somewhere out of sight in the dark choir an old, unsteady voice began to sing. A few others joined it. For a while the frail sound quavered, thin among the stone arches and the shadows. Then it ceased. Shuffling. The dull thud of a heavy door. He turned and walked quickly back down the church, his own footsteps echoing, and out into the rain.

Everywhere the same silence as before lay damp and chill. He went back to the smithy the way he had come, pausing every few yards to look for any sign of the old man. There was none. At the forge he opened one after another the doors that gave on to the yard. Tools, logs, hay. In the hay a litter of kittens mewed, and their mother arched her back and spat. Nothing else. He went into the forge and sat on the floor, close to the banked-up fire. There was a jug with a little cider left in the bottom. He drank it. The rain pattered on the roof. He slept.

Drunken shouts and laughter woke him.

He stumbled out into the yard. The light was failing, and it was still raining. Coming up the lane through the dusk was a loud, disorderly procession. Seven or eight men, abbey servants, carried shoulder-high a hefty body, its arms hanging down, head lolling. Losing their footing in the mud, they marched along, bellowing out the dirge for the dead. The body was the body of his father.

As the procession reached the yard the corpse raised its head. His father saw him standing there gaping, slid to his feet between his bearers, and, his arms still round two necks, shouted and roared with laughter.

He picked up a bucket of water and threw it into his father's face. His father stood there, astonished, dripping; when the other men let go of him, he shook himself like a dog. In the sudden silence the group dissolved. He took his father's arm and pulled him out of the yard.

The wet fields darkened round them as they walked back towards Easterside without a word.

In the wood the sky above the branches still just showed grey. There was no sound among the trees except for the rustle of their boots brushing though piles of last year's leaves.

They almost fell over the old man before they saw him, and his father saw him first, stopping, staggering, with a growl of surprise.

He saw the toe of his father's boot shift a hand that lay open on the leaves.

"Dead", his father said, bending down. "Stone dead. Still warm."

The eyes were open, turned to one side so that the face in death looked no less treacherous, no less terrified, than it had in life.

"I know him—I saw him—he fought for the king."

"Leave him be", his father said. "They'll find him from the abbey. Dig him a grave. Give 'em owt to do."

On the white of one eye a fly crawled.

174

Would they come in the morning and find him also dead, his eyes open, lying across the cellar steps?

From the old man shouting, for comfort, for help, he had run away, but he had not been given leave to escape. He ran away, and the old man lay down to die in his path. And Will, whom he had left at Easterside to be beaten and cursed while he went to the Charterhouse to sleep in a quiet bed, had he not done the same, lain down in his path to die?

He thought of the soldier who had given him water and washed the vomit from his mouth and nose. He himself had only looked and gone away.

He was no longer cold, no longer hungry. He found that by not moving at all and by breathing shallowly he could lie without touching his wet clothes, though his bruised wrists and grazed back still throbbed with pain. The morning would come. After a few days Sunday would come, and the bishop. The bishop and the bear-baiting, both on Sunday. He smiled in the darkness.

Above the cellar where he lay he heard the rain begin once more, gather force, drumming on the earth, a hard, clean downpour like the storm he had walked through from the Tower to the bishop's court. Walking with the soldiers along deserted streets, he had seen torrents flowing down the gutters, carrying towards the river the garbage and filth of dusty, hot weeks.

He listened to the good rain. No bursts of laughter came any longer from the bishop's hall.

Some words came into his mind, sentence by sentence, as if they were being spoken.

"Wash me throughly from mine iniquity and cleanse me from my sin. For I acknowledge my transgressions; and my sin is ever before me. Against thee, thee only have I sinned. Behold, thou desirest truth in the inward parts; and in the hidden part thou shalt make me to know wisdom. Thou desirest not sacrifice; else would I give it; thou delightest not in burnt offering. The sacrifices of God are a broken spirit; a broken and a contrite heart, O God . . ."

He was almost asleep.

The boat pulled away from the bank, into the middle of the stream, and all the others came crowding to the shore, stretching out their hands. There were so many of them, and one small boat. As he watched, someone came towards him across the water, and the great throng of people melted away from the far bank, and with them their longing.

The pain in his body faded as the crowds by the river dissolved from his sight, and he slept.

5

June 1558

Don Gomez Suarez de Figueroa, Count of Feria, at the court of Queen Mary in London, to King Philip of Spain and England, in Brussels; June 1558.

". . . It grieves me greatly to inform your Majesty that I can now offer but little hope of further succour from England in your Majesty's present campaign against the armies of the French king. The truth is that the realm is in no fit condition for war; affairs of state these two years past have been by the queen's unwieldy and contentious council so mismanaged as to appear, were it not for one or two egregious blunders, not to have been managed at all; the harvest promises to be worse even than that of last year; trade has been much interrupted, and is now pursued with less vigour than at any time since I was first in England; above all, the people look sickly upon the war, as an enterprise appertaining to the Kingdom of Spain into which they have against their will been dragged by the accident of the queen's marriage to your Majesty, and there is none in great place who has the inclination to persuade them otherwise.

"I must own to your Majesty that I am, in this regard as in others, sorely disappointed in the cardinal, in whom I had hoped to find a loyal and trusty servant to your Majesty, seeing that it was to you and to your father the emperor that he owed the restoration of his fortunes and indeed, during his many years in exile, the preservation of his very life. But alas, he seems a dead man. His health, though not good, is not so poor that it may altogether account for the sloth with which he chilly conducts even the most pressing business; and although I have in daily conversation with him now and then been able to warm him a little, and the fall of Calais did somewhat stir him, the result is yet far from all I could wish. He has, for example, had the power these three years, and especially since he became archbishop of Canterbury, to send into the shires a good part of her Majesty's Council, thus rendering to the part remaining some semblance of unity and some readiness of decision, but he has done nothing. As to the government of religion in the realm, he has ceased even to urge on the rooting out of heresy with the zeal which it would become so exalted a prince of the Church to show, leaving all to the bishop of London (who has lately become so hated among the common people that riots are feared whenever he goes in the streets of the city). And I have thus far been unable to move the cardinal, for reasons which he will not vouchsafe to me, towards allowing members of the Society of Jesus to come into England for the better instruction and edification of the people, advantageous to the Kingdom though it would in my opinion be to accede to this request of the Society. After these many months in which I have failed in all my endeavours to persuade him to act, I must conclude that the cardinal is a virtuous man, no doubt, but tepid; and I do not believe the tepid go to Paradise."

6

June 1558

A small grating in the cellar roof, at the far end, let in a faint
grey blur. For a few minutes in the middle of most days the sun
sharpened the blur to a bright square on the floor, crossed by
the bars of the grating and further shadowed by the less distinct
leaves of a plant growing near it, perhaps a dandelion. When
there was a breeze outside these shadowed leaves shook a little
across the barred square. Twice it rained at night, and he woke
to hear drops falling through the grating onto the earth floor.
He would have liked to feel the rain on his face and, in the
daytime, to look through the grating up at the summer sky, but
on the first morning they had clamped his ankles in the stocks
screwed to the wall so that he could only sit or lie on one patch
of the floor. They had untied his hands so that he could eat the
bread they brought him once a day, and drink the water. The
water was his consolation. It was clean and cold, and they
brought it in a big jug that held more than he needed to drink.
He used the rest to wash himself as best he could.

The stocks had holes for two more prisoners. He was thankful to be alone. He heard rats but saw none. The fever had left
him weak, and he slept much of the time, so that he was afraid
of losing count of the days. He wanted to be ready for the
bishop on Sunday. The boy who brought him the bread and
water did not come at the same time every day and would not
answer his questions. He put down the things beside him,
picked up the empty jug, and disappeared into the darkness,
locking and bolting the door. Perhaps he was frightened by him.
Perhaps he was sickened by the smell.

179

On Sunday the bishop came.

When the door was opened he heard that there were several people outside and thought they had come to fetch him. He wondered whether he would be able to stand alone. Then he heard someone say: "There he is, my lord." There was a forceful movement, a rustle, and a voice, Bonner's voice, immediately above him, said: "Now, Master Fletcher, how do you like your lodging? We have hidden your preacher's light from the world, have we not? How do you like being kept down here, stored away like old clothes in a cupboard?"

"Stuff is put in the dark, my lord, to keep its colours from fading."

"We have sharpened your wits, eh? Bread and water will soon blunt them." He turned away and said: "Leave him in the stocks. Change nothing."

"My lord."

"What is it, Master Fletcher? Do the stocks bite? They will bite harder by and by, and you will be hungry, and thirsty too if they should chance to forget to bring you both bread and water."

He began to speak, but the bishop raised his voice as if he were in court: "Are you ready to renounce your errors? To acknowledge the right of your ordinary to command your obedience in all the things of religion? Will you tell your followers to leave their heretical ways, throw away their prayerbooks? Will you tell them to cease reviling the pope and the Mass or they will all be burned, every one of them, every man and every woman, and their children will be whipped until they bleed. If you tell them these things—"

"They do not follow me, my lord. They do what they were told by the king in parliament and took for the truth."

"If those who have taught them were to tell them it was not the truth, they would soon alter their minds."

"You are mistaken, my lord."

"You could save their lives, Master Fletcher. And your own life also. If you recant, I will have you taken out of the stocks, washed, fed. If not, you are already condemned. To the stake, if you reach the stake. Otherwise—"

"My lord."

"Your answer?"

"I would ask you that I might be allowed a little straw to lie on."

"Straw! Straw! You lie in my cellar, a filthy heretic, and ask for straw! You know I could have you burned tomorrow."

"If I were a hog, my lord, you would give me straw."

"A hog is a beast and has no evil in him. You will stay here in the stocks, without straw, until you give me proof that you are no longer a heretic defiling the purity of the English Church as your body defiles the ground you lie on, or until, one way or another, you are dead. Seven of your flock at Islington, insolent heretics every one, burn this week at Smithfield. You may yet burn with them, Master Fletcher. It would be most fitting for you to lead them into the flames."

Amid a flurry of respect at the door the bishop left. From halfway up the cellar stairs, where his figure with others was visible in the half-light from the day outside, he shouted down: "I shall send to know how you do."

Then the door was shut, locked, bolted, and the last footsteps receded to silence.

After this he was restless. The bishop's visit had woken him as if from sleep. He craved release from the stocks now, not because they hurt him, not because they pinned him to one filthy patch of floor, but so that he could rub the life back into his numb legs, walk about, think. His swift answers to the bishop had astonished him. If there were that much spirit left in him, there was still time to twist and turn a little before the pack caught up with him. And Bonner's threats: Did not they too imply that there remained something in him that the bishop thought worth pursuing, something he could yet do that the bishop would hasten or prevent? While he had thought himself as good as dead, there had been all the time in the world to die in. Now that there was some time left, some life, some possibility, the time could only be short. How short? He chafed against the darkness, the stocks, his weakness from lack of food. He sat up and enjoyed the sense of his freedom to speak, of the chance there still might be to say something new. He was not old for nothing.

He was now sure that Bonner no longer intended to have him burned. The lesson had at last been learned. The burning at Christmas of John Rough, the last minister of the hidden London Protestants, had only strengthened in those about him the conviction of their own rightness. The bishop and his friends must have understood that in many more people than the spies could ever set down on their lists, ideas that had once been difficult and subtle had been hardened and made simple in the fires of the last four years, most of all in the fires that had burned Cranmer, Latimer, Ridley, and the preachers who had shared the congregations' dangers. They might continue to slaughter the sheep. They would kill no more bell-wethers.

But Bonner had falsely estimated the sheep. If he, now, were to recant, were to sign a paper, as Cranmer had done more than once, saying that he admitted all his errors and would henceforth acknowledge the authority of the bishop and the pope in all particulars, if he were then to be set free to go among his people and tell them of his changed opinion, what then? Did Bonner, after examining scores of them, really believe that they would troop obediently after him to the despised sacrament of penance and the hated Mass, into churches that they regarded as temples of idolatry housing the abominations of Satan? No, they would reject him as a coward and a traitor, a few perhaps daring to say that ill-treatment had curdled an old man's mind. It was too late for one renegade, however much he had been honoured among them, to turn them away from their truth, years and many burnings too late.

Often he had heard them repeat to one another, their faces lit with what each took in the other to be God's own glory: "Blessed are they which suffer persecution for righteousness' sake: for theirs is the Kingdom of Heaven. Blessed are ye when men revile you and persecute you. Rejoice and be glad, for great is your reward in Heaven."

If he were to recant, not out of fear, but because he doubted after all where the bounds of the truth should be fixed, and if he were to go back to these faithful servants of God bearing with him only his sense of a whole somewhere which he had yet to find, would they not persecute him? And whom would they then call blessed?

Where would it all end?

He shifted his body with a groan. It hurt him to move because there were sores on his body from lying on the wet ground. But he was alive. His mind was working. He was very hungry and had to banish from his imagination pictures of cherries in bowls, eggs, cheese, meat sizzling over the fire.

He lay fastened by the feet in the bishop of London's stinking cellar and knew that the bishop was wrong, that there was nothing now to be gained or lost because of him. He had been released, not from pain, not from fear, not from life as he had earlier thought, for before the bishop came he had reckoned himself ready to die, but from responsibility for those he had taught and encouraged in their shining confidence. For months he had known that he would one day be led through crowds to the fire, to a death that he had chosen for their sake when he refused to go to Germany. Now, all at once, he was not going to be burned. The manner of his death had ceased to carry any significance for those he had known in the garrets of Islington. Nor would his recantation after all change anything for anyone except himself.

They were leaving him to rot to death in the dark. He was free to fend alone for his own soul.

His new courage sank to nothing as swiftly as it had flared up.

Where was his soul? What was his soul? Was it not his soul where they were carried, those he had failed? His father, drowned in the swollen river, choked full of spite, too drunk even to struggle against death; Will, whose misery none but he had seen and whom at last he had not taken in from the cold street; Master Husthwaite, whom he had forsaken, as he had forsaken his father and Will, for the peaceful Charterhouse, and whose spirit, when he had found him again, had fled beyond his reach; and Alice. Alice, whom he had brought to guilt and fear when she had known neither, brought to a place where she turned away from his very voice.

He had sinned against them all, and through them against God, and what he had done to them was past his setting right. His soul: What was it but that in him which was of God, for God? And had he not spoiled it, himself broken it past mending into fragments and pieces?

If the king had not pulled down the abbeys, would he not have stayed in the Charterhouse and kept his soul one? Yet the blame was surely his own. All that he had done, all that he had not done, part of the charge God brought. Did he not know, know for sure, that this was so?

The questions swarmed about him like bees, attacking, whining, and he could not hit them away.

He moaned aloud and turned onto his face, his legs, held fast in the stocks, twisted. A hog is a beast and has no evil in him. There had been a vow, made before God, and he had perjured it.

The bolt was slid back, the key turned in the lock, and the cellar door opened. A voice he had heard before said: "Master Fletcher. I've brought you some straw." And then, with some alarm: "Master Fletcher!"

He rolled over and, hoisting himself on his elbows and then his hands, sat up.

"I was here when the bishop came this morning. He's gone into London for more than a week."

To see seven men burn.

"There's none here will carry tales if you have a bit of straw and something to eat."

It was the soldier who had given him a drink in the boat. He threw a bundle of straw down on the ground and went away, returning a moment later with a taper in one hand and a pail of water and a cloth in the other. He washed him, spread out the straw, and lifted him onto it.

"I haven't the key to unfasten the stocks, and the captain of the guard would have me flogged for a thief if I borrowed it, but here's some meat. Eat it slow."

He took a wedge of pie out of his pocket and put it down beside him on the straw.

"Why have you—you know nothing of me—I am not—", he said, through tears. "They've left me here to die. Shall I eat to keep myself alive a few days more?"

"I've seen them worse than you walk out of here right as rain. The bishop may rant and roar, but he's not the beginning and end of everything. A year or two ago, midsummer it was, this time of the year, there were three men down here, heretics, lined up in the stocks and only fit to die. A letter comes from the cardinal to the captain, and out they go, their wives waiting for them at the gate with clean clothes and the bishop not so much as knowing they've gone.

"I'll tell you what. I'll get down here again tomorrow if I can, and I'll bring you paper and pen. You write to the cardinal. They do say he hasn't seen eye to eye with the bishop over half his burnings and whippings, though he's not stopped many when all's said. But you're a learned man. A letter might work wonders for you yet."

"I cannot—I cannot— Thank you."

"You eat your bit of pie, mind."

He went away, with his light.

The sun reached the corner of the yard above, where the dandelion grew by the grating, and the barred square hardened on the floor.

A hog is a beast and has no good in him.

7

23 June 1558

He didn't know what to do with the flowers. He looked at them again, a red rose and a white, cranesbill, marjoram, bright green pennyroyal, and silvery fronds of ladslove, tied together in a bunch with a piece of ribbon. They were limp now and three or four petals dropped from the white rose. The sweetness of the moment, the gift, was fading with their scent.

The air in the room was still, and although one of the casements was open to the summer twilight, the tapers in the tall candlesticks burned with straight clear flames. The table was covered with a heavy velvet cloth, and in its centre was a gilt dish piled high with grapes and plums too early to have been grown in England. He could see trees, motionless, black, outside the window, in full leaf, and beyond them lights on the river. Sounds reached him faintly from the streets, music, laughter, the cries of pedlars selling cockles, sweetmeats, flowers, now and then a cheer from a crowd surrounding a juggler or a group of girls dancing, sometimes a burst of drunken singing.

Midsummer Eve. In the cellar he had kept count only of the days of the week, not of the date. Coming off the boat at Lambeth onto the thronging wharf, he thought he had never seen so many people, so many happy, careless faces, young men sweating as they danced, children eating strawberries, their mouths red with juice, babies crying because of the noise. He had been rowed downstream in the sunshine, past ducks and moorhens busy on the water, swans, the flowery grass high on the bank and the leaves of the willow trees brushing the surface of the river. But it was when the soldier took his arm on the wharf and they began to push through the hot, jostling crowd that he felt he had returned from the dead.

They came to an open space at a street corner where thirty or forty men and girls were dancing in four lines. The crowd watching were clapping the rhythm of the dance, and old women were gathered in the doorways looking on, some of them with tears in their eyes. They could not pass and stood with the rest as the lines of dancers moved towards each other and back. Suddenly, at a shout from one of the men, the rhythm changed. The clapping became faster, more insistent. The dance changed shape, the lines dissolving, the men coming out to the edge of the space and standing in a big untidy ring, clapping too, stamping their feet on the cobbles, while the girls in the middle whirled round and round. They were at the front of the crowd. The soldier began to clap and stamp. They were part of the ring. He clapped with the others, laughing, his heart beating fast, his body warm with new life. Another shout. The clapping and stamping suddenly stopped. The girls in the middle, breathless, dizzy, all of them with flowers in their hands, looked round the circle, ran and stumbled to their sweethearts, into their arms, laughing against them as the men seized the flowers and waved them in the air. The silence was already over, the crowd cheering, when a girl appeared in front of him, dropped him a curtsey, and gave him her flowers. He took them. People surged about him. She was gone. He stood still, looking for the soldier who, after a few moments, pushed through the crowd towards him. He saw the flowers and grinned.

"Lucky in love, eh?" he said, and they went on up the street through the milling crowd of people.

He could not remember even the colour of her hair, the colour of her eyes. He had not heard her voice. She was young and pretty, and she looked at him lightly, with a little mockery because he was old, but returning the warmth in his eyes with hers, mixing her pleasure in her youth and the dance with his.

In an instant over the flowers she laughed with him at the distance between them, and at her boldness, and she was gone.

They came out of the noisy streets into the courtyard of the archbishop's palace, and waited a long time. Clerks, soldiers, messengers came and went. The soldier stopped a few of them, pointed to his prisoner, took out a letter to show them, but they shrugged their shoulders, shook their heads, and hurried on across the court. Once the soldier left him for a few minutes and came back with some bread and cheese, which they shared, sitting on the steps of a mounting-block, their shadows on the brick behind them long in the rays of the setting sun. A woman came to the gate, weeping. She had lost a child in the crowd and had been looking for him since noon. The guards spoke to her kindly as she stood before them, rocking in her arms a baby wrapped in a shawl. No, they had not seen the boy. She told them where she lived, in case anyone should bring him to the palace, and went away, her feet bare in the street.

He was peeled, raw, to the impressions of the day, damp, fresh, frail, like an insect flying for the first time, its grey casing shed.

When the sun had long since withdrawn from the court, though the brick and stone still held their heat in the cooling air, a priest emerged from a door, which he shut behind him, came across to them, and said: "Your name is Robert Fletcher?"

He and the soldier stood up. He was suddenly afraid, and his knees almost gave way. It seemed as if the day, so vivid, that first, new day, might also be the last. He touched the soldier's arm, steadying himself.

"I am Robert Fletcher."

The priest looked at him sharply, then at the paper in his hand.

"You are brought from Fulham at the order of my lord cardinal?" He spoke with a foreign accent.

"Aye—"

"You are to come with me."

He turned in terror, now clutching the soldier's arm. The soldier smiled and gently freed himself.

"God be with you, Master Fletcher", he said, and walked away through the dusk towards the gate.

He followed the priest—perhaps he was Spanish, perhaps Italian—along passages and up stairs until they came to this hushed room with its velvet and its lit tapers. Then the priest said: "Here you will wait", and left him alone. When the door closed he expected the sounds of a key turning, a bolt being shot. They did not come. Was he not even a prisoner any more? Could he open the door and, if he met no one on the dark stairs, go, by himself, somewhere? Where? He thought of York, and of the child he had seen playing in the yard of the Tower. He thought of the long road north, the towns on the way, inns, horses, spies, money, nights after days. He thought of the rat-holes of Islington. He had never imagined further than being caught, imprisoned, tried, burned. Germany? The language he could not speak, angry Englishmen with their factions and their certainties, waiting for the new reign. He thought of Arden, far in the past, himself a child set to watch the sacks filling with grain, shouting out each time one was full. He thought of the Tower, the gaoler coming up to tell him what was happening outside, to other men. He was stripped even of the cellar at Fulham, the soldier bringing him clean straw, the shadow of the dandelion leaves. He was no longer locked in and was the more afraid, the more trapped. Where was there left for him to die? Everywhere and nowhere, as when he had gone out of the Charterhouse gate into the snow.

Shouts came from somewhere in the streets, and a swelling murmur of other voices. A fight had broken out in the crowd. He moved to the window and looked out. He could see nothing but the archbishop's garden, quiet and dark, and the trees beyond. The noise was coming from the other side of the wall on his left. It grew louder, angrier. He could hear the men fighting being egged on, cheers and groans from the crowd as the advantage went this way and that, even, as the bystanders held their breath, the thud of fist on flesh. He remembered the midday crowds, the same crowds, the laughing faces, the dance. These men had stood in the ring and clapped together the rhythm of the dance. Old women watching them had wept for the music and their own youth. Now there were two men fighting, full of hate, their faces cut, their fists covered in blood. They would have to be dragged apart before they killed each other, and the old women were crouching, frightened, behind their bolted doors.

Another silent garden, another wall, with the savage world beyond it, the wild flowers and the fighting deer.

Lamb of God, that taketh away the sins of the world, have mercy upon us.

His garden at the Mountgrace. What had it been after all? A patch of peace marked out against the wilderness? A burrow to hide in from hawk and fox?

Mean by sin a lump. Just as, a few days ago, he lay in the stocks and studied the shattered pieces of his soul, so he had knelt, long ago in his monk's cell, and meant by sin his own body, not only his own body but his own self, beside which God stood, infinite and merciful, to receive his pardoned soul. But was not the lump indivisible, all men born to hatred and pride, all men twisted together in the rope of evil, all men?

The fight beyond the wall grew fiercer. Then there was a woman's scream, a sudden silence. Did one of the men lie dead, bleeding on the cobbles? There was a noise like a sigh as many turned away and began to mutter quietly to each other. He heard a new voice shouting commands, clearing the street, sending the people home, perhaps the voice of one of the soldiers at the gate. He thought of his own soldier. Where was he now? Eating and drinking with the rest in the guardhouse?

Gone back to Fulham or Saint Paul's to take more prisoners for the bishop of London, to bind their hands, fasten them in the stocks, and comfort them? Or had he a home, a door in an alley, a mother, brothers, sisters? Was there also evil in him? He too was twisted into the rope, or his goodness would not so have shone.

He looked across the garden through the still trees to the river. There were fewer lights moving on the water, and after the din of the fight, there was suddenly hardly a sound in the streets close to the palace. He turned round, so that he was facing the room, and listened. No footsteps on the stairs. No voices from the hall. No doors opening and shutting. It was so quiet that he could hear the noise of the burning wicks consuming the wax in the candles. A cloud of tiny insects hovered over each flame. As he watched, a big moth whirred past him towards the light, circled a few times closer and closer to the candle-flame, too close, and dropped to the table with a little tap. Outside, it was almost dark. The candlelight in the room glowed among the shadows with a rich warmth. He walked towards the table, delighting in the freedom of his legs to move. After a fortnight lying in the stocks, woken from every sleep by the pain of his ankles caught in the heavy frame, it was enough to be free to walk, aching and stiff, from the window to the table.

It was to please the soldier that he had written the letter, certain that nothing would come of it.

What did he know of the cardinal? He had once seen a young man who rocked his pruned rose in the earth to test its strength. The young man had after many years become the papal legate in scarlet robes whom he had seen for a moment that night at the palace of Whitehall.

He had since heard talk of him, that he had always been the pope's man, that King Henry had put a price on his head and hired murderers to kill him in Italy, that some had hoped he would marry the queen his cousin, that he hated the Spaniards.

In the spring there had been rumours that he was ill, that his mind had gone, that he kept to his rooms and would not see the queen because the Spanish war, which had lost England Calais, was a war against the pope as well as against France. What was true he had no means of telling. After Cranmer's death, when the cardinal had become Archbishop of Canterbury, he had seen an effigy of him burned in a London street, a straw doll dressed in red cloth, the people cheering as the flames blazed up. He knew that more heretics had been burned in Canterbury than by any other bishop's court except Bonner's; he had never heard that the cardinal had tried a heretic himself. He had written his letter to a name at the centre of contradictory tales, but remembering how many of the cardinal's family King Henry had put to death.

The soldier brought him pen and ink and a scrap of paper, and he sat up in the stocks and wrote against his knee, the soldier holding a guttering light close to the paper.

"May it please your lordship to look mercifully upon your humble servant in Christ, Robert Fletcher, a prisoner in the stocks at Fulham of the lord bishop of London, in the sixty-first year of his age, condemned as a heretic which he is not and has never been."

There was no room to write more. The soldier took the letter, and he let it go without hope, without even desire. He would have forgotten it if the soldier had not looked each day for his release. Nine days passed. And then one morning, the morning of the day not yet over although it seemed long ago, the soldier came down with the captain of the guard and stood by, hardly able to keep his mouth shut, while the stocks were unfastened.

"You are to be carried to Lambeth under guard, Master Fletcher."

He could not stand at first, and the soldier walked him up and down the cellar until some strength returned painfully to his legs. He helped him into some clothes, his own clothes, washed, and they went slowly up the steps and out into the blinding light.

He stood by the table looking down, away from the hovering insects, and saw that there was a carpet at his feet, in front of the dark hearth. The pattern on the carpet reminded him of something. He moved one of the candlesticks closer to the edge of the table and bent down to look. He could not remember. He straightened. His head swam and he almost fell. He went back to the window and leaned out as far as he could, breathing in the cool air. When he felt better he opened his eyes.

Under the window in the blackness of the garden he saw a bush of white roses. It was too dark to see the stems, the leaves, the brick wall, the grass, but the roses shone white with all the light that was left in the day.

Not to have died, there in the cellar, but thus to have come back to life, was a great good.

He heard behind him approaching steps, the creak of a door. As he moved he noticed the withered flowers still in his hand. He threw them out of the window and turned back towards the room.

8

23 June 1558

The man who had opened the door did not come right into the room but stood motionless, looking at him across the flickering tapers. In his left hand he held a light; his right hand gripped the edge of the door as if he were afraid of falling. His eyes were large, tired, and patient, without guile. His whole bearing suggested fineness, a fine gentleness oppressed under a weight of care. His presence made Robert Fletcher feel like an idle boy, overgrown, footloose, clumsy, and it was this shame, this peasant strength before the other's frailty, that brought back their past encounter, so many years before, and told him who had come to fetch him. There was, indeed, a bishop's ring on the hand holding the door.

"You are Master Fletcher?"

"Aye, my lord."

"It is very late. I have not been well today. Will you follow me?"

The voice was weary, contained, like the bearded face.

They went along a gallery where a servant, sitting on a stool under a torch, got up and bowed as the cardinal passed. Another servant held open the door of a well-lighted room and, when they had gone in, closed it behind them. The room was not large and was filled with a warm silence that enveloped his senses like a coat. He had become cold, standing by the open window. Here there were no insects crowding to the candle-flames because thick hangings covered the walls. Books and papers overlapped on the table, and there were more books on a heavy chest against the wall. A fire was lit in the hearth, and in front of it a little black cat was curled, asleep.

For four years Robert Fletcher had been homeless, in danger, changing the place where he slept so as to remove danger from others, taking with him nothing but two books and the clothes he was wearing. For nearly two months he had been a prisoner, waking every morning to the possibility that this would be the day when they would come and take him out to die a horrible death. For two weeks he had lain in a stinking cellar, fastened by his feet to one filthy patch of ground. He looked at the little cat and felt his whole body relax as if rain were falling after a long drought.

It was more than the room, the fire, the cat. It was also that the cardinal had not sent a servant for him, a prisoner, a heretic condemned to death, but had come himself, white and tired, to fetch him from where he had been told to wait and had almost begged his pardon for not coming sooner.

Without disturbing the still air in the room, the cardinal sat down and extended the fingers of one hand, palm upwards, towards the chair facing his own on the other side of the fire.

"Be seated, Master Fletcher. This is not a court."

As he said this he smiled very faintly, but his face immediately resumed its sad, closed expression, and when he spoke again he did not look at him.

"The reason that I have had you brought to me . . ." The quiet voice fell silent, and then began differently, as if it were important for the account to be exact.

"The soldier who came with your letter would not deliver it into any hand but mine, though he had to wait outside all day for me to pass by. He seemed an honest lad and spoke most earnestly for you. 'He's a learned man, my lord', he kept saying, as if . . ."

Again the faint smile, and silence. They both gazed into the fire that burned between them coolly, with low licking flames, because it had not long been lit. He waited, tense again, in his chair. The little cat's black fur rose and fell as it slept. He saw it, but it no longer moved him.

The large eyes were turned to him. The voice, not raised, took on an edge: "You were a monk of the Charterhouse. Why do you lead my sheep into the marsh?"

He looked back into the fire for help. The small flames licked on, giving none. He wanted to tell the truth. The truth, where was that? The truth was a living tree, and he could not break a branch from it without killing the branch.

"It was to firm ground that I tried to lead them, my lord."

"Then you yourself have been misled. Outside the Church there is no firm ground for any man to stand on. The Church is a city built upon a rock. She has walls about her, and solid gates, and her streets are straight and sure. Outside her there is only the pathless fen, and if a man goes out into that darkness, his light may glimmer for a while, but soon both it and he will disappear together. Into that night you have encouraged to follow you souls for whose safety you were accountable to God. Many have died stubbornly refusing to come back to the city and the light."

"My lord, I have led no sect into the dark. Neither I nor those to whom I ministered had left the Church. We were faithful to the Church as it was ordered for the whole realm in the reigns of King Henry and King Edward."

"You speak of them, of yourself and them, in the past. Has your opinion of them altered since you were in prison? You know that we have not caught them all. There are many of them left on your firm ground. They will need ministers still."

He looked across at the tired face. The expression on it was not closed now but open, almost amused. There was no malice in it.

"I am a dead man, my lord."

The cardinal laughed.

"We are all dead men, Master Fletcher."

Then he said: "All that is left for us is the time before we die. No one has more than that."

It had been lightly said. It had been said. He felt like a bird flown from the tree. It would not last. The tree is rooted in the earth, and we cannot fly from it for long. The past is who we are and claims us back, always, again and again, until there is no longer any present.

Softly in the warm room he said: "Any time is too much."

They were both still. Not a sound reached them from the palace, full of guards, servants, priests, from the river, the city, the dark midsummer fields and woods, the hunting owls and the foxes padding the lanes.

The burning logs in the fire fell together as one of them gave way, and some sticks that had not yet caught blazed up briefly, brightening the light. The cat stirred and stretched out a paw, showing its claws for a moment before it drew back the paw and settled again to sleep. The cardinal got up from his chair and walked round the room, very quietly, touching things here and there, a book, a fold of the hangings, the scrolled top of a reading-desk on which a large volume lay open. The bird had flown back and sat among the branches. On the table there was a carved ivory box. The cardinal stopped beside it and ran his finger back and forth over the lid.

"If you were a simple man, Master Fletcher, I should say to you that the Church under the forms now ordered in this realm commands your obedience, and every faithful subject's obedience, no less than she did in the days of King Henry and King Edward. But even for a simple man that would not be honest argument. And as it is . . ."

He stood for a moment longer, his finger resting on the lid of the box. Then he turned suddenly, came back to his chair, and sat down. As he leaned forward, the fire lit his face from below. His eyes were intent and calm.

"As it is, and because once you were a monk in the order

which of all the orders that were in England I had most cause to love, I do not ask you to obey the Church for the reason that such obedience is enjoined by law, although it is. Now, in Queen Mary's days, it is. Lately it has not been—wait, Master Fletcher—and in a year or two it may not be again. Before long, I am much afraid, the time will come again when the law will enjoin us not to obey but to disobey the Church. Then it will be right for us to disobey the law. Then the church in England will call itself the church, certainly, as it did under King Henry and King Edward, but it will be as subjects only that it will be our duty to remain within it, not as souls before God. I am asking you, Master Fletcher, to turn back from the path you have taken, not as a subject of the queen, but as a strayed soul, not because you break the law, but because you are wrong, and your path leads only into the night."

The leaves of the tree hid him again; the pull of the earth was familiar.

"My lord, it was not as a subject only that I chose the path I took, and it is not mere stubborn disobedience that has kept many others in that path since the authority of Rome was restored. They also have run foul of the law for conscience's sake, just as you would have me do if Rome's authority is cast off again. They believe that the English service that every man and woman can understand, the supper of the Lord, the bread and wine freely given to all who ask for God's grace with a contrite heart, are of the Church, are of the ancient Church of God as it was before the corruptions and oppressions of recent times grew up about it as a thorn hedge protecting the power and wealth of a few and concealing the word of God from the poor and ignorant. There are many in England now, and out of it, both simple and learned, who believe that they saw in the last days of King Edward the church as it truly is, and who, as you know well, my lord, are ready not only to break the law for it but to die for it too. They believe that they are right, right before God, and that those who obey the pope are wrong, whatever the law may require, to bring back all the rules and conditions, fines and dues and measured-out days of purgatory, without which, they are told, they shall not see God. They are not wild, unruly men, my lord, nor traitors to the queen. They take their stand in faith, as souls before God, as you would have them do, and the only difference between them and you is that their faith is in the church whose authority is that of God whereas yours is in the church whose authority is that of mortal men."

The cardinal looked at him searchingly over the warming firelight.

"You put their case very skilfully, Master Fletcher. Do you take your stand on it?"

"I put their case because the bishop of London is still burning them, and your court in Canterbury too, my lord, I daresay, and they do not deserve to die, nor can they put their case so well themselves."

"That is no answer to my question. But it answers one I did not ask. You are a priest. You ministered to them, said their service for them, baptized their children, strengthened the dying, taught them. Above all you taught them. You gave them the words through which alone they became able to see themselves as far from God, close to God, sinful men saved in Christ, the words through which alone they were able to grasp the new vision of the church that you were holding up before them. You brought them the word of God. And when they misunderstood, when they were in despair at the weight of their sin or thought that they could save themselves by their own actions, when their zeal carried them away and they wanted to destroy more of the old Church than you thought was right, or when they seized on passages of Scripture and used them in isolation to encourage each other in courses that you knew were wrong, you corrected them. Did you not, Master Fletcher? You corrected them. You fetched them back to the right path with more teaching, more understanding, more words. And what were you using but the authority of a mortal man? And you are using it again, now, to put their case for men who cannot put it for themselves."

The cardinal was flushed, feverish. He had not finished speaking. He got up, threw some wood on the fire, and began to pace about the room.

"Once a part of the Church separates itself from the whole and confines its truth and rightness as the church to those who follow a single leader or those who live in a single land, it has lost the authority that it had as part of the whole, the authority of unity, the authority of tradition. Without what it has lost, it must nevertheless curb the folly of fools and restrain the excesses of the reckless, unless each individual man is to become his own church. So what does it do? What is there left for it to do, having thrown off and despised the ancient authority of the whole Church, but to lean far more, and far more dangerously than ever was done before, on the authority of mortal men? Outside the Church men alone, weak and fallible men, have no choice but to set themselves up to choose for each other what shall or shall not be right, what shall or shall not be the truth. Is that a charge you wish to bear, Master Fletcher? Inside the Church the living truth brought by Christ, the living authority he gave to the Apostles, are guarded by God, and heretics delude themselves who think that, running from the Church, they run from man to God. They run from God to man. Your church is but a limb cut from the body. The limb will die; the body cannot die."

Again the tree. The cardinal also saw the severed bough, the leaves drying, brown against the summer green. But the cardinal's vision was of a whole outside himself. He could see his bright city and the heretics fleeing into the dark. He could see his towering oak from the ground where he stood, and the dead wood fallen beneath it. It was not as simple as that. It had not been like that. His own tree, his own truth, was obscure, hidden inside himself. When he died it would crash to the ground with him and all of it would die together.

He moved in his chair and after a while lifted his gaze reluctantly from the fire. The cardinal, pale as if after great exertion, was standing against the table, supporting himself on it with one hand. He wavered slightly, and the hand on the corner of the table tightened its hold.

"You are not well, my lord."

Robert Fletcher rose towards him, to save him from falling. With a little gesture of his other hand the cardinal stopped him.

"I am well enough. The air is heavy. In London."

He saw the effort that he made. He stood upright, letting go of the table, returned to his chair, and sat down.

"Go back to the beginning, Master Fletcher. Were you ever in the Charterhouse at Sheen, long ago?"

"No, my lord. I was at the Mountgrace, in the county of York, all the years that I was a monk."

"The Mountgrace? I came there once, for Easter as I remember."

"I was there, my lord, when you came."

"Were you? Were you indeed?"

The cardinal looked across at him, his smile for a moment mocking the distances of the time between.

"How many years were you a monk?"

"Twenty years, all but a few months."

"Twenty years. Twenty years is half a life. Yet time in a Charterhouse goes swiftly by, does it not? One year follows another as one hour the next among the changes of the world. The pattern that the monks lay upon time binds it up, reduces the strength of its blows almost to nothing, so that a whole life passed between a man's going into the Charterhouse and his dying there must seem at the end not much more than a short sleep and the awakening from it. That is why . . ."

The cardinal spoke slowly and softly again, as he had at the beginning, and stared into the fire. Robert Fletcher sat quite still, his eyes fixed on the same glowing logs, hearing the words found for what he had thought.

After a pause the cardinal, not moving, said: "When I was a boy I was brought up in the Charterhouse at Sheen. It was a safe place from the world, and I used to think that afterwards, that some day, I should come back there and be given a cell of my own, and a garden, in which to die a quiet death.

"My mother was afraid always. Her father, my grandfather, was secretly murdered. Her forebears for two generations had died on the battlefields of York and Lancaster. And then her brother whom she greatly loved—they had been left, two children alone and hated for their birth—he also was killed, for fear, for revenge.

"I saw the king of Scots myself, when they brought his corpse to Sheen after the battle of Flodden, the wounds on his body black holes, though they had washed the skin.

"And after all it was not I but she who—on the block.

"I was to be a scholar, she said, and not a monk, not yet a monk. But afterwards there was no going back. From time to time I have lived almost as a monk. I have tried to find a monk's peace. But there is no going back."

There was a long silence.

At last Robert Fletcher said: "No, my lord."

The cardinal looked up.

"It grieved you, the being sent out from the priory?"

He thought. Once more the longing for the truth. Not so much to tell it as to know it, to see it whole.

He could argue an opinion with ready speech. Now that they had shed opinion, he spoke haltingly, as the cardinal had.

"It grieved me, aye. To be removed from the cloister was to be removed from my only home. It was the heavier grief because I had been taken from my home before."

"To go into the Charterhouse?"

"No, my lord. When I was seven years old. But although it grieved me to be taken from the cloister, and I had been well content to stay if the king spared the house, which my lord Cromwell promised us that he would, I was nevertheless, after a little while, not glad, but not sorry either. It was perhaps that, instead of being held fast in that sleep, the sleep from which I would have awoken only in death, I was suddenly brought to my senses by being thrust forth into the world, and the unlooked-for waking from sleep was a waking to much more than grief.

"I don't intend by this—I would not have you think, my lord, that I reckoned then, or, in spite of all, that I have reckoned since, the life of a monk in the Charterhouse to be of no more account than a sleep whose period is a holy death. I have in mind only to say that to return to time, as I was forced and would not have chosen to do, was to return to the element that God has set for the souls of men to dwell in. After I had been out of the monastery a while, and in the world, I began to think that to evade time, as monks seek to do, is to evade also the chances and changes, the opportunities and occasions, by which a soul is made. How can there be proof, I thought, where there is no testing? How can there be increase of worth where there is no motion towards God through trouble and disarray but, on the contrary, the same calm offering of denial and obedience, hours and prayers, day after day, year after year? How can there be virtue where a man leaves behind his fellows in their confusion and their misery, as if he were not part of the same fallen race as they, and lives in a peace that is defended from the world, as a garden is walled from the forest outside, as if he were safe with God before his death?

"All this I thought, not all at once, but piece by piece over a number of years as I had to live in the world, in time, again, among people, and saw their need, not just for understanding, of the rightness or wrongness of what they had done, but for assurance, for certain belief, that in Christ they are loved of God. When I went into the Charterhouse, I had left behind my fellows, those for whom I might have discovered such a sure belief, and when I was put back among them, I was glad.

"It was in this way that I came to be grateful to the chance that took me from the cloister where, if things had fallen out differently, I should now, no doubt, be soon to die a comelier death than any that awaits me out of it."

The cardinal did not smile but said: "And it was in this way that you yielded to the new doctrines and drew from them the inferences that so many men have drawn."

"Aye, my lord."

He had become aware as he was speaking of something growing up beside his words, like a mirror image of them, something as true as they were but carrying an exactly opposing weight, as if, even while he spoke, he were disproving, sentence by sentence, what he was saying. It was not a new sensation. He had had it recently, in his room in the Tower, thinking about these things, and had quailed before it as before a choice he was too old to make. But now, because of the quality of the cardinal's attention, because of the warmth there, and the lateness, perhaps he had the courage at last to confront the choice.

He looked down at the little cat, breathing noiselessly beside the fire.

"But in these last weeks, during my imprisonment, I have begun not to be certain any more."

He glanced at the cardinal. The weary eyes met his. The cardinal said: "Do not be afraid, Master Fletcher. No one knows you are here."

He could not now, in any case, have held back.

"I have begun to see the same things, the same difference between a life lived out of the world and a life lived in it, newly, as if—as if, having become accustomed to the evening light, I had passed through the darkness and now see, in the morning sun, all the shadows lying the opposite way. All that I have said, of the necessity for the soul to contend with the changes and occasions of the world, of time as the air we are meant to breathe, the element in which we are meant to dwell, of the trouble through which we may move towards God—all this, I have begun to think, tends in the opposite direction from that which I have followed for so long.

"I do not make myself plain. I am sorry, my lord. Let me try." He paused for a moment and then went on. "If it is wrong for a monk to reckon that by self-denial and certain observances he has earned his salvation, then it is no less wrong for me to require myself, or any man, to earn salvation in the fiercer world outside the cloister. The soul's safety is not to be earned. There is no merit with which we can compel God to redeem us. He has redeemed us. There is only the soul's good, God himself, nearer to us or further from us according to our openness to his grace, according, not to our love for him, but to his love for us. And the monk, of all men, should know this openness of soul, because he has abandoned so much that shelters men from God."

"For we have to live, all of us"—it was the cardinal who went on—"both in time and out of time, and the monk, keeping the cloister, has already defeated some of the power of time though he is in it still."

He remembered the height from which he had watched them scurry in the shadows during the last days at the Mount-grace. Then he remembered the abbey church at Rievaulx, dusty and cold, the old men left alone to sing the office because they were not fit to ride a horse.

"But, my lord, it only should have been so. It was not. I have not been mad all these years. You remember them too, the great abbeys and the small, the riches, the idleness, the decay, faith gone out of them and works performed without love, the wealth of the Church going to waste that should have been the wealth of the poor."

"And has it become the wealth of the poor since the abbeys were brought down, Master Fletcher?"

The cardinal leaned forward in his chair.

"No. That sinful men make little or bad use of rules and customs, books and stones, long ago devised and built for the good of many, is no reason for casting aside the rules, burning the books, and pulling down the stones. It was not that these things made sinful men; it was rather that sinful men brought these things into contempt. The disgrace should have been spared from the things and confessed by the men. And the case of the whole Church is no different."

His voice quickened. "You do not yet know it, but what you have said shows this to be so. I could draw out for you—but tonight it is late, and you are very tired."

Indeed his strength had suddenly left him, and he had begun to tremble with exhaustion. The cardinal rose and stood with his back to the fire, looking down at him, his face in shadow.

"I will say only this. The new light that you have lately seen shining for you from the other side of the sky is no new light but the same sun that shone also in the evening. The sun is the same. The earth is the same. Only the shadows change, and the way they lie. You do not have to choose between one way of seeing all these things and the other, because both are true. The truth is in the whole, Master Fletcher, in the whole. And the Church—what is she, Master Fletcher?"

His face must have been clear in the firelight; something in its expression had halted the cardinal. He looked up at him, who had changed so many times in the hour they had passed to-gether, but whose kindness had not wavered.

Robert Fletcher shook his head.

"I no longer know—anything, my lord."

"You are tired. You shall sleep. Much talking, and the journey from Fulham, and the crowds in the streets, and your days, no doubt, in the bishop of London's cellar, have worn you out. Come."

Getting up out of his chair was slow and painful. His ankles, bruised by the stocks, had become stiff, and when he at last stood upright, he almost fell. The cardinal put a hand under his arm to steady him. Tears came to his eyes. He reached the table and held on to it as the cardinal had. They were both old men, he thought, stumbling among thickets of words.

The cardinal went to the door and spoke to the servant outside. After a moment the man came in with a cup of wine.

"Drink it, Master Fletcher", the cardinal said. "It will give you a little strength."

He sipped the wine, which lessened his trembling and at once made him lightheaded. It had been many hours since he had eaten bread and cheese in the courtyard with the soldier. The soldier . . . If it had not been for the soldier, he would perhaps by now be dead, have died alone, of hunger, in the cellar, watching the shadow of the dandelion shiver in the barred square.

The cardinal was writing on a piece of paper. He scribbled his signature at the bottom, sanded the ink, folded the paper and gave it to the servant.

"Take Master Fletcher to the clerks' chamber and see that he is found meat and drink and a clean bed. The letter is for Signor Bernardi. Be sure that he receives it when he wakes. I have no doubt that he will have been asleep long since."

The faint smile accompanied these last words. Robert Fletcher hoped that he would see it again.

"Good-night, Master Fletcher. God be with you."

"Good-night, my lord, and—good-night."

He left the room, the warmth and light, with the servant, and the servant closed the door behind them.

9

July 1558

By the middle of July he had become accustomed to days in the palace at Lambeth as quiet and ordered and as like to each other as any he had ever spent.

They had given him work to do, a plain English digest to prepare from two heavy Latin volumes of canon law, the decrees of the recent Council at Trent. He knew nothing of the Council and so far had learned little from the ponderous paragraphs of the early decrees. Slowly and carefully he worked away; he had not been set such a task since he was a boy struggling with the difficulties of Master Husthwaite's Cicero.

Every morning, after hearing Lauds sung in the archbishop's chapel, he sat down at his table in the library and applied himself to the books lying ready for him, open at the page he had reached the day before. A change in the light or any noise in the courtyard outside, a shout, the bark of a dog, a door opening, would distract his attention. He laid down his pen and gazed out of the window, scarcely noticing those who came and went through the gate, watching with his mind's eye the pieces of past time that came back to him. After a while the palace clock would chime the quarter, any quarter, and he would return to his thick folio, pick up his pen, and begin to compose his next sentence. He had been given no term for the work, and no one asked him how it went.

No one asked him anything. They addressed him courteously by his name, wished him good-day and good-night, nodded to him at table, and otherwise left him alone. At first he thought they had been told to treat him in this way; after several days, watching those who also sometimes read or wrote in the library, who ate alongside him in the hall, who silently walked ahead of him into the chapel, he saw that few unnecessary words were exchanged between them. This withholding of familiarity in a silence as contained, almost, as that of the Charterhouse was no more than the manner customary in the cardinal's household. Most of the priests and clerks, and some of the servants, were Italians. They wore black clothes, as everyone knew the Spaniards of the queen's court did, but there were no Spaniards at Lambeth.

He had not heard the London Protestants, the burnings, or Bishop Bonner spoken of by anyone.

He sat at his table and watched a light rain falling on the empty courtyard. The cardinal was at Richmond with the queen, for whose recovery from sickness prayers were said every day, and the passage across the court of soldiers, priests, and messengers was less frequent than usual. The rain fell coolly onto the grey cobbles, the brick paths between them, the mounting-block.

From his seat at the table in Master Husthwaite's parlour, long ago, he had looked out, when the Latin was fuddling his head, at the mud cottages on the other side of the lane, their cabbage-plots sloping down to the river, which, higher up the dale, drove the wheel of Arden mill and then flowed past the church, the graveyard.

The graveyard.

He was sitting on the hillside above Laskill one morning in July, watching the Easterside sheep being brought down off the moor for shearing. He was ten or eleven years old. At the bottom of the hill on the far bank of the river stood the abbey woolhouse, a long barn where the fleeces from the whole of Bilsdale would be collected, weighed, packed, and stored until the lines of wagons came from the abbey to take them out of the dale. The Easterside flock was sheared in old stone pens, empty the rest of the year, in the lowest part of the field on the near side of the river.

He watched the sheep pour through a gap in the stone wall. Two sheepdogs ran back and forth in the heather chasing stragglers. When the last few sheep had come through the gap like the last grains of sand through an hourglass, the sheepdogs raced through after them and poles were slung across the gap to close it. His own dog sat beside him. His hand lay on her neck.

The sheep fanned out again over the field. The dogs began to separate them into groups of five or six and chivvy them into the pens where the men were waiting. The first half-dozen sheep were thrown to the ground and pinned, eyes rolling in terror, under the knees of the shearers.

His dog suddenly stiffened under his hand, then shot forward across the grass, running downhill so fast that her belly was almost flat on the ground. In the far corner of the field a strange dog had appeared, a huge black dog that stood with its front paws braced and its tail high, looking at the sheep milling about in the field. He called his dog. She did not hear. The black dog sprang towards the sheep. They scattered in flurries up the hill, their feet pattering on the turf. The sheepdogs lay side by side at the pens, cowering, though Tom and the other men kicked and cursed them. The black dog bounded into the sheep, singled out a three-months lamb still running with its mother, took it by the throat, shook it three or four times like a rat, and dropped it to the ground. Blood leaked over the white wool, dripped from the dog's jaws. A moment later, while the lamb still twitched, the dog had killed an old ewe in the same way. All the men were coming up the hill now, shouting and waving sticks, shears, coats. One or two took stones off the wall as they came, and threw them. But the dog was hunting out of their reach, killing among the running sheep.

Then he saw that his own dog was also among the sheep, hunting with the black dog. He saw her let go a lamb, which dropped and twitched. He saw her bloody muzzle. He screamed her name as he ran, again and again. She never paused or looked towards him. The sheep were crowded into the top corner of the field, dashing this way and that. On the grassy slope behind them ten or twelve lay still. The men had reached the gap. The poles were unslung and the sheep began to stream through into the heather. He could see their fleeces bounce past as the men gathered at the gap, their sticks raised in the air.

"No!" he shrieked, "No!" hurling himself at Tom, who shook him off so that he fell backwards on the grass.

At the very last instant the black dog saw the men, stopped suddenly, raced off down the hill. But his own dog followed the sheep right up to the gap. A coat was flung over her head and the sticks came down on her back. He ran away, along the top of the field, away from the sound of the sticks on her back, past Will, who stood rigid, watching the end, into the lane, down to the beck, up the other side. At last, when the pain in his chest was so great that he could not run any more, he fell with his face in the grass under the hedge and sobbed.

He cried for a long time, his sobs shaking him, choking him, leaving him worn out at last and shivering at the edge of the lane in the sharp grass.

It was quiet in the village, dinner-time, when he walked past the houses. He took the lane up the narrow valley to Arden. It was a lifeless day, overcast and dull. He walked quickly, hearing his footsteps in the empty lane, hearing the absence that accompanied him. The same cow-parsley was high, seedy, musty, by the white stony ruts of the lane as it had been the day Tom fetched him down from Arden to Easterside.

When he reached Arden, he looked down the track that led to the mill. It was not his any more. Smoke came from the chimney, and at the side of the millstream a wagon was being unloaded by two men he did not know.

He went on past the shut gate in the priory wall and round to an old door into the nuns' kitchen garden. The latch had been rotten, was rotten still. There was groundsel growing between the rows of beans and dandelion clocks thick along the path. He looked at the apple trees. Clusters of spurs had grown out unpruned by the greened-over cuts that Robin's knife had made. He heard laughter from the bakehouse door, which was propped open. He went and looked in. A nun he remembered and two other women were standing at the table kneading dough, their arms floury up to the elbows. A warm smell of sweat and yeast blew out at him. The idiot-woman sat on the floor by the oven where she had always sat, rolling together and pulling apart a dirty piece of dough.

After a few moments one of the women saw him. "Well I never! What dost tha' want, lad?"

The nun looked towards him, but he was against the light and she did not recognise him. He shook his head and ran off through the garden. When he was outside he looked back through the crack between the door and the wall and saw the nun standing on the bakehouse step. She peered about, her elbows against her sides and her hands in the air so that flour should not fall on her habit. She shrugged and went in.

He had only come to see.

He walked slowly. The lane back to the village seemed too short. There was nowhere he could go except to Easterside, and he did not want to get there before dark. He found the empty shell of a blackbird's egg lying in the ditch and spent some time hunting about in the hedge until he found the deserted nest. At the bridge he slithered down the bank and stared into the shallows for lurking trout. Not seeing any, he set flat stones spinning across the pool, counting the number of times they jumped.

The village church stood by itself close to the river, a short way down from the bridge. As he passed the gate of the churchyard, he saw something bright through the leaning gravestones. He opened the gate and went down the path. The bright thing was a wreath of flowers, roses and blue cranesbill and lilies of the valley, twined with branches of rue and myrtle and laid on a fresh grave. The squares of turf, their edges cut straight with a spade, had not long been put back on top of the mound of earth. They did not fit close together, so that there were gaps between them through which the bare earth showed. He looked round. The grass on the other graves grew dense and even as in a field, and the mounds were almost level with the ground.

The gaps between the sods oppressed him. He wanted them to grow together quickly so that the grave would be no different from all the others. He knelt down and began trying to push the edges together, but they would not move at all unless he lifted a whole piece and slid it up—they were very heavy—and then he had opened a wider gap further down. He started to cry, seeing that it was useless. He shook his head and gritted his teeth. He would not give up. He would shift them all until they were so close that no earth showed between, and then he would find a spade and cut some turf from somewhere else to cover the spaces he had made.

He stayed on his knees, lifting the lumps of grass and soil with both hands. Some of them broke as he lifted them because they had dried and crumbled easily. He had reached the head of the grave and laid the flowers beside him on the ground when he saw the priest, Master Husthwaite, coming down the path towards him. He sat back on his heels. His hands were black with soil, and he could feel tears dried on his face and smudges where he had pushed his hair out of his eyes. He waited to be shouted at. The priest stopped at the foot of the grave and looked at what he had done, then at him.

"Was she your friend?" he said.

The kindness of the question confused him.

"She was—aye, she was", he said, getting to his feet and

brushing the soil off his hands. "She did it, I know she did it, but it wasn't right of them to kill her for it. It was the black dog made her do it. She's not ever worried sheep, and I know she never would again. It was—"

He saw the blank look on the priest's face and understood his mistake. He looked down at the grave, the uneven patches of bare earth. He did not know, it had not occurred to him even to wonder, whose grave it was.

"No." He stood desolate now, his hands hanging at his sides. "I don't know what they called—her—that's buried here."

"And your dog?"

"This morning, at the shearing. My brother killed her for worrying sheep. I had her from a pup, at Arden."

"You're Thomas Fletcher's boy, from Easterside."

They seldom came down the mile and a half from the farm to the church on a Sunday morning. Now and then his father would wake in a fit of terror, put on a clean shirt, and bellow round the yard that they were all to hear Mass for the peril of his soul. Tom would raise his head, look at his father with contempt, and go on with his work. But he, impressed and afraid, would go with his father and all the way would hear him mutter to himself: "She'll not rest for my evil ways. She'll not rest, not while I'm dead and gone."

They would stand at the noisy back of the church where the young men talked and laughed through the Mass. But his father would be among them stock-still, his eyes closed and tears creeping down his cheeks. Then he would go to the ale-house and get drunk, and he himself would run off to the river and sit until he was hungry, watching the water slip past under the trees.

"Aye, sir."

"Put back the flowers. Good lad."

He straightened up, and the priest said: "The woman who lies here was a good soul, past three-score years, and I have no doubt she rests in peace. Come with me. I shall say Vespers now and pray for all the dead."

In the church he knelt where he was told, at the altar step, while the priest said softly words he did not understand. Afterwards the priest took him back to his house at the bottom of the village. In the dark parlour, where he had never been before, Master Husthwaite gave him bread and butter and strawberries to eat, and milk to drink. While he was eating, there was a knock at the door. The priest went out, telling him to wait until he came back. He looked round the parlour. There was a piece of stuff on the wall, fringed at the ends, with a dark, intricate pattern on it. He touched the pattern with his finger and found that the surface of the stuff was soft, almost like the fur of a cat. There was a chair beside the hearth with arms carved like rolls of parchment. On the seat of the chair he saw a very small book. He picked it up and opened it, taking it to the window so that he could see it better. He had not held a book in his hands since he had been at Easterside.

Some of the letters in the book were different from those in the prioress's hornbook, from which she had taught him the alphabet and the Our Father. The few words he could read meant nothing to him. It must be Latin. He turned the neat pages. Something about the book, its smallness, the fineness of the writing, made him long to be able to read what was written in it.

The priest came back, stopping on the threshold at the sight of him with the book in his hands. He closed it and began to say that he was sorry, but the priest waved a hand towards him and shut the door gently.

"No, no. You did right. But you have not learned to read?"

"No. Aye. The prioress taught me, when I was a lad, at Arden. But there are no books in my father's house, and I have near forgotten. And she never taught me Latin, though she said she would. It's a long while since."

The grey light from the window fell on the priest's face; the look he saw on it gave him the courage to say:

"Will you tell me, sir, what is written in this book?"

"Ah—that book. I copied it myself, long ago, when I was not much older than you are now. I was a student then, in a city far away from here, a city called Padua."

He opened it again. "But it's so gradely done."

The priest laughed. "That was how we all wrote when I was a boy. And we copied those old scripts in Italy, in the sunshine, as if we had travelled the ages ourselves to bring them back."

He took the book from him.

"This one tells of bees."

"Only bees?" He was disappointed.

"Bees. How to care for them, how to make a hive and where to put it, how the bees live and fight, how they raise their young and gather honey."

"But— But the prioress told me Latin was the language of God and the Church."

"The prioress was right. But Latin is the language also of other things. All that is told here of bees and bee-keeping is set down in verses of great beauty. The poet who made them used every skill he had, every device of craft and guile, so that they should be fair and memorable. When you have understood their words and learned their measure, this book will stay with you always, for its grace. You might not be able to repeat a single verse of it, but there is that in the whole which you will never forget."

He stooped to pick up from the floor the cup out of which Robert had drunk his milk.

"The verses are like the chased silver of this cup. It would be possible to read the book for what it teaches of bees, as it would be possible to hold this cup only to drink from it. You did, I daresay. But look at it now."

He held it out. Robert took it and looked, in the weakening light. He saw, delicately drawn and just raised from the silver surface, the figures of a man running, a woman with her hair loose behind her, also running, rippling water, a tree, the same man with his head bent, still and sorrowful. Then he had turned the beaker right round, and there was the man running once more.

"A drink from that cup will quench your thirst no better than if you had drunk it from an earthen pot that you might break tomorrow and think nothing of. The potter has already thrown a hundred more you could not tell from your own. But once you have studied the silver beaker, touched it often, and learned its lines, you will not forget it as long as you live, though you could not draw the smallest part of it."

"What does it mean? Who is he, the man, and why is she running away?"

"He is Apollo, she Daphne. In the tale, Apollo loved Daphne, but she was afraid and ran away from him. He followed her through the fields and between the trees, but she only grew more frightened and ran faster than the wind. At last when he had almost caught her, she reached the bank of the river Peneus. The river was her father, and he changed her into a tree. Then she was free. Only the brightness remained in her, but this too Apollo loved."

He turned the beaker round in his hands. He saw the speed in the running, the fear. He traced with his finger the waters of the river, the leafy branches of the tree, but not Apollo grieving.

He said: "Was it her dying, when she was changed into a tree?"

"Aye. It was her dying."

That night he slept in a bed in Master Husthwaite's house. The next morning he and the priest sat side by side in front of a grammar-book, and he began his first lesson.

Unwillingly, he let the memory fade. After fifty years the whole day had come back to him, as fresh and clear as if it had been today.

He shook his head, to rid it of the past, and worked for a time, his pen scratching in the silent library.

When he looked again out of the window, it had stopped raining. The cobbles in the court gleamed under a white sun.

He looked down at his old hands resting on the book. They had turned Master Husthwaite's silver cup in the twilight. They had held the neat copy of the fourth Georgic and lifted the crumbling sods in the churchyard. When they were already old, they had picked up the child from beside his mother, put him in the cradle, and given him away. Soon they would lie folded in the grave, and the grass would grow together over them and all they had touched.

He stood up and opened the casement. The air was fresh and damp, the dust laid. A man trotted into the court, reined in his horse, and shouted, so that the horse danced sideways on the cobbles: "The cardinal returns tonight!"

He shut his book and stood for a while longer, watching and listening as the palace came to life.

10

July 1558

Don Gomez Suarez de Figueroa, Count of Feria, at the court of Queen Mary at Richmond, to King Philip of Spain and England, in Brussels; July 1558.

". . . Your Majesty's instructions as to my departure from England having been safely received, I shall leave for Flanders with all possible speed, trusting to be of service to your Majesty in whatever negotiations with the ambassadors of the king of France it may be judged expedient to undertake. I shall take my leave of the queen at the earliest opportunity; her Majesty's health is not, I fear, greatly improved of late, although on some days she has been well enough to receive certain councillors in her privy chamber. There is no immediate anxiety for her life; I doubt, however, whether we may now look for any return to that vigour of mind and body which she showed at the start of the war. The cardinal-archbishop ails also, of the quartan fever it is said, and his household so protects him from the demands of state that it is now difficult to approach him even by letter.

"All in all, I must own to your Majesty that I shall not be sorry to quit, for some while, this realm and Kingdom of England, where there is no love or goodwill shown to any Spaniard, so that my servants are afraid to go about the streets on their lawful occasions for the slanders and jostling they may expect to receive, while I myself am in these last weeks addressed with the scantest courtesy by the ministers of the queen. Every honest Catholic councillor has at his back two or three Protestant lords and gentlemen lurking in the shadows in expectation of the coming of the Lady Elizabeth to the throne when the queen shall have departed this mortal life. It is said, moreover, that the common people no longer attend the Mass in the numbers that were seen two or three years gone by and that in the city of London heresy is grown so rife that Bishop Bonner is at his wits' end to know what to do for the best. Seven heretics, the most insolent and loud in error of those taken at Islington in May, were indeed burned in Smithfield on the eve of Saint Peter and Saint Paul, but the uproar and tumult among the mob was so great that it has been resolved to burn a further six outside the city, at a place called Brentford, in order to prevent any other such disturbance of the peace.

"The body politic must without doubt be cleansed of these warts and pustules, but there is scarce any encouragement given to the many who have thus far resisted the blandishments of the new opinions, and for this I cannot but hold the cardinal to blame, sick though he now be. To allow heretics burned at the stake so to become the heroes and exemplars of the meanest rabble (which it is not the custom in London to suppress by force of arms) has been the very grossest fault of policy, though I do hear that in the more distant parts of the realm there are less or none of these disorders and the people there do show a fairer loyalty to the Church of their fathers.

"God willing, I shall be with your Majesty in Flanders, to my great joy, before the month is out."

11

July–August 1558

On his return the cardinal was carried through the courtyard on a litter. He had become very ill at Richmond, and for three weeks after his return he did not leave his room. Robert Fletcher heard no one say that he was close to death, but he saw the worn faces of secretaries and chaplains and how quietly they walked the galleries, as if they were afraid to wake one who slept. Every day a messenger came from the queen and clattered out of the gate ten minutes later, taking with him the letter that had been prepared for him. Meals were eaten in silence. Signor Bernardi and two or three others stayed behind in the chapel after Vespers on their knees, and one night at supper he saw an Italian nobleman who had arrived that afternoon rise from the table having eaten nothing and cover his face with his hands.

He did not feel shut out from their anxiety. He, too, prayed that the cardinal would not die, and beneath his prayer lay both a longing to see him again and sadness for the imminent falling apart of the peaceful household. He was grateful to them all for their discreet courtesy; it was impossible to mistake its source.

At the beginning of August the weather again became hot and sultry. The streets stank, the river at ebb tide flowed low and greasy, and the air was so still that from his window in the library he could hear the shouts of the ferrymen on Millbank. In the space of three days two of the guards and a boy in the kitchen died of the plague. Undressing at night behind the panelled partitions of the clerks' chamber, he knew that the rest, like him, were looking for the reddened swellings that almost certainly meant a rapid, painful death.

The cardinal had been ill too long for his disease to be the plague.

In the second week of the month there were two days of storms. Afterwards the sky cleared and the sun shone as brightly as before, but the air had a new freshness. A breeze agitated the leaves and ruffled the surface of the river. The faces about him lightened; footsteps quickened in the flagged hall; people smiled as they greeted each other in the mornings. The cardinal was better.

His spirits, also, had risen at the change in the weather. He remembered how in the winter of his death even Master Husthwaite had been cheered by a warm day, by an afternoon when he could sit in the doorway and feel the sun on his face. He remembered also that to talk of the weather would bring a little life back to his voice. How many inches of snow had fallen, how quickly it was thawing, whether the wind had shifted to a new quarter, whether the rain had come in time for the sown corn. These were things that were the same as they had been when he was young.

He sat one morning at his table working not at the decrees of the Council but at a Greek Testament someone had left open on a lectern. He had forgotten almost all the bits of Greek he had learned as a boy when a copy of this same Testament had reached the priest's house from Venice like a garden rose carried by chance into a hedgerow and growing among quickthorn and dock. The sounds of the letters had come back to him one by one, and he was beginning to remember the meanings of a few words.

Sunshine streamed through the windows, lighting motes of dust. There was no one else in the library, and he had looked up briefly only when a girl had come out of the door across the court and thrown a bucket of dirty water over the cobbles.

In the beginning was the word. He turned to the first page of Saint John's Gospel because he remembered that the Greek was easy and he knew the text in Latin, in English, by heart. He read through the first four sentences slowly and understood them. He was pleased as his memory took a firmer grip on the Greek in front of him. He read the sentence through again. This time the last three words stopped him as if someone had spoken them aloud. Comprehended it not. That was what they said. Understood it not. And the light shines in darkness, and the darkness understood it not. *Comprehend* was the Latin translation, which the English Bible had taken over, but *understand* was a good English word. The light shines in the darkness, and the darkness understood it not. And what was it now that he thought he understood? He looked at the Greek word again. Seized, it meant, grasped. Held down. That was it. The darkness did not hold it down. To hold down a light is to put it out. Then he noticed the tenses of the verbs. The light shines in the present, always, in darkness, and the darkness did not hold it down. Not with nails driven through the flesh into wood, not with the tomb, not with fear and despair and people running away. Not with man's understanding either. Not then or ever.

The sun shone down on the page. In its yellow light he saw the unevenness of the paper, the tiny shadows cast on its surface by the roughness of its texture, the smooth blackness of the printed letters a little sunk in it.

From far away a new sound reached him. The door closed. Steps came towards him, stopped. He looked up. A servant stood there, who said: "My lord cardinal is in his garden, Master Fletcher, and wishes you to come to him."

He sat for a moment longer without moving, the letters blurred in front of him. Then he cleared his throat, pushed back his chair, and got stiffly to his feet. He walked the length of the library very slowly so that the servant, who had set off ahead of him, had to wait for him at the door.

For nearly two months he had hoped for this, living through the calm days with a quarter of his attention on his task, thinking of the long past. Now he was at a loss. It was as if that night in June had been a dream, a dream of some other peace that might have come in an interval of a fever. He had not been well, after the stocks and the cellar floor. He could feel again in his hand, he could remember throwing out of the window, the wilting bunch of flowers that the girl in the crowd had given him. But the warmth, the kindness, the straight candle-flames, the little cat? He went down some stairs and along a passage after the servant as if he were going to meet a man he might not recognise when he saw him. Only as he walked out into the smell of clipped box in the sun and the light heat of the morning dazzled him did he think of the cardinal's finger tracing the pattern on a carved ivory lid, and was reassured.

Butterflies fluttered above the lavender on either side of the hot path. They met coming towards them the Italian lord he had seen at supper and several times since. He knew now that his name was Signor Priuli and that he spent much of each day with the cardinal. He and the servant stood aside to let him pass. As he bent his head in acknowledgement, Signor Priuli glanced at him for a moment. His look was keen, curious, not un-friendly, and this too encouraged him.

They entered a shady walk between pleached hornbeams. The leafy branches were intertwined overhead, and only the odd diamond of light spangled the path. It was cool, and although there had been only stray bees buzzing in the August flowers, he had the impression of passing from noise into si-lence. At the end of the walk, across a sunny brick path, the cardinal was sitting at a table in an arbour, writing. He stopped as they approached, looked up, and laid down his pen. His face was thinner, the melancholy eyes seemed even larger.

"Master Fletcher, my lord", the servant said.

"Good-day, Master Fletcher", the cardinal said.

The servant bowed and went away, back down the dark walk.

The cardinal nodded to an empty chair at the corner of the table, close up against the honeysuckle. Its flowers were over, and little swarms of gnats hung among its sticky leaves.

"Tell me how you do, Master Fletcher?"

"Well, very well, my lord, thank you."

"I have not forgotten you all this while, although I think it likely that the bishop of London has."

The smile appeared in his eyes for an instant, and then died.

"It is too late, in any case, for that. The queen will not live long, and then . . ."

He looked down at his thin hands folded on the table. Robert Fletcher's, in his lap, were square and broad. He had a big, puckered scar on his left thumb where he had sliced the top off it with a chisel, making the child's cradle.

"And you, Master Fletcher, shall you be content to see the Princess Elizabeth crowned?"

Wanting to tell the truth, not knowing what it was or where to look for it, dizzied him as before. The ground fell away in front of him.

"I do not know, my lord."

Three months ago, four, before he had been caught, he had known, had he not? Then he had thought that only the queen's death, without her having borne a Spanish heir, and the coming of the Lady Elizabeth could bring balm to the wounds of the realm. Now he thought that the wounds were too deep to heal.

The cardinal pressed harder.

"And to see them that wait in Germany come back to claim the government of the church from the bishops? From each other too, no doubt, since they agree only in what they would destroy. A few will welcome them, those to whom you preached and ministered, for example, Master Fletcher, but only a few. Nevertheless I fear that they will not be much resisted."

The bitterness in his voice had passed as quickly as the smile.

"If there had been the time . . ."

The ground was solid again, outside himself. And they were back as they had been in front of the fire. So that he said: "No, my lord. If the queen were to live another ten, another twenty years, there would not be the time to mend what has been done in the last four."

The cardinal looked him full in the face. His mouth quivered before he spoke.

"What do you mean, Master Fletcher? The queen has always desired to restore what was lost, and, as for myself, I came only to mend, to mend what had been broken by others."

"Forgive me, my lord."

But he had already recovered.

"No, no, Master Fletcher. I wish to know what it is you are saying."

He smiled.

"I am long past injury. And also you have been closer than I to England. While you were yet in the Charterhouse I was in exile, and leave was not given me to return until after the queen's marriage, which . . . You have been these many years among the people, in the cities, in the streets, while I, even here . . ."

He waved a hand at the shaded walk, the neat box hedges, and over towards the sunlit orchard where in the distance a man was scything grass under the apple trees.

"The gardens of the great are the same everywhere."

Robert Fletcher thought for several moments before he spoke. What he was to say must be both true and just, not only for his own sake but also for the cardinal's.

Where to begin? When had the breaking, the destruction started? So far back. The abbeys. Heaps of bedding on the frozen ground. The fallen bell. Later, the mob in the street in York. Will with the iron bar raised to strike. The leaf from the psalter patching the cracked pane.

And the word was God, and the darkness understood it not. Yet then he had thought the destruction would clear the

227

darkness, would free the word from a language the people did not know and from laws they had been wrongly taught would save them. The mob that day, what had it freed? Nothing good. The lust to smash and pull down. As the destruction of the Mountgrace had freed only wealth to make needles' eyes for those who might have been better men without it.

He passed his hand across his forehead. How many at the time had seen these things for what they were? He looked again across the table. Perhaps the cardinal had. And yet it was he who, since he had come back, had been the queen's right hand and therefore himself a destroyer.

"When King Edward died, my lord," he began at last, "there were many in England so weary of change, so doubtful, thinking that all they had seen torn down had better been left standing than gone to line the pockets and build the palaces of turncoat lords, that they were willing and glad to see Queen Mary crowned. I had never been in London then, but I know that in the north there was great rejoicing at the old ways brought back, and I feared we should lose all but a few of those we had gained to true faith and freedom through the English Bible and the English prayerbook. There was little grief in York when the archbishop was sent into prison for marriage, and of all the clergy in the city who had taken wives, not more than one or two refused to put them away."

"And of those you were one, Master Fletcher?"

"I was one, aye, my lord."

"Your—wife. Where is she now?"

"She died soon after, of childbed fever."

"Did the child live?"

"Aye. He may yet live. He does not bear my name."

Then the cardinal said: "It was a great betrayal, Master Fletcher, and a weakness I can scarcely understand in one professed for twenty years in the rule of the Charterhouse."

He spoke coolly, as if of a man not present.

He remembered her standing at the door of his garret, brave, frightened, eager. What she had given him had been herself, all that she was, and he had accepted it as a burden to be carried for ever. As a strong beast he had borne her on his back when she was alive, and after she was dead. He bore her still and would until his own death.

"It may have been a betrayal, my lord. If so, it was she that I betrayed, and I am sorry for it. I betrayed nothing of myself in carrying her, and weakness, I am sure, it was not."

There was a silence. Out of the corner of his eye he saw the man scything in the orchard, laying the grass in long swathes to the ground.

"And yet . . ."

And yet had there not after all been weakness? Could he not have given her her own strength, not carried her with his, and taught her to use it for herself? Often he had told her of the God he had newly found, loving, forgiving, and she had listened, loving him, loving the God beyond him whom she had learned to know through him. But at the end he had stood, a dark obstruction, between her and God.

"And yet, Master Fletcher?"

"I brought her only sorrow."

The cardinal made a slight movement of his head and opened his folded hands, signifying that he was willing to let it pass.

"I broke in upon an account I asked you to give. Will you go on, Master Fletcher?"

But the chill of his earlier words remained, and he allowed it to seal his resolution.

"I came to London, my lord, the winter after, and since then until I was taken I lived in hiding doing what I could for those too poor, too encumbered, or too loyal to run away to Germany and wait. Three years I was with them, among them, and during that time I saw them change. I watched the new faith they had been given—given by the king, my lord, by his bishops, his preachers, his prayerbook—become hard and clear in their minds. I saw others join them, among them some whom religion had never troubled before. They listened to what was said, fastened upon it because it was uttered with such certainty, and became in their turn no less clear and hard than their fellows. But this change was for the worse. Refuge from the truth in observances, pride in works, hatred and suspicion—all those things which should have dissolved in the new vision of God's love—have not only returned into souls who once understood their worthlessness, but have increased a hundredfold."

He saw the cardinal look up as if to speak, but he had not reached what he had to say and went on without a pause.

"And what has brought this change about? The burnings, my lord. More than any other thing that has been done these twenty years, the burnings have made men's minds hard and clear where they should be—pliable before God, yielding to his touch, forgiving in their darkness beneath his light.

"And as for the rest, those who were tired of the hasty alterations in religion, those who were sorry to see the chantries gone and much that was old and loved in the churches destroyed before their eyes, those in London who remembered their own grief at the deaths of Sir Thomas More and Bishop Fisher, at the monks in their habits disembowelled in the street for resisting the king's marriage to a whore—there were many such. Where is their goodwill now, my lord, their goodwill towards the queen, towards the old Church and the ways restored to which they had been long accustomed? Gone in the smoke of the fires. They have seen their neighbours burned alive for holding to what they were taught by learned men with all the authority of king and parliament at their backs. Often they cry out to die more quickly. Have you heard them, my lord? They die for the truth they have seen, even if only once, and those who watch them die see in their deaths that truth, and see also the blindness of those who kill them."

As he spoke his gaze was fixed on the cardinal's folded hands. He knew that he should stop, that he was abusing something of great value freely given him, kindness outside the expected cruelties of faction and the law. But his own words had roused in him at last an anger that had gathered slowly over months and years, anger at the stupidity of them all, of those who died, of those who killed, and the sight of the frail, still hands folded peacefully on the half-written page undid what was left of his restraint. He would go on now, to the end.

He leaned forward, putting his own clenched fists on the table, far apart.

"But there is more, my lord. The worst harm that the burnings have done your cause and your Church, the harm that will be the most difficult and the last to mend, is that the people think of those who die that they die not just for the truth but for England too. The queen's marriage was the start of it, then Spanish priests at court and in the universities, Spanish soldiers in the streets, and then the Spanish war we had to fight, and lost because of Spain, and all this time Englishmen roasted to death in the rain in London and Canterbury—yes, my lord—for refusing to accept the queen's foreign Church."

The cardinal raised his hand at last. It shook.

"The Church is not the queen's. She is not foreign. She is not mine. She is the Church of God, the body of Christ, and those who refuse to return to her as she has been in England not for four but for a thousand years refuse to return to the fold that Christ founded for us all when he said to Peter—"

"I know, my lord. I know what you see when you look at the Church. I put no case. I have no case left, myself, neither theirs nor yours. I tell you only what the people see when they look at the Church, now. As children those who are old enough were taught to pray to Saint Thomas of Canterbury, the archbishop who died at the king's hands, a martyr in defence of the Church. Now many of them have seen, or think they have seen, which in the end comes to the same, another archbishop of Canterbury die at the queen's hands, a martyr in defence of the Church."

"But it was Master More and Bishop Fisher who died in the same cause as Saint Thomas of Canterbury, while Cranmer stood at King Henry's side while he had them put to death! For that and for many other things, and above all because he led the English Church into the darkness in defiance of his own consecration oath, he deserved the stake."

"The people do not see it so. In the eyes of the people Master More and Bishop Fisher died because they would not agree to King Henry's marriage."

The cardinal was no longer listening. He had spoken quietly. His hands were again folded on the table, and he sat looking down at them. Then he said, still more quietly: "And yet it may none the less have been folly—"

"Folly? You call it folly, my lord? It was a great wrong!"

Robert Fletcher was standing up and shouting across the table.

"To send to burn a repentant heretic—it was a sin, a sin not only against mercy but even against justice. And to call it folly is to take more account of the anger it caused among the people than of the deed itself, as my lord Cromwell did when he left the Charterhouse monks to rot in prison rather than have them butchered before the people as their prior had been. No, my lord. Archbishop Cranmer was a convicted traitor, and his death on the block would have been no more than the just penalty for his crime under the laws of the realm. But for the always merciful Church—those are Bishop Bonner's words, my lord— to send to the stake an old man who not once but four, five, six times had renounced all those opinions in which he had differed from its doctrine: that was murder, mere revenge by the Church upon a body that housed a soul contrite before it. You will say that he withdrew his recantations at the last. So he did, and thus became the inspiration of many who have since died in the same way for the new religion that he brought to light out of the tangled briars of the old. But it was before the last, my lord—I have heard it from men who were there and saw all that passed—that Doctor Cole in his sermon said to the whole crowd that the archbishop was to be burned to make even the death of Fisher of Rochester. He made mention also of the queen, the council, reasons of state. But this was the burning of a heretic, not the execution of a traitor, and he preached his sermon not as the queen's servant but with the voice of the Church. And what he said that day, my lord, showed our Church in England to be no more than a frightened tyranny exacting vengeance as if its rulers had never heard the words of Christ's forgiveness. By their fruits ye shall know them. There were more than Cranmer made their choice because of what happened that day. Often the people see what is not there; often they do not see what is. That day they saw what was there indeed, and I say they drew from it conclusions that were right."

He stopped. He was very hot, and his pulse was throbbing in his head and in his clenched palms. Slowly his body slackened. There was a long silence, during which he could hear the buzz of a bee out in the sunshine and the gentle sound of the scythe cutting the grass.

"Sit down, Master Fletcher."

He sat down. He had got to the end. He felt limp, empty, close to tears. He had made an accusation, but it was as if what he had said had been a confession.

"Was this why you were ready to go to the stake in the same cause?" the cardinal said.

It was not, or, rather, the reason, whatever it had been, could not be so simply put. But he was too tired, now, to look for more words.

"Aye, my lord."

The silence lengthened as if neither had spoken. Across the brightness the bell in the palace yard chimed the hour. The man stopped mowing and glanced up at the sun. Then he wiped his forehead with his arm, shouldered the scythe, and walked away through the apple trees.

They sat so still that a chaffinch, coming out of the orchard into the shade, alighted on the back of the cardinal's chair, and then on the table, where it hopped about for a minute or two, on the cardinal's papers and off again, before flying up and away into the heat with a quick flash of its wings.

After a long time the cardinal said: "Master Fletcher, you are a guest in my house. I took you from Bishop Bonner because you were once a monk of the Charterhouse, and I kept you here because I thought you an honest man. Perhaps for being out of the world so long with your mind fixed upon the things of God, you have since you came back into the tug of earthly affairs seen more, and more plainly, of all that has befallen England since we were both young men than many of those to whom I have occasion to speak. You saw the abbeys pulled down, the chantries destroyed, much of the wealth of the Church taken into other hands, perhaps not to the true loss of the Church. You saw what you read in the pages of Luther take hold in other men's souls and change them sometimes into better followers of Christ. You preached to them and taught them, and, especially when you saw them suffer for their new-found faith, you helped and comforted them. All this you saw when I was abroad or shut away in palaces seeing none of it for myself. But while I was in those palaces, in Italy, in Rome, at the Council in Trent, I saw other things, greater things, things that forced me to choose . . . Listen to me, Master Fletcher, if you are not too tired, and I will try to tell you."

The cardinal spoke gently, with care, as if to let him know that what he was going tell was a long tale whose end could not be understood unless all were told. He could not answer and only bent his head. He was sitting without moving, in a blessed quietness, his breathing so light that he might have been asleep, but his mind attentive, patient, a slate wiped clean. The cardinal's words were like words of absolution.

"Let me begin with Archbishop Cranmer's death, since that is where you ended. I am ready to grant you that to send him to the stake was not only foolish, because of the anger it caused among the people, but also sinful, him being at the time a repentant heretic—although how heartfelt his repentance was, what happened at the last may show. But whose sin was it? The Church's sin, you say. I say it was the sin of those who had the case in charge, the bishops' sin, the council's sin, the queen's sin, my sin, not the sin of the Church. The Church is one; the Church is God's; the Church cannot sin. By their fruits ye shall know them: you used the words of Christ as if they gave us licence to dwell in one church or another according to how we judge the actions of those who rule them. But we have no such licence. The choice is not between one church and another but between the Church and what is not the Church.

"All men sin. The man has never lived, save Christ and his Mother, in whom God has not found cause for grief, and the sins of those who rule the Church have often been heavy indeed. I could tell you, Master Fletcher, of things I have seen in Rome . . ."

He paused for a moment.

"I shall tell you. We are both old men, and you are one who deserves to come to the truth by way only of the truth.

"Thirty years ago in Rome, the very centre of the Church, there were those in high place, and even in the highest, beside whom England's ignorant parsons, hunting abbots, Cardinal Wolsey himself, might have seemed, did seem to me, paragons of virtue. Cardinals' courtesans displayed in sumptuous finery in the streets, princes' bastards appointed as spoiled boys to the great sees of the world, the peace of the whole Church put at risk to advance the fortunes of the sons and nephews of popes, elderly bishops profiting from the causes of the poor who would not have been able to find their own dioceses on a map. And even now—much is better, but much more remains that is bad, wrong, wicked in the government of the Church, which is to say, but which is only to say, in those who govern the Church. The sins of the Church, like all sins, are ours, the sins of men, and to deduce from them that the remedy is to leave the Church is to reckon the Church no more than a device constructed by men, one among many possible devices, a house built upon sand. But that is not what the Church is, and the remedy is not to leave her. No, Master Fletcher, the remedy is not to forsake the Church for something else that we are pleased to call a better church. The remedy lies in the repentance and reform of the Church, which means nothing more, and nothing less, than repentance within ourselves, reform of ourselves. What more did Luther ask for, what more did he describe, than this? Until mere mortal stubbornness, his own and, alas, that of others who should have seen further than they did, drove him out of the Church and at last beyond return into the darkness where his sect is now riven with faction and sick with the cruel self-righteousness of the French and the Swiss.

"Aye, Master Fletcher. I have read Luther too. I have felt that wind, that fire. Faith in God's unreasonable love. Salvation for our black souls in that faith. But the wind must blow down, the fire must destroy, only our sin. Not the Church. Not the Church. Or what will become of us all, cast off from each other and from the truth?

"When I was young I learned from the great scholars, in Oxford, in Padua. I read Cicero; I studied to write like Cicero so that one would not be able to tell a period of mine from a period of his. A friend of mine resolved to use no single word, no case of a word that Cicero had not used. We thought then that clear understanding, orderly expression, and the example of the ancients could dissolve all the ills of the world, that a man need only follow reason and live with moderation and piety to be happy on this earth and blessed after death. Our bright wits flashed over the surface of things, glittering like a shallow stream. We left far too much, almost everything, out of account. We had no sense of the deep darkness in ourselves, in every man. We had no sense of sin, and without it we could have no sense of the need for God, for his forgiveness in Christ, for his light. Yet to find that sense, to feel that need, what use is clear understanding and orderly expression, what use are Cicero and his Roman dignity? To take the first, the decisive step, what we need is not reason but faith. Luther was right, Master Fletcher, and you are right, you are all right who say that only faith saves, but at the same time . . ."

The cardinal stopped talking and for a few minutes twisted his pen between his fingers.

"Faith is a gift from God. But it comes to us in words, and those words have to be spoken by men.

"Two things changed the young man I was, two things above all. I read the words, the words of Luther, the words of Valdés, the words of Saint Paul, the Letter to the Romans, the Letter to the Ephesians, the great texts of salvation. At the same time . . ."

He smiled at the echo of his own words.

"At the same time the command of King Henry, whom I then loved above any man on earth, forced me to study with diligence and my whole conscience the issue of the supremacy. He had taken upon himself, taken for the crown of England, supreme authority over the Church in England, and he wished me to tell him, as others told him, that he had the right of it. You know the conclusions to which I came, and you also know, I daresay, the consequences they had for me. I lived in Italy. Many times he tried to have me killed. My family he did have killed, all but one who still—"

He stopped, an odd sag to his face, but almost at once went

on as calmly as before: "So that it was at the same time, aye, it was, that I came to understand both the saving power of faith and the necessary unity of the Church. And it was on account of both these things at once that I then began to work, as I have worked ever since, for the reform of the whole Church from within, which can be nothing else but the reform of men's souls within her.

"You may say, or, rather, perhaps", he smiled, "you might have said, that the reform of a man's soul is hidden between that man and God, that the faith which frees him from his sins, as the Gospel freed those Jews who accepted it from the power of the old law, frees him also from his need for the authority of the Church. You may say that any man who has turned towards God in the depths of his soul can henceforth read the words of salvation for himself and live alone without the intervention of the Church, in a secret peace between himself and God. If you were to say this, you would be both right and wrong.—How to put it?"

The cardinal paused, resting his head on his hand. It was the middle of the day. The birds were silent, and in the hot sunshine of the garden nothing stirred.

"We came close to this, on the night you were fetched from prison.

"You would be right because from time to time there is, there can be, a gap, a breach in our mortality through which the light of God shines directly upon us. You would be wrong because at once, before we know it, time is back, shutting out the light. That man whom faith has saved is a sinner still, and he must live until he dies within the world, his resolution weak, his judgement fallible, even his faith uncertain. He must live in the world: therefore he must live in the Church, because the Church in her wholeness, with the Mass at her heart and the ancient, unbroken authority of her councils, is where Christ is in the world, since his Resurrection and Ascension to God. A man in the darkness of the world receives the light of God mediated to him through the sacraments of the Church, hears the word of God spoken to him in the words of the Church. If a man rejects the authority of the Church, where else can he look, in the world, for that light? Where else can he hope to hear the words that will rightly interpret for him the word of God in the Bible?

"I will tell you where, Master Fletcher. Listen to me, and I will tell you what you already know.

"He can look to other men. Or he can look within himself, to his own conscience. There is nowhere else. If he looks to other men, it may be that they are the king and his ministers, the secular power taking upon itself direction of souls. This was the authority that King Henry assumed when he removed the English Church from the Roman obedience. While he lived, King Henry preserved orthodox doctrine. But we have since seen the perils of the path he took: authority over the church in the hands of a child and thus in the hands of unscrupulous lords serving their own ends, confused clerics altering doctrine every year or two as each new voice was heard from Germany or Switzerland—and I am ready to grant that these clerics were honest men. We have seen only the beginning. If the secular power is to hold absolute sway and, without reference to the Church, authorize itself to govern by the law what men may write, or preach, or say to one another, the day may come when it will be called a crime to speak the name of Christ. Then, if by chance the past is permitted to be remembered across the darkness, men will look back to what they now think of as the fetters of the Church and recognise as most bitter slavery what they took for freedom.

"And if we suppose that it is not the state to which we are to look instead of the Church, but other men calling themselves a new, a better church, what then? Then we are hoping too much of men no less fallible than ourselves. They have begun by calling the Church wrong and themselves right, by dividing themselves from the saints and the whole company of the faithful dead. They will go on to quarrel with each other. It has happened already in Germany. Once the unity of the Church is broken, there is no end to division and hatred, infinitely multiplied. Some of these men will no doubt say much that is true; but while they take upon themselves final authority, what they say will always be beset with dangers. Fanatics, deceivers, those who wish only for power over their fellows or for fame and wealth: how will men see them for what they are unless they judge them by the authority of the Church?

"But, you will say, what of conscience? Is it not by looking within himself that a man may judge whom to follow, whether to stay in the Church or leave her, where truth is to be found?

"I will give you an example of conscience at work. Those who followed King Henry out of the Roman obedience because they preferred the authority of the secular power to the authority of the pope and the councils now tell us that Queen Mary must be disobeyed, deposed, murdered even, because their consciences assure them that she is wrong to have taken England back into the Church. The authority of the Church was thrown over by the authority of the state. Twenty years only have passed, and the authority of the state is already thrown over by the authority of conscience. What pride is there! What faith of sinful men not in God but in themselves!

"And this conscience of which they boast so bravely as their sole interpreter of God's will, what is it? They were not born with it already made and formed. It has been formed in them by words, the word of God, yes, but spoken to them, made plain to them, by men. They cannot so lightly as they think separate themselves from the past. But their unacknowledged bondage will not last for ever. The making of consciences outside the Church has not yet gone far. Twenty years ago, fifteen even, it had not gone too far to be reversed. No Christian man is yet so far outside the Church that he has altogether lost his sense of what the Church is, as an idea, a reality in God, for all her human faults. But after a little time it will become easier, and after that, quickly, faster and easier still, to put off the past; and the weakness, the fallibility, the pride will spread like a disease. O Master Fletcher, I fear for those yet unborn, that they are already betrayed. Robbed of the truth we can but inherit, they will know their sins only as misery, and their forgiveness they will not know at all, because they do not know God. Then at last men will be free of the Church. Then they will be slaves indeed."

Robert Fletcher was weeping, the tears running down his cheeks into his beard as he sat looking down at the old oak of the table, the knots smoothed and blackened by time. Whether he wept for himself, for the cardinal, or for the darkness that men choose when they might choose the light, he did not know.

After a silence, during which far away beyond the garden a boatman shouted something over the water and a woman laughed, the cardinal spoke again:

"You will not remember all that I have said. But remember this: we are not to despair. The Church of God is an idea, a vision of wholeness and holiness where there is peace and freedom for the souls of men. But she is also a reality, a reality where every day in the hands of priests bread and wine become the body and blood of Christ. The Church is always obscured from us by the sins and follies of men; now more than for many ages she is hidden from us by the high walls of hatred and division. But we must have faith in her. We must, Master Fletcher. We must have faith in the Church as we have faith in Christ, for the one is the body of the other, the life of one in this world is the life of the other, given us by God to take us from time into eternity. For this faith, for this belief, I myself have—sacrificed much good."

The cardinal looked up. So did Robert Fletcher. Their eyes met across the table. He could feel the tears drying on his face. He wanted to speak but could not.

The cardinal said, in an altered voice: "I shall see you again, Master Fletcher. I should like you to know also how imperfectly I too have . . ."

He stopped. It was an appeal.

But he rose and laid a small book, as a paperweight, on the half-written page.

"God be with you", he said, and, almost inaudibly, "Pray for me."

As he passed behind him he just touched his shoulder. He crossed the sunlit path and went away down the quiet walk under the branches of the hornbeams. Robert Fletcher heard him disappear into the shadows but did not turn his head. His gaze was fixed on the empty chair.

He sat without moving, listening to the stray sounds of the August afternoon. The man came back to the orchard, with a red handkerchief knotted on his head, and began again to scythe the grass.

He sat for a long time by the sticky honeysuckle.

At last he rose, crossed the warm brick, and in his turn entered the shadow of the pleached trees.

When he went into the palace the servant who had taken him to the cardinal was waiting for him.

"There's a lad out in the court to see you, Master Fletcher, a young soldier, that won't take no for an answer."

He walked through the cool rooms, brushing against familiar walls and doors as he went, and out again into the glare of the sun.

The soldier got up from the mounting-block and crossed the courtyard to him.

He thought, he has come to take me back. He almost turned and fled into the palace.

"I have a letter for you, Master Fletcher. The woman who gave it me, thinking you yet a prisoner, said to be sure and see you had it, so I brought it down from Fulham, and here it is."

"That was very good of you." He took the letter, smiling with relief. "I am glad to see you again. I owe to you more—" he began, but the soldier interrupted.

"And I am glad to see you look so well, sir, in your new clothes and all."

He looked down at the black clothes Signor Bernardi had given him, for the first time ill at ease in them.

"I am well, aye, very well."

There was a silence between them. Then the soldier held out his hand. "Good-day to you, sir. I must be off if I'm to be back up river tonight."

He shook hands with the soldier and waved to him when he looked back from the gate.

He took the letter up to his table in the library and opened it.

"We do daily remember and earnestly pray for you in your sore distress and suffering at the hands of our oppressors who shall not, please God, for ever persecute and punish us, faithful children of the Lord, for that we will not betray the truth we have received and know ourselves to be safe in the mercy of Christ for all that some among us may be bound and fastened in the prisons of men. Keep high your courage and despair not a whit, to whatever pass you are brought, even to death itself, for the Lord shall deliver us out of the hand of our enemies and scatter them by his power. When the count is taken of those who have stood fast to the truth, your name shall not be forgotten among them, to the greater glory of the Lord our God. And so we take leave of you, asking you also to remember us in your heart that are yet in the midst of such manifold and great dangers and having no learned men remaining to give us counsel, yet hold to the path of righteousness."

He turned the paper over on the table and spread his hand flat on its blank side, as if to put out the fire that burned in the words.

When the bell in the courtyard began to ring for dinner, he got up, tore the letter into tiny fragments, and mixed them with the ashes in the hearth.

12

October 1558

The air was damp and windless, rank with the smells of smoke, sodden earth, battered and dying grass. A sour chill came off the river that flowed in swift dirty spate, the full tide swollen by weeks of rain. He stood still on the muddy path that skirted Lambeth marsh and looked across to where the square tower of Saint Paul's, the spire of Saint Dunstan's-in-the-East, and the white battlements of the Tower rose above the mist, catching the sun.

It had been the change in the weather that had enticed him out. The silence he had woken to after so much wind, the mist lying on the river early in the morning with the sky lucid blue above it, the sounds, audible again, of someone sweeping the dung from the courtyard, of people's footsteps in the street outside the gate: all this had lured him. For the first time he had walked out of the palace, and the soldier at the gate had nodded to him as he passed. You are a guest in my house.

He watched a big branch, snapped off somewhere upstream by a storm now blown out. It went by quickly, rolled and tossed on the surface of the water like a twig thrown in by a child.

And yet he was not free. He had no money and nothing to sell. He must go back to the palace to eat, or starve, or beg. There was no one he had known in the city to whom he could go: those he had once known would regard him as a coward and a traitor. Was he?

He did not know. Chance and the whim of a man more powerful than his captor had saved him from a slow and painful death, alone in the dark and altogether without the glory he had seen on the faces of those burned at the stake. Yet several times in the last month he had thought almost with envy of himself fastened by the feet on the cellar floor with only the shadow of the dandelion to tell him of the passage of the sun.

He sighed deeply as he stood there. A laden barge pulled heavily upstream against the tide, the ten oars rising and falling together in the mist, a few gulls wheeling round it.

It seemed to him that he had outlived his death, like the green leaves still clinging to the branch he had seen tumbled along on the rushing water. He had been severed from all his past, and an encounter of the day before had made him understand how strict were the bonds of his confinement to the present.

He had been working, or rather sitting at his place, in the library as usual. Since the end of August, when the summer weather had broken for good and the cardinal had again taken to his rooms, more gravely ill, it was said, than before, he had scarcely looked at his decrees. He kept the huge volumes open on a table, as if to remind himself that a task did exist that he had been given to perform. But he passed the time with the Greek Testament in front of him and the Latin beside it, laboriously puzzling out the sense of the language he had never properly learned. He was reading his way slowly through the Gospels, and the new words gave the history of Jesus, what he had done and said, a freshness that, during the hours he spent there, made him forget everything else. He was quite drawn away from the sad, expectant household, the closed faces of men he saw daily but hardly spoke to, the fires lit in every hearth against the buffeting rain. Sometimes the words of Jesus seemed addressed to him, to everyone, with such simple force that he wanted to pick up the book and take it through the silent, guarded rooms to where the cardinal lay dying and read to him, only a sentence or two, to undo the harnessed weight he was dragging to the grave. But the distance between him and the cardinal was much greater than the length of a few rooms, and he would shut the book and fall back into the listlessness that made of every day an indistinguishable lapse of time.

So he had been sitting, idle, the day before, his finger on the Greek word he had reached but his gaze out of the window on the rainy sky, when the door opened and a man dressed in the habit of a Carthusian monk came into the library. He had known for three years that the queen had restored to the priory at Sheen a group of monks from the old Charterhouses, among them even one or two from the Mountgrace. But it had seemed a fact remote from him, and he had never troubled to find out which of his former brethren had chosen to go back to the cell. The monk who walked towards him through the shadows, as he stood dismayed by the window, was a stranger. He might have been a ghost.

He had never thought to see again the habit he had worn for twenty years, and he would not have imagined that the sight of it could so move him. He got to his feet and stepped forward.

"Good day to you, sir", the monk said. "I have leave of Signor Bernardi to borrow for the Charterhouse an old book, Master Hilton's *Ladder of Perfection*. I daresay you know of it. It is a printed book, finely bound. Archbishop Cranmer had it from the library of the London Charterhouse when they took our books away. In those unhappy days we did not dare to hope the time might come when we would be able . . ."

He knew where it was, took it down from its place, and put it into the old monk's hands.

"Thank you, sir. Thank you."

The monk did not turn to go but looked down, weighing the book in his hands.

"You know, sir, this was the book, the very book, the prior gave me to read when I was a novice. Fifty years ago, that was, all but three years. He gave it me because my Latin was not good in those days, only schoolboy Latin I had when I was first a monk, and it was a pleasure to me to read an English book that treated of the things of God. The very same book!

"Little did I think all those years ago that before I saw this book a second time the ladder would be broken under us, the very rungs on which we stood taken out to make us fall . . . But there, young men are full of trust in themselves, which is as it should be, no doubt, or they would never set forth on these perilous climbs . . . Perhaps if I had paid more heed then to what Master Hilton had to say, I would not be here now, telling the tale. In this wicked world yet, in my grey hairs, when others I knew, clearer-sighted than I, though some were young and some were unlettered men, went to their deaths bravely in God's cause."

The old monk raised his watery eyes to look at Robert Fletcher. "Alas, sir, God gives courage only to some. The rest of us he means to learn patience as best we may, and we have the longer road. Aye, we have the longer road."

The frail voice fell silent. Robert Fletcher was unable to reply. After a few moments the old man peered up at him, wrinkling his eyes against the light.

"We have the longer road, but at the last we may reach, with God's grace, the top of the same mountain, may we not?"

When he still said nothing, the old monk shook his head, perhaps taking him for an Italian who did not understand English. He tucked the book under his arm.

"Forgive me, sir . . ." He patted the book. "An old man's memories. An old man's memories."

He held out his hand. It was light and dry.

"God be with you, sir, and thank you."

Then he had gone, closing the door quietly behind him.

The gentle words had stayed in his mind all day, and when he had woken in the morning, this morning, he had wondered for a moment whether the old monk's appearance in the library had not been a dream, so much did what he had said seem to come from inside himself. He had lain still, listening to the new silence of the weather, and slowly his own perplexity had gathered about him like darkness until the monk's innocent hope shone as a taper shines in an alien window on a foggy night, intermittently and far away. Yesterday he had thought that he might have delayed the monk with answers, have revealed to him a little of himself, that he too had once been a novice reading Walter Hilton, and then a monk for whose safety in the cloister others had gone blithely to a horrible death. He might have gone back with him to the Charterhouse at Sheen and disappeared behind its doors for ever, as into the grave. But the thought had been no more than weakness, a wish to escape into the certainty of the past from the bewilderments of the present.

The monastery door was locked to him. It was locked not only because the Charterhouse would never receive into its painfully preserved fidelity a married monk, a contumacious priest, an unrecanted heretic. It was locked also because he himself had rejected for good what lay behind that door.

Had he not?

He picked up a stone from beside the path and threw it furiously into the river. He wished that he had never met the cardinal.

He walked on through the mud towards London Bridge, looking only at the path in front of his feet. What, after all, after sixty years, was he? A monk without a monastery, a priest without a people, a father without a child, a brother who had left his brother lying in the street when he might have taken him home, washed him, fed him, as he himself had been washed and fed when he was lying in the stocks by a young man, a stranger, who, at risk to himself, had tended him as kindly as a son his father. A son his father.

He stopped and looked again, out over the wide, rushing water. The mist was thinning, and the city on the far bank, the houses, the palaces, the many churches, were becoming clearer in the sunshine. At his feet the river swirled on, dark and dangerous, with the litter of autumn carried tumbling on its surface. The thought of his father, and of his father's wretched death, made him angry as he stood on the path by the river and kicked at the stones with his worn shoe like a moody boy.

If he himself had stayed at home and never gone into the Charterhouse to lead that sweet, that free and ordered life, would he have been able, one day, to shift his father from his defiance, his sullen crouch over the smouldering fire?

He kicked another stone into the water. Very likely not. If a man will not forgive himself, other men, death, fate, even God, he cannot himself be forgiven. It had been the same with Master Husthwaite. For all his goodness he had died embittered and without joy, because something had happened to him that he would not forgive.

He shivered, from standing still in the clammy October morning, and began to walk again, more slowly than before. *Requiescant in pace*. The three words of prayer, of farewell, soothed him a little. Had not their souls, the unhappy souls of his father and Master Husthwaite, been gathered long ago into the mercy of God? All souls, however broken, however wordless and maimed, could they not be entrusted to God in the prayers of the living till the end of time, when every man would have vanished from the earth into God's eternity?

As he walked he remembered that not long ago he had told simple men and women that there was no need to pray for the dead, that the idea of purgatory was maintained by the pope and his obedient bishops and priests only to frighten people into thinking that they could buy the safety of their souls, of other souls, with money or good works or a certain number of Masses. The words rose in his mind like a cloud of chaff. Had he not prayed, just now, for the dead, that their souls might be brought clear of misery and sin? What was his prayer but a prayer for the souls in purgatory? And was his prayer not real and shining beside those dusty arguments of the recent past—as Luther's description of faith had shone for him in York among the dusty Masses he had been paid to say for souls he knew nothing of, alone in his Minster chantry?

He shook his head as he walked, and smiled. Surely it was only the truth that shone so. But he had known for years that both could not be true. If a soul were saved only by the faith that was in it, then to pray for the dead was empty folly. If there were a reason to pray for the dead, then the justification of the soul by faith alone must be a false account of salvation. Was this knowledge or was it not? Men had died, men, therefore, had killed, for one of these truths or the other. But suppose that both indeed shone with the light of truth? Suppose it were only the reasoning of men, the dry, excluding words, that set them over against each other? Suppose it were in one mystery that both these things so shone, and men had killed, and died, only for the dust of their own words?

He was walking more briskly again, enjoying the unfamiliar exercise. Perhaps there was something to be said for being old, something to be thankful for in having been cut off from so much. He thought with exhilaration now of the leafy branch tossed over and over on the out-going tide. He hoped, recognising the neatness of the thought with an appreciative nod, that it had not lodged itself against a pier of the bridge. He had never seen the sea.

All at once the last layers of mist rolled away from the surface of the river. The bright sun struck him suddenly in the eyes, and the wide expanse of water to his left sparkled and gleamed in its light. He looked about him. The muddy path had become a muddier lane. He was approaching a row of cottages built along a narrow wharf at the river's edge. The water slapped against the stone wall, only a foot or two from its top. On his right were gardens and orchards glistening in the sun, the leaves on the trees just beginning to turn. On the grass beneath them lay green leaves, twigs, and unripe apples blown down in the gales. In a cobbled yard in front of one of the houses a man was scraping the bottom of an upturned wherry, whistling as he worked. He stopped to watch. There was something consoling in the noise and rhythm of the scraping, in the rhythm of the man's body bending and drawing back, something from long, long ago, and he himself standing and watching.

The man stood upright over his boat, stretching to straighten his back. He sensed his attention, turned towards him, and grinned.

"'Tis a bonny day."

He smiled back. He realised for how long he had been cooped up among books and discreet Italians walking close to the wall with downcast eyes. He opened his mouth to answer, but the man went on: "Mind you, we want a bit of sunshine after all the wet we've had. And wind. I've not seen the river like it's been, not ever. More than once I've thought we'd have it over the top, and a fine pickle we'd be in here if it did that. But there you are, what will be will be, I say. The water's stayed in its proper place, and if we have a few fine days it'll go down soon enough. No use in meeting trouble halfway. You on your way to London, sir?"

"No. Aye. That is, no. I've walked out from Lambeth, because the sun was shining."

"A right mucky road that'll have been in this weather, and you not so young as you were, sir, if you'll pardon me saying so. Now . . ."

He turned back to the boat and ran his hand down the keel. Then he stood away from it and looked it over carefully. He went round to the other side and did the same. Finally he gave it a cheerful kick and said: "She'll do for a few months, I reckon."

He gathered up his tools from the ground, put them in a small sack, and slung it over his shoulder.

"I've to go back home to Southwark for a plank. There's a bit of gunwale rotten that won't see out the winter. Will you walk down with me for a jug of ale—on account of the sun's shining yet?"

Robert Fletcher was almost frightened, and for a moment wished he were back in the safe obscurity of his library. But the man's laugh was friendly, his look open and uncurious, so that he said: "I will. Aye, I'll just walk down to Southwark. Thank you."

He wanted to say that he had no money for his share of the ale, but he looked at the man's face again, passed his hand across his own, and remained silent.

"My name's Kit Tye", his companion said after a few minutes. "I'm a carpenter by trade, as you see, like my father was before me, and a Southwark man born and bred. If you searched the wide world over, you'd never find a better town than Southwark, nor better neighbours than mine. I wouldn't cross the river if you paid me to, not to live. I've a son myself now, God be praised, after three girls, pretty as they be, and it's my only wish he'll be content enough in the house and trade of his father."

The carpenter went on talking, but Robert Fletcher thought of the rabbits in the field at Easterside, the pigeons in the wood at the Mountgrace, now and for ever, the deer, the monks living and dying and being buried in their nameless graves.

"I'm very sorry."

The carpenter had asked him a question.

"You, sir, you'll not be a London man?"

"No. I'm from the north, from York and thereabouts, though I've been in London three or four years now."

He saw the carpenter glance sideways at him as they walked, uncertain, from the evidence of his clothes and manner, what his occupation might be. He saw him almost ask, and then, with a shyness that touched him, decide not to.

"From York?" the carpenter said instead. "Then you'll have

seen something of the great rebellion they had there against King Harry twenty years gone and more?"

"I scarcely saw any part of it. I lived—not much in the world then."

The carpenter laughed.

"That was all I ever heard of the north, that rebellion, never stirring, as I say, further from Southwark than I could help. I was no more than a lad in those days, still making rakes and rolling-pins all day I was, but I remember my father saying: 'They're risking their necks up there in the north, rising against the king, and for what? For a few old abbeys—and the monks won't lift a finger to help themselves, you mark my words.' And he was in the right of it, sure enough. We've never missed the monks since they've gone, have we? Never missed them a day or an hour. Yet there were all those then, your countrymen, ready to lay down their lives to keep them in their abbeys. I don't understand it. Never shall. It's like nowadays, the burnings. Plain men, the likes of me, some of my neighbours among them, and their wives, with children to care for, ready and willing to roast, they are, and to leave their children and their old fathers to starve, and for what? For this Mass or that Mass, for up with the pope or down with the pope, for whether we have a wooden table in the church or an altar-stone, for whether we go to the priest to be shriven or stay at home and trust to God to forgive us our sins—come to that, for Our Father or Paternoster, as if God couldn't hear the different tongues he's given us!"

The carpenter broke off to greet a little old woman with bright eyes who sat in a doorway beside a barrel of salted herring, shouting her wares in a high voice. They were walking now in a narrow, busy street through a thickening crowd of people. The tall bulk of the church of Saint Mary Overy rose above the rooftops on their right.

"Old Mother Starkey", the carpenter explained as they walked on. "She's a good soul. Her son's my sister's husband."

But the old woman had looked at Robert Fletcher sharply as she returned the carpenter's greeting, and he had dropped his eyes.

"No", the carpenter went on, in the same tone as before, waving his free hand as he talked. "It's against all reason, that's what it is. There's this one goes to burn, forces them to take him, almost with his bragging, and that one tears all up by the roots and is off to Germany—Germany!—when he might rest his bones in England that bred him, and the other fellow falls out with his father over it, or his wife, and ends up hating half the folk he's known from a lad—hating them! Foolish days we live in, sir!"

"They're all the days we have", Robert Fletcher said, but the carpenter swept on.

"Foolish and light. To be so pulled about as we are from one side and the other. The great ones that do the pulling, the king, the parliament, and now the queen and the bishops—they chop and change, to be sure—this in, that out, pulling down here, setting up there. But we're to blame as much, the common people, losing our wits, running here, there, and everywhere after our betters, losing our lives along with our wits often enough. Don't folk know, haven't they always known, that if a man loves God and honours the king he can't go badly wrong? If he says his prayers at night, goes to church with his neighbours on Sundays, loves his wife, follows his trade honestly, brings up his children to do the same, owns his sins and trusts to God for a quiet death, what need he fear? There's plenty to do between him and God if he sticks to what he knows, what every Christian man knows, and doesn't go chasing about and about after every new-fangled preacher putting all that's good in the melting-pot. I don't like the preachers for muddling folk, telling us it don't matter what we do if we believe right—what sort of Christian's that they'd have us be?—and turning sound men into silly sheep that dash up and down bleating what they don't understand any more than I do, that confessing sins is wicked and the Mass is blasphemy and the bishops ministers of Satan and I don't know what all. Mind you, I don't like the Spaniards any better that came in with the queen and hide in doorways to catch these same silly sheep—but English sheep, mark you—and carry them off to burn in front of their neighbours. Here, sir."

The carpenter turned into a gap between two houses wide enough to let a horse and cart through. As they crossed the muddy yard towards an open door, on the step of which two children sat playing cat's-cradle, the carpenter added: "But I daresay the worst of it's over when all's said. They say the queen's not likely to see the year out. The Lady Elizabeth's as English as I am and from what I hear not over-fond of either Spaniards or preachers. So much the better for simple folk. There's my wife."

A young woman, smiling, with a nine-month-old baby on her arm, had appeared in the doorway.

"I met this gentleman coming out from Lambeth in the sunshine," said the carpenter, "and he walked down with me for a jug of ale."

She looked from one to the other.

"You talk too much, Kit Tye", she said, still smiling. "Will you come in, sir? Out of the way, Meg and Jenny. There's sawdust everywhere, sir, but a carpenter's house is his shop."

He felt as if he had been walking with a strong wind blowing full in his face so that he could scarcely breathe. Not only what the carpenter had said but the noisy street, the crowd of people buying and selling, crying their wares, pushing past each other; the pretty girls leaning from the windows of the stews; the mounds of apples, cabbages, whelks on stalls; the rabbits and hares hanging head downwards; the smells of bread coming from bakers' shops, blood from butchers', fish, vegetables, beer, plums, roasting chestnuts: it had come at him with violence, all at once like a gale, and he was stunned. He had lived for weeks without impressions, his present an empty space crossed only by the shadows of the past. Suddenly teeming life and words of raw wholesomeness whose flavour he had quite forgotten had rushed into the emptiness, and he stood in the sun, nameless and alive, the past for the moment stilled behind him.

"Thank you", he said as the children got up from the step, one of them carefully holding the string pattern taut on her hands. "You are very kind."

They went in.

He saw the carpenter take the baby from his wife while she went out through another open door into a further yard at the back of the house. The sound of someone sawing came from the yard, and beyond a low wall the river glinted between the branches of an overhanging tree. Along the rays of sunlight streaming in at the door sawdust floated gently. There was no wind. Something stirred far within him. The dry sweetish tickling smell of fresh oak-dust and shavings, mixed with another. His eyes travelled round the room. There—over the fire a black pot of hide glue hung from an iron hook, a curl of acrid vapour twisting from it. Beside the fire an old man sitting on a stool held a half-made bowl between his knees and shaved slivers of wood from it, tapping the end of his chisel very softly with a hammer. The woman came back with a jug in one hand and two pewter cups in the other. She put them on the table and poured out the ale. She gave him a cup.

"It's my own brewing, sir. Kit likes it well enough."

The ale was strong and cold. As he drank she said to her husband: "A man came from Master Phillips about the chest. I said to come back before dark and you'd be sure to be here."

"It's done, all but the last waxing. I'd best be on with it now."

The carpenter downed his ale and made as if to give the baby back to his wife.

"Put him in the cradle if he'll go down. I've things to see to—if you'll pardon me, sir", she said.

The carpenter began to cross the room towards the cradle in the far corner, but as they passed him, the baby suddenly smiled and held out his arms to the stranger standing by the table. Disbelieving, he put his cup down.

"I'll take him for you, if you—"

The carpenter laughed. "You'd better sit down a minute then. He's a fair weight to hold."

He sat on the end of a bench beside the table, and the baby, contented on his lap, his small back firm against his chest and his downy head bent forward, played with the empty cup.

The carpenter took a big lump of beeswax from a shelf. He cut a piece off it with a knife, warmed it in a ladle over the fire, and then stood with his back to the fire rolling it round and round between his palms.

He was watching the wax with such attention that he was startled when the carpenter, paying no heed himself to what he was doing and grinning at the baby, said: "He's a fine little lad."

When the wax was soft enough, the carpenter wrapped it in a linen rag and began to rub with it the panelled surface of a new oak chest that stood against the wall. He rubbed with an even pressure, in a gentle circular action, rubbed and rubbed, until the wax through the linen started to stick a little to the wood, and then he rubbed still more gently, with the same motion, and a shine began to come.

He watched, with the baby heavy on his lap, and a drowsy pleasure gathered in him, a slow warmth spreading through his body. The carpenter talked as he worked: "Master Phillips is a goldsmith, this side of London Bridge. He will have a good shine to his wood if it's only to keep servants' linen in." But he scarcely heard the words. He was back in the mill at Arden, a small boy by the fire on a winter evening, watching Robin as he waxed—what? A new chest for the prioress's chamber, a dish for her table, a butter-tub, a plough-handle, a coffin, a haft for a sickle, a salt-spoon. There was no wooden thing those great hands could not make, and at the end the waxing, the gentle, even rubbing, in soft circles, with a catch now and then as the wax stuck.

He remembered seeing the prioress, on the night of Robin's death, burst into tears at last when she had to send away for a coffin for him.

In York he himself had tried to wax the cradle he had made, without skill, for Alice's baby. He had not the knack, and the wood had been too rough to shine much, but he had rubbed away, kneeling beside the cradle in the room above the baker's shop, and Alice had laughed with pleasure, watching him.

He put his hand on the baby's head. The bones of the skull were not yet joined together and through the skin he felt the pulse beating softly and quickly. He prayed with all the force of the love stored up in him.

God send your father health and a long life so that he may see you grow and flourish here, in the sawdust and the sunshine, and become a man and marry and beget children in your turn.

He got up, carried the child to the cradle, and laid him down. The baby smiled up at him, put two fingers in his mouth and shut his eyes. The carpenter was still waxing the front of the chest, squatting on his haunches and whistling through his teeth. He stood up as Robert Fletcher came towards him.

"I must be on my way, Master Tye. The ale was very good. I thank you for it, and for . . ." He waved a hand at the room.

"You're most welcome, sir. We had a fine talk, coming down, and broke no bones. And the sun's still shining for your going home." He laughed again. "Good-day to you, sir."

They shook hands. As he passed by the fire on his way out the old man lifted his head, with his hammer and chisel still in place, and said very quietly: "God be with you, master."

He walked back to Lambeth through the brilliant autumn noon, hungry, as if he were indeed walking home. The level of the river seemed already to have dropped a little. In the orchards opposite the cottages along the wharf, women and children were looking for windfalls in the wet grass and shaking more apples down from the branches. He wondered without anxiety if he would live to see the spring and, if he did, where he would be when it came. He wondered what sort of man was miller at Arden now, and whether his children were set in turn to watch the sacks of flour fill and shout out when they were ready to be tied and rolled away. If Robin had lived, that man would most likely have been himself. The mill no doubt still stood, still needed a miller, though the nuns were long gone and some stranger would have taken the priory, its woods, and its few fields in the narrow dale, from the king.

Then he would never have gone to Easterside, never known his father or Will, never learned Latin, never have been a monk. He would only have worked. And married.

When he reached the palace it was at once as if he had not been out. On his table in the library the Greek Testament was open at the page he had been reading when the old monk came in. At supper he nodded as usual to the priests and clerks of the cardinal's household and heard them say that the cardinal was no better and no worse. When he went to bed he wished a good-night, as he always did, to those with whom he shared the big clerks' chamber. He blew out his candle and for a moment pressed his face to the casement. The panes were cold, the glass running with moisture from the warmth inside the room. Outside the mist had risen again from the river, and the torches over the gate burned in the dampness with a thick, dim glare. He opened the casement a crack. The mist smelled of salt, of smoke, of winter.

That night he dreamed of Alice as he had not once dreamed since her death. She was there in his bed with him, warm, asleep, her legs entwined with his, her head heavy on his shoulder, her hair close to his mouth. Snow was falling on them as they lay, and was not cold.

13

12 November 1558

"You see how it is with me, Master Fletcher. Every morning they bring me a boiled egg, and when I eat it, with sippets of bread like a weaned child, they tell me I am better today, to be taking meat so well. But the truth is that I lose a little strength, leave this poor corpse at a greater distance from me, each day that passes. To hold a pen so tires my arm that I can scarce write my name, short as it is, before my fingers drop the pen. I can no longer hold a book. And every time the fever returns, it leaves me a little weaker."

The cardinal was lying in his bed supported by a pile of pillows. The great eyes seemed all that was left alive in his worn face; the end of his beard could scarcely be distinguished, in the candlelight, from the fur of the rug drawn up over his chest. His hands rested palms downwards on the fur, thin and wasted, no less white than the sleeves of his shirt, the bishop's ring huge on one of them. He spoke almost merrily, as if it were a jest to be shared, his knowing how much closer to death he was than anyone had told him.

"I am very sorry to hear it, my lord", Robert Fletcher said, nevertheless.

"Sorry? No, Master Fletcher. The fever is not Satan, coming back each time fiercer than the last. It is not bad in itself, not evil, not good. It is—a storm, that is all, which when it comes will blow down only the tree that is ready to fall. It is not to be feared because it is not to be fought."

A smile lit the great eyes.

"But sit down, Master Fletcher. I think there is a chair."

He moved his eyes without turning his head. Robert Fletcher saw the chair near the side of the bed, placed to face the cardinal. He crossed the room slowly and quietly, as if not to frighten a deer or a bird, and sat down. In the last weeks he had accustomed himself to the certainty that he would never see the cardinal again. The drift of feeling at Lambeth reminded him of the last few months at the Mountgrace. Though no more than usual was said, and each day passed in the same orderly manner as ever, the whole household was disquieted, unable to live contented in a present that had no purpose because it had no future. Two or three of the Italians had already left for home, fearing the hardships of a journey in the worst months of winter. As at the Charterhouse, he observed the common uneasiness and found himself almost untouched by it. He had thought scarcely at all of what he should do after the cardinal's death.

For a few days after his meeting with the Southwark carpenter, he had wanted to talk once more to the cardinal, to explain to him the discovery he felt he had made that morning. But during the weeks that followed he heard how weak the cardinal had become, that he no longer left his bed, that he could not eat without help, that he saw no one but his chaplain and Signor Priuli and one or two of his most devoted servants. Already at the end of October it was said that his thoughts were now entirely fixed on death and that he asked for nothing but the same few passages from the Gospels to be read to him each day. He would not see him again.

So today's summons had moved and shaken him as if it had come from beyond the grave.

"Has all been well with you, these past months, Master Fletcher?"

"With me, my lord? If it were not for . . . Aye, very well, my lord, thanks to your great kindness."

"If it were not for what, Master Fletcher?"

The round eyes were fixed on him with complete attention, as they had been in August in the garden, in June in the study next door.

"I began to say, my lord, that if it were not for your kindness, I should have been dead before July was out."

The cardinal smiled.

"But you thought that no fit speech to make to a dying man—if that, in truth, was what you had begun to say."

He could not meet the cardinal's look, and dropped his eyes. In the silence the fingers of one of the thin hands moved slightly, backwards and forwards in the fur.

"Have you wished, would you have wished, that I had left you to die, in the summer, in the bishop's cellar?"

"No, my lord. That is to say, perhaps if . . . It is hard for me to find words, and it is not that I am ungrateful, unmindful of all that you have done for me. But it would have been . . . No, my lord." He looked up. "No man should wish to have died before it is the will of God to take him from the world. In any case, now is by no means the time for me to speak of such things."

"Aye, Master Fletcher. Now is the time. Yesterday, if I am not mistaken, was Martinmas. The winter is drawing on. It is very cold outside, they tell me, and the air full of fog, which has ever caused me harm. I shall not see Advent come again. After a few days, a knock or two more from the fever, I doubt that I shall be able to speak to you, even so feebly as today. That is why I sent for you when I did. I wished to ask you—to tell you—while it is yet in my power . . . But tell me first . . ."

There was a pause. The cardinal waited.

"It would have been easier, my lord, to die in the stocks as the bishop left me to do. Even then I had begun to be uncertain, not of the rightness of my cause perhaps, but of the rightness of how it was being upheld, the deaths, the hatred, the pride, the simple statements that seemed to have reduced to law

263

and letter once more what had been spirit and life. But at least, then, I knew that I had in some ways tried for the best, the best that had been open to me, as I saw it in those days, and, once they had fixed me to the ground and bolted the door and ceased to bring me food and water, there would have been nothing left for me to do, nothing that I had to choose, but only to die as well as I was able. I had forsaken the world for God, though I had been forced to it, as entirely as if I had again been a monk in a cell at the Charterhouse. But now . . ."

He stopped. The cardinal's eyes were closed, his face motionless. He half rose from the chair.

"But now?"

The lips had moved. The voice was as quiet as before, and no less firm.

"I am tiring you, my lord."

The eyes opened and the cardinal smiled again.

"No, Master Fletcher, you are not. I have never felt less tired than now, when I am about to sleep for ever. I close my eyes because my eyelids are as weak as my fingers, my arms, my legs. But I am listening. Go on, if you please."

He sat back in his chair. He clasped his hands together in his lap, clenching them against each other until they hurt, and then relaxed them. For a moment he was angry that before this man, this dying prince of a Church whose authority he had long ago rejected for ever, he must try to give an account of the darkness that had settled on his soul like the fog outside. Yet he must. He was also glad that he must.

"Now, my lord, I am alive when I no longer looked for life. I am stronger than I have been for years because I have plenty to eat and sleep in a warm bed. No one questions my presence here or troubles, so far as I can tell, even to find out what I have been. Every day in the chapel on my knees with the rest I pray to God for a quiet mind and a contented spirit and ask forgiveness for my many sins. And yet now that I have life ahead of me, not many years of life because I am already old, but life instead of only death, I am compelled again to choose. What I have been is still what I am. I am alive; therefore I am required to judge, and cannot leave the judgement all to God.

"I must discover where my sin lay, what was falsehood and what truth, where I have been misled and where I have misled others, what I should hold to and what give over, to whom, if to anyone under God, I owe my duty and my love. And I do not know, my lord. I have had hours, day, months to think on all these things, and it seems to me that I know less, both of myself and of God, than when I first came to Lambeth. The words of Jesus—I have been trying to read the Gospels in Greek, my lord, in your library—the words of Jesus are simple and true. Yet in the world, in the Church, under the authority of these bishops and those, of the queen, the officers of state, of laws and changes in the laws, of books of theology old and new: where, among all these, and among all these things is where we have to live, is there any simplicity, any certain truth to be found? In the past, not once but several times, I thought I knew, and altered my life so that it should be in accord with what I had discovered. But each discovery melted into mist as the last had done, and now I am sure of nothing but my loss, my own loss and the loss of all that I have ever found."

He took out his handkerchief to wipe his face. It was of linen, starched, and the slight rustle it made as he crumpled it in his hand seemed to him, in the absolute stillness of the room, a loud noise. He glanced at the cardinal. The eyes were again closed and there was no change in the quiet face on the pillow. There was one thing more to say. He no longer knew whether he cared if the cardinal were listening or not.

"One day last month I met a man, a Southwark carpenter. He talked to me. I could tell him nothing. I saw his house, his wife, his children, his old father. I wished, then, that I had never known—I mourned one moment, one mischance, one fall in a hayfield fifty years ago that killed a man and sent me from home, for ever.

"I tell you, my lord, that Southwark carpenter is living out his life in the world, in the very thick of all the warring accounts of God and man, Church and state, that have lately led men into so much confusion and darkness. He is not slow-witted. He understands much of what he sees about him. But it has not defeated him. He lives in simplicity and truth, while I, a learned man, I, who have been a monk, a priest, a teacher of others, I live out of the world, under the protection of your peaceful house—in confusion and darkness. I doubt if he has given his death two serious thoughts together, yet when the Lord comes as a thief in the night, he will be ready for him. While I, passing my days between life and death and considering both with all the powers I have, am fit neither for the one nor for the other."

He wiped his face again and put his handkerchief back in his sleeve. The cardinal lay still, giving no sign that he had heard anything he had said.

The only sounds came from the fire flickering steadily in the hearth behind him. Beyond the leaded panes of the window the opaque grey light of the November afternoon dulled towards blackness. No wisp of the fog, no breath of the cold outside found its way into the room, and a candle-flame reflected in the glass burned straight and clear.

His words had come, and gone, taking a great heaviness with them. He was emptied. The awe that had weighed on him when he first came into the room had also gone, and he looked round as if he had just sat down to wait in a strange house. The cardinal neither moved nor spoke. The covers over his chest rose and fell very gently, regularly. Perhaps he was after all asleep.

Perhaps he should get up and go quietly away; but any movement, however careful, might wake the dying man. He sat on without stirring, like a mother beside a sleeping child.

He watched the daylight fade until the darkness at the window could deepen no further. Then his gaze returned to the room, and it seemed warmer, smaller, quieter than before.

On the far side of the bed was a reading-desk placed, so that the cardinal could see it, on top of a chest that had been pulled away from the wall. Most of what he had taken for a book open on the desk was hidden from him by the curtains of the bed. He leaned forward a little and saw that it was not a book but a picture in a gilded frame, lit by two candles burning on either side of the desk. He stared at it. He had never before seen anything like it. There was no colour, no definite outline. It was grey and black like the thickening night outside the window. The dead figure of Christ naked on the cross, the head fallen forward between the outstretched arms so that the face could not be seen: this shape was dark and heavy, pressed forward by its own weight as if the lifeless body would crash to the ground, pulling out of the wood the nails hammered into the hands. More lightly drawn, hard to see from a distance against the blank grey space behind them, were two living figures. Shadowy and hesitant, huddled close up against the hanging Christ as if seeking the protection of his dead arms extended far above them, they seemed at the same time to be stumbling forward, bearing the weight of his rigid body like a great battle-standard between them. He thought he had never seen such grief as was drawn into these two human figures, one male, one female, alive under the burden of Jesus dead.

"What shall you do, Master Fletcher, after I am dead?"

He moved his head sharply and lost sight of the picture. But he did not lose the sense of its presence there, lit and dark behind the curtain, like a third person in the room.

The cardinal had spoken in the same level voice as before. He had not slept. Still he did not open his eyes.

"Do, my lord?"

He felt the weight of his uncertainty come down upon him

again as if he had never hoisted it into speech. He did not remember what he had said. He knew only that behind him, across a darkness that he could not penetrate, lay an unrecoverable good. That was what he had tried to say.

"If I could make amends . . .", he began.

What he saw as he said this was the starved face of Will propped against a step in the desolate street.

"My brother—I left my brother to—"

The cardinal raised one hand an inch or two from the fur, to stop him.

"You are right to say that it is easier to die than to live. Perhaps I know this even more nearly than you do, not only because there is so little of life left to me now, but because I have so many times been compelled to return to the wretched affairs of the world from the retirement in which I have always preferred to pass my days, and very bitter the coming back has often been to me. But we are all dead men, Master Fletcher, do you remember? I said this to you once before. I say it to you again now, now that I am almost in fact a dead man myself. It is living, not dying, that has never seemed easier to me than in these last weeks. Yet I too have on my conscience more than you will ever know. Living and dying are all one. No man is fit for one unless he is fit for the other, as you said of the simple man you found in Southwark. You are not a simple man. You must seek your safety in knowing how far you are . . ."

Suddenly the cardinal opened his eyes and looked him full in the face.

"Master Fletcher, you do not believe that in Christ's death we are forgiven our sins. You do not believe it."

"My lord, I—"

"You have believed it. I do not doubt that you have believed it. Was it not in this very belief that you rejected the mediating authority of the Church and set yourself up to free others from the prison of trusting in their own merit, their own power to

268

earn salvation? But now, Master Fletcher, where now is that faith which once burned so clear in you?"

He did not shift his eyes from the cardinal's, but thought of the candle shining in the window-pane, and the night outside.

"Let me try to tell you what I can only guess. When you read the words of Luther and were convinced of their truth, you turned away from the past, from your own past and that of the whole Church, persuaded that if only men could be helped to see what you had seen a new faith would be born in them as it had been in you. They would lead Christian lives from love rather than from fear, the laws and proscriptions of popes and bishops would cease to be necessary, the darkness keeping men's souls from the knowledge of God's grace would be dispelled, the world would become—better. I know this vision. I saw it myself, long ago, and thought then, as you did, that all that was needed was to spread the sight that lit it, the capacity to see it, far and wide.

"But what came after, when you had left behind so much on account of your vision? You saw the world become no better, worse even for the faction and hatred, cruelty and fear, into which opposing claims to the truth had led men. Though obscurely as yet, you began to understand, because you are a good man—aye, Master Fletcher—an honest man and no fool, that the vision you had been granted, and had watched forming in other souls, was not by itself enough. By itself it seemed to bring, indeed, greater dangers than those which, at its first appearance, you thought it had vanquished for ever. It was so, with the past ruined behind you and the future before you no less ruined, that you faced your death in the bishop's cellar with a good grace. You were alone with God in the present, and the present is where each of us must seek him, always, for he is nowhere else.

"You returned to life, to the constraints, as you say, of judgement and choice. You came to my house, to me, and your resistance to the old case for the Church began to weaken. All that you had turned away from, in yourself, in what you had been, and in the long history of the Church, laid a new hold on you. But you could not welcome it. You no longer saw the vision of salvation that once shone before you, but you remembered the sight of it, and you believed that to accept the past again, to bow again to judgements you had resolutely put aside, would be to blot out that vision for ever. So that you are left, now, with nothing. But all is there within you, Master Fletcher, all is there."

The cardinal stopped speaking and closed his eyes. The pale forehead contracted into a frown and then became smooth again. Robert Fletcher neither moved nor spoke. The cardinal opened his eyes.

"The vision does not cancel the past; nor does the past cancel the vision. We live, perhaps, moving always between the two. We know for a moment our salvation in the love of God. The moment fades into the past, and the shadows close about us. Faith in the power of Christ's death to free us from our sins shines within us, none the less, invisible to others, invisible to ourselves, but visible to God, who works in us in ways beyond our understanding. Each of us must turn again and again, not once only but always, to God, believing in his salvation given to us in Christ. This belief, this faith, will make us whole, will find us in the eye of God, but first we must know that we are lost, broken; and all, both faith and knowledge, must be held, together, in the present. *Simul iustus simul peccator.* Luther's words, Master Fletcher. Do not desert them because the past presses hard upon you. Do not desert them. They tell the truth. They tell of what is in what has been, of the light shining in the darkness, of the love of God—in us and for us."

The cardinal closed his eyes. His forehead was damp with sweat.

"Master Fletcher—the cup of water."

On a table beyond the fire were more lit candles, a gilt cup and two silver jugs, a pile of folded linen cloths. He crossed the floor softly, bent down and sniffed the jugs. One contained wine. He poured some water from the other into the cup.

"A few drops of wine—in the water."

He brought the cup back to the bed. The thin hands lay still on the fur rug, so he held the cup to the cardinal's lips. As the sick man drank, in small sips, he thought that he would gladly lift him from his bed and carry him somewhere, anywhere, away from the danger of death.

The cardinal choked and water dribbled from his mouth into his beard. Robert Fletcher went back to the table to fetch one of the white cloths. He wiped the cardinal's mouth and wiped away the drops from his beard.

He remembered Master Husthwaite blind and helpless in his chair through the long winter of his death. He had fed him with a spoon, washed him, changed his clothes. He had talked to him and read to him day after day, yet nothing he could do had reached the spring of his despair and dried it for him.

And now a dying man had spent some of his last, most precious strength to comfort him. He was ashamed.

After a while the cardinal opened his eyes and smiled.

"Thank you, my friend. I can do nothing, now, for myself . . . But when is it not so, Master Fletcher? When do we not need the help of other men? We think we stand alone. A dream, Master Fletcher, a dream. We wake and find that we are no more than a part—and the Church, what after all is the Church but the common bond of all Christian men, Christ himself within us, for each other, the bread broken and broken to feed us all?"

His eyes were fixed on Robert Fletcher, looking at him, and beyond him. Then his face changed. He laughed.

"But I have not said what I sent for you to tell you. There is so little time. Another night of fever, and I may not remember, may not know you."

271

He had spoken lightly. But for a few moments he studied him keenly, as if making up his mind whether or not to trust him.

"When I am dead, Master Fletcher, all those of my household who are here only on account of me must go their ways. I fear the queen will not long outlive me, and after her death the Church in England will again sound to a babel of contentious voices. I shall not hear them. Nor shall I live to find myself again in exile, followed through all the courts of Christendom by murderers and spies, last and most hated of the house of York, most detestable and traitorous Pole. I shall be lying in an English grave. But you, Master Fletcher, who shall you be? A monk forgotten of his cloister, a heretic forgotten of his fellows, a servant of Pole left homeless by his master, a man without a name.

"There is almost nothing, now, that I can set right. But you, you may have left a few years of life.

"When I am dead, they will give you some money, not much, but enough to keep you from hunger for a while. Also they will give you a letter, a letter to the prior of the Grande Chartreuse. In it I have asked that you, as a monk turned out of his cell through no fault of his or of his monastery, as a penitent and friend of mine who has lived under my roof a life of patient obedience, as a heretic who has—not persisted in his heresy, may be absolved of the breach of your vows into which you were partly led by false laws passed in this land, and that you may be received again into the order that bore you blameless within it for half your life.

"All this I have written, Master Fletcher. What you choose to do with this letter I can but leave to you. I know that now, today, you are no penitent of mine. But should you, after my death and somewhere else but in my house, be given absolution through another mouth but this, I think that you will nevertheless be a penitent of mine. The letter will be—no more than what you have left of me when I am no longer here, my hope for you, for the true end of all that, so far as I can tell, you have been and are still."

Robert Fletcher could no longer bear the weight of the cardinal's gaze. He buried his face in his hands and saw instead the dark figure of the dead Christ in the picture on the other side of the bed, and the two beneath it grieving under their load as they faltered forward.

The cardinal said, more softly than ever, as if nursing the little power he had left with which to speak: "One thing more. When you have the letter in your hands and do not know, as you will not, whether to cast it in the fire or to allow what it says of you . . . to be the truth, ask yourself what they were, those vows you made as a lad of twenty, and who it was that made them. If it were you, yourself, for all that you are old now and have seen much change, that which does not change—"

The cardinal stopped speaking suddenly, as if interrupted by pain or alarm. Robert Fletcher raised his head from his hands and looked round the room. Nothing had stirred. The candles still burned straight and clear. The fire still flickered in the hearth.

The cardinal had lifted his head a little from the pillows and was listening, his mouth open and his face rigid with attention. Both his hands clutched the fur of the rug.

"What is it, my lord?"

As he spoke he heard the sound of a man shouting, hoarsely and some distance away, perhaps in the hall of the palace, or the courtyard. He went to the window but could see nothing for the fog, pressing dark against the glass. He turned and listened himself. Silence.

"A drunken soldier in the guardroom."

The cardinal's head shook in a convulsive spasm.

"No—no—I know that—"

The shouts came again, much closer now, and again, closer still and mingled with other raised voices. The door burst open, banging against something as it did so, and a servant fell into the room backwards as if pushed by a violent force. The confusion of voices in the doorway suddenly ceased. A man stood there, panting, dishevelled, a crowd of frightened faces behind him. He had a knife in his hand. The blade glinted in the firelight. There was frost on the fur of his cloak.

Robert Fletcher was on his feet, heavy and resolute, standing so as to shield the cardinal. But the stillness that had fallen on them all came from behind him, from the dying man lying motionless in his bed, and after a few moments he moved aside and stood in the shadows near the head of the bed. He did not turn to look at the cardinal, but he knew that the fear had gone from his eyes.

The man in the doorway dropped the knife. It clattered as it hit the floor, and he began to laugh, a high-pitched demented laugh that changed to tearful sobbing.

The knife was not a dagger but a common carving knife. The blade was dirty.

"They would have kept me out. They bolted the door against me. I heard the bolts go. One. Two. Have I no right to see you? Have I no right? When they're all dead but you and me? They know me! They tried to stop me, twenty of them! You set them on me! You set twenty men on me, and I wouldn't hurt a soul. You shouldn't have left a knife there. I might have killed someone. It would have been your doing if I had killed—killed—"

He broke off, quiet suddenly as if a new thought had struck him. He bent down and picked up the knife. He felt the blade with his thumb.

"It's blunt. Blunt I tell you!" he shouted in the small, warm room. "Why does he give me knives that are blunt? I'll tell you why!"

He rounded on the four or five men who had edged into the room behind him, and they shrank back.

"Because I am not to be trusted. That's the reason, the good,

274

the excellent reason. I—am—not—to—be—trusted! Have you heard of the house of York? Have you? The blood of kings? The blood of traitors? I killed them all, all, mother, brother, cousins, all. They said they would rack me, and I killed them all."

He turned back towards the room and lowered his head. His voice had sunk to a hiss.

"All but one. He was not there to be killed. He was not there to be racked. He was somewhere else. And yet it was all for him . . . that . . . that . . ."

He seemed to lose hold of what he was saying. His face sagged, and his eyes became dull, stupid. He looked down and saw the knife in his hand. He turned it over and over in his fingers, staring at it as if he had never seen it before.

"Put it away."

The cardinal's voice was mild and steady. The slight stir it caused among those at the door did not make the man with the knife look towards them. He walked slowly to the table and put down the knife. He poured out a cup of wine with a shaking hand and drank it all. Then he turned round in a slow circle where he stood, looking at the faces by the door, one by one, at Robert Fletcher's, peering as though his sight were weak, at last at the cardinal. He came to the foot of the bed.

"Why are you here? I thought you lived in Rome." He spoke peevishly, like a fretful child.

"This is my house. I lie here because I am not well."

"Not well? What do you think I am? I am never well. Several times they thought I would die. Why do you not speak to me? And why are all these men here? Can I not be trusted to see you alone?"

"Sit down, Geoffrey. There is a chair."

He backed away from the bed. "Oh, no, I'll not sit down. I'm a grown man. I can choose for myself. I'll not sit down again with you to be told . . . to be told . . ."

Then he stopped. His eyes widened without blinking, stared horribly.

"You are white", he whispered. "White. And not moving. That's it! That's why they've brought me here. You are dying!" At the last word his voice rose to a shriek of terror. A shudder ran through the lookers-on at the door. Robert Fletcher took a menacing step forward. But at once the man began to laugh again, retreating from his fear, the same ghastly laugh as before.

"You are dying. Even you. Even you cannot live for ever. I expect you think you will join them in paradise.

"How can you die and leave me, after all I've suffered for you? The blood of traitors! My blood. And yours too!"

He shook with laughter, then quietened suddenly, his eyes narrowing with suspicion.

"Why have you had me brought here? To watch at your deathbed? For you to ask my forgiveness? And theirs? How can they forgive you from the cold grave? No. You have a reason. A good and Christian reason. Always a good, Christian reason! I have it! Before you die you will forgive me! That's your reason! That would be like your grace, your holiness! But we've played this scene before. That was in Rome. No one to watch. Have we to play it again, in England, before honest English witnesses? Very well! We shall play it. Listen! All of you!"

He turned, flinging his arms wide.

"See how the coward, the traitor, grovels before the brave, the virtuous, the blameless cardinal!"

"Geoffrey, I beseech you . . ."

But he was on his knees, hands clasped together, eyes raised to heaven.

He began to recite in a loud, harsh monotone, not pausing between the words: "I confess to almighty God to blessed Mary ever-virgin to blessed Michael the archangel to blessed John the Baptist to the holy apostles Peter and Paul to all the saints and to you brethren that I have . . . that I have . . . that . . ."

He faltered. His face crumpled suddenly, and his eyes stared wildly round like the eyes of a terrified animal. They came to rest on Robert Fletcher.

"What have I done?" he cried out with a breaking voice, and then, more quietly, pleading, "What have I done?"

He still knelt. His hands were still clasped together as he bent forward, straining as if to see through the shadows. His eyes were fixed on him, begging for an answer.

Robert Fletcher shook his head.

The kneeling man toppled forward to the floor and wept, this time really wept, his head between his outstretched arms, bowed by a shaking grief.

It was plain that the fury had gone out of him, and when at last he raised his head from the floor, two men came from where they had been standing near the door and helped him to his feet. He did not shrug them off but stood forlorn between them as they held him gently by the arms.

"Take me home", he said.

They led him from the room. He walked unsteadily, his shoulders twitched by sobs. He did not look at the cardinal again.

The others followed, murmuring among themselves as they went. Only the servant remained. He came to the foot of the bed, anxious inquiry in his face.

"Leave us."

The cardinal's voice was just audible.

The servant left the room, shutting the door behind him. Robert Fletcher returned to the chair and sat down.

The cardinal's eyes were closed. Tears escaped from under his eyelids and rolled down his cheeks into his beard.

The tears stopped. After some time he spoke.

"Are you there, Master Fletcher?"

"Aye, my lord."

"That was—that is—my brother. You saw and heard—"

"Aye, my lord."

You will understand, now, how it is that I too am often so far—so far from certitude. Behind me also, and not left behind me but here with me, within me, is that suffering, that pain. I must bear it, not only because, as you see, he cannot, but because it is true that—because, Master Fletcher, I was indeed the cause of it."

He waited through a long silence for the cardinal to speak again. He sensed him gathering what was left of his strength for a new effort.

During this silence the little black cat of the summer, which must have slipped into the room while the door was open, jumped onto the bed and rubbed its head against the cardinal's motionless fingers. With a faint rasping sound, it began to lick a finger, which responded by straightening slightly. Then it curled up and went to sleep beside the thin hand with the heavy ring.

The cardinal opened his eyes and smiled.

"Bring me a little wine, Master Fletcher, and I will tell you a tale that will make you glad you were not born to great estate."

The wine brought, after a few moments, a trace of colour to the cardinal's drawn face and a brightness to his eyes. He did not close them again but looked across at him with an eager intensity, as if he had at last reached a decision long foreseen.

"If you will bear with me."

"My lord . . ." He spread his hands, to receive whatever it might be that he should be given.

The cardinal looked down for an instant, and then back at him.

"Very well." He paused.

"My brother Geoffrey was of all my family the least strong, the least able to stand firm against the blandishments and the menace of the world. We learned at our mother's knee of blood most unjustly spilled by royal command, of her father Clarence secretly murdered in the Tower, of her brother Warwick executed by King Henry Tudor on no charge worthy of the name. Her courage in the telling of these stories hardened the rest of us to face the dangers of our inheritance with a like courage. Geoffrey would wake night after night screaming, terrified by dreams of blood and drowning. As a man he found only in spendthrift, reckless living some refuge from his fears.

"When we were young, King Harry, perhaps in reparation for his father's killing of my uncle, treated us with very great kindness and liberality, myself most of all. He kept me in state at Oxford, in the university at Padua, at Venice. He offered me the see of York at Wolsey's death when I was barely thirty. I refused it because he already demanded as condition that I should think him right in the matter of his divorce. I could not think him right then; later, as you know, after his destruction of the unity of the Church, I could still less think him right, for all the love I bore him.

"I loved the king when I was a boy, Master Fletcher. To me he was everything a great prince should be. I loved him.

"I returned to Italy and lived as an exile. I wrote a book against the king's proceedings. I did not publish it but sent it to the king, hoping that he might thereby come to see the peril he was in. His rage against me was terrible. Because I had called him wrong, misled, he branded me a rebel, a traitor, a viper he had nursed, and all my family with me, though none of them had raised a finger against him. He was a man whose fury, once roused, must find a vent. Master Cromwell knew how to break a weak link where he saw one. Geoffrey was taken, imprisoned in the Tower, a place of horror to him since he was a child, examined seven times, threatened with the rack. In the end he laid false evidence against my elder brother, my cousin Exeter, and some others, that they had spoken treasonably, intending harm to the king. They were executed. My mother was kept in the Tower several years, several years, Master Fletcher, an old woman of great goodness and fidelity, in cold and want, and at last executed also, on no charge at all.

"Twice in the Tower Geoffrey tried to take his own life, once with a knife. Aye. Since he was freed he has been at intervals as you see him now, driven quite from his wits by the terror of the past. At other times he is quiet, spiritless, without the will to put on his clothes or eat or talk. I have seen him sit all day on the same stool, not even coming to the window for light or to the fire for warmth. Remorse has wasted him these twenty years, remorse that he has not the power to turn to penitence. Yet whose is the guilt for the sin that so torments him? Who put him to the test that he could not but fail? Not he himself, not Master Cromwell and his obedient lords, but I—I, with my clarity of mind, my stubbornness, my learned assurance that I was in the right, I, far away in Italy among my friends, left him, who had none of these things, to be brought to this wretchedness, this despair. He was no more than the miserable agent of my family's destruction. I was the cause."

Except of his mother the cardinal had spoken levelly, as if he had many times been through these events in his mind and long ago become accustomed to his account of them. He was silent for a moment.

Then he said in a different voice: "You said that you had a brother, Master Fletcher."

"I had two, my lord. The elder hated me because my father loved my mother and not his. He would not let me into my father's house when I came back from the Mountgrace. Perhaps he feared that I would be a charge on him, though I wished only to know whether my father still lived. My father was dead.

"My second brother was also the son of my father's first wife. They reckoned him an idiot. He was mute and solitary. He did strange things. But he was not an idiot, and he was not deaf. He did not speak because—because, over what I could not tell, his heart was broken.

280

"My father paid no more heed to him than to a dog. My elder brother kicked him, cursed him, beat him. He never resisted. Sometimes he would break things. He broke a great stone trough to pieces with a pick and all the water ran out over the yard. The day I left to go to the Charterhouse I could not find him, though he was always afraid to go far. I looked for him all day. Afterwards I feared that grief at my going had made him run away. As a boy I was smaller, weaker than he was. He would follow me to places where he would not go alone. I think he loved me then, so far as he was able, though as I grew up he came with me less and less. All the years at the Charterhouse I never knew whether or not he had run away that day. If he had, they would not have gone after him.

"When I came back I could discover no news of him. He was altogether forgotten in the village, even among the old people, as if he had never been. Later, in York, years later, I saw him one day. After the chantries were dissolved. There was a mob running wild in the streets, breaking, plundering the churches. I saw him among them, older than all the rest, and taller, strong still, with a great iron bar in his hands. Soldiers took them from the church, and afterwards I could not find him, not in the prison, not anywhere in the city.

"But he was there. I think he was in York, God knows in what wretchedness, what filthy hovel, all the time that I was living there. For it was in York that I saw him the last time, the time I could not—did not . . . It was cold, a bitter wind blowing. I had gone out for eggs. I had money at home, meat, bread, warm clothes, firewood. I saw him in the street, lying in the gutter. I pretended to myself that I was not certain it was he. It was he. I saw him lying where he had fallen. People hurried past, going home, as I was. It was almost dark. I stood still outside my door. I had to choose. It was so cold, though it was April, that there was ice over the running ditch. I went in. My wife was there, great with child. I said to myself that it was for her I had left him there. She was much afraid, had many dreams. But it was not because of her. It was I that was afraid. I had peace, warmth, safety. I was afraid that he would take them from me. I begrudged him them. I looked on him and passed by on the other side. Soon after, it began to snow. He died, very likely, that same night. Very likely the watch found him dead before morning. My lord—"

"Calm yourself, Master Fletcher."

"My lord, I read, this morning, Jesus' words. I have read them many times before. 'If thou bring thy gift to the altar and there rememberest that thy brother hath aught against thee, leave there thy gift before the altar and go thy way; first be reconciled to thy brother, and then come and offer thy gift.' He is dead. My brother is dead. What is there that I can do?"

"Or I, Master Fletcher, though my brother be alive?"

There was silence in the room, among the burning candles.

He got out his handkerchief, mopped his face, blew his nose, put back the handkerchief. He looked up at the cardinal. The large eyes, patient and thoughtful, returned his look.

"I am a coward, my lord. I have always been a coward. Once when I was a lad I met a beggar, a horrible old man, hungry, frightened, full of hatred. I was afraid. I ran away. I was afraid of my father, of my brothers, both of them, of the bitterness and hatred that was in the house. I ran away to the cloister, to my quiet cell, my garden, and stopped my ears to the misery of those I left behind. Much later when my old schoolmaster was dying I cared for him, fed him, read to him because he was blind, but I never spoke to him of the despair I knew was in him. I was afraid of his grief. And Alice—my wife—poor child. She died alone because I had gone out to find someone else to help her die. And my brother, that last day. And my own son.

"I have been a coward, my lord, I know it now. I have been afraid, always afraid, to love."

"But not to bear the blame."

282

The cardinal's gaze was steady; the few words had been spoken very softly, as if to himself. Then he said: "Put some wood on the fire, Master Fletcher, and lift me up a little higher. If I am ever to try, it must be now."

There were great logs stacked beside the hearth. He picked up two, one after the other, and laid them across the iron bars. Those that were there already, consumed almost to ash, crumbled beneath them and dropped into the burning embers. He returned to the bed, took the dying man gently by the shoulders and, as he braced his back, raised him a little on the pillows. He was lighter to hold than the fresh logs.

He sat down.

"Soon they will bring my supper." The cardinal smiled. "Which I shall not be able to eat. And before I sleep the fever will be back upon me. What I have told you already, many people know. There is more. I tell you this tale for you. I begin with myself, but I shall end with you. In a few days, a week or two at the most, I shall be dead. But you, you will be alive, you will have the time, perhaps, to—to think.

"I too have been afraid. I too have run away, and many times failed to find safety either in running or in staying still. Always I have loved books, a study, solitude, gardens—gardens above all. Sometimes I have thought that I love trees more even than my friends, although my friends have been—the health of my life. But fortune has thrust me among great causes, great affairs of Church and state. They said in England, and no doubt led the king to believe, that ambition took me to Rome and made a traitor of me. It was not so. At first I refused the cardinal's hat. But I had chosen to obey the pope. So I obeyed him. And I was persuaded then that the best means I had of restoring what had been destroyed in England was to stay in Rome and labour for the reform of the whole Church. And yet to leave England then was also to run away. Others stayed. Others stayed and were killed. Bishop Fisher, Thomas More, my family. My family died because I was not there, and I was afraid to return.

"And the Council, the great Council of the whole Church, of which we hoped for so much, which was so often delayed and for such unworthy reasons that we who worked for it in Rome felt that all our efforts were no more than the struggling of flies in syrup—

"I remember Cardinal Contarini, the best man I ever knew. Long ago, long before the Council, he saw the pope one day at Ostia. He gave him our report on the Dataria, that sink which swallowed up the money of the poor and made the very name of Rome hated and feared throughout the Church. Yes, the pope agreed that reforms were necessary. Yes, a commission would be appointed. Yes, our report was accepted and its condemnation of corrupt, grasping officials. We rejoiced. A few days later Contarini came to my room. He looked old, worn out. The report? I asked him. He said nothing, only shrugged his shoulders. We heard no more of the reform of the Dataria. When at last the Council was called, it was too late. Contarini was dead, had died in disgrace because he had tried to piece together the unity of the Church when the rifts were already too deep to mend. But the truth, the truth—it was too late for unity, but it can never be too late for the truth.

"The pope appointed three legates to the Council. I was one. At the beginning I spoke to the whole Council. I begged them, pleaded with them, the bishops, cardinals, princes of the Church, to take upon themselves the charge and trust that was theirs and with it the burden of guilt, no less theirs, for the evils and errors that neglect had allowed to flourish. I was full of hope. Soon the Council reached the question of justification, of our salvation in Christ, the very centre of our belief, the heart of our faith. They would define in a few words, a few articles, a mystery that can never be perfectly defined in the language of law. And the words they chose must have nothing in common, nothing, with the words Luther had used. So the Jesuits said, especially the Jesuits. As if everything that Luther ever wrote must be false because he wrote it. I implored them to change their minds, to understand, to return to the New Testament, to Saint Paul. I did all I could to show them that it was not agreement with the Protestants I sought but that we should not limit and confine the truth out of fear of agreement with the Protestants. I spoke in vain, utterly in vain. And when I saw how it would be, I went away. Again, I did not stay. I became ill and left the city, left the Council, did not stay to hear a Jesuit declare, and carry all the Council with him, that the throne of divine justice must not be turned into a throne of mercy—as if—as if Christ had never come to tell us that it is indeed so, to be, himself, for us, that mercy, that forgiveness. O Master Fletcher . . ."

The cardinal looked at him with pleading eyes.

"I had forsaken my country, sacrificed my family to a tyrant's revenge, and myself lived in constant danger of murder, all for the sake of loyalty to the one, holy, Catholic Church. I had to watch that Church exclude from orthodoxy things I knew in conscience to be of the truth of God.

"What could I do? You will ask, what did I do? I ran away. I obeyed the Church, and I ran away. After that I never again spoke of those things that I had known and understood when they were not heresy because the very Council for which I had toiled so long and in which I had put all my trust had declared them—heresy. Yet they are there, Master Fletcher, they are there, not only in Luther but in Saint Bernard, in Saint Augustine, in Saint Paul, where Luther found them, and the day will come when this truth also will be told.

"After that I lost the will to act, the will to move. Perhaps there was nowhere else that I could run to. I only waited, and let what would befall me. Nine years ago, during the Conclave that elected Pope Julius, I found one morning that I myself lacked but one single vote. I might be pope. I might myself rule the Church I had loved so long, for which I had lost so much. I might myself have brought about the reforms for which I had striven in vain . . . There was a silence, a great silence. I waited for a voice to speak. One more vote. I remember that I was thinking of a friend of mine who lay dying at my house in Rome. I thought that if I should be elected, I would be able to leave the Conclave and see him again before he died. No one spoke. The vote was not cast. Some of my friends were sorry. I was—neither sorry nor glad. That silence had been for me—had been a momentary chill, as if a cloud had moved across the sun."

He paused, looking down, into the past. His face was white again, quiet and sad.

"Did you see your friend before he died?"

He smiled.

"I did. The Conclave lasted another two months, but he did not die until a few days after it ended. Now he, and several others among my friends, and I myself are disgraced, abused, in Rome. But that comes at the end of this tale.

"Five more years I waited. I did nothing. I said nothing. To call it patience would be to fasten a fine word to what was no more than staying still. King Edward died. My cousin the Princess Mary, whom I knew when she was a child, a proud, brave, dutiful, frightened child, was queen. Then I was for a little while again full of hope. I came home after all to England. The Church was restored. All that I had longed for since the king first broke with Rome seemed at last to be coming to pass. And yet . . ."

He sighed a deep, rasping sigh that shook the whole of his frail body.

"Perhaps it was only that it was too late. Too late for England, too late for the queen, too late for me. Perhaps I should never have accepted the burden of an office that in my numbness, my lethargy, my unhappy sleep, I was unfit to bear.

"But it has been unjust!"

His voice suddenly rose to a feverish cry.

"It has been unjust, Master Fletcher. It has been more than I, more than even I, have deserved."

He was leaning forward, his back for the first time unsupported by the pillows. Both hands grasped the fur. The little cat stirred in its sleep.

"The pope, Master Fletcher, the pope for the sake of whose authority I sacrificed my family and have allowed misguided Englishmen in their scores to burn and have kept silence many years even at the price of the whole truth—the pope has lately condemned me as a heretic, revoked my legatine commission, and recalled me to Rome to be questioned by the Inquisition. I know him well. He is a man, like King Harry, whom I loved for most of my life. Twenty years ago I persuaded Pope Paul to make him a cardinal when another man was already chosen in his place. And now he also calls me a traitor.

"Friends of mine he has put in prison for no other reason than that they are friends of mine. Twenty years ago and more, in Venice, he and I and Cardinal Contarini and others used to discuss day after day the healing of the Church, in the garden of San Giorgio with the monks, under the trees, and the light on the water—the years of hope—we saw what must be done—we knew—the pope must not exercise power as a prince of this world, we said. The pope must be in truth as he is called, the servant of the servants of God. And now this man, this good man as I thought, but old and hard and jealous of that very power he used to scorn, has waged on behalf of his family and Naples a war, a bloody war against half of Christendom. He has set France against Spain to save the worldly power of Rome as the popes have done for fifty years. Long ago I heard the Emperor Charles plead before another pope, at what if anywhere on earth should be the throne of justice and peace, only for justice and peace. In vain then. In vain now. Nothing changes. And yet the world I leave is worse than the world then, for what we understood and failed to perform, for what we glimpsed and failed to build.

"And I myself, an exile after all, in England and an exile from the Church, pronounced a heretic though I obeyed, though I left the Council and never spoke after."

He leaned back against the pillows and said quietly, the pain gone from his voice: "The queen refused to allow me to go to Rome, refused to allow me to be replaced as legate on the pope's command. So that I who staked my life, my family's lives, my very soul, on obedience to the Church in defiance of the crown of England now die at last obedient to the crown of England and in defiance of the Church."

He laughed, without bitterness.

"What will you? I am too ill—as you said of yourself in Bishop Bonner's cellar, there is nothing left for me to do now but to die—and God . . ."

He paused and laid his hand on the cat's head.

"God forgives us, as—when—we forgive them who injure us—and ourselves. These last weeks I think I have understood what many times in the past I thought I knew—but we never know—we never reach the end of understanding—the understanding of God—the mystery of his love . . .

"I have hated them both, the king and the pope, most deeply hated them, or, rather, not them but the blindness, the cruelty, the injustice in them. But what is the use of hate? I wrote my book to the king, and the blackness in him became blacker still. Last summer I wrote a long letter to the pope. It had in it all that I have told you and more. It was to justify myself before him who had unjustly cast me off. I threw it in the fire. But as I watched it burn, I was full of anger. I burned it because it would have served no purpose, not because I had forgiven him the wrong I had suffered. Now—now at last I see that the wrong is one wrong, the sin, their sin and mine, all one, the mud that holds us back, the bog in which we struggle, ourselves—and at the end there is none but God to free us, not the king and all his laws, not even the Church and her authority, her discipline, her tradition, but only Christ, his hands held out to each of us, to take or not to take. Faith. Forgiveness.

"All this time I failed to forgive because I felt them stronger than I. They threatened and condemned me, and I ran away into my righteous silence, my nothingness. I would not bear any blame. I would be innocent of sin. But who is innocent?

"With you it has been altogether different. Listen, Master Fletcher, listen . . ."

His eyes shone with the brightness of clear discovery.

"You have always felt yourself to be the stronger one— stronger than your brother, your father, your wife, the people you preached to, all. You have taken upon yourself the charge, the guilt. Where there was fault, it was yours. Because you have courage and understanding, where there was lack of courage and understanding, it was your lack. You think you have failed, again and again. You have failed. No man is innocent. But you have borne all the blame. You judge only yourself. Others you do not hold to account. You forgive them. Therefore, therefore, Master Fletcher, you are yourself forgiven. You have but to accept forgiveness, to take the hands—they are there. I in my weakness would not forgive; you in your strength will not be forgiven. The result is the same—to be stuck fast—caught—and the remedy also is the same. The remedy—look there, Master Fletcher."

Without moving his hand from the bed the cardinal raised one finger and pointed in the direction of the picture on the chest.

He had not forgotten it. He leaned forward and saw it again. The contrast between the heavy dead figure and the live ones struggling forward beneath it struck him more violently even than before.

"Look there. Many hours I have lain here alone, my eyes fixed upon that—and thought that there is all the sorrow of the world, and all its cure. That piece of paper scratched on by an old, shaking hand has brought me as I am dying further into . . . life than all the definitions of theology and all the books I ever read."

The cardinal's voice dropped to a whisper as he said:

> Né pinger, né scolpir sie più che quieti
> l'anima, volta a quell' amor divino
> Ch'aperse, a prender noi, in croce le braccie.

How they come, grieving, bearing their ruined hope. We are given the day, the hour. We hear the word of God. We recognise his love, as they recognised Christ. Then, as they did, we run away. They watched him taken prisoner, condemned to a slave's death, and they ran away. At last they turned and saw him there, as we must turn, again and again. He was among the dead. He, they, all of us were among the dead. But the third day came.

"What has he done for us? What have we done to him? Look at him there. He was—he is—God with us. He has borne our griefs and carried our sorrows. He has. It is all done, yet all to do, over and over, in every soul. And he is—see how they carry him there, pleading, with hope and trust—he is of us, with God. He told us, he came to tell us, and to be, in us and for us . . . That is all. It is enough."

The cardinal stopped speaking and lay quiet, his eyes, in his exhausted face, fixed on the picture.

Very softly Robert Fletcher said: "It is enough."

When he looked up again the cardinal's eyes were closed.

He sat on in his chair, watching now only the still flames of the tapers burning on either side of the picture. Silence lapped them. There was nothing left to be said.

After a while the cardinal opened his eyes and smiled.

"I am tired now. I shall sleep. I think perhaps the fever will not come tonight. Not tonight. But soon, very soon. Go now. When I am dead, you will go your own way. You are a man without a name. What is the cardinal of England to you? It is because of that that I have tried to tell you, you out of them all . . . You shall have my letter. Do with it what you will."

Robert Fletcher got up and stood beside the bed for a moment, his head bowed, as if beside a grave.

"Farewell, Master Fletcher. *Dominus tecum.*"

"*Et cum spiritu tuo.* Good-night, my lord."

He walked to the door and, as he reached it, turned to look back. He saw the friendly eyes regarding him across the firelight, the long beard mingled with the fur of the rug, the hand resting on the cat's head.

"Farewell, my lord."

He closed the door behind him, nodded to the servant outside it, and went away through the cold rooms of the palace.

14

November 1558

Don Gomez Suarez de Figueroa, Count of Feria, at the court of Queen Mary in London, to King Philip of Spain and England, in Brussels; November 1558.

" . . . On my return to London I was deeply shocked and grieved to discover the serious worsening of the queen's condition. I fear that her Majesty's expectation of life must now be counted in days rather than weeks and that it has therefore become necessary for me, as your Majesty's ambassador to what will shortly become no longer your Majesty's Kingdom, to consider the dispositions that may with most benefit to your Majesty's concerns be made for the next reign. It is my belief that the accession of the Lady Elizabeth to the realm of England will be welcomed both at court and by the common people and that the crown will pass to her with no tumult or disturbance save that of general rejoicing. Her likely regulation of the Church is as yet an open question: she has conducted herself and her household in recent years with a discretion that leaves her intention as to the future government of the religious affairs of the realm a matter for speculation. Certain it is that she would be ill-advised to take any harsh or precipitate action in these matters, and, from all I learn of her, and of those who have her ear, she will tread cautiously for a while for the sake of quiet among the people (she is said to be a woman of sound judgement, though also of a merry wit and high spirit). Since the cardinal's case is hardly less grave than that of the queen, it is likely that the new queen will early be given the opportunity to appoint an archbishop of Canterbury of her own choosing, to lead the Church in whatever direction her opinion may tend. Thanks to his long indolence in affairs of state and his fall from favour in Rome, the cardinal, alas, will leave no loyal followers at court to further the cause of Rome after his death, though I myself shall, it need not be said, do all that is in my power.

"As to the matter of the Lady Elizabeth's marriage, there can be no doubt that the surest way to protect your Majesty's interests both in England and in the Netherlands would be for your Majesty to gain her hand, and with it the continuation of the present alliance (the necessary dispensation from Rome should be forthcoming in the next papal reign if not in this: even his Holiness cannot live for ever). To the arrangement of this most advantageous match, which could not but strengthen the cause of the Catholic Church in England, I shall devote my best endeavours whenever her Majesty shall have reached the term of her natural life. She is said to be calm in mind and spirit and suffering no great pain, and to speak often of your Majesty with the deepest affection."

15

January 1559

"Will you lend me the warmth of your fire? It's bitter walking now the sun is set."

"Aye. It will be."

The man looked him up and down. He waited, leaning on his staff. His cloak, which had been new a month ago, was caked with dried mud and torn where a dog had snatched it in its teeth.

"You're an old man to be on t' road for nowt at t' year's worst end. Be you a pilgrim of some sort?"

"Of some sort, aye."

"Sit there. On yon side. We've work to do before dark."

But the man picked up an empty sack, shook it free of the chips of wood that had fallen on it, and laid it down by the fire for him to sit on. He nodded his thanks, pulled his hat further over his eyes, wrapped his cloak round him, and sat down. The land was black already, without colour, as if the sky had taken to itself such light as the afternoon still kept. The moon was up but could cast neither light nor shadow on the earth while the sky was not yet dark. Even the flames of the fire had no brightness in them but only flapped from the burning brushwood like dirty rags. The fire gave out some heat nevertheless, and he was very cold. Walking over frozen ruts and trying not to slip on iced-over puddles had worn him out more than trudging through the mud earlier on his journey.

He watched them working, three of them. Two were thinning and laying the old, overgrown thorn hedge that ran beside the road, the first man chopping out branches with an axe, the second cutting half through the rest, bending them over and lacing them together to make a close fence for the spring to cover with leaves. The third man, the one he had spoken to, looked at each branch as it fell, sliced off the thorny twigs with a few strokes of his billhook, and threw some onto the fire and some onto a pile for faggots. Then he plunged the blade into the top of the stripped branch and split it down to the bottom in one rapid, accurate stroke, twisting his hand as the billhook went down, to avoid the knots in the wood. The two laths he had made fell apart, and he tossed them behind him to a heap of others. The fresh-split surfaces shone white with a little light from the sky as the roses had on midsummer eve, under the cardinal's window.

Since Christmas, perhaps because it had been so cold, he had lost count of the days. One night, on his straw pallet in some inn, he had woken to hear church bells ringing for the end of the old year and the start of the new. He lay for a while listening to them, praying again for the cardinal, who had known he would not hear another year rung in. He tried to turn his thoughts from the dead to the living, to himself, still bound by years and hours, cold at midnight on a straw bed in spite of his cloak. He tried to look forward, to the new year, the morrow, the north. But he was tired and saw only the dying man, his hand on the cat's head, and the lights burning again in the quiet room, and slept. That had been four nights ago, or five.

Now he was only a mile or two from the gates of York. He had seen the Minster in the afternoon, distant across the flat, frozen plain, and Clifford's Tower on its mound. He sat by the fire delaying, as the sky darkened, and wished that he had not come.

Early in the morning of the seventeenth of November, when the fog outside had not yet paled after the night, those who slept in the clerks' chamber had been summoned to the chapel. There the whole household, expecting to hear that the cardinal had not lived through the night, was told that the queen was dead. The news seemed to reach them from far off, and when, at dinner that day, someone said that the streets of London were full of people come out to greet the Lady Elizabeth, sent for from Hatfield to be queen at last, it was as if he spoke of another country. In the evening they heard that the cardinal had said that it would be fitting if God were to put an end on the same day to the lives of himself and the queen, which had so much resembled each other. These were the last words of his that he had heard reported, and he cherished them for the smile he knew must have accompanied them. Later that night, as they stood in silent groups waiting in the hall with the fire piled high against the dank cold, Signor Priuli came slowly down the stairs and on the last step said: "E morto."

It was still the seventeenth of November. He knelt the following dawn, during the first of many requiems, and hoped that the cardinal knew that it was the feast of Saint Hugh of Lincoln. In the intervals of the singing, the sound of several men hammering came from different parts of the palace. Later they filed past a lead coffin standing alone among candles in the middle of a room hung with black cloth. Others wept, but he had looked at it without sadness. It was part of the past. The man he had talked to through those hours was of the present, would stay alive in him always. And after he himself was dead, both of them would live in God, who is nowhere else but in the present.

He got stiffly to his feet and sat down again with his back to the way he had come, so as to warm his other side. The northern sky was no longer clear but laden with a heaviness that obscured the fading light. It would snow. If it snowed the air might become less cold. He looked up at the sky, one side of his face hot, the other already cold again, while behind him the chopping and splitting, the rustle of brushwood hitting the frozen grass, went on.

Death. There seemed to be so much difference between life and death, between himself, now, tired, hungry, and cold, and the cardinal, who had been freed from it all, from winter and nightfall, weariness, the hard ruts of the road, and from the body, the closed dead eyes, the skin and bones wrapped in scarlet, that lay in the lead coffin. Yet was there so much difference? Had not the cardinal, lying in his bed, his gaze fixed on the picture, only the picture, of Christ crucified, the first day before the third, been free already? The souls of the just are in the hand of God. Who are the just? The just are those who are in the hand of God, both the living and the dead.

He clasped his cloak tighter round his legs and rested his head on his knees, looking into the fire, which glowed brightly, now, in the deepening dusk. The heat hurt his eyes, and he shut them.

And the way. I am the way. No man comes to the Father but by me. He was sixty years old and never yet had he understood. Thy will be done on earth as it is in heaven. Was this what it meant? The will of God done on earth in the life and death of Christ, Christ in the souls of the living and the dead, and no such difference between them as we falsely perceive. Was it not this that the cardinal had seen at last, after all that he had suffered and made others suffer, was it not this? Thy will be done.

Some phrases came to him that he had read long ago. I was in the land where all is different from you, and I heard your voice calling, "I am the food of full-grown men. Grow, and you shall feed on me. But you shall not change me into yourself. Instead you shall be changed into me." He had not understood. Thy will be done.

It was hot, too hot, and the glare scorched his closed eyelids. The blazing sticks crackled loud beside him. He had not the power to move. Were they burning him after all? There was no pain, then, not the pain he had feared.

Something fell with a thud to the ground beside him, and a

hand pushed him roughly away from the fire so that he almost toppled over.

"You'll be catching alight, old fellow, nodding so near t' fire."

He had put out a hand to save himself from falling, and his palm was full of thorns. He pulled off his mittens and brushed stupidly at the thorns. Some went deeper into his flesh. He sat staring at his hand in the firelight which gleamed back dully from the blade of the axe the man had thrown down beside him. He felt tears rising in his throat.

"You'll not fetch those out while daylight", the man said.

He shook his head.

"If you've a bed to find in t' city you'd best be on your way. Been freezing fast since dinner-time, it has, and likely an hour or two'll see it colder yet."

The sounds of work had ceased, and the three of them stood in the dusk looking down at him as if at a sick animal. The fire burned on. He did not want to leave it.

Again he shook his head.

Without a word two of them bent down, took him by the arms and helped him to his feet. It was painful to stand, and he swayed, light-headed for a moment, between them. They held him upright until the third man gave him his staff and he leaned on it, steadying himself.

"He'd be dead by sunrise an he slept out here", one of them said. "Frozen stiff."

"Can he walk that far, d'you reckon? A mile and a half? Reckon you can walk a mile and a half, old man?"

"I've walked from London."

One laughed, but the others still looked at him uncertainly. "I can walk", he said again, to take the burden from them. They let him take it, stooped and picked up their tools. One of them kicked the unburned ends of stick into the fire.

"Good-night, then", they said. "Good-night."

He watched them go down the road together, the way he had

come. When he had almost lost sight of them, one of them turned his head. He saw his face, pale in the darkness. He waved, to show that they had done right to leave him. For a few moments after he could no longer see them, he heard their footsteps fading into silence.

He looked down at the fire. If he had passed by a little later, now, after they had gone, he would have sat down here for the warmth, and slept perhaps, and . . . He raised his staff with both hands and brought it down hard on top of the fire. The brushwood fell together lightly, easily. There was almost nothing left to burn. The fire would soon be out and the cold might not have woken him. They would have come back in the morning to finish the hedge. He glanced again towards the northern sky, from which small gusts of icy wind were beginning to blow. There would have been snow, no doubt, lying unmelted on his frozen face. The sun would have risen, red over the snow; other eyes would have seen it, not his. He poked with his staff at the place where he had sat.

He moved away from the fire, crossed the uneven ground to the road, and began to walk towards the city, the cold wind from the north making his eyes smart.

Was that why he had set out, stubborn, for York instead of travelling across the sea with the Italians, to France, with his letter in his pocket? He put his hand to the belt that he wore under his cloak. It was there, folded small in a leather bag with the money they had given him. There would have been enough to pay for his burial, and the letter would have told them his name.

He smiled, under his hat in the darkness.

The moon, two or three days from the full, shone down on the cold fields and lit the road ahead of him so that he could see the ruts clearly, the shadows they cast, and here and there ice gleaming. A dog was barking, far off. He gripped his staff tighter as he walked and felt the thorns in his hand. He was hungry. The meat was already sizzling on some spit that he should eat before he slept.

The cardinal, whose kindness had put the money in his purse to pay for his supper, who had himself loved gardens, loved trees as he had loved his friends, had learned to hold life cheap. Why could he not do the same? There was a resignation, a knowledge, that he had caught sight of many times, as just now when he had almost fallen asleep beside the fire. Yet always he lost it, again and again. The moonlight, the hard road, the barking dog, for example, drew him back, and gladly he came. The earth. It was only the earth, not life, that the cardinal had learned to hold cheap. Did he not believe, as the cardinal believed, that life, which is in God, does not cease when the eyes no longer see the sun rising, when the ears no longer hear and thorns no longer sting the hand? Then why could he not let go?

After the Tower and the bishop of London's cellar, Lambeth had been no prison. He was held there, nevertheless, from the earth, as he had been, for years before they took him, in the alleys and garrets of London. These last weeks, walking the length of England in fair weather and foul, he had rejoiced in his freedom as he had that day, long ago, when he walked from Hawnby in the spring after Master Husthwaite's death. After another man's death. Another man had died, and he had not. And his freedom, what was that? Money in his purse from the dead.

For nearly three weeks after the cardinal's death he had done nothing. Of course he had to leave. They had given him the letter. He hesitated. Was what it said of him the truth? In the months of warmth and safety he had thought too much. Now he could not think. And his child?

One afternoon he was standing at the window where he had waited on midsummer eve. Behind him servants were moving chests and tables and packing the cardinal's candlesticks in straw. There was no fire in the hearth, only ash that no one had swept.

The casement was shut. Outside in the fog the leafless branches of the trees were faint, the river beyond them altogether hidden in whiteness. Damp leaves lay rotting on the ground where they had fallen, here and there among them the stalks of long-spent flowers, which would not bend if they were trodden on, but snap. A wren flew into the grey branches of an apple tree and perched on the single apple that still hung there, an apple as grey, in the fog, as the leafless branches. He watched the little bird peck at the apple over and over again, and its hardness and sweetness pierced him as he stood at the closed window. The apple did not fall under the wren's weight. Some thin flow of sap, some life, still joined it to the twig that had blossomed in the spring. The wren flew away.

He turned from the window and went down to the great hall where Signor Priuli sat at the table with a pen in his hand, an inventory in front of him and a pile of rolled-up tapestries on the floor beside him.

"I shall leave in the morning, my lord."

"For France?"

"For the north, my lord. For York, where I once lived."

Signor Priuli looked up at him for a moment, bringing back all his attention from the dismantling of the household. But he only said: "*Bene*, Signor Fletcher. *Dominus tecum.*"

He bowed and went away. In the morning someone else gave him money and new clothes. Signor Priuli's look, and the five words he had spoken, were the last breath of Italy upon him.

Italy: he smiled again as he tramped along the frozen road. Padua and Venice Master Husthwaite had described to him long ago as they sat, priest and listening boy, under some tree in the high dale in summer. Impressions of weight and richness, great stone palaces, marble steps leading down into water, long black boats rowed from the back by an oarsman standing—Master Husthwaite had sketched one for him later with his scratchy quill—had formed in his mind to be forgotten for fifty years.

Afterwards, in York, Luther. Italy had become only Rome, the glittering edifice of power and law lying heavy over the truths of God so as to bury them from simple men, bloated princes defending their treasure from every just attack.

But in the last months, in the cardinal's household, he had caught sight many times of an ancient gravity, a wealth not of jewels and gold but of books and manners, that had reminded him of a particular wistful love in Master Husthwaite's voice: "In Italy we had all to learn. The light that strikes us in the north only from the words we read, Virgil, Tully, in Italy has never ceased to shine. And the gardens. The gardens among the stone." Italy—where the silver cup had been made, and the cardinal's picture drawn, where Master Husthwaite had carefully copied thousands of verses, and the cardinal and his friends had designed the reform of the whole Church in the garden of San Giorgio. Venice. Venice above all he wished he had seen. The great market of the world, the crowds of people speaking in a score of tongues, the wharves piled high with carpets, bales of silk, silver, and beaten copper, the galleys coming and going on the water, Africa, Arabia.

He stopped on the road. To either side there lay under the moon the flat marshes of the Knavesmire, the common outside the walls of the city where the poor grazed their beasts. They had come out here in their hundreds to see the Dutch heretics burn. Near him some sheep munched at turnip-ends. His breath, and the sheep's, were forming little clouds of vapour in the icy air. The walls were not far now, dark under the sky, and within them the long shape of the Minster. Torches flamed on either side of Micklegate Bar. The wicket would still be open in the gate. He listened to the scrabblings of the sheep and the low murmur, with now and then a faint shout, that reached him from the city. An owl flew across the road, a heavy shadow, and disappeared without a sound into the darkness. Beyond the sheep in a hollow of the ground among clumps of coarse grass stiff in the cold was a pond, frozen over, its surface giving off a dull, even shine.

Italy! He laughed, half-aloud so that the sheep raised their heads. He had not even seen the sea.

He began to walk again, with firm steps, towards the city.

And in any case, what odds were there? Italy, England, Venice, York, France. What odds before God, whose freedom was not that of the traveller over the beloved earth, the man with money in his purse and new clothes on his back, but that of the prisoner in his chains, the oppressed man whom his oppressors cannot overcome? See that ye love not the world. If any man love the world, the love of the Father is not in him.

He reached the gate, out of breath because he had quickened his pace up the last slope from the quiet common. No one challenged him as he passed through the wicket, and the air, as he stood still for a moment on the cobbles to get his breath, seemed at once warmer, thick with the life of the whole city huddled against the winter. He walked slowly down the steep familiar street towards the river. People brushed against him as he walked, overtaking him or coming the other way, their eyes bright in their muffled faces. Lights burned inside steamy windows, and fires lit in iron baskets smoked at the corners of streets. Smells hung in the air with the smoke, horse-dung, roasting meat, dirty clothes on warm dirty bodies, ale from the taverns, singed hoof from the open door of a smithy. A boy pushed past him leading a goat, and he felt the rough, thin, stinking flank of the goat against his leg. A beggar sat in the entrance to an alley, a filthy bandage over his eyes and a hand holding a bowl stuck out of his rags. A donkey with an old woman at its head pulled a sledge loaded with sawn logs up the hill. Dogs nosed about in the rubbish. A baker stood in his doorway clapping his hands together because of the cold, a smell of loaves and currants coming past him into the street. The great bell of the Minster tolled the hour from across the river.

He walked slowly, not stopping, down the middle of the street. Alice. All his carefully assembled resolution, his weeks and months of calm, had dissolved into the anguish of her name. He had not looked for this. When he reached the river there were tears freezing on his cheeks at the emptiness at his side, the emptiness of his hand. He stopped on the bridge, at his old gap between the houses. Mist, silvery in the moonlight, curled off the black, fast-flowing water. Here she turned away, from the knowledge of him he offered her, and therefore from him.

He shivered at the chill of the stone under his mittened hand. The water that flowed there, black and quiet, came down from the moors, from the icicle-hung pools and the rattling becks. They were the river: they made the river. He hit the coping of the wall hard, with the flat of his hand. The stone hurt him, and the thorns in his palm.

He left the gap on the bridge and walked again, up through the narrow streets, the market place, the shambles, towards the Minster. He was alone again, as on the road across the Knavesmire, the emptiness gone from his side. He no longer looked at the people hurrying past. Once he slipped and would have fallen but for his staff. After that he looked only down, at the icy cobbles, and put his staff in the spaces between them as he walked.

He thought of Arden, as a temptation. It was two days' walk, that was all, perhaps three now that he was old. He could go back, like an old fox to his earth. But it was not his, had never been. If he went to the mill and asked to stop, they would turn him away, with his torn cloak and his staff, a stranger, too old for useful work.

He went along Goodramgate and stopped in front of the baker's shop. He gazed up at the window. A light was burning. Someone else, another life, someone warm in the yeasty warmth that came up from the shop. But the sense of her, her presence, her absence, had altogether left him, and his sorrow was only for himself, out in the cold street, in the fallen night. He remembered suddenly, as clearly as if he were there, the blessed peace of his cell at the Mountgrace on winter nights, the fire, the habit that was his and not his own, the two or three books, his and not his own, the cloister wall at the back of the garden standing high against the weather and against the nettles and brambles of the wood. Many times his world had been taken from him. That peace, that world out of the world: Was that the loss he had never repaired? And the cardinal's letter, his chance to repair it?

He set off again, faster now, jabbing his staff into the ground. The crowds of people in the city were like the thoughts crowding his head. He did not know them. He knew nothing. He had not the time. He could taste the bitterness in his throat as he could feel the cold air he breathed in, icy in his lungs.

He came out of the huddle of little streets into the space in front of the silent vastness of the Minster. His heart was thudding in his chest, and his whole body was hot with a fever of rage and misery. Why was he here? Why had he come two hundred miles to find his spoiled hopes thronging the lanes and alleys, crouching in doorways from the cold, pleading for his attention like the beggar holding out his bowl? He was a fool, stubborn and a fool. He should have turned his back on the north, which had cast him out, from Arden, from the Charterhouse, from York, and gone with the courteous Italians among people whose language he could not speak. He leaned on his staff and cursed himself aloud.

The words died feebly into the night. A woman passing gave him a frightened look. He heard her quick footsteps vanish among the houses. The great church stood before him in the darkness, its windows lit with a dim glow, like a lake into whose still depths many streams clatter and are quenched. The moon was a milky blur, hidden behind clouds, and against the clouds the three towers and the long roof waited in the sky, massive and black. The streets behind him, the seething passages, what were they? Mud and clay, wattle and daub, wood, thatch, plaster, huts, and cabins to shelter the body, to eat and sleep and couple in. Like the bodies they kept warm, and the rats that ran from one to the other, and the lice in the clothes, they would not last long. Others would come to take their place, others and others again. But the hearthless cathedral, which sheltered no one, in which no one was born or died, was it not here in the stone silences that the crowding people found—the love of the Father? And the crowding thoughts?

He could no longer hear his heart beating. His anger had left him weak, so that his legs trembled as he crossed the shadowed space. The wicket in the southwest door was unfastened, and he went into the cathedral. Warmer and darker than outside, the air was full of smoke from hundreds of tapers. There were groups of people, men, women, children, babies in arms, gathered in the immense obscurity of the nave. A low mutter rose from them as they thronged forward towards a cluster of lights in the transept. He was taller than most of them, but he could seen nothing over their heads except the blaze of light. The mutter ceased as a chant began in the choir, twenty or thirty voices high up in the church beyond the screen from which the carved faces of the kings of England looked down, appearing alive in the candlelight. The heads in front of him were all turned towards the south door. Suddenly the bells of the Minster rang out, overwhelming the chant in their clangour and clash of sound, and a cheer went up from the people, who pressed forward more eagerly than before. Through the craning heads he saw a golden crown move slowly along the transept towards the cluster of tapers, then another, and a third. He understood. It was the feast of the Epiphany. As a chantry-priest, he had stood in the choir, beyond the rood-screen and hidden from the body of the church, and sung the Vespers of the feast with the rest of the Minster clergy. He had heard the peal of the bells and the people cheer. But the ceremony had been stopped at the time the chantries were dissolved. He had never seen the kings come in with their gifts.

The crowns disappeared one by one behind the crowd as the kings knelt in turn before the massed candles. He could not see the child, picture or painted wood or gilded image, to whom they knelt. Out of his sight they set down the gold, the frankincense, the myrrh, and the hush among the people while the bells still pealed was so deep that he bent his head over his staff and asked forgiveness for his rage and the jostling tumult of his thoughts as if he had indeed been a pilgrim.

The bells stopped, and as their echoes faded, leaving the solemn line of the chant audible once more, the people broke up into groups and began to murmur again among themselves. In threes and fours they came back down the nave. The great west door was open now, and the freezing night air blew in, laying the flames of all the tapers flat. Before he also turned to go, he looked once more towards the rood-screen. He saw only the dark forms of the crowd moving about in front of the light. Above them the stone kings still looked down, their grave features mild in the smoky haze.

Outside on the cobbles a pedlar with a tray round his neck was selling sweet pies and roasted nuts to the people leaving the church. He was caught in the press close to him, and among those who pushed past him to buy from the pedlar's tray was one of the three kings. He was laughing under his pasteboard crown, and as he brushed against him he smelled the tarnished gilt on his robe.

The crowd thinned. The people went away into the streets, soothing crying children, wishing each other good-night.

He walked quickly to the house of Alice's father. He knocked on the door. He waited on the steps in the cold night, fighting down the past. He knocked again. The door was opened by a servant he did not know.

"Is your mistress at home?"

"Aye, sir. She's in her chamber, with the boy. The master's from home, at the Guildhall. What would you . . . ?"

The man stared at him.

"Tell your mistress Robert Fletcher is here. She will know the name. Ask her if she would be so good as to come down."

The man let him in and shut the door behind him. After another puzzled glance he went away, up the stairs.

A huge fire was burning in the hall. He crossed the flags and stood with his back to it. He tried to breathe evenly, but the beating of his heart was choking him.

On the settle by the fire he saw a hornbook lying, just such a hornbook as that with which the prioress at Arden had taught him to read. He picked it up. It too had the alphabet on one side and the Our Father on the other, but was less scratched with age. He bent down to see it more clearly by the light of the fire.

He saw looking out at him from the smooth horn his father's face, the face of old Tom Fletcher, haggard and stubborn, laden with grief, lit from below by the flickering flames of the fire. He closed his eyes and his hand, holding the hornbook, dropped to his side.

He opened his eyes, put the hornbook back on the settle, and stood for a moment, motionless in front of the fire. He heard voices somewhere in the upper part of the house. Fumbling under his cloak in his haste, he took from his bag the cardinal's letter. He turned it over once in his fingers. Then he laid it down on top of his son's hornbook and left the house.

Outside, snow was falling. He walked through the quiet streets. The white flakes floated softly towards him. God be praised, he said to himself over and over again. God be praised.

16

May 1559

"Il Schifanoia", anonymous agent of the Signory of Venice, in London, to the Ambassador of the Duke of Mantua at the court of King Philip II of Spain, in Brussels; May 1559.

". . . Since I last wrote to you, most excellent friend, the affairs of religion in this Kingdom have gone from bad to worse. Already at Christmas the queen would not sit devoutly through the Mass; cobblers and others of the meaner sort usurped the pulpits in the churches of the city and with impunity mocked and abused the blessed memory of the late queen; statues were broken in the churches, especially any remaining of Saint Thomas of Canterbury; and on the feast of Epiphany there was permitted a most scandalous revel at court: wolves representing abbots, asses habited as monks, and a crow clad in the scarlet robes of a cardinal were marched up and down in ribald procession, to the great merriment and delight of all. Now the Mass is altogether forbidden, the parliament has bestowed again upon the queen the title of supreme head of the church, first assumed by her father, King Henry, and there is not one left standing of all the late queen's acts, those of Cardinal Pole being likewise annulled. All men marvel, however, at the constancy of the old bishops left alive from the late queen's time, some of whom are now in prison, and I hear that, owing to this great constancy, it is secretly determined, from the fear of some insurrection among the people, to proceed more adroitly than formerly in enforcing the oath to observe the statutes, and that many will be exempted from the obligation to swear to it.

"As to the matter of the queen's marriage, speculation is rife at court and will never abate until she choose one or other of her suitors. The earl of Arundel is now generally thought to be out of contention on account of his advanced age; a pretty boy at court whom the queen has favoured with many a smile and glance of her eyes is reckoned too young and green even by his own family; a third contender, judged at this present to lead the field, is a certain nobleman who has not yet returned from France, in which realm he has dwelt these past several years on account of his religion. Although he has not, as yet, made his appearance, it is known—by what means I cannot tell—how greatly the queen has loved and still loves him. He is a very handsome gentleman, whose name I forget. All are agreed in wishing her to take an Englishman. Without doubt, the poor count of Feria failed utterly in his master's suit, leaving at last for Flanders having spoken only once with the queen, in the little chamber leading out of the privy chamber, where she conversed with him very merrily to no purpose whatsoever. She knows well that even if the people have to wait ten years for her to wed, they will have no more of the king of Spain.

"Before he went away, the count of Feria did obtain leave from the queen's council for all the religious, monks, friars, and nuns, who were in the habit at the time of the other schism, to depart this realm for Flanders if that be their wish. They are, however, very few in number, and aged men and women, and their going will scarcely be noticed among the people and still less at court, whence the Catholic lords have for the most part long since withdrawn themselves and their wives to distant shires of the realm.

"There is so little love now shown to foreigners in England that I shall be glad myself to return again into Italy. My departure hence depends only upon that of Signor Priuli, in whose house and under whose protection I am living. He is much occupied, and weak from a recurring fever, and has not yet executed all the bequests of his beloved cardinal. As soon as he is able, he will, I think, be content to leave these shores, where he has known naught but grief, and I look forward before long to seeing again my dear friends in Brussels, which city we shall without fail pass through on our journey to Venice . . ."

"*Post scriptum*: I have heard this day that a married priest who was chaplain to Queen Anne Boleyn is made archbishop of Canterbury."

17

June 1559

With an effort of will he forced his terror back and tried to piece together his memories of the day before. He had been given a ride on an ox-cart. The oxen plodded through the heat more slowly than he would have walked, but there was no reason for haste, and he had ceased even to ask how many miles there were to the next village. He sat in silence beside the carter, his back against the flowery hay, and watched the rocking of the yoke as the cart jolted over stones in the road. But was the ox-cart the day before, or another day, further north? And the roses. He saw the first dog-roses of the year, blooming in the hedges, whiter than they were in England. When was that? After the ox-cart or before?

He had no means of telling how long he had been here. Had he been ill for days, without knowing, and eaten nothing? Was it because he had had no food that he could not move? At first he thought that the weight on his chest that prevented him from moving was a sack of flour, a stone, an iron bar, that he could push away with his hands. But when he tried to lift the weight from his chest, his hands had not moved. His head was propped up on a straw bolster. He looked down. His arms lay straight down by his sides, outside the blanket that covered him. He could not move them. There was nothing on his chest but the blanket, a thin, worn blanket. Terror had made him shut his eyes. For a while he had not tried to move. He breathed shallowly, under the weight. Perhaps he had slept. When he opened his eyes he knew that it was morning because there was more light than before. Nothing else had changed.

Since then he had lain in the slowly increasing light and fought down his fear until he succeeded in busying his mind, for minutes together, with other sensations, other kinds of thought. Then, forgetting that he could not, he would try to move, and fail, and the terror returned, rising up to cover all else, to choke him. There was nothing on his chest but a thin blanket. What was the weight that so pressed him down?

Looking down, he could see from his arms that he was wearing only his shirt. What had happened to his cloak, his coat? He breathed as deeply as he could, making the weight heavier, to discover whether his belt was still round his waist. As far as he could tell, it was not. Never once on his journey had he taken off his belt. It held what was left of his money. Someone else must have taken off his clothes. Where had they been put?

From where he lay he could see a big square of light, open to the sky. He looked at it for some time, and at the uneven chink of light beneath it on one side, before he realised that it was the top half of a stable door. Outside, the wooden shutter must be fastened back, hooked to an iron ring in the wall. His picture of this shutter, flat against the wall so that it should not bang, consoled him. The top edge of the square was a jagged line, spiked with ends of straw because the thatch overhung the lintel. He watched the dawn light gaining on the night, and when a swallow flew across the square, and then another, he knew that he had been expecting them.

Somewhere else, long ago, he used to lie still and watch the day grow light through the open top of a stable door.

How had he come here? He was certain that he had not shut that door himself, leaning over the hard edge of the planks to shoot the bolt on the outside. He had knocked at no house to ask leave to sleep in the stable. Barns he had slept in several times as the nights had got warmer, but with his coat folded under his head and his cloak wrapped round him. He had not much money left, and, except at the monasteries, he had to pay for his food. It cost nothing to sleep on straw in a barn. Lately, once or twice, there had been new hay. He was lying now on bracken, he knew it by the smell, and someone had put a bolster under his head. Bracken. That, too, reminded him . . .

They must have carried him here. He did not remember falling. He did not remember the last village, the last night he had lain down to sleep, the last meal. He did not remember the road, the woods, the look of the hills, the weather . . .

The images of his journey were jumbled together as if it had been during only a long, single day that he had tramped the roads of France, always southwards, always towards the summer and the mountains. He walked all morning with the sun on his left. The shadows shortened as he walked, and the sun moved up the sky ahead of him until it blazed full in his face. At noon he rested under a tree. He ate his bread and cheese and drank from his water-bottle, and slept in the tree's shade for a while. Afterwards he walked on while the sun descended on his right and pushed the shadows further and further across the fields. He would find a meal and a bed before dark. That was all. Before the early morning mist cleared, some geese had crossed the road, seven of them, one behind the other. They had marched across his path without a sound, as white as the morning, and disappeared over the wet grass into the mist. Later there had been showers, each a few minutes of fine warm rain. He had seen them travelling the hills, the rays of the sun white bars shining through them. In the afternoon he had met men coming from work with unfamiliar tools on their shoulders and seen rows of vines growing in the flinty earth, strings between the stakes that supported them. And always the villages, the whitewashed villages, the plane-trees, the dung-heaps, and the bare churches. He did not know their names. In the morning there were women scrubbing clothes at the pump and children playing barefoot in the white dust. In the evening swallows screamed as they dived above the roofs of the cottages, and swifts skimmed the surface of the village pond for flies.

Would the power to move come back to him? He shut his eyes. Outside all the birds were singing, the dawn din of early June with the cooing of pigeons thick in the leaves and far off a cuckoo, always far off. Was he going to die here without ever again moving his arms, his hands? Beneath the noise of the birds he thought he could hear the clatter of a stream, the soft roar of falling water. Could he?

There was some knowledge, some gathering together of the hooked-back shutter, the swallows, the bracken, the sound of water, that lay in wait for him. He would come to it presently. He would give himself time. First he would have to let go his hold, to sink, to sink down under the weight on his chest, the weight of all his life . . .

He was woken by the hard rim of a cup held to his lips. He drank cold water. A woman he had never seen before was leaning over him. He was thirsty. She put her arm behind his head and raised it a little so that he could drink more easily. He finished the water, and she laid his head gently on the bolster. At once a piercing pain seized his stomach. He made as if to clasp his belly with both hands. They did not move. Fresh anguish rose in his throat. He had forgotten, in his sleep, his foolish sleep—forgotten.

The woman stood, looking down at him, one side of her face lit by the daylight from the open square, which now had a golden tinge to it although the sun was not shining directly in. The bottom half of the door was still shut. There must be another door into the stable, from the house. Was that the way they had carried him here?

Then he saw a child, a small girl clutching her mother's dress and staring at him with terrified eyes. He smiled at her, but the fear in her face did not go away.

The woman bent forward and asked him a question. He

thought she asked him his name. He opened his mouth to answer. No sound came. He tried again. Nothing, except a faint croak in the back of his throat. She shook her head and then put her finger to her lips as if it were good that he should not speak. She took the child by the hand and went away into the darkness behind his head.

If he could not speak, he would not be able to tell them where he was going. He would not be able to ask which road to take. It was when he understood that it did not matter, when he understood that if he could not move—if he could not walk—when he saw the simple future that he had built himself vanish like smoke twirling and thinning quickly, quickly into clear air, that he cried out. He cried out, only once, a wordless cry, and he heard the echoes of his cry, a howl like a dog's howl, fade into the emptiness of the stable. It was not much that he had promised himself. Someone else's garden. Now he would never reach it. He had not come as far even as the foothills of the mountains.

He bit his lip to stop himself crying out again and was glad to find that his teeth did sink into his flesh. If he could bite, why could he not speak? He forced himself to become calm, breathing slowly so as to quieten the beating of his heart and pleading for the words to shape themselves in his mouth.

Dear God—he tried to whisper—dear God. Nothing. Nothing but the same croak as before. This time he wept. Soundlessly the tears flowed down his cheeks for several minutes, and when they ceased his prayer had changed. He had become acquainted with his muteness, the silence of his body as of his voice, and was thankful, now, for the bed on which he lay, the water he had drunk, the peace of the stable.

This peace, the peace after tears that he would not again let go, was it not like the peace he had felt in the cellar, waiting only to die? There too he had been held fast, in the stocks, able to move hardly more than he could now. There, although he had not lost the power to speak, he had thought that there was no one left for him to speak to, nothing left for him to say. He was wrong. There had been the cardinal. New words. The cardinal's and his own.

How long ago had it been, the cellar? He had lost count of time before he crossed the sea from England. He had been walking for many months. By the length of the days, the hay, the roses in the hedge, he knew it was June now, almost midsummer. A year ago it had been, a year ago he had lain in the cellar, expecting death. Then his life had been a load he still carried, a burden he almost wanted to unshoulder, to set down before God. Now he was free of it, freed from it, although he had shed no part of it, although he bore it all within him, sealed into his silence, as England was within him as he walked away from it, through France.

What had freed him? Not the cardinal's death. Not the new reign in England. Not the changes that would come, again, in the Church. None of these. But his journey to York, what he had done there, what he had not done, had freed him at last.

He had left the cardinal's letter, for Alice's parents and later, if they chose, for his son, and the leaving of it had absolved him from choice. He would go to the Grande Chartreuse, but not as the cardinal's penitent. He would ask to see the prior, and without help he would tell him the simplest truth. After that, he would obey. They would not receive him back into the cloister. He hoped only to be given work, and he had allowed himself to build a picture of his days. A garden. Beans to be sown in rows, onions to be hoed, vines he would learn how to prune. Goat's milk he would set to curdle for cheese, hens he would shut up for the night from foxes, bees. On feast-days he would stand with the lay brothers at the back of the church and listen to the monks singing, and he would speak to no one because no one would understand his foreign tongue.

Sometimes on his journey people had asked him where he

was going. "La Grande Chartreuse", he had said. In the villages they had looked at him blankly, not knowing the name. In the monasteries one or two had stared at him, taking him for a messenger too old for his task, and shaken their heads at the distance he still had to travel.

If they turned him away . . .

Every so often on his journey he had compelled himself to admit that they might. If they turned him away, he would go on, walk to Rome, to Jerusalem, to the deserts of Egypt. If they turned him away, those to whom he had vowed obedience as a boy of twenty, whatever else had come between, if they sent him from their garden, which he no longer hoped to dwell in but only to tend for them, then indeed his last debt would be discharged. Hundreds of miles he would have walked to find them, but if they ordered him after all to walk past them, he would obey. He had walked through white dust, between hedges, while the sun moved through the sky, and thought that if they shut their garden against him it would be no different from how it was now.

We are strangers before thee, and sojourners, as were all our fathers.

But he had hoped.

A grating sound made him open his eyes, a sound he knew at once for the rusty bolt on the outside of the stable door being pulled back. The door swung open. No one came in. He heard light footsteps retreating. He waited for what he knew would happen next.

Through the doorway he could see the beaten earth on the flat bridge over the stream, a gate into a steep field, daisies in the grass. Only the trees were not the same, a big oak in the field and alders by the water instead of the birches and the rowans. The early morning sun shone down from behind the stable, throwing sharp shadows across the grass, and the leaves of the trees were ruffled by a breeze that seemed to come off the surface of the stream. A fine red cockerel stalked across the bridge. He watched the inquisitive jerks of his head as he looked about him, the delicate placing of his yellow feet on the dried mud. Birds still sang, less noisily than before. A summery breath, the early freshness of a hot day, reached him in the dark corner of the stable where he lay. They would come from the pasture, which was downstream. Now he could hear them, the shutting of a gate, the lazy amble of their walk up the trodden path.

A heavy shape filled the doorway. The cow stopped, because he was there, and then, pushed from behind by a second cow, went to her place and stood quietly in the straw at the far end of the stable. The second cow followed. A girl came in after them, a pail in her hand. She crossed the stable and stood beside him, her head bent. He could not see her face because she had her back to the light, but she did not seem to be afraid. What had happened when they brought him here? Had he spoken to them then? She said a few words to him, or perhaps to herself. This time he did not try to answer. Instead he smiled, as he had to the child. She put out her hand towards him, uncertainly, as if to lay it on his forehead to see if he were feverish, or as if to ward off any danger that might be in him. He could not tell. She withdrew her hand and went back to the cows, pulling a milking-stool out from the wall as she went. The cows were waiting for her, large and warm in the dusty shadows. He knew that there would be ropes hanging by their heads, from iron rings in the wall, and that she would not bother to fasten them.

He lay with his eyes closed and listened to the old sounds: the scrape of the pail on the flags as she wedged it between her knees, the murmur of her voice as she settled the cow, the same few phrases repeated like the nonsense with which a woman soothes a restless baby, then the rhythmic spurting of the milk into the pail, on and on while the birds sang outside and the swallows flew across the doorway to their nest in the thatch.

Then he had been too young to receive words except as an

319

animal receives them, as tones of voice, sounds of comfort, of command. Now, dying in a foreign land, it was the same.

He heard her push the stool back on the stone. She had finished the first cow. He waited, and it came, the sound of her pouring the milk into a pitcher. She slapped the cow's rump and told it to move over, using a word he did not know. The cow started, shifting its clumsy feet in the straw. Then all the sounds began again with the second cow, and the spurting of the milk had a new ring because the pail was empty.

Yet it was not the same. The weight. Between then and now lay the weight on his chest, the weight of his whole life, all the words, the long years of the past . . . He had thought that this was what he had left behind, for the wordless present of his journey through France, his single day.

He remembered turning his back, on the past, on the future, on England, walking down steps, and then more steps, and then down the long empty nave of Canterbury cathedral, and out into the morning—turning his back.

In March, it was, in a white windy morning. He woke in Canterbury, at an inn. They had been pleased to give him a good bed, cheap, because there were no pilgrims any more and too many beds in the town for the travellers who passed through. He walked alone to the cathedral, whose walls rose high at the ends of streets as the Minster's did in York. Inside the church there was a great silence and the cold of winter not yet gone from the stone. He walked up the south aisle, hearing only the sound of his own footsteps and the tap of his staff. There was no one anywhere in the church. He went up the broad steps and into the deserted choir. A second transept, more steps, up and up he walked, and still there was no one. He thought of the crowds of people in the Minster nave, the blaze of tapers, the pasteboard crowns, the cheers. There was nothing here but the level daylight quiet above him and the empty steps leading him up.

After the last steps he walked round a long semi-circle of

enormous tombs. Sleeping effigies lay on them, their hands joined in the attitude of prayer. In the centre of the chapel, inside the circle of tombs, was a raw space. Fresh-cut stone slabs had recently been laid; the new mortar between them was rough and clean. He stood by a tomb, his hand on the cold marble of a carved edge, and looked into the space. This was where the shrine had been, the shrine of Saint Thomas of Canterbury, the richest place of pilgrimage in England. He remembered the prior telling them, in the chapter-house of the Mountgrace, that the shrine of Saint Thomas had been pulled down and all the treasure sold. The prior read from a letter that the great ruby of France, the shrine's most precious jewel, had been made into a thumb-ring for King Henry, and all the monks had winced. And had not he himself come to think such destruction right and good because it took from simple minds the false hope of salvation earned by gifts left at holy places?

He looked at the bare, patched stone, and back, over his shoulder, at the unpeopled stillness of the church below him.

A king had had an archbishop murdered here, because the archbishop defended the Church against the king's encroachments. He ran his finger back and forth on the corner of the tomb, and the dust made his finger grey. This was Cranmer's church too, Cranmer who had been Archbishop of Canterbury for twenty years and had seen the ruby every day on the king's thumb, Cranmer who was himself to be killed.

All had changed. He hit the edge of the tomb with his clenched fist. That was it. When Thomas Becket died, the scandal reached the ends of Christendom and the king had done penance on his knees under the lash of the monks of Canterbury. When Bishop Fisher and Thomas More died, and Becket's shrine was stripped for spoil, the scandal had been hardly less great, but the king had ground his teeth and gone on his way. When Thomas Cranmer died, what was left of Catholic Christendom had stood by and applauded.

He thought of the ruby, the great glowing jewel that the king of France had given to the shrine. There had been a time when kings themselves feared God as he was made known to them in the Church, the Church, the body of Christ in the hands of men. It was no longer so. And that it was no longer so was less the fault of kings than of the Church, of the men in whose hands . . .

The king who had Becket killed sent for monks from France as a sign of his contrition, the monks who were the first English Carthusians. One of them, Hugh of Avalon from the Grande Chartreuse—he had read the story of his life at the Mount-grace—had afterwards become that king's dearest friend, Bishop of Lincoln, a saint of the Church.

Now all the English Charterhouses were in ruins and the tomb of Saint Hugh at Lincoln smashed and robbed as the tomb of Saint Thomas at Canterbury had been. Hugh of Avalon, who had come from France as the ruby had come, blessed Saint Hugh, on whose feast-day the cardinal had died, the cardinal who had tried to save the Church Saint Hugh had known and loved, and had set his own murderous King Henry only to rage more furiously against that Church, the cardinal who at last had failed even to . . . the cardinal . . . archbishop . . .

He turned suddenly and looked from tomb to tomb as if he had not all along seen them standing there in the silence. In Becket's crown, he had heard them say at Lambeth. In Becket's crown. From the heaviest and most decorated tomb he caught the calm stare of a gold knight gazing up to heaven. He crossed the space to him, hearing his own footsteps again. The knight lay open-eyed in his shining armour, his hands in their spiked gauntlets just touching at the finger-tips in prayer, the arms of England on his surcoat and a crowned lion under his head. Edward Plantagenet, Prince of Wales. He looked up. There they were above him, hanging in his bronze gaze, his helmet, gloves and coat, and his shield, not gleaming and graven as on the effigy, but old, battered, the very ones he had worn at Crécy, at Poitiers.

He laughed aloud. This tomb would not be destroyed. This shrine to the butcher of ten thousand Frenchmen would stand for ever, because the knight, the king's son, held no meaning but his own, his own glory and England's, as the victor of so many bloody battles. The ruby of France and Hugh of Avalon were already forgotten, what they had signified returned into God for whom they had come. The Black Prince would not be forgotten.

He traced with his finger the line of the long, brazen nose. Put not your trust in princes . . .

He looked about him, slowly now, tomb by tomb. He would not be here, the cardinal, not here among these monuments to worldly glory. There, at the very top, the very end of the whole church, was a round apse lit with a white light and empty of effigies and carvings. Becket's crown. He walked through the arch into the apse and saw a new stone, bare in the light, and three words on it. *Depositum Cardinalis Poli*. He stood in front of it for a long time and thought of the warm room at Lambeth, the mad brother, the tapers burning each side of the picture of Christ, the fog outside.

Put not your trust in princes, nor in any child of man; for when the breath of man goeth forth he shall turn again to his earth.

At last he shook his head and went away, walking away down the great church, an old man in a ragged cloak leaning on his staff as he walked, his heart light, light. He waved as he passed the Black Prince. Keep your shield safe, lad, and your spiked gloves.

He had gone away to France, where the ruby had come from, and Saint Hugh, where he knew nothing and no one and would not understand what people said.

And now he lay, unable to speak, unable to move, on a bed of bracken in a stable and smiled once more as he remembered that morning in Canterbury and listened to a girl milking a cow.

It was done. She poured the second pailful of milk into the pitcher and picked it up. She needed both hands to carry it, so that she had to put it down on the ground in order to unlatch the door behind his head, into the house. He heard a little milk slop over onto the floor as she picked it up again, heard her pull the door open with her foot as she went through. The sound of women's voices, the high voice of a child, reached him from behind the door. Then she came back, shutting the door behind her. She stopped beside him, but he did not open his eyes. He did not want to see her face. He wanted to pretend for a little longer that he was back, after all, at the beginning, in the narrow dale, and that the girl, the miller's daughter, was she who had nursed him because her own baby had died . . . He knew, certainly he knew, that it was not true. It was only a game he was playing with himself. All the same, beneath what he knew not to be true there was a truth, a truth, if there would be time to find it, that had to do with time and with what was not lost, not ever, and with God . . .

His shoulders had begun to ache under the weight on his chest. If he could have moved on his bed, if he could have hoisted himself up on the bolster, if he could . . . He felt himself slipping down further and further under the weight.

She went away from his side, and he opened his eyes to keep himself from falling asleep. He must not waste what was left of the day. The dazzle and glint of the morning outside the door he had forgotten while his eyes were shut. He heard the unfamiliar sound he made in his throat, but she did not turn towards him as she sent the cows out in front of her down to the pasture. She left the picture empty, quiet except for the birds and the rattle of the stream over pebbles. The cockerel did not pass by. After a while she came back. She came into the stable, fetched the pail, and took it to the stream. She knelt on the bridge and tipped up the pail to drink the last of the milk. He saw her throat move as she drank. Then she rinsed the pail in the stream, swilling it out twice, three times, in the clean water.

He felt a great weakness as he watched her, as if, under the pressure of the stones, something in his chest had given way. Tears rose again in his throat. He closed his eyes because he did not want to see her go. Shut in his own darkness he listened to the beating of his heart, loud and irregular as if it might stop, as if the next beat, the next thud inside his head, his ears, might not come, might never come.

He breathed as slowly as he could, and little by little the beat became firmer and quicker. He felt the sweat on his forehead roll down into his closed eyes, down his cheeks, into his beard. He must not let go, not yet, not quite yet . . . There was something that he had to find out, something that had to do with the difference between then and now, between the child in the early morning with the day before him and the old man holding on to his breath for a few more beats of his heart—with the difference, and with what was the same . . .

He knew that it was a question of words. It was not that the words and his life were one, the weight on his chest. The weight was only his life, the fallen stones. Sixty years, seventy, and he would have lain, here or elsewhere, under their weight with the strength crushed out of him, seeping away. It was not that the words and his life were one, and the fact that they were not one . . . He closed his eyes more tightly, frowning as he tried to bring it clear. The fact that they were not one was part of whatever it was that he had to find.

Had not always been one. There. That was solid ground to stand on, to begin from. The muscles of his face relaxed.

Perhaps in the Charterhouse, during the years of silence in which the hours, measured out by the tolling bell, were nevertheless full of words, perhaps there the words and his life had been one. Perhaps that oneness had been the very thing, the jewel, the ruby, that the king had stolen from him when he sent commissioners to strip the wainscotting from his cell and the habit from his back, from his days. Those long days had been the loss, their singleness of life and word, when all that he had done had been in the meaning, and all the meaning had been in what he had done.

He saw them coming into the church at night, their faces hidden by their cowls, their hands inside the sleeves of their habits, one light burning at the lectern, men without names, hidden in God. Each monk as he passed the light stopped for a moment and looked across at him, and each face, lit from below by the flame flickering in the draught, was full of reproach.

He shrank back into the darkness. Surely it had not been only he who had gone away. They had all gone. They had not chosen to go. But they had gone. Still they came, one after another, more and more of them, and disappeared into the dark, more monks than there had ever been at the Mountgrace, all the Carthusians, risen from their unnamed graves, and each stopped at the taper and looked towards him, reproaching him.

He opened his eyes. There was no one there, no one in the stable, no one on the bridge, no one in the field, no one.

O God be merciful to me, a sinner.

He was hot, burning hot. If only he could be free of this burden, free of the weight on his chest, the stones he had pulled over on himself, the weight of sin.

Yet he had almost reached . . . When he had fallen asleep he had almost reached the understanding that lay in wait for him, close to him. But it was hard, beneath the fallen stones, a hard struggle to find his way through, and now he had lost the ground he had gained. To find his way back he had to stay awake, not to let his eyes close, not to sleep . . .

He looked out through the open door. The June heat was gathering in the day. The birds no longer sang, except for now and then a short note uttered into the sunshine, and the leaves of the trees were still, even over the stream. The girl had gone; the cockerel had gone. No one came over the bridge, not even a cat. There would be a cat, and it would be lying stretched out somewhere, in the shade, asleep. He heard a man shout, and far away, perhaps in the yard beyond the mill, the rumble of wheels, a dog barking. He saw the oxen standing in the heat, the miller unloading sacks of grain from the cart, lifting them one by one onto his back from where the carter stood them ready, hens pecking in the dust among the shadowed spokes of the wheels for the odd grain of corn that fell when the sacks were shifted. Soon the great stones would start to grind, and they would call him to come and watch the sack fill . . . And always the sound of the water, the even roar of the mill-race, the nearer rattle of the shallows . . .

"Nay, Master Fletcher", the gaoler said, rattling the keys at him. "They had me lock you in. You won't get out a second time."

"But the sack—I have to watch the sack. If it fills too full the flour spills over and goes to waste—"

"I can't help that, Master Fletcher. They had me lock you in, and you'll stay here until they come to fetch you away to the trial. Then you'll have to answer for the wasted flour, then you will, so you'd best not drop off. Don't you dare fall asleep—and don't you try to move. That's what my keys are for, to keep you from moving. I'll let you have a window, mind. You can watch the others die. Out there on the green, in the sunshine, that's where they die. But in your case it's all a pretence. A pretence, is it not, Master Fletcher? For England, did you say? To die for England? You want armour to die for England. Golden armour, and gauntlets with spikes on the knuckles. You have no armour. You have only your bare hands and the scar on your thumb. Or is it the Church you would die for? Which one, Master Fletcher—ah! Which one?"

The gaoler came nearer and stood over him as he lay.

"Where is your brother, Master Fletcher? You never found him. You left him to face the rack and the cruel lords, didn't you? And you could have saved him. He was always afraid of the river. And the river got him in the end, ten foot deep in the middle, it was, and the wheels stuck between rocks, and him drowned as he sat there on the wagon in the dark. Go out there! Go out in the cold and find him! Bury him in the snow, or the crows will get his eyes!"

He felt the gaoler's hot breath on his face as he leaned over him.

"All the birds in the air fell a-sighing and a- . . . Robin is dead. They are bringing him now, bringing him in from the field with the pitchfork in his belly, carrying him on their shoulders who never but walked, tall and strong. He'll not jump down from their shoulders. They'll not clap him on the back and laugh, all of them together. He's dead. He'll not come back at the mill door, taking the light in the doorway, to tie your sack and lift it away. He'll not come back. And the sack, Master Fletcher, the sack! Look there! Full to the top and running over! The flour pouring out on the dusty ground, all going to waste! Shout! Shout for Robin to come! Shout!"

A bursting pain in his chest woke him. He could not shout, he could not.

A big black dog stood beside him, panting into his face, its tongue hanging out. A black dog . . . The sheep . . . He saw a lamb twitching on the grass, blood spreading from its throat.

Someone called the dog, and it went quietly away. He heard it lie down in the straw at the far end of the stable, its tail thump the ground.

Sweat trickled down his face, his neck, his chest. He saw an egg hit an old man in a street, without a sound, and trickle down his face.

O God, be merciful to me, a sinner.

If he could breathe evenly, if he could steady his heart, the pain would cease. If the pain would cease he would have the time, a little time . . . and the meaning would come back to the words.

O God, be merciful . . .

There was something he had yet to do. The gaoler had said, the gaoler had known—but he had not understood. He had not listened to the words. And now they were gone.

A man was there, a man he knew, his bulk solid in the shadows. His hand was stretched out behind him to keep the dog quiet. There was flour on his clothes; he saw it on his shoulder, his thigh, in the light from the door. It was Robin.

He closed his eyes. The gaoler had been wrong, and the dream—a dream. He had shouted, and Robin had come. He would tie the sack and roll it away, out into the yard where the oxen were standing, and lift it onto the cart . . . lift it off his chest . . . up off his chest so that he could breathe . . . so that he could move, run, run out into the day . . .

Someone was talking as he ran. Words. But he shook off the words.

He ran down the path by the stream and vaulted the gate into the pasture. He ran through the high grass and the buttercups. The cows were standing under the trees in the shade. He ran down to the ford and waded into the river. The water was cold, the stones sharp under his feet. He splashed his face, his hair, his shirt, with the water and drank from his cupped hands. Then he ran up the steep field on the other side, scattering the sheep as he ran, and out to the open moor, higher and higher along the narrow path the sheep had made, winding upwards through the heather. He reached the place where a great flat ledge of rock stuck out of the moor with bracken growing under it and a green space of turf. Out of breath from running, he threw himself down on the turf. He looked down. He saw the heather below him, the field, the sheep quiet again, the river shining between the trees, the mill quiet . . . quiet in the sun. No one came out of the open door. No one crossed the bridge. He could not get his breath. His whole body hurt from running, and he could not get his breath. The pain in his chest made him gasp.

He had to go back. Down there. To the mill, the silent mill. He had to go back. No one came out because they were gathered inside, waiting. A man lay dying there, an old man, a stranger, and he had to go back because he had something to tell him, something the old man needed to know, something no one could tell him but himself. He must hurry, he must run, or it would be too late. But he could not get up from the grass. His breath would not come. He could not move for the pain. He could not move. He opened his eyes. The stable was empty. Sunlight flowed in at the door, dense, warm, light with the dust gently rising in it, and lit a patch of the flags so that he could see the cracks between them, and the straws lying, and the bits of chaff . . .

The pain suddenly faded. The rasp of his breathing stopped. That was it. That was all. Not to fight any more. Not to struggle. He looked at the uneven flags, the straw, the chaff, lit in the heavy light. That was all. Only to love. The bread and the wine.

He saw a bearded figure leaning against the jamb of the door, arms folded, head down, waiting.

Then he knew that he had come to fetch him, and he watched.

At last the figure turned and came towards him through the light. He watched, and he was not afraid.

The cardinal spoke, so that, with his eyes open, he heard these words: "I saw a new heaven and a new earth. The tabernacle of God is with men and he will dwell with them."

And the earth was the flagstones and the straw and the shadows of the straw.

There was enough money left to pay for a coffin and a priest. They buried him the next day in the village churchyard beside the river. When the priest reached the prayer: "O God, we humbly pray to thee for the soul of thy servant", he looked across the coffin at the miller. The miller shook his head and the priest read the prayer again. "O God, we humbly pray to thee for the soul of thy servant. Let him not go into oblivion, for in thee he put his trust."

By the end of the summer the grass had grown together over his grave.